I0659203

# Whatever
# Is
# Done

Bridgett Henson

Empowered Publications, Inc.
Leroy, Alabama
www.empoweredpublicationsinc.com

Scripture quotations are taken from the King James Version.

This novel is a work of fiction. All characters are a product of the author's imagination. Any resemblances to actual people or events are purely coincidental.

Published by Empowered Publications, Inc.
26812 Highway 43
Leroy, Alabama 36548
ISBN 978-0-9909542-1-7

## *Acknowledgments*

I thank my God and Savior for calling me into this unique ministry. I couldn't have written this series without the Holy Ghost's anointing. There are hidden prayers on these pages. I thank God for answering the secret desires of my heart.

As always, I thank my editor Tyler Chastain, and my proofreader Diane Brown. Any errors you find in this book are my own despite their valiant effort to save me from misplaced modifiers and sentence fragments.

My sincere thanks to Garfield Chambers. You, my friend, are a mighty man of valor. I pray that you continue to allow the Lord to bring glory to His kingdom through you. May He bless your ministry in abundance.

I'm thankful for every testimony received by email, social media comment and private message from my readers. I encourage each of you to grow in the faith. Let God direct your life, and you'll be amazed at where He takes you.

And to my family...whew. I'd say it's over, but Zack is demanding to be heard. Here we go again. Thank you, for loving your "genius" mother. I love you.

In loving memory of
## Charles Devin Giles.
July 10, 1988
to
March 25, 2013

*Chapter One*

One small boy crouched alone at the grassy edge of the water. Around the perimeter of the huge pond, adult-child, two-person teams competed for the best catch. The kid frowned at the toddler-sized rod and reel in his hand. Ray searched the crowded bank for the boy's dad and then waited for someone to lend him a hand.

No one stepped forward.

A little brow wrinkled in concentration as the boy peered about ten feet to his right and watched James demonstrate how to press the button and release the line.

Curious what the boy would do next, Ray eased nearer with his own pole. Little fingers struggled with the release button and then slumped in defeat.

As Ray moved closer, the boy gritted his teeth and squeezed with both thumbs. A hard plastic fish splashed into the water's edge and sank six inches to the sandy bottom. The line had no hook, no weight, and no cork. Ray shook his head. There was no way possible for the boy to catch a real fish.

Yet the little cherub face grinned and yelled over at James. "I did it."

James—Ray's oldest friend in the world—cast a line into the water and handed the pole to one of his sons. "That's great, Trevor. Don't fall in or your mom will kill me."

Trevor stared into the water at the plastic fish attached to his line. "Yes, sir."

Why didn't James rig up Trevor's line? The kid wasn't much younger than the twins. And the rod he held was way too small for a boy his age.

"Ouch." James howled and pushed the end of a pole out of his face. "Be careful with that son. You 'bout caught your dad."

Both twins giggled. One peered up at James and said, "Sorry, Daddy."

Ray laughed at his friend's terrified expression.

"They do it all of the times." The little fisherman's gray eyes sparkled with mischief.

"Oh, yeah." Ray grinned. "What do they do?"

"Break stuff."

Full blown laughter escaped from Ray. That was one way to describe the twins. He stepped beside Trevor and whispered, "That's why I call them the Twin Terrors."

Little giggles floated off into the morning sunshine. Trevor lifted his pole and tilted his head at the fake fish. He sighed and dropped it back into the water.

James's voice boomed along the breeze as he removed a fish from a line. "Great job, son."

The ripples from Trevor's pole spread out into deeper water.

"Your dad must be at the office, huh?"

"He doesn't go to work." The little boy concentrated on the water.

"Oh." A dead beat dad? Ray glanced at Trevor's well-kept appearance, designer clothes, and the bulging backpack at his feet. "Well, your mom must take good care of you."

"Yep." Trevor nodded. "She loves me." The line was pulled up again and plopped back into the water. He squinted over at Ray and then leaned around him. "Where's your kid?"

Ray dropped his tackle on the shore. "I don't have one." Over the years working construction, he'd carefully insured that he'd not become a weekend dad like so many of the men on his construction crew.

"Not even in heaven?" Trevor peered into the bright sunlight.

Ray's heart dropped. "Is that where your father is?"

The sad little smile pierced Ray's gut. "Sometimes he swims the clouds with my sister. Momma says he watches me." He jiggled his pole again. "If I catch a fish and win the prize, he'll see me and say it."

"What will he say?"

The little head tilted as Trevor tucked his chin and mimicked in a low voice. "Good job, Trevor."

The steel cage around Ray's heart melted. Every boy should have a dad, and every man should have a son. Maybe that's why Ray had empathy with the kid. Neither one of them had either of those things. The modern-day, father-son fishing tournament included a few women and girls. Ray didn't see any reason for him and Trevor not to enter the competition. "James!" Ray waited until his friend turned his way. "Is there a rule against non-related fishing partners?"

"No." James looked pointedly at Trevor. "But if you're thinking what I think you're thinking…don't. His mom will stroke out if you put a real H-O-O-K on that line."

Ray rubbed the hairs on his chin and eyed the little boy. "Well, we don't want to upset your mom."

The little boy swung his line out of the water. Animated sparks flew from his eyes. "Grandmother says if momma ain't here, she don't matter."

The cutest smile pleaded with Ray. Was the mother really that bad? He looked back at James.

His friend shrugged. "Go ahead. She can't kill you if you're half way around the country on another job."

Yeah, but he'd be in town for at least six weeks. The boy grinning up at him in expectation was skinny as a steel beam. Was his mom just as petite? Few women worked construction and none on his crew, but there were some stout women out there who could heft twice their weight. He'd never raised a hand toward a female, not even in self-defense. "Trev, what's your mom do for a living?"

"She feeds people."

A waitress? Some could be tough, but he'd never met a woman yet that he couldn't sweet talk. "What's she look like?"

"Don't go there, Ray." James shook his head. "She's an old, widow woman. She's not your type at all. Come over here, Trevor. And leave Mr. Simmons alone."

If the crestfallen look on the little boy's face didn't cave Ray in, his next words would have. "But Mr. James. He don't got a kid. He needs me."

"Yes. I do." Ray reached out and ruffled the silky red hair. He wanted to help the boy, especially if his mom was one of those paranoid freaks that didn't let their kids get dirty. He called over to

James, "What do you think? Should Trevor and I fish? Or are you and the boys afraid to lose?"

James laughed. "Fine. Enter the competition, but promise me you'll stay away from his mom."

Why would James think he'd want a widow saddled with a kid? Cute though he may be. Ray shrugged. "What's one woman in a vast sea of females?"

Ray ignored James's pointed look and focused on his new fishing buddy. "Well…if we're gonna catch something…you need some bait. Swing your line over here."

Using his pocket knife, Ray cut the fake fish off Trevor's line. "Hand me my tackle box behind you."

Trevor hefted the box over and Ray rigged up the pole. Then he showed Trevor how to cast. Without thinking, he said, "Catching fish is like catching women, Trev. Keep your hook sharp, your line tight, and your bait fresh. Then all you have to do is sit back and reel 'em in."

Around the curve of the pond, a group of teenage boys high-fived and laughed. James's face had turned a purple hue. He hissed, "This is a church fundraiser."

Ray'd been watching his words real close to avoid saying any profanity. What did he say wrong?

He welcomed the buzz of his phone. He reached in his pocket. The last time he'd been in town, he'd split his time off work enjoying the company of two waitresses. He just arrived in the city yesterday and made that knowledge public via social media. He'd wondered who'd make the first contact. He smiled as he read Shelia's comment.

*Glad you're in town. Buy me a drink?*

"Where'd it go?" Trevor peered into the water. His cork had gone under.

Ray lay his phone on the grass beside him. "You've got a fish. Pull him in." He crouched down beside the boy and helped Trevor reel in a bream the size of a man's hand. "That's a nice one." Ray grabbed his phone. "Hold it by the string and smile." Women loved pictures of their kids. If the widow got too ornery, Ray'd show her this. He took several shots, and then a selfie with Trevor and the fish. "We'll win this thing yet."

ဆာလ

The new shingles and fresh paint may have changed the appearance of the old wood house, but Cindy's mind's eye saw the prison of her youth. She pushed past the memories as she bustled through the commercial glass door, and went to work preparing sandwiches for the needy.

Minutes later, the empty stare of the bruised child standing in front of her reflected Cindy's own childhood. The little girl couldn't be more than thirteen. Yet the hand reaching for a brown bag trembled. The girl winced and then touched her swollen lip. "Can I have two? Dad'll freak if there isn't food when he wakes up."

"Sure." Cindy dropped a second sandwich and another apple into the bag. She wanted to do more. "I can help. If you let me." She softened her voice. "Did your father hurt you?"

"No." Panic flashed in wide brown eyes. "He didn't. Please, don't tell."

A sour odor reached across the stainless steel countertop and stabbed Cindy through the heart as the girl pivoted away. She smelled of bodily fluids that couldn't possibly be her own. Cindy gagged as the girl rushed out. She wanted to protect the child, but unless the girl confessed the truth to the authorities, the abuse would continue.

The back door slammed.

For the next thirty minutes, the line of hungry people continued through the doors of what once was Cindy's childhood home—the house she, her brother, and her sister had shared with their abusive father. The new varnish on the old hardwood floors couldn't cover the dirty feeling in the bottom of Cindy's stomach every time she stood in this room.

Five years ago, Cole had paid to convert the wood building into a distribution center for the hungry. Part of her was glad the dwelling was used for good. Another part of her—the part that couldn't escape the haunted look in a young girl's eyes—wanted to burn the place to the ground. Instead of striking a match, she smiled at the helpless people trickling through the lunch line.

She nodded encouragement to a young woman with two small children and shoved the memory of trying to feed her sister to the back of her mind. Grubby hands reached for the brown bags that held lunch for the hungry family. Cindy wished she could offer the woman a place to rest from the southern heat, but the permit Cole had gotten for her, prohibited consumption on site. Since his death, she'd knocked down a few walls, but the minor remodeling didn't give her room to grow.

She missed him.

Blinking away the nightmare of her youth, she recalled the good memories of her deceased husband. Cole had saved her. He'd given her love and a home.

He'd given her a son.

Cindy prayed that Trevor would never taste the pangs of hunger. After a horrible miscarriage, her son was an unexpected blessing. One that arrived eight months after Cole's funeral. He was her reason for living. Her motivation to survive. Cindy thanked God for him every day.

"That's the end of the line." Maria, Cindy's sister shut the commercial glass door and twisted the lock. One hand smoothed her pixie cut, dark hair as she crossed to where the kitchen used to be—where their friend Joni stood counting leftover bags.

Cindy drummed her knuckles on the bar. "What's today's totals?"

Joni held up a finger. Her golden head bobbed in rhythm with the flip of the bags. Then she looked up. "Two hundred twelve." She stacked the empty bags into a perfect rectangle. "I saw her too. Should I dial up Detective Simmons, or did you want to make the call?"

"While you're at it, tell the detective to quit hanging around here. He makes our clients edgy." Maria swigged from a water bottle. "DZ's Boys came in, snatched two bags and lit out the back door knocking Mrs. Peterson off her walker."

Cindy joined in the cleaning by replacing unused loaves of bread in the pantry. "The boys need to eat." She leaned close to her sister and whispered, "If you'd stop hitting the green stuff, you could tell the detective yourself." She swiped a wet rag across the countertop. "But, if I was gonna call someone, it wouldn't be him. Besides, there's nothing he can do. We all know without proof, notifying the authorities will make the situation worse."

Joni's smile disappeared with a grim nod. "Proving a parent unfit in the Alabama court system is next to impossible. If his biological mother hadn't voluntarily signed consent, James's son would still be on the streets. I'll be so glad when we open our intervention clinic." Joni moved to the other side of the room.

Maria leaned close to Cindy and whispered, "I'm not using. It's just sometimes I need a smoke to calm my nerves."

Cindy blew out a breath and wished her sister would give her life to God. "I don't want to know details."

ଅୟଓ

Ray held tight to the wiggly, little boy with one hand and knocked on the blue apartment door with the other.

No one answered.

Skinny arms latched around his neck. "Am I back by five?"

With one hand, Ray checked the time on his phone. "We're early." He lowered Trevor's feet to the landing and hunkered down beside him on the cool concrete. "We'll have to wait."

Trevor blew out an exaggerated breath. Little legs scampered to the rail and peered through the bars to the luxury cars below. "Where's momma?"

From where Ray sat, the welds appeared solid, but the landing was thirty feet high. "She'll be here in a minute. Move away from the edge."

Curious feet wandered further down the landing. Ray opened his mouth to call Trevor back to his side when singsong music danced from the parking lot below.

Little eyes widened and his mouth opened as he gasped. "Ice cream." In a flash, the little boy disappeared down the stairwell.

Ray scrambled to his feet and ran to the top of the stairs. His heart dropped as Trevor rounded the corner out of sight. "Trevor!" All day the kid had been an angel, why did he all of a sudden go rogue? Pulse racing, Ray descended the steps three at a time. He left the brick building and spotted his target following a crowd of children toward the parking lot. In two strides, Ray snatched the little boy off his feet. "Don't ever run off again."

Gray eyes morphed like drops of mercury as tears gathered.

Each of Trevor's sobs punched Ray in the gut. Maybe he'd been a little rough. He cradled the boy close and whispered, "It's okay, Trev. You scared me. Please don't cry."

One final sniff and it was over. Ray caught a glimpse of an innocent smile before Trevor rested his forehead against his. Eye to eye. Nose to nose. "Uncle Ray, I want ice cream."

Uncle Ray? His heartbeat tripped. The Twin Terrors claimed him as an uncle, although they weren't blood related. Trevor probably thought Uncle Ray was his name.

A sweet kiss fluttered against Ray's cheek. "Please."

Warmth flooded through his coldblooded veins as he hugged the little boy close. "Sure thing, Trev. Uncle Ray will buy you as much ice cream as you want."

A precious giggle was thank you enough as they waited their turn in line. Across the small crowd of parents and children, more than one pair of eyes glanced his way. Nothing new there. He was used to the appreciative looks from women. One stared with open admiration. Ray ignored her and lifted his wiggling bundle onto his shoulders.

Little hands propped on top of Ray's head. "I see the big chocolate."

He kept a firm grip on Trevor's ankles. "Go ahead and pick which one you want."

"Excuse me." The woman had maneuvered to their side and brushed her hip against his leg. "Hi, Trevor. Where's your mom? And who's your friend?"

Ray recognized the invitation in her eyes, but the gold band on her finger answered for him. He stepped to the side ending the bodily contact. "Ray Simmons."

"You're Trevor's uncle. You must be Cindy's…brother?"

At least a dozen pairs of ears besides her two pierced ones leaned close. He kept his answer short. "No."

Gold hoops dangled beneath her short bleached hair as she laughed. "Brother-in-law?"

"Nope." His rude answer didn't seem to faze her. Thankfully, two preteen girls waved from the front. "They're waving for your attention."

She huffed and rolled her eyes. "My girls." Her eyes violated him once more. "I'm in the apartment below Cindy's, if you need to borrow a cup of sugar or anything. I'm always available." With one last, wide smile, she turned and walked away. The heels on her sandals sank into the soft lawn as she moved to the front of the line. The exaggerated sway of her ample hips did nothing to flatter her rounded figure.

One of the few men in the crowd whispered, "Her husband is a good man, unfortunately, he travels a lot. My guess is she's lonely."

Lonely meant clingy. Ray didn't want a lonely woman. And he definitely didn't want a married one. Soft fingers tightened on Ray's chin. He glanced upward and a little face pressed against his.

"Momma says she's a floozy." Several snickers sounded near them. An elbow bit into Ray's skull. "Momma says we don't like people who—"

Ray flipped Trevor over his head and swung him around his back. Giggles erupted, drowning whatever the little munchkin had planned to say next. Ray tossed the little boy high into the air and caught him airplane style. Disaster avoided, Ray perched the giggly, little boy on his forearm and stepped to the counter. "Okay, Trevor. Choose."

"The big one."

Behind the opened, sliding-glass window, the ice-cream man's hat twisted at an odd angle. A wrinkled hand offered a frozen yogurt bar. "This is what Miss Cindy buys."

"No thanks. Real men don't eat fluff." Ray pointed to a large cartooned head on the chart of gooey confections. "Give us two of those." He set Trevor on his feet and reached for his wallet.

The man hesitated but palmed the offered bills. "His mom isn't gonna like this."

Trevor grinned and accepted the opened package. The ice cream was three times the size of Trevor's hand. One bite and both cheeks were smeared.

Ray held his little elbow, and steered him away from the crowd. A few feet later, a pretty blonde blocked his path. She was cute, but too young for his taste. He searched his brain for a polite refusal as her smile trembled.

"Hi." Color infused her cheeks. "My husband and I attend church with Cindy at Bible Tabernacle." Long slender fingers threaded and a knuckle popped. "We would love to see you this Sunday."

He lifted one brow. The husband wasn't in sight.

"I'm sure Cindy's already invited you." Sweat beads materialized on her forehead. "James Preston and his wife sing most Sundays." One huff feathered the hair out of her eyes. "Except when they have other engagements."

"James and Joni are friends of mine."

"Oh." Her eyes widened against her pale skin. She ducked her head. "Sorry for bothering you."

He studied the strange creature who'd issued an offer he'd never encountered. "It was no bother." What did her husband think of her asking men to church? "I doubt I'll make it Sunday, but thanks."

Kind eyes met his. "You're welcome. Tell Cindy I said hi." She turned and with a little wave, pushed a baby stroller across the neat lawn. "Bye, Trevor."

Melted from the hot evening sun, ice cream dribbled down Trevor's arm. "She's nice."

"Yeah. A little weird though." Ray's mawmaw had forced him to attend church every Sunday morning. As a child, he'd sat on the hard pew in starchy clothes while a man talked forever.

Mawmaw would pinch his side when he'd fall asleep. So he studied the architecture of the building and decided to build things. Though, then, he'd never suspected he'd work industrial construction. He'd dreamed of building his own house for years. Maybe he'd start on it while he was working local.

The invitation to church surprised him. James and Joni asked him occasionally, but they'd never waited for an answer like the shy girl had.

At a young age, Ray'd said the required prayer to make it through the pearly gates. He believed in God and His son, Jesus. What was the point of listening to a boring sermon?

"Let's head back. Your mom could be here any minute."

Sitting on the bottom steps, Ray bit into his treat. The ice cream had gumballs protruding from the etched cartoon face on the front. "Trev, check this out." Ray chewed and then blew a bubble. A loud pop echoed in the stairwell.

"Me too." Trevor plucked out the eyeballs made from gum and chewed.

"Like this." Ray demonstrated again. Trevor giggled as the bubble deflated on one side.

His phone buzzed and he read the text from Charlotte. *You in my neck of the woods? Let's get together.*

Charlotte? Who was Charlotte? Was she the teacher or the dancer? Oh, wait. She was the girl that drove the Jeep.

Beside Ray, the little boy blew on the gum but no bubble formed. "Keep trying. You almost got it."

Ray replied to the message on his phone. *Sorry my schedule's full.*

ഇരു

Long, jean-clad legs ended at scruffy work boots. Cindy sucked in a breath as she rounded into the stairwell and pressed a hand to her fluttering abdomen. The unknown man looked far too comfortable sitting on the step above Trevor.

Green eyes lifted to hers and widened in surprise. A hand holding an ice cream paused halfway to his open mouth. Full lips curled as he stood, and then tossed the treat in the nearby trashcan.

She stalked toward him. "Who are you? And what are you doing with my son?"

"Momma!" Trevor vaulted from the bottom step and shoved something behind his back smearing a mess along the side of his shirt.

The gorgeous hunk of man towered above her. His smile elevated the foreign heat in her belly. "Mrs. Maxwell, relax. Trevor's safe with me."

Cindy lifted her chin. Ignoring the sizzle in the air, she stepped closer and focused on his jade colored eyes. "Where's James?"

"Ah, you see, Mrs. Maxwell." The man ran a hand through his short, sandy brown hair. The unabashed little-boy-lost look that covered his handsome face seemed genuine. "James had a run-in with a fish hook. And then one of the twin terrors dropped his knife and well…Mr. Preston drove James and the twins to the emergency room. To save 'em some time, I volunteered to bring your son home."

Sitting on the bottom step, Trevor's eyes widened. "Mr. James bleeded." And then he pulled his hand back around and licked what little remained of an ice cream.

She didn't doubt Joni's twin boys created the chaos described, but that didn't answer her original question. "Who are you?"

His stance widened and his voice rose an octave. "I'm Ray. Ray Simmons. I'm a good friend of James's. I was with them when the accident happened."

Her nerves untangled as she searched her memory. "The friend from James's construction days that always gets him into trouble?"

He shrugged and muscles bulged beneath his brown tee shirt. "Well…"

He definitely looked like trouble. "Joni's mentioned you."

*Chapter Two*

Ray rubbed sticky fingers against his thumb and silently cursed James to the pits of perdition. Old widow woman indeed? He swallowed against his dry mouth as a gentle breeze tossed her strawberry hair over cherry lips. James was crazy if he thought Ray wouldn't be interested. He hadn't been this interested…ever.

She stooped down and lifted Trevor in her arms. "Thank you for looking out for my son."

Ray'd had fun with Trevor, but if he'd known his mom looked like this, they'd have come home hours ago. "You're very welcome."

Surprise flickered in her blue eyes as she scanned him from head to toe. The frown dissolved into a thin line. "And thank you for bringing him home." Slim shoulders rose and then fell. She turned to Trevor and kissed his brow. "I shouldn't have let him go."

"It was fun, momma. We caught fishes. I rolled 'em in." Trevor lunged and Ray caught him in his arms. "And we winned a trophy."

She rubbed her hands together. "You're sticky."

"Uncle Ray buyed ice cream."

Her frown reappeared and one delicate brow arched. "Uncle Ray?"

He kicked a loose pebble across the concrete stairwell. "That's what The Twin Terrors call me."

"Oh." Soft arms brushed his as she reclaimed her son.

"Momma, you're squishing me."

"Sorry, baby." A slender hand fluffed his hair, and Trevor quit squirming. "Sweetie, Ray isn't your unc—"

"I don't mind."

She peeked through luscious lashes and blinked. "Well, thank you again."

She wasn't going to dismiss him that easy. Ray held her gaze.

"Anytime." They were at a standstill. He didn't turn to go and neither did she.

"I have groceries in the car so if you don't mind?"

"Not at all. Mawmaw would bust my hide if I didn't carry in your things. Where did you park?"

"I. I wasn't." She stuttered. "I wasn't asking you to help."

"I know." He flashed the smile that always got him what he wanted. "I want to."

Delicate shoulders lifted. "Thank you." Sleek, toned legs hurried away.

He'd held some beautiful women in his arms, but there was something about her natural beauty that made him want to follow her further than to a dusty garage.

She lowered Trevor to his feet and opened the white door of an older BMW. While leaning in, she bumped her head and reared back.

Never being one to waste an opportunity, he stepped close. He bent his knees and met her gaze, but the blue depths drew his heart into a place he'd never imagined existed. His fingers brushed a lock of silky hair away from her forehead. Except for a red patch from the car door, her skin was flawless. Blood hummed through his veins. "I don't think it will bruise."

She swallowed and then her breath teased the hairs on his forearm. "Good." She sprang from his touch and backed into the front fender. "Maybe you should...um...you know...just..." An agitated hand waved at the plastic bags in the backseat. "Yeah."

Definitely, yeah.

A little tug pulled on his hand. "Can I help, Uncle Ray?"

Ray ruffled the kid's hair. "Sure thing, Trev."

Reaching in the backseat, he lifted a bag filled with leafy produce and handed it to Trevor. A carton of eggs and a loaf of whole wheat bread shared a plastic bag. This he held towards Trevor's mom. "You may want to carry these. I don't have a good track record with fragile items."

Three quick steps and she stood within reach. Though her lips smiled, the hand reaching toward him trembled. He pulled the bag away and searched her wide eyes. Her gaze flitted to the open doorway and then to Trevor. No woman had a reason to fear him.

Ever. "I would never hurt you. Or Trevor."

"Momma, don't you like Uncle Ray? He's a good guy." Trevor laid his head against her leg and a slender hand caressed his cheek.

Her eyes closed briefly, but then she met his direct gaze. "I'm not afraid of you. I've never...never mind." A hand stretched forward. "Give me the bread."

He released the plastic handles, but held her hand as he searched the depths of her blue eyes. "If you aren't afraid of me? Then why are you so jumpy?"

Her gaze traveled around the garage and finally settled somewhere near his feet. "I'm just...I'm worried for Joni. They haven't heard from—"

"That's understandable. I'm worried about the little guy, too. James and I already have plans to check into it." He remembered how James and Joni had struggled to protect James's son Isaac from his abusive mother years ago. When they'd finally got the ammunition to sue for full custody, a negative paternity test had rocked their world. Adoption by the mother's half-sister had secured Isaac's safety. The monthly emails reassuring them that Isaac was fine abruptly ended a few weeks ago. Tremors shook her left hand. "I'd hug you, but I'm afraid you might freak out."

Her smile kicked him in the gut. "I'm fine, Ray. But thanks for your offer."

Hearing his name on her lips sent shivers down his spine. "No problem." Crouching into the backseat once again, he looped the remaining plastic bags on his own arms and stood. "Can you close the door?"

"Of course." She did as asked and then led them around a brick wall to an elevator. Separated by the loaf of bread squished against her chest and the plastic bags hooked on his arms, she stared. "Those look heavy. Can I help?"

He waited until her flitting gaze settled on his. "Yes. You can tell me your name."

"Cindy." Color tinted her cheeks. "Cindy Maxwell."

ℰᏆᏣ

According to Joni, Ray was the most fun loving person on the planet, and half the female population had firsthand experience.

Despite his bulging biceps, fear wasn't the emotion he evoked—
which was new for her.

Stepping into the elevator, Cindy admired the subtle flexes of
strength from a safe distance. His corded forearms bulged as his
hands gripped the many bags. Oh. My. Goodness. She swallowed
and jerked her eyes to his face.

He smiled at Trevor and her heart warmed. Her son was right.
Ray was a good guy, and that's why she should be afraid. Friend of
James's or not, he had to go. He stirred feelings in her that she hadn't
known existed. As soon as he brought in her groceries, she'd politely
ask him to leave.

Jade eyes caught her stare and heat bloomed in her cheeks.

"Lik dis, unte 'ay." Trevor's gum protruded between his lips.

"Almost." Ray's lips twitched. "You gotta use your tongue.
Watch me."

She melted against the opposite wall as Ray blew a huge bubble.
Trevor giggled and then laughed when it popped covering Ray's face
with pink goo.

Spontaneous laughter escaped her.

Ray sucked the gum in his mouth and grinned. "So much for
my poise and charm."

A thin circle of pink surrounded his mustache and the hairs on
his chin. She dug into her purse, and held out a wet wipe. His arms
swung to the side making a path through the many bags.

Surely he didn't mean for her to touch him?

His chin lifted in a challenge that she couldn't ignore. She'd
cleaned Trevor's face a thousand times. Surely this would be no
different. She stepped close. Ray shivered with her first wipe and
her hand paused. "Cold?"

"No." Those dangerous eyes held her captive.

A whiff of his cologne secreted through her senses. As the spicy
scent burned through her lungs, she swallowed against the knot in
her throat and wished the slow elevator would hurry for once. For
some reason, she longed to wrap her arms around his trim waist,
rest her cheek on his chest, and claim the previously offered hug.
Instead, she stepped away from his controlled strength.

His heated gaze followed. "Thank you."

She stared at the wet wipe in her hand as the tension swirled around them.

The elevator dinged.

The doors swished open.

Breath gushed forth from her deepest being. "You're welcome." She blinked away her crazy thoughts, and escaped the close confines of Ray's presence.

Trevor bounced in front of them leading the way to their apartment.

She fumbled with the keys and then finally held the door open. "If you don't mind, put the bags on the counter." At least her rare case of nerves hadn't affected her voice.

"Sure thing, sweetness." His wink buckled her knees.

Cindy usually hated it when men used clichéd endearments, but Ray's words made her feel sweet. Pausing at the entrance, she took a moment to reign in her hormones. She was a Maxwell, and Maxwell's didn't show emotion. The door clicked as she leaned against it and caught her breath. Decadent male laughter rumbled from inside the apartment, and strummed her nerve endings like violin strings. Shoving away from the door, she ignored the rush of feelings fluttering through her body.

He had to go. Now. She hurried into the kitchen, but paused.

Trevor pursed his lips and blew. As a small bubble emerged, his eyes crossed at his nose. A poof ended the bubble's short life span. "I did it, Uncle Ray." Her son danced across the ceramic tile. "Did you see me?"

"Air five." Ray swiped his hand through the air. "I knew you could. You just have to keep practicing."

Trevor spotted her in the doorway. "Momma, I blew a bubble!" He ran toward her and lunged.

She dropped the bread on the counter and caught her precious son. "It was the best bubble I've ever seen." She hugged him close. "You are awesome, but you are also a sticky mess." She tickled his ribs and savored his giggle. "Go change your shirt and wash your hands."

Coward that she was, she kept her back to Ray as she crammed the groceries into overflowing cabinets. Though her eyes couldn't see him, she felt his heated gaze linger. "Thanks again for bringing everything up. And for teaching Trevor to blow a bubble. He hasn't been this excited in a while."

The refrigerator hummed.

She turned.

Like a jaguar stalking his prey, jade eyes pinned her feet to the floor. "Not a problem. I liked teaching Trevor, and I don't mind helping you."

Her phone rang. Grateful for the distraction, she dug it out of her purse and then frowned at the caller id. "Hello?"

"Hey, this is James. Joni gave me your number. Did Ray find you?"

The object of their conversation leaned against her refrigerator and watched her with smoldering eyes.

"He helped unload the car."

"Tell him to leave. Ray has a gift with women. You won't be able to resist him, and he'll break your heart." James's voice confused her further. "Just say no, Cindy. Just say no."

She turned her back to Ray and lowered her voice. "What kind of drugs did they give you, James?" It wasn't like Joni's arrogant husband to tell her what to do? Why start now?

Over her shoulder, Ray shoved off the appliance. He lifted both brows and bit his lip. Through the earpiece, James stuttered something about friends looking out for one another. Across the kitchen, with a half shake of his head, Ray closed his eyes.

Cindy had heard enough. "Goodbye, now. I'm hanging up. Thank you for your concern." She disconnected. James had no authority over her actions, and Ray had been nice to Trevor. "Do you want to stay for dinner?"

Ray's grin sent her heartbeat galloping. "I'd love to." Sidewalk Prophets sang Love from his pocket. He slipped out his phone and winced at his screen. One swipe ignored the call. "But I'd better not."

"Oh." Disappointment settled around her like freshly erected bricks. She'd rejected countless invitations in the five years since Cole's death, and issued only one. This one. And he said no. "Okay then." Pivoting on her heel, she lined the pasta cans in straight rows.

Behind her, Ray cleared his throat. "Do you mind if I wash my hands before I go?"

She didn't turn around. "The bathroom's down the hall on the left." She may not have felt this burning desire before, but she knew when a man was interested. What happened? One minute Ray was flirting and then…nothing.

The carpet muffled his retreating footsteps. Not that she wanted him to stay. The only reason she'd invited him for dinner was because James thought she shouldn't. She hated being told what to do. She'd fought hard for her freedom.

Down the hall, Ray asked Trevor for a towel. She hurried to the laundry room next to the guest bath, and selected an embroidered cloth from the stack of linens she'd yet to put away.

Why couldn't James mind his own business? But then again, what would she have done if Ray would've said yes?

She stepped into the open bathroom doorway. "I don't have many guests, but here's a clean towel."

His easy smile returned. "Don't worry about it. I'm not complaining."

She gave a nod and escaped to the kitchen, but once there she longed to be near him. The bleach belonged on the top shelf of the hall closet. She grabbed the gallon jug by the handle and retraced her steps.

Through the open bathroom door, Ray used the towel to dry Trevor's hands.

She turned her back on the endearing sight. Stretching on tiptoe, she couldn't quite reach the top shelf in the closet. Why didn't she bring the step stool?

"Here." Strong arms reached around each side of her. "Let me help you."

She relinquished the plastic bottle, but held tight to her heart as inviting arms ensconced her, and placed the jug out of reach. The urge to lean against him overwhelmed.

Especially when a calloused hand settled on her shoulder. "Cindy, I'd love to stay for dinner, but I promised James I'd do something altogether different. He's a good friend."

"He and Joni both are." Except for acting all crazy today.

She stiffened her spine. The comfort lifted from her shoulder as Ray moved backward.

She led the way to the front door.

James had overreacted. Friendship was all she needed. She was used to being alone.

A gentle breeze blew in as she opened the door. "Thanks again for bringing Trevor home."

Ray paused just outside and turned. Something—regret maybe—flashed in his eyes. His lips curled as he winked.

And then he was gone.

*Chapter Three*

The sun peeked through her bedroom curtain and pricked her tired, burning eyes. The whirl of the ceiling fan above her mingled with silence. She would give anything to hear Cole's morning prayers again.

Curling into the body pillow, she hid under the covers.

The nights were the hardest. After all this time, she still dreamed of his arms around her.

Pain rolled over her like a rogue wave. Lingering images of last night's dream stole her breath, and her lungs turned to stone. Everyone said the pain would lessen with time.

So far, they were wrong.

The clock's alarm renewed her determination to survive.

Trevor needed breakfast, and they both needed to dress for church. Just once she'd like to sleep in. But if she didn't show for Sunday school, others would judge her for the fraud that she was.

Cindy couldn't disappoint Cole. He'd want her to go.

She rolled out of bed and padded to her bathroom. Breathing in the morning air, she brushed her teeth. Cold water sloshed over her back tooth and pain sliced through her jaw. She gripped the sink's edge and tried to think of anything except the pain.

Ray's offered hug returned to her memory. The throbbing ache eased as she gobbed pain gel over her gums and tooth. Joni had said Ray was in town for a few weeks, but the odds of seeing him again were slim. She should have accepted the hug when she had a chance.

She spit. Her hand cradled her cheek and the other reached for the bottle of antibiotics. No, she shouldn't have.

Ray was dangerous.

Cindy had lived almost five, tortuous years without Cole. She'd endured a troubled pregnancy, and fought to bring Trevor into this world. She'd won the battle against Mrs. Maxwell to raise Trevor on her own. Her life had meaning. She had learned to survive. She didn't need anyone else. Even if the sleepless nights never ended.

𝔰𝔬𝔠𝔯

The only available parking space was on the back row. Ray slid from the truck and then hurried through the graveled lot.

Pausing on the steps, he checked his boots for mud and then swiped his phone for the time. Ray didn't tolerate tardiness from his crewmen, and he doubted God did either. He walked through the double doors at exactly ten fifty-seven.

The church opened into a foyer.

A bean pole of a young man offered him a program. "Good morning, sir. Nice catch yesterday."

Ray recognized the gangly teen from the tournament yesterday. "Thank you." Another set of double doors stood open behind him.

People loitered inside the church.

The few empty pews held purses or blankets. He wished everyone would sit. That way, he could tell which seats were vacant. At the front, Joni waved and then tapped James's shoulder with a microphone. Propping on a crutch, James greeted Ray with a nod and a surprised smile. Relief that his friend was okay with his attending church, didn't help him find a seat.

A gray haired matron appeared and gripped both of his shoulders. "Good to have you here this morning, son."

"Thank you, ma'am."

The tall beehived woman moved on to her next target, and he stepped out of the fresh line of traffic surging from a side door. Twisting the program into a scroll, he tapped his toe.

"Uncle Ray!"

He turned. Trevor rounded a long beaded skirt and headed straight for him. Ray squatted down and lifted the welcomed bundle of energy. "Hey, Trev."

Skinny arms wrapped around his neck and held tight. "You comed here."

Everyone within hearing distance stared. Ray swallowed. He needed to find somewhere to sit and quick. A young man and the pretty girl who'd invited him yesterday appeared. The man—barely old enough to shave—held out his hand. "I'm Wesley. I believe you met my wife Dawn yesterday."

Ray shook the baby smooth hands. "Ray Simmons."

The wife smiled sweetly. "We're glad you could make it."

The husband jerked his head toward the left side of the building. "Cindy and Trevor share a pew with us. This way."

Ray shrugged. "Thanks, but ah…she's not expecting me."

"Oh. What a nice surprise."

As he followed the couple across the church, he wondered what Cindy would think when she saw him in her pew. But about middle ways, she stepped through a side door and entered the sanctuary. A long skirt flowed past her ankles. She paused mid-step as their eyes locked. Smoothing her skirt, she waited until he reached her side.

Trevor reached for her. "Look momma, Uncle Ray's here."

Her arm brushed his as she took her son. "Why did you frown?"

"What?"

She kept her voice at a whisper. "When you looked at my dress, you frowned. Why? Is something wrong with it? Do I have a stain? Or a wrinkle?"

He leaned close. "No, its fine. You're beautiful."

"Then why the frown?"

"I'll tell you later." He tugged her elbow toward the young couple, hoping she'd drop the subject and follow them.

They hugged the wall and got about three steps. Then she turned. "Tell me now. If you don't, I'll worry about it all service. Is there a loose thread?"

A shake of his head prompted her forward again. Piano notes rang as they reached the pew.

"Ray, please tell me."

He couldn't ignore her whispered plea. Under the cover of the music he answered. "Your skirt is too long."

She entered the pew after the young couple and put Trevor on her other side. Both hands smoothed her skirt down her lap. "What? Why would you say that?"

He sat on the outside end and draped his arm along the wood rail behind her.

One delicate brow lifted into a perfect arch. "Ray? What's

wrong with my skirt?"

He leaned over and whispered in her ear. "Nothing. I wanted a glimpse of those long legs of yours."

Her soft gasp didn't surprise him. She swiveled to face him with red cheeks shining. "I cannot believe you said that in church."

He shrugged and grinned. "You demanded an answer, and I can't lie in God's house."

She poked his side. "You are bad, Ray Simmons."

"Yeah. I am." He leaned near once again. "But you like me anyway."

Although her eyes rolled toward the ceiling, he didn't miss the smile peeking out sideways.

Church was fun. James and Joni sounded like professionals, and the preacher's antics kept Ray awake. At one point, he thought the man would disrobe. But in the end, he'd only removed his coat and tie.

Ray's favorite part was the prayer suggestions. Some of them were vague, like James's request for Isaac. Others were lengthy, bordering on gossip sessions. Ray hoped he never needed prayer. He could only imagine what people might say about him.

Now, most everyone knelt at the front—even the children. Ray grinned as Trevor bowed his little head on a carpeted bench. He couldn't see Cindy, but she was down there—somewhere. After a few minutes, Trevor lifted his head and bounced toward Ray.

Trevor climbed in his lap. "You don't talk to Jesus?"

He smoothed the baby fine hair. "I did once when I was a little bit older than you."

"I like talking to Him. My daddy lives up there." Trevor snuggled against Ray's hollow heart.

ഇ൪ന

Cindy kissed Trevor and hugged him tight. "Have fun at Papa's and I'll see you this evening."

"Okay, momma."

Mr. Maxwell grinned as he lifted his grandson. "Are you sure you won't join us for lunch? Marquetta made your favorite—stuffed flounder."

Cindy shook her head. Mr. Maxwell always included her in the invitation for Sunday lunch, but Cindy would rather be alone than spend the day under Cole's mother's scrutiny.

Trevor smiled at someone behind Cindy. "Me and Uncle Ray catched fishes, Papa. And blowed bubbles."

"Well, that sounds like fun." Cole's father turned his attention back to Cindy. "I didn't know you and Zack had a brother, but he's welcome to join us for lunch."

"Uncle Ray!" Trevor yelled across the wide porch. "Let's eat!" His outburst turned all heads toward them.

Cindy sucked in a breath and explained. "Ray's not my brother." She didn't want the Maxwell's to get the wrong idea. The words spilled from her mouth as Ray walked away from James and moved toward them. "He's James's best friend. The twins call him Uncle Ray. Trevor thinks that's his name. I tried to correct—" She broke off her words as Ray stepped beside her.

Trevor lunged forward and before she could blink, Ray caught her son in his arms. Mr. Maxwell tilted his head. As his gaze inspected Trevor and Ray, he smiled. One hand extended. "I'm Alexander Maxwell."

Ray swung Trevor high on one arm, and shook Cole's father's hand with the other. "Ray Simmons. It's nice to meet you, sir."

After a brief handshake, the elder man shoved his hands in his pockets and rocked back on his heels. "We were just discussing our lunch plans. You and Cindy are more than welcome to join us."

Ray's easy smile faltered. "Uh." He looked to her with raised brows.

Pain shot through her mouth. She winced. The gel she'd used earlier had worn off, and the dull toothache now throbbed.

"Momma's face hurts." Trevor's little head rested against Rays.

He turned toward her. While holding Trevor with one hand, he caressed her cheek with the other. "Where? From when you bumped your head on the car yesterday?" Ray's gentle touch confused her thoughts.

"No. I have a toothache. That's all."

Mr. Maxwell cleared his throat and Ray removed his hand. Genuine concern lined her father-in-law's expression. "Why didn't you request prayer?"

Was he worried about her pain, or Ray? "I have another appointment Tuesday. I'll be okay 'till then, but I don't feel like lunch. Tell Marquetta I said thanks for thinking of me."

"Alright. If the pain becomes unbearable I have Dr. Benson's cell number. He owes me a favor, and I'm sure he can work you in sooner. Come on, Trevor. Grandmother is waiting in the car." He reached out. Trevor kissed Ray's cheek and then Mr. Maxwell pulled his grandson into his arms. "If you change your mind, come on over. Both of you are welcome."

Trevor waved over his grandfather's shoulder. "Bye Uncle Ray. See you later, momma."

She smiled and waved until Mr. Maxwell walked behind a minivan, blocking her view of her small son. Her jaw throbbed, but she'd learned to live with pain.

Ray's shoulders brushed against hers. Her guilty conscious wondered who invited him to church. James thought she did. She hadn't, but if it rankled Joni's arrogant husband to think she'd invited Ray, so be it.

Joni had added her warning to James's. What made her friends think she needed protecting? Ray was a harmless flirt, and she had no intentions of acting on the feelings he provoked.

Car doors slammed, and gravel crunched as families left the Sunday morning services. Ray returned Trevor's wave as the Maxwell's luxury sedan passed the front of the building.

She lifted a hand, shielding her eyes from the noonday sun as they stepped into the sunshine. "Sorry about the lunch invitation. Mr. Maxwell means well but…he's like a father to me and I think that he thought—never mind."

"Cindy! Wait up!" Phillip jogged across the parking lot toward them.

She groaned as Cole's friend caught his breath and blocked her path.

"I wanted to talk to you." He glanced at Ray. "Hi, I'm Phillip." And then turned back to Cindy. "This year's rent is due on the storage unit. Have you made your decision? My offer is more than fair, and Cole's Harley is rusting away."

He already knew her answer. She sidestepped him and kept

walking. They'd been through this a thousand times. "I won't sell the motorcycle until I can ride one more time. And you refuse to take me. My decision is no."

He groaned and ran around her again. "I told you. It won't look right for us to ride together. People will talk." He pursed his lips and looked to Ray. "Let your boyfriend take you."

Cindy was losing patience. "He's not my boyfriend, and stop being rude. I already said no."

Ray stepped in between them, facing Phillip. Steel entered his voice. "She said no. Take your offer elsewhere and leave her alone."

Phillip's face paled in the bright sunlight. He stepped back. His blonde hair lifted with the wind. "You've got it all wrong. I'm helping her."

Warmth bubbled within her. Ray was taking her side, without judging her actions. Now maybe Phillip would accept her answer. She gripped Ray's thick upper arms and stood on tiptoe to glare over his shoulder. "I don't want your help."

"Fine. When you change your mind, call me." Phillip hurried away.

Ray turned toward her and her arms slid to his chest. His body heat burned her fingertips through the thin cotton shirt. She snatched her traitorous hands to her sides and started for her car. Her lips curled. Ray had shielded her. And she'd let him.

He kept pace with her. "I didn't realize that Cole was a biker."

A gentle wind stirred the distracting scent of his aftershave. She caught herself inhaling the delicious fragrance. "Not many people did. Phillip wants to buy the Harley, but I keep hoping that I can ride again."

They stopped beside her car, and he leaned against the front driver's fender. "It's a crime to own a Harley without being able to ride her."

Yes, it was. And she longed to feel the wind in her hair. "Is there a chance that you can you captain a sailboat?"

"No, why?" Ray's dazzling smile accelerated her pulse. "Do you own one of those too?"

"Not anymore." She still didn't understand why Cole had sold it to the District Attorney. "But I do have the motorcycle. For now."

Ray's head tilted as he studied her. "During the preacher's sermon about finances, I couldn't help but notice your fidgeting."

She braced herself. It wouldn't be the first time someone asked her for a handout, but she'd hoped Ray was different. "I don't want to talk about money. It'll ruin the day."

Ray shot her a half smile. "I've worked since I was eighteen. Haven't had that many expenses to speak of. You've been without a provider for a few years. I could spot you a loan if you need one."

She fell against the car door to steady her weakened knees. He wasn't asking for money. He was offering. "That's the nicest thing anyone has said to me in a long time. Thank you, Ray. But Cole left me plenty of money. This morning, I realized that I haven't been generous enough in my giving. Your offer just now kind of cinched it."

His gaze recaptured hers. "If you don't have to sell it, I could teach you to drive the bike, or I could take you for a ride?"

She pressed the car's remote unlock button. Could she do this? "Do you worry about other people's opinions?"

"No." His wink gave the butterflies in her stomach flight. "But, James is watching us from his truck."

One glance proved Ray's words. "Why can't he mind his own business?" She forced a smile and waved.

James didn't acknowledge her, but shifted into gear and the truck slowly crossed the parking lot.

"He's a good friend."

As she opened the driver's door, the truth hit her like crumbling bricks. "He's the reason you didn't stay for dinner yesterday. He warned you not to be friends with me." Through the windshield of the truck, James pretended to talk on his phone as he turned onto the highway. "He did, didn't he?" Ray's grin was gone. "Like Joni listed your many sins to me."

His shoved off the front fender and towered over her. The car door separated them. "Don't believe everything you hear."

She lifted her chin. "So you don't have two women in every city?" His head tilted and she explained, "One with a broken heart, and one waiting for your return?"

His grin was back. "Not in every city."

She tossed her purse on the front seat. "What did they say about me?"

Those dangerous jade eyes captured hers. "That you weren't ready for a relationship and you'd break my heart."

"Better yours than mine." She couldn't look away. "But they are right. I'm not ready, and I may never be." She wanted to see Cole again in heaven. She wouldn't jeopardize that for anything or anyone. "Regardless of James's opinion or anyone else's…I could never date anyone who wasn't a Christian. And if half the rumors are true…you are a very good sinner."

He covered her hand resting on top of the car door between them. "I admit it. I am a horrible wretched sinner." His thumb drew sizzling circles around her knuckle. "But, I believe that Jesus died on a cross to forgive my sins." He grinned and her stomach flip-flopped. He lifted her hand until his mouth hovered a breath away from her skin. "And that—my sweetness—makes me just as much a Christian as you are."

With one touch of his lips, she forgot why she was waiting.

*Chapter Four*

The occasional childhood nightmare was expected, but last night's dream was frightening in a different way. Cindy'd dreamt of Cole as she always did, but just when the dream got good—or bad depending on your perception—Ray's face leaned down and kissed her. She covered her head with her body pillow, and tried not to think of what happened next.

She shouldn't be feeling this way. Because of her abusive childhood, and until she'd met her husband, she'd never desired a man's touch. Cole's love had been a comforting warmth. Not a hot burning flame that jumbled her insides. It wasn't right. The dream. The longing. Sunday, she'd been tempted by Ray. And she shouldn't have been? How could she see Cole in heaven if she succumbed to Ray's allure? She couldn't. So she wouldn't. Then why did she want to, if she didn't want to?

Ugh.

It was a dream. It wasn't real. According to Joni, Ray and James would work fourteen hours a day for the next few weeks. Then she'd never see him again. That could be a good thing.

She rolled out from the covers and headed to the shower to wash the images from her mind.

Her morning went downhill from there. Trevor's pullup was wet, again. He was four years old. Her mothering skills needed tweaking.

They were late for preschool. Cindy signed Trevor in, and bent to kiss his cheek. "Have a good day sweetie."

"Okay, momma." Trevor's backpack bounced as he ran down the hall toward his classroom.

Stuck at a red light, Cindy drummed her fingers on the BMW's steering wheel. Every year the church ladies put together care packages for an orphanage in Guatemala. This year they were meeting at Joni's house. One, because she had the most room, and two because the fellowship hall was being retiled.

In the flow of traffic, a blue dodge truck passed and Ray entered her thoughts, again. She shook her head. Get a grip. A horn beeped, and she drove through the intersection. She was the last to arrive, but took time to brew a cup of tea before joining the group in the family room. Folding chairs were lined around the sectional furniture.

Cindy stepped into the room. Directly across Joni's living room sat Mrs. Maxwell, Rachel, and a petite blonde deep in conversation. Rachel dabbed the corner of her eye and suspicion curled in Cindy's gut. Something was up. But after her hectic morning, she didn't have the patience to deal with Cole's mother nor his want-to-be girlfriend—Rachel. Granny used to say "Keep your friends close, but your enemies closer." Cindy maneuvered around the furniture so she could hear their hush conversation.

Mrs. Maxwell patted Rachel on the hand. "Dear, You're like a daughter to me. You don't need an invitation to visit. We're family. Come any time."

"I'm sorry for your loss." The stranger hugged Rachel. "The death of a spouse is hard. My sister lost her husband two years ago. I'll keep you in my prayers."

The tea in Cindy's cup spilled over as the cup rattled against the saucer. "Thank you."

Mrs. Maxwell's eyes rounded in shock. "Cindy." Her mother-in-law nodded in greeting and then lowered her head to sip her tea.

Ignoring the fiery darts shooting from Rachel's eyes, Cindy forced a smile at the woman sitting between the two thorns in her side. "Yes. The death of a spouse is hard. I miss Cole every minute of every day. September 9, it will be five years."

The blonde looked to Rachel and frowned. Then she looked up at Cindy and bit her lip. "I'm sorry. We haven't met."

"Cindy Maxwell. Cole's wife. Mrs. Maxwell's daughter-in-law."

A dainty hand covered her gapping mouth. "Oh. I'm so sorry." She pointed at Rachel. "I thought she was the—." A blush stained the newcomer's cheeks. "Oh please, forgive me."

Cindy waved a hand as she stood. "Nothing to forgive. Rachel's been trying to steal my husband since before he died. I'm used to it." Mumbled gasps and a few snickers followed Cindy out of the room, and into the empty kitchen. Rachel's outrageous claim stirred a familiar anger inside her, but Mrs. Maxwell's betrayal cut deeper than she wanted to admit. She leaned against the kitchen counter and closed her eyes trying to escape the world she was trapped in.

Cole had picked Cindy up off the side of the road. He loved her though she didn't deserve it. He introduced her to the power of his God. He worked a deal with the judge and got her felonies reduced to time served.

And, oh how she loved him. Everything she did was to make him proud. Both Cole and their baby girl looked down on her and Trevor from heaven. Her shameful past was a blight on the Maxwell name even before Cole died. She wasn't good enough to be his wife. Everyone, all his friends, the people in his church, and especially his mother wished he'd married Rachel. But Cole had loved Cindy, and she wasn't about to give up the claim to his heart.

"He loved me first." Rachel hissed from the open door.

"Then why didn't he marry you?"

Rachel pranced into the kitchen. "Because he loved me enough not to make me a widow."

"I don't have the time or patience to listen to your craziness. If he loved you, he would have married you. Not me."

Rachel's eyes glowed with hatred and something else, a secret. "Cole knew he was dying. If you don't believe me ask Dr. Glover or James. They'll confirm it." Strong conviction lined her words. Whether they were true or not Rachel believed them.

But Cindy knew better than to show a weakness to an enemy. "It doesn't matter how he died. The fact is my husband is gone. And I'd appreciate it if you didn't trample his memory with your lies."

James's and Joni's voice floated in through the thin walls separating the kitchen and the living room but their words were too muffled to understand. Rachel's gaze flickered to the hallway and then back to Cindy. "Your very existence tramples his memory. He loved me his whole life. But when he knew he was dying, he turned away to protect my feelings. In some since of chivalry, he turned to you. I wish he would've died three months earlier. Before he met you. Before he forgot his Christian upbringing. Before his memory was tainted by—"

Heavy footsteps sounded behind Cindy. Ray's cologne reached her nostrils a split second before his large hand cupped her shoulder.

Grateful for the interruption, Cindy ignored the unseen knife shredding her heart to ribbons. Turning slightly so that she still had Rachel in sight, she looked up into Ray's handsome face and forced a smile, "Hey. What are you doing here?"

His grin twinkled in his eyes. "We had a delay on the job. James needed something from the den. We won't be here long, but seeing you is an unexpected surprise."

A huff sounded from Rachel. "I bet it is."

Cindy had done nothing wrong, and she refused to cower beneath Rachel's unvoiced accusation. "It's good to see you, too."

"Humph." Rachel pivoted on her toes and fled the kitchen.

Cindy breathed easier. Slowly the tightness in her chest loosened.

Ray's thumb drew circles into her shoulder. "Cole's ex?"

She stepped away from his tempting arms. "No. But she wanted to be."

"I overheard some of the things she said. I know that hurt. I'm sorry you had to endure that."

"I'm fine." Her mind replayed Rachel's accusations. Had Cole known he was dying? How could that be possible? Ask Dr. Glover or James? How did Rachel know who Cole's doctor was? Needing support, Cindy reached for the counter top, but it was Ray's arm that steadied her. His forearm muscles were warm and solid beneath her palm. She dismissed Rachel's words and focused on Ray's voice.

"Others used to tell me she didn't love me, but I refused to believe them."

"Wait." She leaned back in order to see him. "You were married?"

A sad smile adorned his face. "No. I was in love with a different kind of woman. My mother. She disappeared when I was seven, and left me with my Great Aunt. The other kids used to say it was my fault. They said she left because I was too ugly to be loved."

Cindy squeezed his arm for reassurance. "That's awful. You were right not to believe them. Kids can be cruel. I'm sure your mom loved you very much."

Her heart tripped over his full blown grin. "Maybe. It really doesn't matter if she did or not. It's what I choose to believe that effects me." His free hand covered hers on his arm. "I used to make up these wild stories about how she was abducted by aliens and she was fighting her way back to me. Silly stuff, but it got me through middle school."

She ached for the little boy he used to be. "Did you ever find her?"

"No. The adult in me knows she probably overdosed in some remote location. But the kid in me imagines that she's flying in her spacecraft toward the Milkyway this very moment."

A giggle slipped from between her lips. "Maybe we can negotiate a trade with the aliens. Rachel for your mom."

Ray tilted his head back and laughed.

"What's so funny?" James narrowed his eyes at their joined hands. "What's going on in here?"

"Treaty negotiations." Ray winked at Cindy.

Belatedly, she snatched her hand from his arm, and shoved both hands behind her back.

"Well, if you're done, it's time to hit the road."

An hour later, Cindy fell into Joni's empty loveseat and dangled her feet across the armrest. "Have you ever had bad thoughts?"

"Yes. I'm having a few right now about my husband. Not to mention Sara ordered the Jesus-loves-me pencils late and they may not be here in time." Joni's pen scratched across the notepad. "But no matter how much she irritates, you can't kill Rachel. You know what it's like to miscarry a baby. I don't like to gossip, but Rachel's had four. Her family is worried that it's affecting her mental state. Pray the Lord will heal her, and then hopefully, her obsession with Trevor will go away."

"As long as Rachel stays in Birmingham, she's not my problem. Anyway, I wasn't talking about mad thoughts. I meant bad ones. You know…about men."

"Oh!" Her friend's blonde head came up with a start. "Lustful thoughts?"

Cindy's faced flamed. She'd never lusted after any man. Not even Cole. "Not quite that vivid." She stood and blew out a breath. "Never mind."

"Well. Um." Joni perched on the sofa. "I had lustful thoughts about James, but now that we're married it's kind of fun. Maybe you should remarry."

"I don't think so." Besides, the man invading her dreams wasn't the marrying kind. But he did look good in those jeans.

"Look. Ignore Rachel's snarky comments. Cole's been gone for years, and he wouldn't want you and Trevor to be alone. Tom has had his eye on you since the hay ride last year."

"Not interested." Cindy paced the living area. No one could replace her husband.

"Why not? Personally, I figured you'd have found someone to marry before now. And it's normal for you to desire the love of a man."

Before Cole, she'd hated sex. If Cole could wait twenty-eight years for their wedding night, she could wait until she joined him in heaven. Not that people had sex in heaven. But then it wouldn't matter. Her forehead fell against the wall as a groan escaped her tight throat. What was wrong with her?

"Or you could fast?"

She lifted her head and stared at her friend. "What?"

"Yes, that's what you should do." Joni stood and paced the length of the room. "Just because you're having normal urges doesn't mean that it's not sinful if you act upon them. So…you need to fast and pray. The Lord will help you."

Heat blazed a trail up her neck. She'd fasted with Cole, before their wedding. She couldn't fast for Ray. That would be blasphemy.

"The solution's simple really." Joni pivoted on her heel. "Paul said it best. It's better to marry than to burn. And I don't think he meant hell. He could have meant burning with unfulfilled desire."

Cindy blinked at her friend and grabbed her bag out from behind the bookshelf. "Thank you for your advice, but that's not what I meant. I'm going to change clothes. The realtor's supposed to meet us at two."

"Well…" Joni shrugged. "It may cost more to bring the place up to code than to buy a new lot and start over. Remember what happened last year when we had that electrical problem?"

"You may be right, but the location is perfect."

Joni cleared her throat. "I asked James to meet us. He can give us a few rough figures."

Probably, but…he would also try to talk her out of buying the place. He was overprotective of Joni and he'd voiced his opinion long ago. And every day since. He didn't want his wife anywhere in that neighborhood. But the people they were reaching had no transportation. As much as Cindy hated the place, their facility had to remain where it was.

Cindy nodded to her friend. "Let me worry about the cost. You just concentrate on passing your finals and getting your degree."

Forty-five minutes later, she fell into the old squeaky chair she'd bought at a thrift store, and rested her forehead on the metal desk in her office. She needed one minute alone from Joni's incessant chatter to gather her thoughts.

"Cindy, you have a visitor!" Maria yelled from the other room.

Rolling her shoulders, Cindy peeked out of the office to find her sister preening with one hip propped against the counter. Maria turned toward Cindy and fanned her face. Then she mouthed, "Wow."

Cindy glanced around her. Ray stepped in her line of vision and her breath hitched. "Ray? What are you doing here?"

"I'm with James. I hope you don't mind me tagging along."

Maria nudged her in the back, and Cindy stumbled forward.

"Not at all. I'm glad you're here."

Maria pulled her purse strap over her shoulder. "My shift starts in twenty, so…I'm outta here." A smooch landed on Cindy's cheek. On her way to the door, Maria waved over her shoulder. "Call me tonight. I want details."

Cindy forced a smile and prayed her sister wouldn't say anything more embarrassing. She breathed a sigh of relief as the door shut.

"So…" Ray frowned at the electric panel box and closed the cover. "This is where the miracles happen?"

Cindy fought the heat that crawled up her neck. "I don't know about miracles, but we feed about two hundred a day."

Ray let out a long whistle. "Impressive. What kind of project do you need James's advice about?"

"I don't. Joni wants his opinion. We don't have a dining room. Our permit won't allow one because we lack the square footage. Plus, Joni graduates in December. After she gets her license for social work, we can offer abused and neglected women and children a safe place to sleep."

Cindy showed him around the small house that Cole had named Lulu's Place—in memory of the baby girl they'd lost. Ray silently scrutinized everything. At the backdoor, she held the base of the handle while she twisted the loose knob. Over the years the house had settled. She pushed her shoulder against the wood and it popped open.

Ray's hands steadied her.

"Thank you. This place could use a few repairs, but the house behind me is for sale. I'm gonna buy it and connect both buildings. Using one to prepare and one to serve. The new addition in the middle will become the safe house. The realtor should be here any minute." She stopped at the wood privacy fence that divided the two properties.

James had his arm around Joni's waist who said, "We can drive around."

Ray ripped off a few rotten boards, creating a hole big enough for them to squeeze through. "No need."

James ducked through first, knocking away the spider webs for his wife who carefully stepped through the fence.

Ray steadied Cindy's hand as she stepped over the base board. Her arm jolted with the now familiar spark.

ജ്ഞാ

Wisteria grew wild in the huge magnolia in the small backyard. Mimosas and popcorn trees camouflaged the old, dumpy house. Why did she want to fix this up? It would take a small fortune to bring it to code.

"What do you think?" One glimpse of her smile and he couldn't break her heart.

Behind her back, James arched his eyebrows. "There are other options."

Her smile disappeared. Ray lifted her hand instinctively. "The lot has potential, but the house...eh?"

A portion of cinderblock crumbled to the ground revealing solid pine floor joists. If the roof was intact, it was doable. Expensive and impractical, but doable. On the drive here James had voiced his intentions of trying to change Cindy's mind about buying the place, but Ray had an inexplicable urge to give her what she wanted. "Do you want to check out the roof?"

James reached and touched the facial board. "Why not? Boost me up."

Joni gasped. "What about your stitches?"

Ray cupped his hands low. "Ready?"

James stepped in with his good foot. "Go."

Ray sprang up as James scrambled onto the eave of the house.

A soft touch landed on Ray's arm as Cindy gasped beside him. "I can't believe he made it."

Footsteps crunched above them. "Pretty sound up here. A few shingles missing though."

Ray latched onto Cindy's hand and took a few steps back.

Joni glared at her husband. "Please come down."

"In a minute, beautiful." He bounced on the roof. "No penetration. There's a lower side over here. I'll climb down.

Cindy reclaimed her hand as Joni hurried around the side of the house. Ray missed her touch.

Blue eyes held his gaze. "So, it's good?"

Ray didn't know how to tell her she would be wasting money. "It depends on the inside."

Tires scrunched around front and voices greeted one another. Cindy's smile stole his breath. "That must be the real estate agent. Let's go."

In the front of the house, Cindy and Joni greeted the business woman as James nudged Ray. "I hope she listens to you."

Cindy looked over her shoulder from the doorway. "You guys coming in?"

"Sure. James?"

"I'm gonna check on my truck. Someone might have stolen my hubcaps."

James's truck had alloy wheels. Ray noticed his friend's limp and remembered James's injury. "You okay?"

"Yeah." James slapped Ray's shoulder and lowered his voice. "Let her down easy."

Joni wrapped her arm around James, and helped him cross the yard. His friends were depending on him to convince Cindy not to purchase the building, but he couldn't hurt her.

Ray stepped around the broken concrete steps and focused on the old house. There must be some way to make it work. It would make a good hunting camp. He gave the inside a courtesy inspection thinking more and more that's what the house was suited for. The one she was using now had multiple code infractions.

The agent gave her best pitch about the convenience of the location and then asked, "Are you ready to make an offer?"

He stilled himself for the question that was coming his way, but Cindy surprised him. "Not yet, but thank you for the tour. I'll let you know."

Relieved, he followed the women outside. Baby cedars enclosed the porch. Empty beer cans and cigarette butts littered the wood floor. Someone was using the old place as a party. The agent left. Ray waited until her car reversed into the street, and then turned toward Cindy. "Did you change your mind?"

Her laughter poured sunshine into his heart. "No. But I don't like pushy salespeople, and I wanted to talk to you about estimated costs." She turned in a circle. "What do you think?"

Ray was brutally honest. "I think you're the most beautiful woman in the world."

Her lips twitched and then she pressed them together.

"Your smile dances in those big, blue eyes."

Color flushed her cheeks making her even more beautiful. "What do you think about me buying the house?"

"Oh that. Tell me again why you want it."

"Ray." She tilted her head, and a hand landed on her hip. "I need a dining room."

"Then it is my expert opinion that you buy the lot. Demolish both houses. And build a new multipurpose building."

Her smile vanished. "It's that bad?"

"Yep. During the tour of your current facility, I couldn't help but wonder how well you knew the Health Inspector?"

She cringed. "He let a few things slide when I pretended an interest in dinner. Date night arrived and I had a convenient headache." She stared at his boots as her cheeks turned pink. "He finally quit calling. I doubt he'll be as forgiving as before."

Ray didn't like her answer. "It's gonna cost you more than dinner for *this* building to pass."

"Ray!"

"Seriously, buy the lot. You can save demolition costs by offering the house free to someone who moves it to their hunting club." His hands cupped her shoulders, and turned her toward the back lot. The sweet scent of vanilla captured his thoughts. He inhaled, blinked and refocused on the narrow view through the hole in the fence. "Then build your building. With both lots, you'll have plenty of room. When you're done, have the green house removed and use the space for a parking lot or a picnic pavilion."

She relaxed back into his chest. His hands slid down her arms and curled around her waist drawing her closer. A sweet savor lured his lips to her neck.

The simple kiss snatched her beyond his reach. She stood three feet away and glared at a dead weed. "Thank you, Ray." Her wavering gaze lifted to his. Fear flickered, but disappeared with a blink.

He hadn't intended to kiss her, but he wouldn't apologize. "Before you do anything, check the zoning restrictions."

"Thanks. I will. What do I owe you?"

"Dinner." He touched her forehead. "Headache free."

*Chapter Five*

The shipment of steel, needed to begin construction, was delayed again the next day. Normally, Ray would be beyond aggravated, but he smiled and drove to Cindy's in hopes of claiming the dinner she owed him. He figured he stood a better chance of persuading her to say yes if he asked in person.

The apartment complex gate was open. As he drove through, unease churned in his gut. The day he'd brought Trevor home, he had to wait and follow another resident in.

Cindy's car jutted at an odd angle halfway outside the garage. He parked beside it and slid out of the truck. The rolling door couldn't be secured without crushing the trunk of her car. The BMW's engine ticked in the cool afternoon.

His fists landed on his hips. He turned toward Trevor's battery powered jeep charging in one corner. Plastic tubs lined the adjacent wall.

An unseen hand gripped his heart and an urgency spurred his feet into motion. Something was wrong.

Ray ran up the stairs. A child's cries penetrated the thick oak door of Cindy's apartment. "Trevor? Is that you, bud?"

The sobs hushed. Ray pounded on the door and called out again. "Trevor, it's Uncle Ray. Is your mom home?"

The movement on the other side was muffled by Trevor's voice. "Momma fell down."

Ray shoved open the door, but the safety chain caught. Through the six inch gap, Cindy's unconscious body lay facedown on the carpet. "Trevor, step away from the door."

"Momma don't talk."

"Move, Trevor!"

The boy flinched and ran to his mother.

One kick against the solid oak door snapped the flimsy chain. Ray rushed to Cindy's side. He rolled her in his arms. Her face was flushed. He lay the back of his hand against her lips. Her faint breath warmed his skin. "Sweetness, wake up." One jaw was swollen. Using his thumb, he lifted an eye lid.

She moaned, and a tear trailed down her cheek. Her lips muttered. "Trevor?"

"Right here, momma."

She went limp in Ray's arms and he jiggled her. "Talk to me." Drugged eyes couldn't focus. "What did you take?"

Her head moved in slow motion, and her mouth opened. Bloody cotton packed the inside of her jaw. "Dentist." With that slurred word she crumbled against his chest.

Heart pounding, he lifted her. "Follow me, Trevor. We need to take her to the doctor." Ray nodded to a set of keys on the floor. "Grab those. We'll take your mom's car, so you'll be safe."

Ray needed a free hand to help Trevor, so he slung Cindy over his shoulder, and lifted Trevor by the waist. In the parking lot, Trevor pressed the unlock pad and Ray eased Cindy into the passenger seat. "Get in."

Trevor scrambled into the back. Ray shut both doors and raced to the driver's side. On the wild ride to the emergency room, an occasional groan from Cindy stabbed his heart, but at least he knew she was breathing. Skidding to a stop under the hospital canopy, Ray braked hard and shifted into park.

Trevor's little body slammed into the back of Ray's seat. Trevor regained his feet, leaned over and stroked his mother's hair.

Ray jumped out of the driver's side and flung open the rear door. "Why aren't you buckled up?"

Little gray eyes blinked. "I don't know how."

It was too late to argue about it. Ray ran around the hood, and lifted the unconscious woman to his shoulder. "Come on, Trevor. Stay close."

A nurse waved them into the back and indicated a bed behind a curtain.

A doctor rushed into the cubicle and shined a light in Cindy's eyes. "What happened?"

Ray caught his breath and lifted a pale Trevor in his arms. "I'm not sure. She went to the dentist and passed out three feet inside the door when she got home."

The doctor placed one end of a stethoscope on Cindy's chest, and held up a finger. Ray held his breath until the doctor yanked the things out of his ears and said, "Her airway is closing. I believe she's having an adverse reaction. Possibly to Epinephrine in Novocain. Though normally not this severe, it's fairly common."

Her eyes didn't open and Ray wanted to argue, but Trevor's question refrained him. "Momma's okay, now?"

"Yeah, Trev. Momma's okay."

The nurse touched his arm. "We have some paperwork for you. And then you can wait out front until we stabilize your wife's heart rate and open her breathing passages."

Her words didn't reassure him, but he forced a smile for Trevor's benefit. "I need to move the car, and then we'll fill out whatever you need."

℘ℭ

The bright lights of the patient pickup canopy blinded her. Letting Ray push her out in a wheelchair when she was able to walk was foolish. Yet, she didn't remember blacking out, nor the drive to the hospital.

She squinted against the pain behind her eyes. Maybe she should've stayed overnight like the doctor wanted, but Trevor had never stayed away from her.

She stood and reached for the car door handle. Darkness tunneled in, and she swayed on her feet. A strong arm steadied her, and helped her into the seat. "Thank you, Ray. Where's Trevor?"

His little voice came from the backseat. "Uncle Ray teached me how to buckle up this time."

Ray slid under the steering wheel. "Sorry, I was preoccupied on the way here."

Heavy weights closed her lids. What had they given her to make her so sleepy? The clank of the garage door jolted her awake. Ray appeared at her side and cradled her in his arms. They were at the apartment? Already? Ray insisted on carrying her up the stairs. Why? The elevator is around the corner.

"You heard the doctor. You'll be dizzy and disoriented, but after a couple days rest you'll be good as new."

She didn't have the strength to argue. Burying her face in his solid chest, she murmured, "Thank you, Ray."

"You're welcome." Keys rattled. "Trevor, can you open the door?"

"Yes, sir."

Sounds faded. Her bedroom dresser focused. She reached for the body pillow and encountered emptiness. Ray's laughter mingled with Trevor's somewhere in the distant fog. Her lips curled as she drifted off to a dreamland where Ray's arms held her close.

&#8480;&#8475;

"Where are you? I need some help." Ray didn't think Cindy would appreciate waking up to find him in her house, so he'd called James.

"I'm at the farm going over some paperwork with my uncles. They think they can locate Sam's last known address. What's up? What's wrong?"

Ray paced the apartment's kitchen and quickly explained Cindy's adverse reaction to the dental work.

"What did the doctor say? Will she be alright?"

Before he could answer, Joni's voice sounded in the background. "Cindy's sick?" Joni's chatter grew as James relayed the information to his wife.

Then Joni came on the line. "Ray, the twins are asleep. We can't make it back tonight. Cindy keeps emergency numbers written in Trevor's shoe. Call Mr. Maxwell and explain the situation. He'll either come over or send Marquetta."

"Hold on." Ray walked into the living area where Trevor watched cartoons. He tugged off a little shoe. Giggles erupted from the little boy, and he kicked off the second shoe and curled on the couch.

Three phone numbers were written in permanent marker on the inside sole. Ray recognized one as Cindy's cell. "I got 'em. Thanks, Joni. I got it from here."

"Ray." Her voice hesitated. "I know you are a good guy and want to help and all, but no matter what happens, you can't stay there tonight."

He clenched his jaw. "I've never been that desperate for a woman."

"That's not what I meant." A sigh breezed through the earpiece. "Because of her past, gossips have always targeted Cindy. If you stay the night, no one will consider the circumstances. If you can't reach Mr. Maxwell, go downstairs to the apartment below Cindy's. I forget the woman's name, but she has a teenage daughter who babysits Trevor sometimes. I'll be there in the morning."

Ray reassured Joni he wouldn't do anything unseemly, and disconnected. He shuddered at the thought of asking Mrs. Foloosy for a favor. The second number listed in Trevor's shoe went to Mr. Maxwell's voicemail. "Mr. Maxwell this is Ray Simmons." He swallowed. "Cindy had a reaction to something the dentist gave her today. She's fine. Trevor's good. I just..." He rubbed his chin. "I thought you might like to know."

He ended the call and hit himself in the head with the phone. That was the stupidest message he'd ever left.

There was one more number to try.

A feminine voice answered. "Hello?"

Ray released a breath. "Yeah. This is Ray Simmons. I know this is weird, but...who am I talking to?"

A drunken giggle swelled down the line. "This is Maria McDuffie. Who were you hoping would answer?"

Maria? Maria? He snapped his fingers. "Cindy's sister?"

"Oh." The voice sobered. "Yes. And you must be that fine specimen eyeballing my sister yesterday?"

"Uh." Ray laughed. "Come over to her place. She and Trevor need someone to look after them."

Laughter purred. "No can do, Ray baby. I'm not much for hobnobbing with the richies. She'd probably prefer your company to mine anyways."

"She's sick."

"What's wrong with her?"

Ray explained Cindy's reaction.

Her sister sighed. "And you can't stay the night because all the self-righteous hypocrites will tear her apart. Fine. Don't go anywhere, I'll be there in thirty minutes."

Three hours later, as Ray tucked a sleeping Trevor into bed, the front door banged open. He hurried up the hall, and found a red eyed Maria stumbling across the living area.

He caught her before she fell and cringed at the amount of alcohol on her breath. "Had a few drinks, did you?"

"Shhh." She waved her hand. "Don't tell Shindy" Her words slurred together as she folded onto the couch.

He glared down at the sister. "How are you supposed to take care of Trevor? You can't even take care of yourself."

Maria sniffed and started bawling. "I'm sorry." Hiccup. "Sorry. Sorry. Sorry."

Great! Joni may not like it, but he wasn't leaving Cindy or Trevor in the hands of a drunk. He walked down the hall and peered into what he thought was the extra bedroom. With a flip of a switch, light flooded the room. Dust covered a huge wood desk. A large set of drums took up what little space remained. Ray'd have to sleep in the recliner.

On his way back up the hall, a scream sounded from Cindy's room. He burst through the doorway as she kicked and punched the covers. He dove on the bed, but held her gently. "It's okay. I'm here. It's just a dream."

"Cole, don't leave me." Her hands gripped his back and she buried her face in his chest. "Don't leave me, again."

෨෬

"Wake up, sweetness." Ray's unshaven face focused.

She blinked and sat up in the bed. Pain shot down the left side of her jaw. She wiped the drool from her cheek. The bedside clock read 8:13 am. Through the fog of pain, reality collided. Sunshine poured in the window and Ray was in her apartment. Her breath hitched. "Please tell me you didn't stay the night."

The curve of his lips held no regrets. "The doctor said not to leave you."

"You slept with me? In the bed?" No wonder her pillow smelled so good.

"The extra bedroom doesn't have a bed and the couch is occupied. Hey, relax. I'm innocent. You're innocent. Nothing happened." His lips quirked into a half smile. "Except a few screams and snores on your part. And those were some pretty hellish nightmares, babe."

Her face throbbed. "I do not snore."

"Whatever you say, sweetness."

Her traitorous lips tried to smile, and she winced in pain. "Do I look like a chipmunk?"

"Only on one side."

"For mercy sakes, get out of here before the neighbors see you and think the worst."

His weight dented the mattress beside her. "After suffering the heart attack of finding you unconscious on the floor? I'm not leaving until you're in perfect health. But if you're worried about being alone with me, don't. Your sister is here."

"Maria?" She threw off the covers and stood, putting the bed between them. "I'm sure you have more important things to do than babysit me. I'm fine. See? All better." The room swirled.

Ray's gaze locked on her bare legs. "I see."

She swayed and grabbed for the bedpost. He folded the covers back, and she collapsed onto the sheets. The impact rocked her teeth. She curled on her side and held her throbbing jaw. As Ray tucked her in, she whispered, "Don't go."

The mattress dipped and his hand propped on her other side. He leaned over her and stroked her temple. "I'm not going anywhere, sweetness. I came in to see if you wanted breakfast. Trevor and I have eaten already, but it looks like you need something for pain. Why didn't the doctor give you something?"

"I told them not to."

"Do you have anything here?"

"No. I can't. I'll be fine."

"Rest. I'll be back in a minute."

She missed his closeness, but refrained from calling him back to her side. She suffered through greater losses. She would survive this.

೧೧೧

The thick, red tomato juice threaten to slosh over the sides of the tall glass as Ray placed it on the coffee table. The sister squinted against the morning sunlight. One eye closed. "What?"

"Drink it." He'd been on the receiving end of his share of hangovers, but never had he neglected his family in favor of a binge.

She blinked. Her eyes were clear. "I'm not putting that crap in my mouth." Maria frowned, and then screwed up her mouth in distaste.

"It will help with your hangover."

Maria swung her jean clad legs over the edge of the sofa. "Who died and made you king of the castle?"

Cole. The name wasn't spoken yet it lingered as a ghost from the past.

Maria flinched. "Sorry. I didn't think. He was good for her. Not that you're not. But he…well…never mind."

Ray didn't want to think about the man Cindy loved. Last night he'd remained silent so that she could rest, but in the light of the morning, he didn't want to compete with a ghost. "Are you sober?"

"Always." Maria lifted her phone from the coffee table and winced at the screen. "Who wakes up this early?" She snuggled into the cushions and pulled the afghan over her. "Wake me up at nine-thirty. Lulu's Place opens at eleven."

Trevor bounced up the hall. "I'm ready, Uncle Ray."

"Ugh. Please, sweetie. Aunt Maria has another hour to sleep."

Trevor kissed his aunt's forehead. "I'm not a sleepy head."

Maria yawned. "That's nice, Trever-Wever, but I am."

Trevor giggled as he tucked the blanket under his aunt's chin. "Me and Uncle Ray'll be back by five."

She propped up on her elbows. Sleepy eyes stared at Ray. "Where are you going?"

"Trev and I are going for some ibuprofen. I don't know why the doctor didn't give her something for pain."

"Because, she wouldn't take it. And she won't take whatever you buy either. You might as well save your money."

"Why not?"

"My big sis doesn't flirt with the dragon."

Ray glared at the sister until she explained.

"She's afraid she'll relapse. She won't take any drugs. Not even over the counter."

"Relapse?" From what?

Her pale eyes widened and she swore. "You don't know?"

"Know what?" Ray had a feeling he didn't want an answer to his question. Cindy was the perfect mother to Trevor. She was poised, beautiful and sweet.

"Her arrests are a matter of public record, but don't tell her I told. She'll kill me. But you might as well know now. She was a junkie and a dealer. The best cook in the county. Until she met Cole. He saved her. Guilt drives her to be perfect."

&#8359;&#8360;

An eternity later, Ray's comforting arms returned. Cindy tried to snuggle close, but the bands warded her off. "I missed you."

Trevor's voice answered. "Me and Uncle Ray buyed you some medicine, momma."

"Ray?" Pain stabbed through her jaw.

"Are you an alcoholic?" He sounded angry.

"I never could stand the taste of beer." A knife dug through her molars. A moan sounded and a glass pressed against her lips.

"Good. Drink."

Fire burned down her throat, and she gasped for breath. She choked and then swallowed again. Hot coals filled her mouth and lava flowed into her belly.

&#8359;&#8360;

"Momma's silly." Trevor bounced up the hall, carrying the empty pudding cup.

At least Cindy ate something. Ray relaxed against the couch cushions. Drinking on an empty stomach was a bad idea. "Yeah. Silliness is a side effect of her medicine."

"She laughed at her pillow." Trevor giggled and rounded the bar that separated the living and dining areas. A cabinet door slammed signaling he'd trashed the plastic container.

Off key humming grew in volume and despite his early resolve to keep his distance, Ray smiled. Cindy staggered in the hall and he stood from the couch. She braced an elbow on the wall and a hand on her hip.

She was one sexy drunk. Her words slurred together. "I'm tired of sleeping alone." Her tee shirt barely covered the tops of her thighs. Her chin lifted. "I'm getting up."

Ray shook his head to clear his thoughts, and reminded himself of her past. He didn't want to get involved with an addict. "Okay, then. Have a seat."

She flung off his hand. "I can do it."

He stayed close by her side. Sure at any moment, she would face-plant into the carpet. "Can you make it to the recliner?"

"I want to sit by you. On the couch."

"Here, momma." Trevor lifted his blankie so his mother could sit. The little boy smoothed the fabric over his mom's bare legs, and then climbed on the couch behind her.

Her hazy eyes zeroed in on the sketch pad on the coffee table. "What's this?"

Trevor leaned over her shoulder. "That's Uncle Ray's new house. I'm gonna help build it."

One blue eye closed, as she tilted her head. Ray sat beside her to protect the image he'd worked on for hours. Unbidden memories flashed through his mind. His mom had once used his drawings for rolling paper.

Cindy dragged the coffee table flush to her shins. "Puh." A finger tapped the page. "That's so stupid." She huffed and fell over onto the cushions. "Just like a man."

"Whoa. What's wrong with my house?"

She stretched her legs out on the cushions and rested her head on his knee. "Dirty laundry."

He lifted the notebook and scanned the drawing. Her drunken slurs made no sense. "What does that mean?"

Her hair fanned his thigh as she sang. "Upstairs. Downstairs. We all fall down."

The bedrooms were upstairs. He'd designed it that way. He wanted to be able to protect his family. He couldn't do that if the rooms were on separate floors of the house. The laundry room was downstairs next to the garage. "You think the washer and dryer need to be near the bedrooms?"

"Ding. Ding. Ding. Folks, we have a winner."

Alright, it made sense. Taking the pencil, he boxed off a portion of the bonus room for an upstairs laundry noting that it shared an interior wall with a bathroom. He wouldn't have to reroute the water pipes. "What do I do with this space down here?" He didn't expect an answer.

She rolled and reached toward the carpet. Her fingertip trailed delicious sensations along the top of his bare foot and curved to slide around his ankle. Never had a woman's touch been so sensuous.

Her lopsided smile promised future pleasures. "Where are your boots?"

He flexed his foot and enjoyed her simple touch. "By the door."

Her brows rose and her lips smirked. "With mud?"

He swallowed as she wrapped an arm around his knee, and rested her head on his thigh. "Yeah."

"Good. I'm a take a nap. You clean the mudroom."

The mudroom? She snuggled into the couch, and pressed the back of her head against his stomach. He lifted her up and propped her against the cushions. She slumped slightly as he filled another shot glass. "Drink this first."

She slung the glass back. "Ugh!" Her shoulders quivered and her eyes closed. When they opened, she smiled. "I'm sleepy." Her head fell into his lap.

He cradled her in his arms and carried her to her bedroom. Trevor bounced along behind him. Once Cindy was tucked into the bed, the boy kissed his mother's cheek.

Back in the living room, Trevor climbed in the recliner and then jumped off the armrest. "Can I watch cartoons?"

Ray lifted the remote control and flipped to an educational show. "Yeah, but keep it down. Your mom needs her rest." When Trevor was occupied, Ray's thoughts strayed to Cindy. She may never forgive him when she realized he'd given her whiskey, but he'd rather deal with a flirty drunk than listen to her moans of pain. After the first cup, the rest went down surprisingly well.

Pencil in hand, he changed the downstairs laundry into a mudroom with utility hook ups. It would be a good place for storage and maybe an extra freezer for the deer meat and vegetables his mawmaw preserved.

Did Cindy like the rest of the layout? Or was she too drunk to understand what she'd seen? Including the full basement for hurricane season and the second floor upstairs, the house was over four thousand square feet. More space than one person needed. It was designed for a family. His family. He stared down the empty hall. Too bad Cindy and Trevor belonged to Cole.

&#8286;&#8286;

The pounding in her head overpowered the ache in her jaw. She was going to kill Ray. He'd gotten her drunk, and now she had an awful hangover.

Trevor and Ray's laughter floated down the hall as Cindy struggled to her feet. The early afternoon sunlight twirled and spun with the shadows creating a kaleidoscope of light and darkness. She placed a hand on her churning stomach, and ran her thick tongue over her dry teeth. The room stilled, and she eased her way to the bathroom.

Leaning against the doorframe, she inhaled the delicious scent of Ray. Holding on to the sink with one hand, she lifted his bottle of aftershave to her nose. Mmmmm. She replaced the bottle beside his razor and turned for the tub.

Water droplets clung to the shower curtain.

She blinked away the image her mind conjured up. It wasn't right to imagine Ray bathing. Forcing the thoughts from her mind, she turned on the hot water and reached into the closet for a towel.

After a quick scrub, she secured the bathrobe around her and glanced into the mirror. One cheek was swollen. She wrapped the towel around her head and gently brushed the film from her teeth. At least Ray would see her without shadows under her eyes.

Now that her mind and body were back to normal, he couldn't stay another night. The doorbell sounded over her hairdryer, and she shut the device off.

Her breath caught. *Someone was here. What would they think?* She fluffed her still damp hair with her fingers, and tightened the belt around her robe. One last glance in the mirror and she hurried up the hall.

"Did you stay all night?" Mr. Maxwell's voice brought her to a halt. She closed her eyes and leaned against the wall.

"Aunt Maria is a sleepy head."

"Oh." The relief in Cole's father's voice echoed that in Cindy's shoulders. "I see. Where is Aunt Maria?"

Cindy continued up the hall as Ray related yesterday and this morning's events to Mr. Maxwell.

Their voices became clearer as she stepped into the living area. "I'll have the church send over a few volunteers to help with the food distribution until Cindy is fully recuperated."

She didn't want anyone looking down their noses at the people in need. "That's not necessary." She forced a smile through the pain. "I'll be good as new tomorrow."

"Momma!" Trevor leapt into her arms.

She stumbled, but luckily Ray's arm was there to support her.

"Trev, momma needs to rest." With one hand Ray swung Trevor around his shoulder and onto his back.

Her son clung to Ray's neck, and rested his chin on top of Ray's head. "I'm thirsty."

The support wrapped around her waist tightened as Ray led her to the couch. "There." He studied her face. "Do you think you can eat something?"

She shook her head.

"You can try." Ray disappeared into the kitchen with Trevor clinging to his back.

"He seems like a good man." Mr. Maxwell lowered into the leather recliner. Elbows resting on his knees, he leaned toward her.

She didn't want to know what Mr. Maxwell thought about Ray. First seeing them together at church, and now here in her apartment. "He's a good friend."

"Yes. I can see that." Mr. Maxwell leaned back and placed his hands behind his head. Just like Cole used to do when he was satisfied with something. He opened his mouth to say more, but thankfully the doorbell interrupted.

"I got it!" Trevor's footsteps raced to the front door. "Yes! The Twin Terrors."

Cindy bit back a laugh as Joni scolded Ray for the nickname he'd given to her precious angels.

"Ray." James stepped in, and slapped Ray across the shoulder. "I'm glad you came back." He stepped further into the apartment and greeted Mr. Maxwell.

Trevor and the twins raced down the hall as the adults gathered in the living area. Weak from her ordeal yesterday, Cindy kept her seat on the sofa.

Joni sat beside her. "How are you feeling? Why didn't you call me?" Her friend angled her head toward Ray, and lifted her brows.

"I couldn't. Anyways, Ray said you were at the farm."

"Yes, but—" Joni smoothed her skirt down her lap. "At least Mr. Maxwell was available."

Joni obviously thought Cole's father had arrived last night. Cindy wasn't about to reveal the truth, but how did Mr. Maxwell know she was sick? "Who called you?"

"I did." Ray sat on the armrest beside her while James sat on the couch next to Joni. "I called your sister too. She stayed last night."

Joni huffed toward Cindy. "*You* should've called me."

"She was unconscious." Ray's statement staled the conversation between James and Mr. Maxwell.

"What?" Joni asked the question. "You said allergic reaction—like Benadryl."

Ray narrowed his eyes on Joni. "It was more like race to the hospital and hope she's still breathing when we got there."

"Oh, good grief." Joni reached for Cindy's hand. "I'm sorry. I had no idea."

Genuine concern reflected in Mr. Maxwell's eyes. "If it was that severe, you should've been hospitalized."

Cindy had refused to stay overnight. "I'm fine. If you'll excuse me, I need to dress."

Joni stood. "You're going back to bed. Men are so insensitive. Mr. Maxwell should've never let you get up."

Joni wouldn't take no for an answer, and Cindy found herself gently tucked underneath the covers.

"I should've came sooner. I didn't realize—"

"Knock. Knock." Ray stood in the bedroom doorway holding a bowl and a spoon. "With all the commotion, you didn't eat your ice cream."

Joni pointed to the bedside table. "Just leave it there."

Even with the intrusion of visitors, Ray hadn't abandoned her. He looked like he had something he wanted to say. Instinctively, Cindy knew he was leaving. She didn't want to say goodbye with an audience. "Joni, will you go in the kitchen and fix me a glass of water?"

Joni looked from Ray to Cindy. "Now?"

Jade eyes locked on Cindy's as he spoke to Joni. "Take your time."

"Oh." Joni flapped her hands in agitation. "I don't know if this is a good idea."

Cindy glared at her friend. "It's a glass of water. How hard can it be?"

Joni held up a finger, and then sighed. "I'll be right back."

Ray entered the room as Joni scurried up the hall. He placed the bowl on the table, and sat on the bed beside her. "James and I are leaving. We're going to look for Isaac. Though, I doubt we'll find anything."

"I'll pray that you do. Thank you for taking care of me."

"You're welcome." Ray's knuckle caressed her temple as he brushed a wayward strand of hair off her forehead. His touch sent quivers down her spine.

"I'm sorry…" She twisted the comforter between her fingers. "I'm not ready to…" She raised her gaze to his steady one. "You're a great guy Ray, but Trevor and I—" She exhaled slowly. "It wouldn't work out."

His teeth captured his bottom lip as he slowly nodded. Then his tongue flicked. "You're probably right." He stood and winked. "I hope you feel better soon."

"Thank you again for taking care of me."

His smile didn't quite reach his eyes. "Anytime, sweetness."

*Chapter Six*

"Momma." Trevor climbed on the bed. "Is it time for school?"

Thankful that the pain in her jaw was gone, she stuck her head out from under her pillow. Trevor's shirt was inside out. She laughed and pulled her son into her arms. "Today's Saturday. No school. But the twins' birthday party is this afternoon. We can go there."

"Yes." Miniature gray eyes sparkled with excitement—eyes just like his father's. Little arms hugged her quick before he bounded out of her bed. "I gotta pee." He bounced up the hall.

The bathroom door slammed open. Trevor insisted he didn't need pullups anymore. She was grateful, but a mother's love had her following Trevor into the bathroom. She leaned against the doorframe in silence.

Little hands wadded some tissue and tossed it into the toilet. "Die you bloodthirsty cutthroats."

Her jaw slacked as her little angel drowned the makeshift boats. Pirate ships didn't stand a chance against a little boy with a full bladder.

"Trevor, is that really necessary?"

"Uncle Ray said a man needs something to aim for."

Ray. She should've known. Wonder what else he'd taught her son? She slipped into the kitchen. His whiskey had dulled the pain, and his solid embrace had brought peaceful sleep. She missed him.

Not that it mattered. According to Joni, the delay on Ray's job was corrected, and he and James had worked fourteen hours a day for the past few days.

On impulse, she reached for her phone, but she couldn't bring herself to call. She'd texted him instead.

*Thanks for the potty training lesson. The pirates haven't stepped foot on dry land since you were here.* She sent the message and then opened the refrigerator for the eggs. Her phone chimed from the counter. She swiped her finger down the screen.

*Anytime, sweetness.* He'd punctuated his reply with a wink.

Her laughter echoed through the empty kitchen. Clamping her lips together, she shook off the feeling and scrambled Trevor's breakfast.

&#8518;&#8450;&#8511;

Half a dozen children sat on the protective pads surrounding the trampoline as they competed to see who could jump the highest. Darla—Andrea's oldest girl—reached out and prevented Trevor from colliding with one of the twins.

Satisfied that her son would be looked after, Cindy retraced her steps toward the house.

Thin puffs of smoke rose from the grill. James cooked the best hamburgers she'd ever tasted. Cindy had forced herself not to return for seconds. She ducked under the "Happy Birthday" streamers flowing from the deck and entered Joni's family room.

"Are the kids okay?" Every mother's head turned to hear the answer to Joni's question.

Cindy nodded to assure them. "They're good."

Everyone returned to their own conversations.

Sara and Mark were on the short side of the sectional. Andrea and Derick shared the sofa part with Mr. and Mrs. Preston while Joni and James each claimed a recliner. Tom smiled from the loveseat and removed a throw pillow from the cushion next to him. Had he saved her a seat?

The father of four lost his wife to cancer two years ago. He was a nice person, but Cindy didn't want to encourage his over friendly smiles. She perched on the edge and wished another seat was available.

Across the room, Joni nudged Andrea. Through Cindy's peripheral vision, Tom slid his arm along the top of the seatback. Both women smiled in Cindy's direction. She stood, and escaped the blatant attempt at matchmaking.

A few serving platters were empty. She collected them from the table and circled into the kitchen.

"Sorry, I'm late." Her ears honed in to Ray's deep voice.

Joni introduced him to the other adults and then offered him the recliner and a slice of cake.

The urge to see him startled Cindy. She exhaled and filled the sink with soapy water. What would it matter if she dated Ray? She was tired of being the third wheel. Her feet took one step forward. But then she remembered the dirty dishes.

&#8180;&#8183;

The moist cake stuck in his throat. Cindy was the reason he'd rushed to the party. He'd given the twins their gifts yesterday.

Trevor was out in the yard. Where was his mother? His heart ached since the day she sent him away, but her message this morning gave him hope. He could deal with her past, but he needed to know where he stood. Ignoring the chatter around him, he slipped out his phone and texted. *Where are you?*

He didn't have to wait long for her reply. *Kitchen.*

In the mock window between the kitchen and the family room, she dried a large plate with a hand towel. *Why aren't you in here?*

Her teeth flashed as she reached for her phone, and then her thumbs tapped against the device in her hand. He felt her gaze as he read her message. *No available seat.*

He bounced his leg and patted his knee.

Tinkling laughter floated through the mock window.

"You've been moping for days." James stared from the other recliner. "What's with the grin?"

Ray held his smile. "Who knows?"

His friend nodded at the phone. "Your girls are welcome here."

Curiosity lined the faces around him. Ray kept his tone light. "I couldn't bring someone to the twin's party." In his peripheral vision, Cindy disappeared from the window.

James's smile grated on his nerves. "You could have. Unless you're ashamed of her."

Joni abandoned the girl talk with the other women and leaned over James's recliner. "Who's Ray ashamed of?"

Cindy appeared in the entryway and crossed to stand behind the sofa. Her blue eyes sparkled, and her beauty stole his breath. She wasn't like his mother. She would never sell Trevor's toys to buy a bottle of pills. "I'm not ashamed of her."

"Who is she?" Joni never gave up. "Another plastic Barbie without a brain in her head?"

Cindy raised her brow, and Ray wished he could muzzle his friend's wife.

Before he could reply, James said, "I don't know. For the past five minutes, he's grinned like an idiot every time he received a text."

He needed to put a stop to their speculation before they revealed his venerability to Cindy. "I don't have a girlfriend."

James barked a laugh. "Yeah right. When have you ever been without female companionship?"

Over James's shoulder, Ray caught and held Cindy's gaze. "Since the girl I want said no."

Joni snorted. "Bet that's never happened before."

"Maybe she regrets turning you down." Cindy's words slammed him, and revealed her position to the others. Her face reddened at her blunder as every head swiveled in her direction. "What I mean is that…if you like her…maybe you should ask again." She studied her fingernails for three silent seconds, and then lifted her warm blue eyes. "Her answer may have changed."

"Good grief. If the girl said no, then she doesn't deserve a second chance." Joni had never been one to hide her opinion. "Don't listen to Cindy. She doesn't know anything about dating."

Cindy's sweet laughter flowed over him. "I know more than you think." She moved in Ray's direction, and his pulse danced in his gut.

Her sweet presence tied his tongue. He should say something. "I…"

She leaned close and removed the empty plate from his hand. The teasing scent of her perfume lingered as she sashayed toward the kitchen.

Another lady pushed off the couch. "Wait. Did you meet someone?"

Joni gasped. "Who is he? Do I know him?"

The women followed her from his view while firing off questions. "Where?" "When?" "Why didn't you tell us?"

Ray blinked at the green carpet. What just happened? He missed something. She wasn't ready to date anyone. Was she?

James narrowed his eyes, and arched one brow.

A bald guy stood from the short couch. "It's time for me to gather my bunch and head home. Thanks for the invitation. I'm sure the kids had tons of fun."

James scratched his chin. "Don't forget those party bag things on the picnic table. After Joni made me put them together, someone needs to eat all that candy."

"We'll do." Baldy smiled and turned for the door.

The men's conversation refocused on the upcoming college football schedule. Ray pretended an interest as he tried to figure out the meaning in Cindy's previous comment.

Three girls burst through the backdoor. Their words raced over one another's. "Trevor's crying."

Ray kicked in the recliner's foot rest, and zeroed in on the door.

A small voice said, "The twins called him stupid."

Ray stood. Where was Trevor?

"Cause he couldn't catch the ball."

Derick held up a hand. "Girls, stop tattling."

Ray started for the door as the little guy slumped inside the room. The misery pooled in his eyes stabbed Ray through the heart. He held out his arms and Trevor ran into them. With Trevor safely enfolded against his chest, Ray fell back into the rocker-recliner.

Sobs shook Trevor's small frame. "They won't let me plaaaaaay!"

Ray held tight and pressed his cheek against the little head. The smell of baby shampoo swirled around them as he let Trevor cry. It wasn't his fault that he didn't have a dad to teach him the game. He shouldn't be teased for something he had no control over.

Ray speared James with a glance. He should have included Trevor when he taught the twins, not give them license to bully others less fortunate.

Trevor sniffed against Ray's shoulder and lifted his head.

Ray wiped wet cheeks with his shirt tail. "You done crying?"

Trevor sniffed once more. "Yes, sir."

"Good. 'Cause I'm ready for some football. You want to play on my team?"

A wide smile flashed. And then vanished. "I don't catch it."

Ray hooked his forefinger under Trevor's chin, and lifted the little boy's gaze to meet his own. "Because no one has taught you. You learn to catch by catching. I'll teach you the game as we go along."

"Don't leave us out." Derick and Mr. Preston stood from the couch and headed out the door. Mr. Preston paused in the doorway. "James, are you and Mark in?"

James's left brow was elevated. "Yeah." The wheels in is brain must be working overtime. He stood. "Cole would want us to show Trevor how to play."

Ray let the comment go, and crossed the room with Trevor in his arms. Mark and James followed.

Cindy rushed around the dining table. "Trevor baby, what's wrong?"

The little arm around Ray's neck flinched. "Nuffing now."

James eyed them from the exit as Cindy's gaze pinned Ray's feet to the floor. "The girls said Trevor was crying."

Ray wanted to kiss the worry from her face, but James hovered like a bad squall. Ray kept his voice light. "It was guy stuff. I fixed it."

James stepped outside and Ray winked at Cindy behind his friend's back. She straightened as color flooded her cheeks.

ഇൻ

Heat bubbled from her heart and climbed her throat. Concern for Trevor evaporated the moment she'd seen her small son wrapped in Ray's muscular arms.

Oh, how she longed to be held. Cindy swallowed and willed her pulse to slow. Before the end of the day, she'd invite Ray over. She bit her smile and pivoted on her heel.

Joni frowned from the kitchen doorway. "Why did he wink at you?"

Cindy tamped down her panic and shrugged. "Ray's a flirt. He winks at all the ladies."

"No. He doesn't. Women flock to him and he chooses one. He's never preferred one over the other. What's going on with you two?"

"I don't know what you're talking about." She brushed around her friend into the safety of the kitchen.

ഇൻ

Outside, a rough hand clamped on Ray's shoulder. James narrowed his eyes. "Anything you want to tell me?"

"Yeah." Ray lifted Trevor onto his shoulders, knocking James's hand aside with a little shoe. "I hope you're ready to lose because Trev and I are about to whoop some tail."

Trevor giggled and gripped Ray's neck. "You're gonna lose, Mr. James."

Ray shook his head at the polite little voice. "Remind me later to teach you how to talk smack."

The other men laughed.

Bouncing a giggling Trevor to the center of the yard, Ray jogged across the lawn and swung Trevor to the ground.

Mr. Preston snagged the football from the other boys and tossed it to James. "Four downs. The maple and the sweet gum are goals. Fair enough?"

James spiraled the ball to Mark. "Derick, you guys can receive first."

Ray nodded to Derick before facing James. "Bring it on."

"Wait! We want to play."

Ray ignored the cries from the other kids. They should have thought about that before they hurt Trevor's feelings. Thankfully, the other men refused to let the older offspring play, stating that they were too small to play with adults.

"That's not fair. Trevor's playing."

Mr. Preston answered. "Derick and Ray needed a teammate. They chose Trevor."

Whines and complaints followed, but the adults stood firm on their decision.

Ray ignored the crybabies and focused on Trevor. "Alright. Mr. James will throw it off. I'll catch it and pass it to you. Derick will block. You run toward the swings. Got it?"

"Yes, sir."

James whistled and the ball sailed toward them. Ray caught it on a bounce. He tucked the ball into the little boy's arms. "Go!" Ray ran beside him. James came out of nowhere, and the impact left both men on the ground.

"Gotcha."

Trevor giggled and swung from Mark's arms.

With a grin, Ray crawled to his feet and accepted the friendly challenge in James's eyes. "Game on, dude." His phone cut into his hip bone. Ray removed it from his front pocket and his wallet from the back.

"Here." James held out his phone. "If I shatter another screen, Joni will kill me."

Ray collected all electronics and tossed them into the cedar clippings surrounding a rose bush. "Come here, Trev." At the line of scrimmage, he looped his arm around the tiny shoulders. "I'll hike the ball and you run out a few feet. Turn around and catch it. Okay?"

Trevor shook his head. "I can't." He looked over his shoulder at the opposing forces and winced.

Derick leaned close. "Don't worry about those guys. I'll handle them."

Ray knelt in front of his teammate. Placing a hand on each side of Trevor's little head he leaned close. "Yes, you can."

The first time Ray threw the ball too hard. He winced as it bounced off Trevor's chest. Tears gathered but didn't fall. "Almost Trev. Let's try it again."

The men lined up again. All focus was on Trevor. "Hut."

Trevor and Derick ran a few steps out.

"One Mississippi, two Mississippi…" James counted in front of Ray. He'd rush when he got to ten. Ray's competitive streak surfaced. Teaching Trevor was fun. He flipped the ball.

Surprise widened Trevor's eyes as it fell into his arms.

"Run!"

Little legs took off in the wrong direction. James's laughter sounded as Ray grabbed Trevor by the waist, lifted him off his feet, and pointed him toward the goal. "That way. Go, boy. Go!"

Mark stayed on Trevor's heels. "I'm gonna getcha."

When Trevor reached the end zone, Ray was there waiting. "Touchdown!" Ray swung Trevor in a victory celebration.

"Wahoo! I did it. I caught it, Uncle Ray. And I runned super fast."

A twin yelled from the trampoline. "Way to go, Trevor!"

Ray cherished the sweet kiss that landed on his cheek. "Good job, Trevor."

The little boy beamed as Ray set him on his feet. "What do you think? Shall we invite the others to play? It might be fun to whip the twins?"

"Yes, sir. Let's whip lots of tail."

৪৩

The goodie bag table was almost empty. Cindy looked over the lawn and watched Trevor play ball with the remaining children. The men seemed to be enjoying the roughhousing as much as the boys.

Cindy laughed as Trevor spiked the ball near the Maple. Ray winked across the yard and sent her heart into palpitations. She smiled and held his gaze for a few seconds until he turned and he and Trevor faced the others.

Joni cleared her throat. "That's interesting. Another wink?"

Cindy stuffed paper cups and plates into a plastic garbage bag. She had been so focused on Ray and Trevor she hadn't heard anyone walk up beside her. "What?"

"I've known Ray for a long time. He's never not had a girl on his arm. Last night when he was over for dinner, a girl called and invited him for drinks. He declined. That's not the Ray I know. He all but admitted to caring about the girl that turned him down. You were her. Weren't you?"

What could Cindy say? Yes, she'd turned Ray down, but she wasn't so sure if he was still interested. Not that she blamed him. With Joni's twenty questions and James's scowls maybe they shouldn't date. She'd piqued Joni's interest with her earlier comments. How could she dissuade her now without outright lying?

"Well?" Joni tapped her sandal against the wooden deck planks.

"Joni!" James yelled from beside the trampoline. "Bring me some paper towels." Blood spurted from one of the twin's noses. Joni grabbed a handful of party napkins and ran down the steps. "My goodness! What did you do to my baby?"

Saved, for now, Cindy released a breath. The injury ended the game and the party. Trevor spotted her and waved. He ran across the yard and bounded up the steps. "Momma. Did you see me catch the ball?"

She swung him into her arms. "I did. I'm so proud of you."

"Uncle Ray taught me." He squirmed and she set him on his

feet. He ran through the sliding doors following the other twin into the play room.

Ray stopped beside her and propped his corded forearms on the railing. Her heart pounded at his nearness.

The breeze carried the scent of his cologne. Even after playing football, he smelled good. She leaned back against the wood and studied his face. "Why do you wink at me?"

His lips curled. His pearly whites dazzled her.

She stared at the base of his throat and swallowed. Did he not hear her question? "Ray, why do you wink at me?"

"Because it makes your heart stumble. I'm praying that one day you won't catch your balance, and my arms will be there to catch you when you fall."

Laughter swelled inside her. She bit her lip but couldn't hold the merriment in. "That has got to be the worse line I've ever heard. But coming from you, it almost sounds sincere."

He laughed with her. "It *was* sincere." His hand covered hers on the railing and he threaded their fingers together. By sheer will, she resisted the urge to fall into his arms to see if he really would catch her. Instead, she enjoyed his simple touch as the sun set before them.

"Excuse me." Joni glanced at their joined hands and then faced Cindy. "I wanted to talk to you before you left. Do you have a minute?"

"Sure." Cindy followed Joni through the sliding glass doors and into the empty dining room. "What's going on? Did you find out anything about Isaac?"

Sadness laced Joni's nervous smile. "No. Not yet, but…" Joni sucked in a breath. "I do have some really great news." She pulled out a chair. "Have a seat."

The formal invitation set Cindy on guard. She and Joni had been friends for years. Something wasn't right here. She swallowed against the dry lump in her throat, and sat alone at the table for six.

Joni paced before the glistening china cabinet. "I'm glad you decided to scrap the older houses and build one multipurpose building. But as a social worker, I have some concerns about housing protected children, and offering help to those who are abusing and neglecting them."

"The women that we'll be helping are on the road to recovery. We won't just pick them up off the street. They'll have to go through a rehab program first."

Joni paused. "I know, but I've planned this speech since yesterday, so hear me out."

Cindy crossed her ankles, but kept her spine straight against the wood backed chair. "Okay."

Joni ran a slender hand through her long blonde hair and then pursed her lips. Pivoting in her dainty sandals, she paced away from Cindy, turned toward her and then blurted, "I've accepted a fulltime position at Twila's House."

Cindy stood. "What about our plans to safeguard children and help parents act responsibly? To feed the hungry? What? Joni, I can't open a new facility without a licensed social worker."

"I know, but there's this girl I graduate with that would be a perfect fit for your plans. And I'm willing to help out from time to time."

Cindy turned her back on her friend, and blinked against the sting in her eyes. "I can't believe you're abandoning me."

"I'm not. James doesn't want me in that neighborhood, and in light of recent discovery I agree it isn't the safest place to be."

Cindy sucked in the hurt and breathed deep. "He's right. Your sunny dresses and perky sandals don't belong there. Don't worry. I'll figure something out."

A slender hand landed on her shoulder. "Don't be mad."

Cindy shrugged and stepped away from the touch. "I'm not mad. I guess I should've seen this coming, but I'm—" She faced her best friend in the world and forced a smile. "I wish you the best at your new job. Maybe, I'll send you some clients."

"Like the young girl from last week?"

"Maybe." Cindy accepted the awkward hug and then went in search of Trevor. She needed to leave before she embarrassed herself with unnecessary tears.

&#8270;&#8270;&#8270;

The scent of butter filled the air. Ray propped his feet on the scarred coffee table, and kept an eye on the wood stairs leading up from the basement and into the main house.

James's sharp eyes turned his way. "Don't like the movie?"

Ray flashed a grin. "Movie's fine." In fact, he'd seen it in the theatres when it was first released. Cindy had disappeared with Joni, but she'd come looking for Trevor sooner or later.

On a piece of carpet in front of the big screen television, Trevor lay on his stomach next to the twins. Sneakered feet dangled in the air as the three boys munched on popcorn.

A door creaked and rapid footsteps descended the stairs. Cindy marched across the sparsely furnished room. "Come on, Trevor. It's time to go."

Ray stood. "What's wrong?"

"Ray." She turned his way and paused. He didn't like the pain lacing her eyes. "I thought you left."

He could joke about his presence, but he sensed she needed reassurance. "I waited for you. Are you okay?"

Her chin lifted. "I'm fine."

She didn't look fine. She looked on the verge of tears. Who hurt her?

Joni stepped into his line of vision over Cindy's shoulder. Movie forgotten, James crossed to his wife. "You told her?"

"Not everything."

"What did you say to her?" Ray moved in between them.

Warmth circled around his wrist. Cindy peered up at him and smiled. "It doesn't matter."

James had his arm around his wife. "Joni and I are expecting an addition to our family."

Cindy sighed beside Ray. "So that's why you abandoned me?" She crossed her hands over her chest and then rubbed her arms. "Congratulations."

Joni pressed her palm low on her own belly and smiled up at James. "It wasn't planned, but I can't wait to hold this sweet baby. The twins aren't still long enough for me to cuddle."

"We don't want no sister." The twins had rolled on their backs. "A brother is all."

James grinned down into his wife's face as the evening sun dipped dimming the natural light coming through the glass door. "We'll take whatever God gives us."

James had two sons. Three if you counted Isaac. Ray had no one, and Cindy looked so alone. He cleared his throat. "Congratulations, but how does that affect Cindy."

James held Ray's stare. "I don't want my pregnant wife working in a bad neighborhood. She's accepted another position."

No wonder Cindy looked devastated. "But she's building a new building to expand for Jo—"

"It doesn't matter." Cindy's smile waivered. "I'll figure something out."

Trevor rested his head on her hip. "I'm sleepy."

Cindy focused on her son. "Let's go home, Trevor. It's almost your bedtime."

Ray claimed the little boy and lifted him in his arms. "I'll carry him to the car."

Her gaze hid from his as she murmured, "Thank you." She turned to Joni. "Good night. And congratulations. I'm truly happy for you."

Cindy preceded him out the sliding glass doors and around the house to the driveway. At her car, she fumbled around in her purse. The streetlight illuminated her pink thumbnail as she pressed the remote unlock, and opened the rear passenger door.

He laid Trevor in the safety seat and buckled him in. Stepping away from the car, he shut the door.

Cindy lifted her face and smiled. "Thank you."

"You turned me down the last time I offered, but…" He held his arms wide. "Everyone needs a hug every once in a while."

She squinted at the concrete and shuffled her feet. Then she stepped into his arms. He widened his stance to keep his balance as he wrapped her against him. Rubbing his cheek against her hair, he simply held her tight.

The hint of vanilla teased his nostrils as he breathed her in. The tension in her shoulder vanished as she melted into him. She fit perfect in his arms. He didn't let go even as the curtains swayed.

Cindy lifted her head. Slowly her lips curled. "Joni's watching us from the window."

"I know." He barely refrained from kissing her. "But I'm following you home anyway. Trev's eyes are drooping and I can't let you carry him up the stairs."

She bit her bottom lip. "I've carried him by myself since he was born."

Ray ignored her arguments and opened her door. His truck had her car blocked in. She couldn't go anywhere until he moved. "I want to help. With Trevor tonight, and with the building."

She slid into the driver's seat. "You're leaving in a few weeks. How can you help me then?"

"I don't know, but we'll figure something out." He closed her door and whistled to his truck.

Fourteen minutes later, he parked behind her garage. As he suspected, Trevor was asleep. Ray pressed a finger to his lips and reached for the little boy. They walked up the stairs in silence. The keys rattled until she opened the door. As he walked past her, he noticed that wariness had replaced the earlier hurt in her eyes.

Ray counted the steps to Trevor's room. He needed to tread carefully. This was a game he'd never played. He wasn't sure of the rules, but he knew better than to pressure her. One wrong move, and he'd lose to the fear lurking behind her smile.

She waited in Trevor's bedroom doorway as Ray tugged off little sneakers and placed the boy on the bed. As bad as he hated it, Ray walked past Cindy and up the hall. His hand reached for the doorknob.

"Wait." She hurried toward him, but stalled a few feet away. "Would you—" She blinked and swallowed. "Would you like to come to the services in the morning? You're welcome to sit with Trevor and me again. If you want to? You don't have to sit with us. But if you do…"

His heart lightened. "I'll go. Will you have lunch with me afterward?"

Her smile spoke more than her words. "Yes."

"Until tomorrow then." The cold doorknob turned under his hand. He walked out the door, but paused and then turned around. He caught her gaze and winked.

## Chapter Seven

With a purpose, Ray walked into the building. As he strode to Cindy's pew, a few adults dotted the rows. He swiped his phone to check the time.

Eighteen minutes early.

A door opened on the side of the church and middle aged men entered. Ray recognized some of them from the fishing outing when he'd met Trevor, and a few others from the first time he'd been to church here. He nodded across the huge room to those that waved. Like soldiers, they surrounded the stage and lay flat on the carpet.

Seconds later their deep voices mingled. Prayers? Ray stood and leaned against the wall. From this view, he watched as one pounded his fist into the carpet. All their faces were hidden, but their words were similar in meaning. Phrases like anointing, liberty, boldness, and glory reached him.

Ray's heartbeat dropped into his stomach and an eerie calm descended like fog as the men groaned and prayed in a foreign language. He worked with a lot of Hispanic men, but none of the phrases sounded familiar. German? No, there were too many l's and vowels.

The door opened once again. Younger men entered. James stooped at an empty space on the carpet, but smiled as he spotted Ray. He stood, and walked the aisle.

Ray waited until his friend was within hearing. "What are they saying?"

James looked over his shoulder. "They're praying."

Did he think Ray was stupid? "I got that part. But the actual words are a mystery to me. I don't recognize their language. What is it? Greek? Hebrew?"

James stepped back and rubbed a hand down his face. "It's not a language you can learn. It's uttered by the Holy Spirit on their behalf, and on the behalf of others."

Now Ray did feel stupid because that made no sense whatsoever. How could you speak words that couldn't be learned? He shrugged. "Okay then."

James grinned. "I'm glad you came back today. Do you have plans for lunch? Joni has a hunk of meat in the oven."

Ray didn't tell James about his plans with Cindy. "Thanks, but I already have plans."

"Um hey, listen. You can sit with us." James widened his stance and lowered his voice. "People might think you're with Cindy if you stay in her pew. Not that you should worry about what people think. Everyone here is very friendly. It's just that you don't want to give anyone the wrong idea."

Several of the men's prayers had ended and a few groups stood around talking. A few glances fell his way. "It wouldn't be the wrong idea. Unlike you and Joni, I won't abandon her."

James hissed a warning. "No one is abandoning her. I just want my wife and unborn child safe. And about Cindy, I promised Cole I'd look out for her. I can't have you messing with her head. She's not one of your pretty-playthings."

It was time to put an end to James's meddling. "I didn't ask for your permission."

James blocked Ray's exit. "Cole's been gone five years. In all that time Cindy's never dated anyone, though plenty of men have shown an interest. I can't in good conscience let you take advantage of her loneliness."

Ray didn't want to think about other men's interest in Cindy. "It's just lunch."

"With you, it's never just lunch." He blinked once and blew out a breath. "Cindy is a Christian. She doesn't party and she doesn't sleep around. I don't understand why you're so interested. I don't want her or Trevor hurt when you leave."

Ray wanted to tell James to mind his own business, but years of friendship held back the words. Yet, there was some truth in James's concerns. "Maybe, I'll stay."

James ran a hand down his face. "Please tell me you're not…

That you haven't…?" The tone of his voice warned of caution.

"I'm not telling you anything. It's your own sick mind imagining the worst. Okay, so I'm lower than pond scum. Not fit to touch Cole's precious wife. The black sinner among all you saints. But, what I do isn't your business, and neither is Cindy." Ray shoved his way around his friend.

"Wait!" James grabbed his arm. An old lady huffed their way and his voiced lowered. "I'm worried about you, too. Cindy may never get over Cole. She still loves him."

"Uncle Ray, look what we made." Trevor and the twins surrounded them. Each pushing coloring pages at Ray.

He shook off James's warning and smiled at Trevor. "Those are some good looking dogs."

Trevor laughed. "I drawed camels."

One twin—Ray couldn't tell them apart—tugged on James's sleeve. "Can we sit with Uncle Ray? It's not fair that Trevor can and we don't."

The other twin joined in. "Please, daddy. We promise to be good."

"Ray?" James probably thought the boys would be a buffer between him and Cindy.

"Fine by me."

"Yes." The boys scrambled on the pew as the music began. James frowned. "Be good, boys." His eyes included Ray in his warning. And then he hurried down the aisle.

Saving a place for Cindy on the outside end of the pew, Ray sat and was bombarded by three little bodies all wanting to sit on his lap. An argument escalated as Cindy walked through a side door. Her sleek legs quickened their pace, and he couldn't tear his eyes away from the subtle lift of her skirt as she hurried toward them. Once again her knees were hidden. His fingers itched to touch, and he gripped the back of the pew. Last night, it had taken every ounce of willpower he possessed to walk away from her door.

Her hard jaw pressed her lips together. Fingers snapped and a long pink nail froze the boys in motion. "Enough. Sit."

The authority in her voice sent a chill through him. Her face flushed, but her eyes sparked with a passionate fire. A fire he longed to redirect. She reached for Trevor and lifted him in her arms. Trevor's shoe caught on her hem as she sat on the pew and teased Ray with a glimpse of knee and thigh. Cindy huffed and smoothed her skirt. "Be still, Trevor."

The twins squirmed on the pew. From the platform, James pinned the boys with a stare and held up one finger.

Cindy jerked on Ray's hand. "Sit down Ray, the boys have caused enough ruckus."

He didn't bother to hide his smile as the boys crowded him next to her. Draping an arm on the pew behind her, he flinched at the ice in the blue of her eyes. "It's not my fault, babe. The twins wanted to sit with us, and James said okay."

Her breath hitched and her chest expanded stretching the fabric of her shirt.

Ray swallowed and whispered in her ear. "I'm sorry."

Her cheek rubbed his as she faced him. Their touch sparked her smile. She glanced down and then up into his gaze. "You're forgiven. Don't let it happen again."

Trevor propped his foot on Ray's knee. The twin sitting closest knocked it off and squirmed onto Ray's lap. The other twin followed seconds later. Despite the empty space in the pew, the five of them were now crowded together. Trevor in Cindy's lap and a twin on each of Ray's legs. "Where's Wesley and his wife?"

"He's preaching at the church down the road."

"Oh." So that's why they'd been so friendly. They were preachers in disguise.

Trevor's eyes narrowed on the twins and peered at Ray. It wasn't fair. The twins had James. Trevor had no one. Ray smiled at Trevor, and pushed the boys off his lap. They all stood with the rest of the congregation. As people sang around them, he maneuvered the twins to his right. "Scoot down. Make room for Trevor." He pulled Trevor to stand in between him and James's boys.

Trevor grinned and the twins frowned. That wasn't fair either.

Ray slipped his arm around Cindy's waist and pulled her in front of him while he moved behind her. Their dance resulted in the twins standing on the far end, then Trevor who was next to Cindy, and then Ray.

The singing ended and everyone sat in order. Cindy's smile stole his breath. "Thank you." She dropped a pamphlet and Ray bent toward the carpet. He couldn't resist sliding the back of his hand against her calf as he straightened.

Stuffing the paper into the songbook, he captured her gaze with his. "You're welcome."

After the service, Joni hurried to Cindy's side to collect the twins. "Sorry to rush, but I have a roast cooking. Do you want to come over for lunch?"

After the betrayal of yesterday, Cindy needed some time away from her best friend. "No." Joni tilted her head and Cindy added. "Thanks though."

James and Ray shook hands, and then the twins were herded out the door. Mrs. Maxwell walked over and smiled at Trevor. "Are you ready, sweetie?"

Trevor looked at Cindy. "Can I go with you and Uncle Ray?"

Mrs. Maxwell's smile waivered. "Trevor. Grandmother has a special surprise."

Trevor had never not wanted to go to the Maxwell's. Cindy had no obligation to them. Did she?

Cole's father stepped between Trevor and his grandmother and held out his hand. "Come on, Trevor. We have a fun afternoon planned."

"Can Uncle Ray come too?"

Ray cut his eyes at Cindy and frowned.

"Trevor, Uncle Ray has other plans." The tension lifted.

Mr. Maxwell claimed Trevor and faced Ray. "When your schedule permits it, we'd love to have you over."

"Thank you, sir. I'll keep that in mind." Ray leaned against the wood end of the pew. As the older couple left with Trevor, Ray held out his hand. "Are you ready for your surprise?"

Heat climbed her cheeks. She ignored the curious glances as she accepted his hand. "You didn't have to buy me anything."

Ray let out a whistle. "Good, because I didn't."

The flames licking her face intensified as they laughed their way out the door. "Sorry."

He led her through the near empty parking lot to the side of a van and stopped.

Curious, she glanced his way.

With a grin, he winked. "Wait for it."

The minivan pulled out of the lot.

She blinked as light reflected in her eye. A chromed out Harley occupied the space beyond where the van had been.

Happiness and anticipation burst from her. "Please tell me this is my surprise."

He shrugged and gave that little-boy-lost look as he frowned at her skirt. "Yes. Although, I'm not so sure this is going to work?"

From the church porch, Mrs. Briggs pointed in their direction. But Cindy wasn't turning down this opportunity. She grabbed one of the twin helmets, as Ray did the same. Lifting her chin, she buckled the straps. "Hold the bike while I climb on first." She straddled the seat and then smoothed her skirt down to her knees. "See. Now let's ride." Before the biggest church gossip took a picture and posted it on the announcement screen.

He swung his leg over the seat, reminding her of the intimacy and close proximity of riding together. The motor purred to life.

She swallowed an uneasy breath as he gripped the handlebars. His shoulders were wider than Cole's, but she held them anyway as they crawled across the parking lot.

At the street, he paused for incoming traffic. "You good?"

Anticipation made her shiver. She'd waited for this day for years. "Yes!"

He gassed the engine, and they soared onto the roadway. The passing wind stole her laughter. Cole would've never driven so fast. Her hold tightened on Ray's shoulders as she imagined her baby girl smiling down from heaven.

Ray changed gears and increased their speed. She pressed her forehead between his shoulder blades. He blocked the wind from her face, but at this speed, she couldn't gaze into the clouds. Closing her eyes, she tried to imagine Cole. His face was blurred by the distance between them. Cindy leaned away from Ray's torso, but an invisible magnet molded her body along his. She stiffened her back once again, and resisted the pull of Ray's movements.

They headed south, and then east following the coast line. He signaled right at a local shrimp shack and they shared a relaxed lunch on the boardwalk.

When they returned to the bike, he swiveled around in the seat and smiled. "I promise I won't drop you, so there's no reason for you to be afraid."

She didn't understand. "I trust you."

Confusion arched his brow. "But when we ride, you're stiff as a board."

"Yes, but—" Cole had told her to stay upright or he'd lose his balance. Evidently, Ray didn't drive like her husband. "What do I need to do?"

His irresistible grin flashed. "Move with me, but follow my lead. You can't experience true freedom on a bike unless you're in perfect sync with your partner."

His thumb brushed her cheek as he rebuckled her helmet, and then turned toward the front to replace his own. Once again she gripped his shoulders, but his hands covered hers and tugged them down and locked them around his waist. "Hold tight to me."

The engine rumbled to life and Ray accelerated. She was plastered against his back and felt his muscles shift. Closing her eyes, she moved with him and equilibrium surged with their speed.

Grappling for balance, she tightened her hold on him, and her index finger accidentally slid into the fabric between his shirt buttons. Ray wasn't wearing an undershirt. His marbled flesh singed her fingertip welding her to his velvet skin.

The miles passed and her grip relaxed as her traitorous index finger painted the ripples on his abdomen. His hand covered hers, and she couldn't snatch away.

Cindy wiggled her finger out of the fabric. His touch vanished and she breathed easy.

This ride was a mistake.

How could she have thought that riding with Ray would bring memories of Cole to life? The two men were nothing alike. Trees blurred and Cindy recognized the rural road Ray had taken north.

He stopped at a four-way stop. "You good?"

"I'm done."

"Too fast?"

She let the tears fall, thankful that Ray couldn't see her. "I want to go home."

He squeezed her hand. "Sure thing, sweetness."

She released a shaky breath when Ray wheeled the bike around in the other direction. Without thinking, she kissed his shoulder, thankful that he cared enough to listen to her.

He took a curve and his muscles moved beneath her hand. Her palm pressed flat against his belly. She didn't know how to deal with this inexplicable desire to touch him. One by one her fingers pressed against his shirt, measuring the indentions of his skin. She rubbed her cheek against his back and committed his scent to memory.

The wind ceased and she opened her eyes. They were stopped at an intersection. Ray's feet held the bike upright. He snatched his shirt from under her hands as a magician would snatch a cloth from a table. Untucked, the cotton now covered her arms from elbows to fingernails. His heated skin burned beneath her touch. The light signaled green, and he drove on as if her world hadn't just tilted.

They rounded a curve and his muscles contracted. He'd all but given her permission to touch him. Curiosity guided her hands over heated skin. Breathing through her nose, she mapped the dips and ripples below his rib cage. He was sculpted steel, covered in a layer of satin.

She blinked as the church sign focused. Ray slowed as he turned and brought them to a stop next to the BMW. She snatched her hands out from Ray's shirt.

Not a word was spoken as he swung off the seat. He held the bike upright with one hand and extended the other toward her. At his touch, electricity zinged up her arm.

His shirttail flapped in the breeze, and heat climbed her face at his knowing grin.

What had she been thinking? Touching Ray? She hadn't thought. She'd felt. Dangerous vibes reached for her, but she ducked under his arm and hurried toward Cole's car.

Ray kicked the stand down, and cornered her at the driver's door. Hunger flamed in his eyes.

"I—"

His mouth silenced her apology. A rainbow of colors bloomed and then exploded as his kiss consumed her. His lips lingered above hers. "Let me follow you home."

*Chapter Eight*

The parking lot was near empty when they exited the church the following Sunday. Ray had worked sixteen hours a day for the past week, and Cindy hadn't seen him since that mind numbing kiss. She craved his touch, but she couldn't risk anyone seeing them in a heated embrace. Especially since Andrea said the rumor mill was already churning.

Cindy ignored the pointed stares. She had bigger problems to face this Sunday. Specifically, lunch with Ray's grandmother. "We'll leave my car here, but we need Trevor's booster chair."

"Not a problem." Ray tossed Trevor high in the air and her heart stopped.

She gulped air as Trevor landed safely in Ray's hands. "Please don't do that."

"Why not? I promise to catch him."

Cindy imagined Trevor splattered on the payment. "Please, Ray. Just don't." She crossed the lot to her car and reached in for the booster seat. Gravel crunched behind her as she re-locked the door. Trevor waved from Ray's lap and jiggled the steering wheel as the truck crawled to a stop.

Trying her best to ignore how good her son looked on Ray's lap, she opened the rear door. Moving a hard hat to the side, She searched for the buckle and then secured the booster in the backseat. "Come on, Trevor. You'll be safe back here."

Her son stepped over the seat and left sandy footprints in his wake. "Trevor!" She swatted them and sand rolled.

Ray's hand covered hers. "I've got it. You buckle him in."

Cindy escaped from his touch. Trembling fingers buckled her son securely. Ray stood inside the front driver's door and brushed little sneaker prints off his dress pants.

"Oh, Ray. I'm so sorry." She reached toward him, but her intentions registered mere millimeters before she touched his thighs.

Ray looked from her outstretched hand to her face. Perfect teeth flashed and flames engulfed her face.

Ducking her head, she slunk around the bed of the truck. What had she almost done? It was nothing. Maternal instinct. Ray didn't mention it and neither did she as she climbed into his truck and buckled her own seatbelt.

His phone rang and she tried not to eavesdrop. "Yes, ma'am. We're on our way. And set another place, Trevor's with us."

Trevor had begged to come with them. Beverly Maxwell hadn't liked it, but Ray invited Trevor too. And Cindy didn't see any reason to make her son cry.

Ray turned east on County Road 32. "Four. I think?" He lifted one brow at Cindy as if to confirm Trevor's age.

"I'll be five my birfday."

Cindy smiled at Trevor's comment. And Ray's next words. "Yeah, he's precious. Okay, see you in about twenty minutes."

The air conditioner had cooled the interior of the truck and she shivered.

"Are you cold?" Ray reached for the control.

She confessed, "A little."

"You're nervous." It wasn't a question.

Cindy forced a smile. "A little."

"Don't be. My grandmother is a wonderful lady. She goes to church. You'll like her."

"Me, too?" Trevor swung his legs in the back.

Ray glanced in the mirror. "Of course, Trev. Mawmaw will spoil you rotten."

Trevor squinched his face. "I don't want to be boiled."

Ray laughed and the wave in Cindy's stomach grew violent as he reassured Trevor his grandmother wouldn't fry him for dinner. Cindy shouldn't have agreed to lunch. She and Trevor should be at Cole's apartment—where they belonged.

Ray turned into the driveway of a brick ranch-styled house. Several cars lined the long drive. Cindy's pulse drummed against her temple. "What's this? You said lunch with your grandmother."

Ray scratched the back of his neck and shifted into park. "Mawmaw didn't mention any other guests, but I recognize the vehicles. The way I work, I don't get home often. I guess they decided to make it a family thing."

Meet his entire family? There were at least eight different vehicles in the drive. She swallowed against her parched throat. Yet, she'd met many influential people when she married Cole. She'd smile at Ray's family, and be polite. Not a problem. *Jesus, please don't let me embarrass Ray.*

He had Trevor unbuckled and in his arms. He waved at a group of kids playing football on the lawn, and opened her door. His lips quirked into a half grin, and her frazzled nerves pinged.

"They're gonna love you. I promise." His playful wink released her stupor and she swung her legs out of the truck.

Too late, she remembered her short skirt. Ray's eyes rounded as she slid from the truck and then tugged down the fabric.

His teeth cut into his lip as hunger flashed in his eyes. The vibes traveled across the small space between them and she wet her dry lips. His gaze transferred to her mouth. All week she'd relived his sizzling kiss. She wanted two seconds alone with him. Just two seconds. Ugh!

"Ray!" Someone called from the vicinity of the house.

He blinked and stepped back, allowing her room to walk around the opened passenger door. The group of kids on the lawn called again. "Mawmaw said hurry up!"

His free hand shut the door and then linked with hers.

೧೪

He hadn't expected the crowd, or Cindy's attack of nerves. She always seemed so poised. Even now, as her hand trembled in his, her spine was straight. She was good at faking. He paused at the closed door. She needed to loosen up. His mouth covered hers in quick possession. She froze, swayed, and then leaned into him. The need to breathe forced him to lift his head. The fear was gone from her eyes.

"Ray." Her giggle relieved him. "I'm good."

Trevor leaned his face between them. "Don't kiss."

Their laughter rang through the house as Ray opened the

door. Cindy stepped in front of him and led the way. The buzz of conversation hushed as everyone stared. He didn't like the appreciation of his male relatives, even though they were harmless.

The women smiled.

Mawmaw waved them in. "Oh, my dears. Come in. Come in. Ray, close the door. You weren't raised in a barn."

He reached behind him and did as he was told. Then, he draped an arm around Cindy's shoulders. "We weren't expecting the whole clan."

"Oh hush." Mawmaw stepped forward. "We all wanted to meet your lady."

Trevor clung to Ray's neck. Beside him, Cindy's smile waivered.

"Everyone, this is Cindy and Trevor. Be nice."

Cindy seemed frozen to the oak plank flooring he and Uncle Tony installed last summer, so Ray squeezed her shoulder and led her into the dining room. "Is the food ready? We're starved."

With this many people, his family had set out the many dishes on several card tables along the wall, buffet style. His Aunt Bertie carried in a sweet potato casserole.

Cindy turned to Ray. "Why didn't you tell me about this? I should've brought something to contribute."

His female relatives swarmed her. "Nonsense, dear. You're the guest of honor."

"Ray's never brought a girl home before."

"You're his first."

"Really?" One eyebrow lifted as she studied him.

Uncle Tony cleared his throat. "Now that everyone is here, let's bow our heads."

After his uncle blessed the food, Cindy followed the women in order to fix Trevor a plate while Ray deposited the little boy at the kid table in the game room. Ray's young cousins were all too eager to help the cute, little boy feel at home. Trevor smiled at the attention. Ray guessed he was starved for it. With the exception of The Twin Terrors, Trevor had no one to torture him with pranks and such.

The cling of plates and silverware rang throughout the three rooms. The oak table in the dining room held eight chairs. In the kitchen, a breakfast hutch seated six and the teenagers migrated to the patio. Cindy entered the game room and set a plate with macaroni and chicken strips in front of Trevor.

"Ketchup, please."

She shook her head and placed a small cup of iced tea beside the plate. "We are guests. Remember what the bible says. Eat whatever is put before you."

"But momma, I gotta have it."

Cindy tilted her head and Trevor frowned. "Yes, ma'am." As she turned back to the dining room, Trevor bowed his head. Ray caught his whispered prayer. "Dear Jesus, bless this food. And please send ketchup."

Ray smuggled a jar from the refrigerator, returned to the game room and gobbed a spoonful onto Trevor's plate. He met Cindy's frown as he returned and set the jar on the oak table.

"What is that?"

"Mawmaw's homemade ketchup." He grinned and pulled out her chair.

Cindy sat down her plate, scooted her chair up to the table and turned to his grandmother. "Homemade?" The women entered the unknown realm of recipes as Ray devoured his lunch. Living on the road, a good home cooked meal was rare.

When the conversation lulled, his uncle Tony asked. "So Cindy, what do you do for a living?"

Her smile faltered. "Being Trevor's mom takes up most of my time."

Ray joined the conversation. "She runs a soup kitchen in Mobile."

Her gaze flickered to his. "It's not really a soup kitchen. We just hand out sandwiches. And, I'm sure your family doesn't want to hear about that."

He reached for her hand. "You're too modest, sweetness. Sure they do." Her grip squeezed as he told his family of her plans to build an addition at Lulu's Place so she could serve dinner.

His mawmaw smiled at Cindy. "That's wonderful. Do you have a garden to supply fresh vegetables?"

Cindy turned. "No, ma'am. We don't have a large enough plot

for a garden and I wouldn't know what to do with it anyway. I'm a city girl. I've always wanted to learn how to preserve food, but…" She shrugged. "I never had the chance."

"Well honey, have we got a deal for you." Laughter flowed around the table. "Half an acre of fall peas have to be picked tomorrow. We could use an extra set of hands." His mawmaw turned to Ray. "Bring her back in the morning."

He lowered his sweet tea. "Can't. My crew's working six 12's and I have to be there at least an hour before they arrive." He draped an arm on the back of Cindy's chair and looked into her eyes. "But you should come over. And then, when you have that extra lot space, you'll have a use for it. That way when you dump me again, you'll have something to remember me by."

Cindy's cheeks shone red. "Ray, stop teasing."

Everyone at the table gawked. His uncle Tony laughed. "You dumped him?"

Ray's free hand linked with hers. "Like a sack of potatoes."

She fidgeted next to him. "Next time you can break up with me."

He winked and said, "Not in this lifetime, babe."

&#8500;&#8505;

Construction noise deafened the yard. Ray's phone vibrated on his side. He checked the screen. Cindy. "Hold on, a minute!" He yelled into the phone, over the generators as he hurried toward the trailer. He jumped over the first three steps and snatched open the door. Doug and three other crewmen were going over the blueprint. Ray spoke into the phone. "Alright, sweetness. I can hear you now. What's up?"

"Were you serious, when you said you wouldn't mind if I went to your grandmother's?"

"Of course, babe. Go ahead."

Three pairs of nosy eyes watched him. Ray turned his back to the men and listened as Cindy recounted Mawmaw's latest invitation. He could listen to her sweet voice all day.

"I didn't want it to be awkward between us if I went."

Where did she get these ideas? "Sweetness, my family is your family. Knock yourself out, okay. I gotta get back to work. I'll see you tonight." He disconnected and faced his crew. "Don't you people have better things to do?"

Doug grinned. "Sure thing, sweetness."

Laughter echoed in the trailer.

ဆဝ

"I don't know why you won't let us use the pea sheller?"

Cindy's laughter joined the other women's as they sat in mixmatched chairs under the covered patio that ran the length of Ray's grandmother's house. Each had a bowl of pea pods in their laps.

"Because it smashes the peas and leaves bits of hull behind. Quit yapping and work faster. We're almost done." Ray's mawmaw wielded authority, but peeled more of the purple pods than any of the other women. "Cindy-dear, give me your pan. You and Monica can start looking them."

What?

Monica—one of the cousins—stood and stretched her back. "Thank God the hard work is almost over. Come on Cindy, I've been dying to ask how you met Ray."

Another cousin stood. "Oh don't leave me out."

"Stay!" Ray's grandmother pointed a pod at the teen. "You shell. And stay out of other people's business. Cindy doesn't need an interrogation."

The girl slumped in the swing and huffed.

Cindy took pity on her. "I don't mind, Mrs. Simmons. Ray and I met through a mutual friend." Although James tried his hardest to keep them apart.

"That's nice dear, but none of that Mrs. Simmons stuff. I'm mawmaw to everyone here. You included."

Cindy didn't know how to respond. She stood and followed Monica into the modern kitchen.

All along the cloth covered table, peas glistened in the afternoon sun that filtered through the panes of the French doors leading to the back porch. Monica showed Cindy how to roll the peas around and pluck out any with brown spots or bits of hull. As they worked, Cindy laughed at the antics of a younger Ray.

"I envied him. When family time was over we all went home, but he lived here on the farm with Mawmaw and Pawpaw. Oh, and he could do no wrong, believe me. He would make up these elaborate schemes, and when we got caught. Everyone was in trouble, but Ray. Used to drive me crazy."

"I can imagine Ray making mischief."

"One day while all of us cousins were playing hide-and-seek in the hay barn—which was an absolute no no—he dared me to run and scatter the cows." She laughed. "I was fine until I stepped in a patty. Surrounded by the huge beasts, I stood there and screamed my head off—which scared the bull. He came charging. Next thing I know, Ray grabs my hand and runs, dragging me after him. We ended up tangled in the electric fence, and the bull cut out through the corn field." She grabbed her stomach and howled.

Cindy laughed until she cried, picturing Ray tangling with a mean bull.

When their laughter subsided, Monica rolled her eyes. "Of course I was in trouble and Ray was a hero for saving me." She sighed. "But those were the good ol' days."

Days of idyllic, childhood freedom Cindy had dreamt about. How much of her life would've been different if she had been raised on a farm like this?

Monica leaned over the mountain of peas and resumed looking. Determined to help, Cindy pushed aside the longing and rolled the peas through her fingers.

The fan in the corner whirled.

The screen door screeched and Ray's grandmother and Lillian walked in, both carrying small tubs of peas. "Don't have all the fun without us. Let us in on the joke."

Monica looked up and smiled at her grandmother. "I was sharing some childhood stories with Cindy."

"What about you, Cindy? Were you a mischief maker back in your day?"

"No, ma'am. I avoided trouble whenever I could."

"So opposites attract with you and Ray. That's nice. You're good for him. Ray's always worked hard and played hard. Sunday was the most relaxed I've ever seen him."

"Cindy Maxwell?" Detective Simmons stood in the kitchen doorway. His mouth moved but no words sounded. With a tilt of his head, his mouth snapped shut. Crossed arms hid the badge she knew was pinned to his starched shirt.

Her heartbeat jumped into her throat, and she struggled to swallow it back down. What was he doing on this side of the bay? And why was he in Ray's mawmaw's house?

"Why are you in my grandmother's house?"

Detective Simmons? A groan escaped her, and she closed her eyes as the pieces connected. Ray's cousin. She should've known this moment was too good to be true. When would she learn that happily-ever-after wasn't for people like her?

Monica's voice brought Cindy out of her shock. "Dale, what's wrong with you? Have you met Ray's girlfriend Cindy?"

"Oh yeah. We've met."

Cindy's heart thundered in the following silence. Detective Simmons was the first cop to arrest her during her life as a dealer. She couldn't stay there while he bared all her sins to Ray's family? "I'm sorry. I have to go." She grabbed her purse and shoved her way around him.

"Wait." Footsteps hurried behind her. "I didn't mean that like it sounded. I'm surprised to see you, but. Wait. You're Ray's lady?"

She kept moving. Detective Simmons gave up the chase, but Mawmaw caught her on the porch. "Why are you leaving? What's wrong?"

Cindy lifted her chin and blinked against the humiliation stinging her eyes. "I didn't grow up on a nice farm—not that that's an excuse for my horrible childhood. I'm a bad person. I've done bad things. Things I'm not proud of."

The elder lady sighed. "Oh, my dear. I'm so sorry. I had no idea."

⊄⊃

Misery lined her eyes. Ray stepped further into the apartment and caressed her jaw. He kissed her forehead and lay his head against hers. "Sweetness, please tell me. Who hurt you?" And God help them when he found the culprit.

"They were so nice. We were laughing and having a good time and then—" Cindy's shoulders quivered.

Ray pulled her close.

"Why didn't you tell me Detective Simmons was your cousin?"

Dale worked for Mobile County Task Force. His district covered the downtown area. The area where Cindy grew up. "I didn't think it mattered. Why? What did he say to you?"

"Nothing much." She stepped away and closed the door.

"Has he ever arrested you?"

Hardness entered her eyes. "Twice, but I was only guilty one time."

He had trouble suppressing a grin. "Sweetness, I know about your past. I'm over it, but if he hurt you... Just say the word, and I can promise it won't happen again."

Her gaze lingered near his boots. "He didn't do anything. I was shocked when he walked in. And then your grandmother—when she found out about my past, she…"

Ray's heart clenched. He pulled her into his arms. He'd been sure Mawmaw would love Cindy. "What'd she do?"

Her cheek rested against his chest. "She hugged me, Ray."

"She hugged you?"

"Yes. Like a real grandmother and I've never—"

Ray rubbed her back. What was the problem here? He was glad that his relatives had taken Cindy in. She'd never experienced a loving family, and he was glad to have given her a little taste of that life.

Cindy leaned back in his arms. A tear glistened in the corner of her eye, but didn't fall. "What do I do?"

He brushed his lips across hers. "Love her back."

"I can't. When you leave and I have to go on with my life. I won't want to let her go. I never…I never had a nice grandmother. I always thought they lived in fairy tales."

The tear still hadn't fallen.

Ray scooped Cindy up in his arms and crossed to the recliner. "I've never had a grandmother either. Mawmaw is my great aunt." He lowered into the chair and cradled her close.

In a rare moment of weakness, she snuggled against him and sighed.

He loved the feel of her in his arms. The tingle of her fingers as she toyed with the buttons on his shirt. He kissed the top of her head and tightened his embrace. "I don't like bad break-ups. Usually, I have the end figured out before the beginning." Ray swallowed. "But with you, everything is different, and I love it. I can't see where we're going yet, but let's just enjoy the ride."

She stirred in his lap. "When you leav—"

A simple kiss stifled her protest. He traced her bottom lip with his finger. "However this thing works out between you and me? My family now belongs to you."

Her tear morphed into a sparkle of mischief. "You can't give your family away. Believe me. I've tried."

"Sure I can. I'm not in town enough to claim them. So why not? Mawmaw isn't getting any younger. Everyone else in my family is loaded down with other responsibilities. And you should have a mother figure in your life. So even after you've kicked me to the side, they're yours. Problem solved. Besides, I like the idea of you cooking with the women in my family while I'm at work."

Her laughter erupted. "Like you're Tarzan. I'm Jane."

"No, babe. More like…I'm Fred and you're Wilma."

Her eyes widened and she scrambled off his lap. "Ray, we could never have that kind of relationship."

His arms felt empty without her. "Why not?"

Her stance widened and her fists parked on her hips. "I have no intention of being anyone's wife but Cole's."

His thoughts hadn't gone there, but maybe they should. "Did I propose?"

Her arms fell at her sides. "The Bible forbids physical intimacy without marriage. And I have no intention of crossing that line."

Ray looped his hands behind his head, captured her gaze and then winked. "Intentions change, babe. Lines fade. Especially when they're drawn in sand. And most especially when you're standing on the other side."

Chapter Nine

"What did you say to my lady?"

Ray's cousin lifted his head from the mountain of paperwork covering his desk. "Nothing. She caught me off guard. Imagine my shock when I learned that Cynthia McDuffie was your lady love."

Ray folded into the hardback chair in front of the desk. "Watch what you say. I don't care about her past. And I know who she is."

Dale's shoulders shook with laughter. "Yeah, but does she know who you are?"

Ray stretched his long legs out in front of him. "She knows I've had a few superficial relationships."

"Is that what you call them?" Dale shook his head. "Anyways, that's not what I meant. You haven't put the pieces together? Let me enlighten you. Six years ago, you called me and told me about a drug deal going down. My team arrested a small time seller. After a few months of sitting in a cell, Kathy gave us the name of the supplier we'd been searching for."

Ray's heart seized. "Who?"

His cousin grinned, and leaned back in his chair. "If I haven't thanked you before now…thanks. Your tip led to the arrest of the best cook in the county—Cynthia LouAnn McDuffie."

&#8258;&#8258;

"Uncle, Ray. Uncle Ray!"

The crowd in the mall muffled the small sound. Ray searched for the owner of the voice.

"Uncle Ray!"

"Trevor." He switched the bag holding his new suit to his left hand, and swung the little boy up with his right. "What are you doing here?" He searched the crowd of shoppers, but Cindy wasn't in sight. "Where's your mother?"

"At Papa's desk. She had to sign papers. And Mrs. Beven said come along dear and here I am."

Mrs. Beven? Who also wasn't in sight. Trevor was alone. Ray's throat constricted. A million horrors could've befallen the little munchkin. Thank God, Ray found him. He held Trevor close and inhaled the clean scent of innocence.

A sweet kiss landed on his cheek. "Then I see'd you. I wanted to say hi."

Ray pieced the puzzled together. It's a miracle Trevor caught him. "You shouldn't have chased after me. You could've been lost. Or hurt. Your babysitter is probably worried out of her mind."

A little lip quivered and tears pooled in gray eyes. "You didn't want to say hello?"

Ray snuggled the little body against his chest and turned in the opposite direction. How did you explain the dangers of a crowded shopping mall to a four year old? "Yes, I wanted to say hi, but I walk fast and I didn't see you. What if somebody stepped on you? Or worse?"

"You're mad?"

"No, but promise you won't run away again."

"Promise."

"Good." Ray kissed the silky hair. "Now help me find Mrs. Beven."

A skinny arm hooked around Ray's neck and Trevor's head pressed against his own. "She smelled that stuff."

Ray turned toward the candle shop Mawmaw loved. A lady with a gray bun gasped and clamped a hand over her mouth. By her side, a skinny security guard touched his holster.

Seriously, the guy probably had all of two weeks training. He wouldn't know what to do with a real threat.

The two quickened their pace and Ray met them in front of a row of benches.

"I found Uncle Ray." Trevor pushed at the wrinkled hands reaching for him. "And I didn't lose me."

"Trevor Coleman Maxwell, you scared ten years off my life." Her shoulders sagged with apparent relief and looked at Ray for the first time. "Thank you, Mr…"

Ray shifted the energetic bundle in his arms and held out his right hand. "Ray Simmons at your service ma'am. Rescuer of wayward children, and damsels in distress."

"Oh, my. I didn't realize Cindy had a second brother?"

He redoubled his effort to smile. "I'm a friend." Or at least he was until Cindy learned his part in her initial arrest. He stood in silence as the elder woman inspected him from his ball cap to his work boots. Not the usual appreciative inspection he received from both old and young, but a deep character assessing perusal. Her look said the jury was still deliberating.

She turned to the security guard. "Thank you, but we're not in need of your services."

The man nodded and walked away.

Mrs. Beven turned back toward Ray. "Come along, Trevor. We have more shopping to do."

"But, I don't want to shop. I want to play with Uncle Ray."

Before Ray could open his mouth, Mrs. Beven cut him off. "That's unacceptable young man. Now, let's be off."

Little arms squeezed Ray's neck and another precious kiss graced his skin. "I hafta go now. Can you come over and play? I hafta be home by five."

Ray touched his forehead to Trevor's. Nose to nose. Eye to eye. "We'll have to ask your momma first."

"Nonsense." Mrs. Beven transferred her purse from one shoulder to the other. "I'll inform Cindy of the play date. Six o'clock. As a thank you for rescuing Trevor."

Ray reared back a step. This lady was more than a nanny. He didn't know what to say. Yesterday was one big headache. He hadn't left the jobsite until after ten. Too late to visit his sweetness. He'd intended to stop by Cindy's apartment sometime this evening, but he didn't feel the liberty to say so.

Little arms wrapped around Ray's head. "I'll tell Momma to bake cookies and we can build the bridge."

Trevor wiggled and Ray set him down. He suppressed the urge to pull him into the safety of his arms as Trevor bounced a few feet away. "Mrs. Beven, hold his hand. You never know when Trev will run."

One brow arched into a point as the elder lady tilted her head. "Thank you, I'll keep that in mind."

℘℘℘

Only Mrs. Beven had the nerve to schedule an at home playdate without consulting her. Cindy slammed the cookie sheet in the oven, and set the timer. She didn't have the time or the patience to entertain a child and his mother.

Mr. Maxwell took care of the legal stuff for Lulu's Place, but Cindy needed to go over her building permit denial and see what went wrong.

The many mandates of the historical society and the permit restrictions of the City of Mobile merged together. Papers littered the breakfast table. How could she ever make sense of this jumbled mess?

If she called Ray, he could translate their requirements, but his job wasn't going right. Four men hadn't shown for work, so he was shorthanded. He'd called after nine last night and hinted to come over, but she was exhausted and knew he'd break through her defenses.

How long would he work tonight? She wanted his advice and after this playdate, she'd need a hug. But only a hug. Kisses erased the reason for holding him at a distance.

The doorbell sounded.

*Lord, please don't let it be Michael and if it is, please let his mother have given him his medicine.*

"I'll get it." Trevor bounced to the door.

Cindy hurried to the door as she remembered the broken chain. He was a trusting soul, like his father. He was reaching for the knob as she entered. "No, Trevor. Don't open the door to strangers."

"It ain't a stranger, momma. It's Uncle Ray." Trevor danced around the living room and whooped his excitement.

"Ray?" She moved the chair and opened the door. Propped in the doorway, he held several boxes in front of him. His wink sent her pulse into an erratic dance. "Surprise."

The boxes in Ray's hands focused and she recognized several elaborate construction blocks. "You? You're the surprise affair? Scheduled by Mrs. Beven?"

He nodded slowly. "Yep."

No Michael or his nosy mother. A sense of gratitude washed over her. "Thank you." She stepped toe to toe with her savior and framed his face in her hands. His smile vanished as she pressed her lips against his. A buzz sounded and she pivoted on her heel. On her way to rescue the cookies, she glanced over her shoulder. "Come in, and close the door." She escaped from his hungry eyes into the kitchen.

The wave of warmth from the oven did nothing to cool her already heated cheeks. She switched off the oven and turned to find the object of her musings grinning down at her.

"Can we try that again? While my hands are free?"

"No." She didn't pretend not to know what he was referring to. "But if you play nice with Trevor you can have some cookies and milk." The metal pan slid on the cooling rack.

Ray peeled off her oven mitts and tossed them onto the ceramic countertop. "I'd rather you kissed me again."

She lifted her face. The intensity in his eyes held her captive. His kiss wouldn't be a quick peck on the lips that zinged through her blood. Her heart thundered in her chest as his fingertips caressed her cheek.

"Cindy?" His raspy voice breathed her name, soothing the ache inside her soul. He lowered his head and pressed his lips to hers. His kiss carried her away on a fantasy. One she didn't want to end.

"Uncle Ray?" Trevor's voice broke the spell. "He comed to play with me, momma."

Ray lifted his head and grinned.

She bet he did. Cindy didn't bother hiding her smile, but hoped Ray couldn't sense the passionate storm brewing underneath her skin. "Now that he is here. He can help me with a small project."

Trevor whined to Ray. "We gotta build the bridge."

Cindy answered, "You can build it later."

Ray lifted Trevor and followed her to the small sunroom. "What's all this?"

"Problems, courtesy of Mobile Historic Society. The plans drawn up by the contractor don't pass neighborhood requirements. I can't understand the rest of their jargon, but our building permit was denied, until we submit plans approved by the board."

He ruffled Trevor's hair. "Let me help your momma and then we'll build the biggest bridge ever." Trevor frowned as Ray lowered his feet to the carpet. Ray's smiling eyes focused on Cindy. "How can I help?"

She spread her fingers over the papers littering the small table. "Anyway, you can. Explain all this red tape? Draw up new plans according to the specifications? Find someone to buy the old building?" She bit her lip and smiled. "Or have dinner with the starchy lady in charge of building permits?"

Jade eyes swung to her as he grinned. "You'd sell me to the other side."

She shrugged. "It'll be more like renting you out." The mock horror on his face ignited her laugh.

He sat in her vacated chair. "How about I make sense of this mess first? Then maybe you'll show a little mercy."

"I'll even throw in dinner. With Trevor and me. I've got chicken, asparagus, and broccoli casserole?"

"Ugh." He exaggerated a shudder. "Sounds delicious." He made a face at Trevor and little giggles exploded into the air.

"It tastes better than it sounds."

Ray lifted a piece of paper. "I hope so."

Cindy escaped into the kitchen and checked on dinner. She and Trevor didn't eat that much. She needed something to supplement Ray's appetite. When dessert was cooking beside the bread, she tidied the mess and checked on her son.

Trevor lay on his stomach in front of the television. Around the corner in the sunroom, Ray's head bent over a stack of documents. They were no longer scattered over the table. The notebook she'd scribbled on held a complex drawing. "What's that?" She handed him a glass of sweet tea and leaned over his shoulder.

"A few rough ideas."

It was a floor plan. A long counter-top divided the room which could be used for serving. Behind the counter, an elaborate design featured a modern kitchen with a double commercial oven, lots of food storage, and a preparation counter. A walk-in cooler surprised her. Why hadn't she thought of that? "Wow. You did this?"

A hint of color entered his cheeks as he swigged the tea. "Yeah. It kinda popped into my head."

Cindy pulled a chair beside him. "What else do you have up there?"

"You like it?"

"Yes, but I need an office, and I wanted to expand to offer the girls fresh out of rehab a temporary place to stay. Ninety-five percent return to drugs after completing a program. I think it's because they have no choice but to return to a drug filled environment. Most fathers, boyfriends, husbands, and friends are users. They need somewhere to launch their new life. Have someone boost them in the right direction. Have an apartment referral. Job listings. Things like that. So make sure we can add on another floor later."

"If you want two stories it's cheaper to do it now. Most of their requirements are for structural and outward appearance. And if you want a second floor we need more support beams. What about putting the girls in a basement? You can have your offices on the top floor, with your referral stations. Lulu's Place itself will be on ground level.

"You're a genius." She kissed him without thinking.

The oven timer beeped and she jumped a step back.

After dinner, Cindy curled on the couch and watched her two favorite guys build with the blocks. Trevor's was a square. Ray's arched into an intricate bridge. He caught her stare and heat climbed her cheeks. His knowing smile sent her heart galloping. He stretched out on the floor and patted the carpet beside him. The offer was tempting, but Cindy shook her head and maintained her position on the couch.

Trevor ran down the hall. "Be right back."

Ray captured Cindy's gaze and his smile prompted her own. He propped on his elbow never breaking eye contact.

Little feet pounded toward them. Cindy's pillow crumbled against Ray's head breaking the electrifying stare.

Trevor giggled and pounced on Ray's back. "Momma likes the way you make her pillow smell."

Heat flushed Cindy's face and she refused to look at Ray. The dishwasher needed loading. She stood but Ray's words stopped her.

"Do you want my help?"

"No thanks." In the kitchen, she breathed deep and got to work. As she straightened the kitchen, Trevor's giggles and Ray's roaring laughter slowly subsided. Tiptoeing in the living room, she smiled at the mess. Toys littered the plush carpet and a tent constructed of three blankets stretched across the back of the sofa to the entertainment center. Ray's sock clad feet stuck out one end. She circled around the room, gathering toys as she went. On the other end, Trevor's little head rested between Ray's side and his corded bicep.

Would it hurt Trevor when Ray moved on to the next city?

Keeping quiet as to not wake them, she straightened the chaos of the room and disassembled the tent. Trevor wasn't a problem as she carried him to his room and tucked him beneath the covers. Ray, on the other hand, looked so peaceful she didn't want to wake him.

His empty arms were flung out at his side. The vacant spot left by Trevor called to the long nights of the past years. Was the memory of sleeping in Ray's arms real? Without allowing herself to think of the possible consequences, Cindy crawled alongside him.

Lips slightly parted in sleep were harmless. If she kissed him now, no doubt he would awaken. She'd have to do the right thing and send him home.

Without further thought, she eased down and curled next to him without touching. He groaned in his sleep and rolled on his side ensconcing her in his male scent, daring her to snuggle closer. The hard floor wasn't comfortable, but his soft tee shirt was the perfect mattress. Inhaling his cologne, she drifted into a peaceful dreamland.

⁸⁰∞⁸

A faint scent of vanilla teased him awake. The floor beneath him was hard and uncomfortable, but finding Cindy in his arms softened his heart.

She nestled her cheek against his chest and sighed. "Go back to sleep, Ray."

His sleepy brain didn't remember how she got there, but he wasn't ready to let her go.

Though clothed, their entwined legs had him gasping for breath. "Not that I'm complaining but...uh."

Her head tilted, and blue eyes opened. Her seductive smile chased away all thoughts of sleep. "I don't want to make you leave yet, so let's pretend like this is a dream."

His dream come true. He rubbed his cheek against her hair. Cradling her against him, he stood.

Indecision clouded her eyes.

He brushed a kiss across her lips. The taste of her was tempting, but his next move was her choice. "Cindy?" His mouth hovered a breath away from hers as he waited.

Her arm curled around his neck as she whispered, "Yes."

*Chapter Ten*

Naked and alone. That's how the dream ended for Cindy.

Ray! Her eyes popped open. Clutching the sheet to her chest, she sprang up in the bed.

On the floor, her body-pillow lay crumbled against the dresser. He had slung it across the room last night when it got between them. She hadn't minded. Who needed a pillow when you were entangled in Ray's arms?

She floated back against the mattress and closed her eyes, living in the sweet memory of Ray's touch. Pure pleasure hummed through her veins. She never would have imagined…she never would have dreamed…

Years ago, she got high to dull the pain of reality. Sleeping with Ray introduced her to a new level of pleasure. And now she just wanted to bask in it.

"Momma?" Trevor's little face peeked around the door.

Cindy gasped and pulled the sheet to her neck. "Trevor."

He bounded on the bed as he did every morning, and she tightened her grip on the covers.

Little arms wrapped around her neck and a sweet kiss wet her cheek. "I'm hungry."

"Go watch cartoons." Her voice trembled. "I'll be there in a minute."

He jumped off the bed and landed on both feet.

"Close the door on your way out."

The door slammed, and she breathed easy.

Cole smiled from the picture beside the bed. Her heart seized and heat waved over her face. "What have I done?" She tucked the sheet under her arms and swung her legs off the bed. One finger caressed the silver frame.

Tears doused the flames of desire. "I'm sorry, Cole. I didn't mean to...It's just...I needed a hug." She sucked in the pain. "You weren't here." Gasping for breath, she choked on a sob as the tears rolled. "Please forgive me. I won't do it again. I swear."

৪০৫৪

Pineapple and cinnamon swirled into a delicious mix of flavors as the sugary pastry melted in her mouth. Never again would she settle for plain cream cheese. Next time she wanted lemon and maybe then raspberry.

"Hello? Earth to Cindy." Joni stared from the end of the kitchen counter and refilled everyone's coffee. Individual Bibles rested in front of Joni, Andrea, and Dawn. "Are you paying attention?"

Weekly bible study was about to start, and Cindy's mind had drifted into the delicious memories of Ray. She stared at the ceramic tile and cleared her head. "Of course."

Andrea stirred her cup. "Sure you are. And what's with the smile? You look like you've found the perfect sugary confection with zero carbs."

"And tasted every one of them." Dawn licked her fingers.

All eyes were upon Cindy. Happiness snuck past her pressed lips. Andrea gasped. "It's Ray, isn't it? Joni told me you're dating him. He's the reason for your smile."

Powdered sugar puffed out of Joni's mouth. "That was a secret."

Dawn spilled her coffee and Sara's jaw dropped.

"Is that a bad thing?" Cindy held her breath and tapped her thumb against the table, waiting. Her friends didn't utter a sound. "You guys?"

Sara came around the bar and hugged her. "You deserve some happiness. Cole's been gone for five years. That's a long time to be alone."

Andrea reached over and squeezed her hand. "It's good to see you smile."

Dawn leaned forward and hugged her. "I knew that we're-just-friends speech was for show."

Laughter sounded around the table.

"I suppose you're talking about that redneck who's corrupting my grandson." Mrs. Maxwell dropped her designer handbag on the table, and pierced Cindy with an I'm-better-than-you stare. "If you must parade a man in front of Trevor, you could at least choose a more suitable candidate."

"Surprise!" Rachel popped into the room. "Look who's in town for the rest of the summer."

Hot tea scorched Cindy's hand as gasps circled the room. Cole's want-to-be-girlfriend was the last person she needed to see.

Joni pressed a wad of napkins in Cindy's hand. "Well, this is a surprise." She crossed the room and hugged the intruder. Cindy kept her seat as the other women followed suit. Her gaze met the gleam in Mrs. Maxwell's eyes. Cindy's glorious morning plummeted into the pits of darkness. She lifted her cup and retreated into the kitchen.

Andrea slipped beside her. "Are you okay?"

"I'm fine. Did you know she was in town?"

"Yes, but I didn't know she'd be here this morning. I was going to warn you today." Andrea's voice dropped. "She's here for good. You know how reliable church gossip is, but she and Blaine are divorcing. I heard he was arrested for domestic violence."

Cindy had no sympathy for the thorn in her side these past years. "As long as she stays away from Ray and Trevor, I don't care."

Andrea nodded. "About Ray, I'm glad you found someone, but seriously, you do need to guard your heart. Joni's right about him leaving in a few weeks, and he isn't a Christian. You know what the Bible says about being unequally yoked."

Though the frantic rhythm of her heart pumped out of control, Cindy kept her voice light. "Ray accepted Jesus as a child."

Andrea smiled. "Sweetie, there's a difference between professing Christianity and keeping Christ's commandments. Just be careful. Temptation can be a powerful thing to resist."

Cindy endured the awkward hug. What had she done? The full reality of sleeping with Ray slammed her. She knew better. She wanted to grab her purse and escape, but if she left now, the girls would be suspicious and Rachel would take it as a sign of victory. Crossing the room, she trashed the remainder of her pastry and resumed her seat at the bar. She tried not to think of Ray, but sweet memories wouldn't cooperate.

Rachel's voice rose above the chatter. "You could always sue for grandparent's rights."

A hush descended.

Color entered Mrs. Maxwell's cheeks. "Why Rachel, I'm sure that won't be necessary."

Cindy had missed something. "What's not necessary?"

Mrs. Maxwell flashed a nervous smile. "We were discussing the family reunion in a few weeks. Of course, since he's now potty trained and out of diapers, you'll let Trevor join us for the yearly trip to Atlanta?"

Uh, no. And what were grandparent's rights? "Sorry, Mother Maxwell, but Trevor isn't quite old enough to travel on his own."

"But dear, he'll be with family."

Cindy had heard enough. "I said, no."

Joni cleared her throat as she sat at the end of the counter and opened her bible. "Before we begin, I have a very special prayer request." Her lips pressed in a fine line and she blinked rapidly. "All of you remember James's son, Isaac?" She fanned her face. "Well he isn't his biological child, but James thought that he was and we cared for him for two years." A tear trailed down her cheek.

Cindy reached over and covered Joni's hand. "We remember. And I don't know about everyone else, but I consider James to be his dad. He certainly loved him like he was his own."

Joni sniffed. "Yes, and so did I. Sam still isn't answering my emails. James and I are both worried. I don't know what's happening, but we need God's reassurance that everything is okay. We're thinking of hiring an investigator. Will ya'll please pray for us and for Isaac?"

Andrea stood. "Of course, let's start right now." Everyone bowed their heads. Prayers sounded around the kitchen.

Cindy said the words, but for the first time, she couldn't feel the communication between herself and God. Was it because of Ray? Of course, it was. Cole said God wouldn't bless sin, and she'd sinned with Ray. Tears pricked her eyes. But she wasn't crying for Isaac. She cried for her own loss. The loss of her savior. Would she ever find him again?

After bible study, she drove to Lulu's Place. A new kid—who

couldn't have been more than ten—lifted a bag and turned toward her. Brown eyes smiled. "Thank you."

"You're welcome." Someone had taught him manners. His designer clothes were filthy, and dirt smudged his cheeks. Most of the children were abused, as well as, neglected. At his age, he'd probably learned to keep out of his parent's way. Seeing him made her want to pray for Isaac again, but Cole always said that God wouldn't hear a sinner's prayer without repentance.

Cindy wiped a tear from her eye and hid in her office. When she was younger, the room had five deadbolts to keep out unwanted advances. She twisted the simple lock and collapsed in her desk chair.

"Forgive me, Jesus. What have I done? Please forgive me. Please Lord." Panic crawled into her heart.

What if someone found out?

What if the church people knew?

She could lose everything. Trevor? Lulu's Place? Her position in church?

Oh, God. What about Mr. Maxwell?

She promised Cole to never shame his name. Her heart raced in her hollow chest. No one could ever know. Ray could never visit again.

Her pleas for forgiveness couldn't drive out the guilt. Last night, she'd felt special and cherished. Today, she felt dirty and used.

Her phone pinged a notification. She reached in her purse and slid a finger across the screen. Someone had tagged Cole's memorial profile in a photo. She pressed the link. This morning's sugary pastry soured in her stomach as a picture of a younger Cole and Rachel came on the screen. His arm relaxed on her shoulder, and his easy smile aimed for the camera. Cindy swallowed the knot in her throat as she read Rachel's caption. *Needing someone to talk to. Wish you were here.*

Rage boiled through Cindy's veins. As admin of Cole's sight, she could delete the post.

Her jittery finger traced the dark waves of his hair. Cole died three months after their marriage. The two pictures on her nightstand, and her memories were all she had to remember him by.

She couldn't bring herself to erase this small token of his life.

When had the photo been taken? Cole never battled thick facial hair, but here his cheeks were baby smooth. High school? Oh, how she wished she'd known him then. There was a lot of things she didn't know about his life. But she cherished every memory.

Ray's sexy grin popped in her mind. With effort, she thrust the vision aside. Cole was in heaven. No sinners allowed. As of now, she wasn't worthy enough to enter into heaven. She needed to be careful. She needed to be good.

Regardless of the pleasure she found in Ray's arms, their actions could never be repeated.

By the time she pulled into Trevor's preschool, she vowed to never to see him again. When she arrived home, a rental car was parked beside her garage. Rachel smiled and waved.

Cindy gritted her teeth. "Trevor, stay in the car."

"But momma, I gotta—"

"No, Trevor."

"Yes, ma'am."

Rachel walked into the garage as Cindy parked. She slid from the driver's seat, and pressed the lock button on the car's remote. After securing her son's safety she addressed the threat. "What are you doing here?"

Rachel's plastic smile widened. "Can't I visit my best friend's widow and son? Cole would want me to check up on ya'll."

"You were never Cole's best friend, and you aren't welcome here."

"I was his confidant." The intruder's eyes narrowed. "He wanted me to tell you after he was gone, but I was so lost in grief that I couldn't bring myself to do it."

Cindy huffed and rolled her shoulders. She was tired of Rachel's games, especially this new one. "Tell me what?"

"About his sickness."

Cindy closed the gap between them. "*You* are delusional. Stay away from me, and stay away from my son."

"Cole would want me to be in Trevor's life." Rachel stepped back as her smile turned malicious. "I should've been his wife. I should've been Trevor's mother. He only stayed with you, because he was dying and he pitied you."

"You're crazy. Get out of here before I call the cops." Cindy held Rachel's stare.

The woman turned and retreated out of the garage. Cindy waited until the rental car disappeared out the apartment gates before closing the garage door and unlocking Trevor's door.

Inside the apartment, she turned on his favorite cartoon and sought sanctuary in Cole's office.

Pencil shavings littered the surface of the desk.

Cindy shoved thoughts of Ray aside and stared at Cole's drums. Leaning back in his chair, she closed her eyes and tried to remember.

The central air conditioner kicked on.

Cindy planted her feet on the floor and twirled around in the chair. Cole's bible lay in the middle of the desk.

She opened the desk drawer to replace the sacred book. Two prescription bottles lay on their side. Trembling hands lifted them. They were prescribed to Coleman Maxwell. She'd never known what the pills were for. Now, she wondered.

Mr. Maxwell's voice from long ago filtered through her mind. "If we'd known about his condition, we could've prayed…"

Trembling fingers powered on the laptop, and entered the name of the first medicine. It was a blood thinner. Her own heart raced as she searched the name of the second prescription. It was used to lower blood pressure.

She dropped the plastic containers like someone caught making change in the offering plate.

Her vision hazed as anger rose inside her. Rachel was right. Cole knew he was sick. But how did Rachel find out? Had Cole confided in her? Surely not. Cole didn't keep secrets from Cindy. Did he? If he knew he was sick, why hadn't he prayed? God always answered Cole's prayers. Always. He'd answered by bringing them together. He'd answered when the judge had suspended her sentence. Even by using Harry to drop the charges against her. Why hadn't Cole asked God to heal him?

Her lungs shrunk. She couldn't breathe. Pain climbed her throat and escaped into sobs. Her body shook with the force of his betrayal. Had her entire life with Cole been a lie?

"Momma?" Trevor climbed in her lap. "Don't cry."

"I'm not. I'm okay." Cindy wiped away the twin rivers flowing down her cheeks, and hugged her son close. Her marriage may have been a fairytale, but at least she had Trevor. And no one would ever take him away. She kissed the top of his head. "Go grab your pajamas. It's time for your bath."

For once, Trevor didn't argue and Cindy concentrated on splashing and cleaning her son. She didn't want to think about Cole's betrayal.

Her phone rang from the vanity. Ray's number lit up the screen. She reached for the welcomed distraction. "Ray?"

"Can I come in? I'm outside in the truck."

"That isn't a good idea. Trevor's in the tub and it's his bedtime. If he sees you, he won't go to sleep." She should tell him that last night was a mistake. She should tell him not to call again.

His sigh shivered through her. "I'm sorry I'm late. Things on the job ran over, again. I want to hold you."

After her encounter with Rachel and discovering Cole's treachery, she needed to be held. But she couldn't. She wouldn't. Her body ached with the remembrance of his arms. The thrill of his touch.

No.

She'd let him in, but only to tell him it was over. "Don't ring the bell. The door's unlocked. We need to talk."

While she dried Trevor and dressed him in pajamas, the apartment door clicked open and then shut. She blew out a breath and focused on the bedtime story. Her words stumbled as she envisioned Ray waiting. By the time Trevor was asleep, her trembling hands barely held the book. She switched off the bedside lamp and kissed his forehead. "Good night, sweetie."

Now to deal with Ray.

Her tank top and sleep pants were damp from Trevor's bath water. Her hair was in a ponytail. One look at her disheveled state and Ray'd run for the hills. The soft carpet muffled her footsteps. Pausing in the hall, she tightened the drawstring on her pajamas.

&#8480;&#8473;

Ray fumbled in the predawn light for his boots, tying not to wake his sleeping beauty. He found his work badge beside the big pillow under the bed, and tiptoed up the hall. In the living room, he sat on the couch and unrolled a clean pair of socks.

Soft light flooded the room as Cindy flipped a switch. His baggy tee shirt clung to her curves and hung off one shoulder. The problem with having a kid in the house was that you couldn't sleep naked. Sleepy eyes smiled. "Come back to bed."

He pulled her down on his lap and claimed a quick kiss. "Can't. My alarm clock went off ten minutes ago. Only I wasn't there to hear it."

The arms looped around his neck stiffened. She blinked and stood. "Ray, we never talked."

"Can it wait?" He didn't tolerate tardiness on the job, but the look on her face worried him. He pulled her back into his arms and held her rigid body. "I can spare a few minutes."

"Last night." She swallowed and bit her lip. "You weren't supposed to stay."

He didn't like the regret in her eyes. "I fell asleep."

"No. I mean…I intended to break up with you."

Again? He'd always been a love 'em and leave 'em type of guy, but with Cindy, he wanted to linger. To lean in for those long hugs. To cuddle after their passion was spent. He couldn't say goodbye. Not yet. "Why didn't you?"

"My body and my brain aren't seeing eye to eye on our…" Her shoulders relaxed as she leaned against him. "…whatever we are."

Last night her body had begged him to stay. The problem was with her brain. She thought too much. "Anything I can do to convince your brain that I'm an okay guy?"

"It's not about you. There's the church rules. And, I don't want to be just another girl in a different city."

She'd been talking to Joni, again. He claimed her hand and kissed her knuckles.

Her fingers caressed his unshaven jaw. "I don't do this. If anyone at church suspected that we—that I—anyway, I have a lot at stake here."

His heart slowed its frantic pace. She was scared. He could kiss her a few times and avoid answering her concerns, or he could be real and tell her the truth.

He chose the latter. "I've never done this kind of thing either."

Her brows rose in disbelief.

He clarified. "There's been other girls. Lots of them."

Her forehead landed hard against his.

Dipping her back against his arm, he captured her gaze. "But none who I wanted exclusively. This is new for me. I've always hated clingy people, but I find myself wanting to be near you every free minute of the day. I want to hear your voice and pick up the phone a hundred times. I'm freaking myself out." He'd said too much, but he couldn't stop there. "I don't know how to handle these feelings." He kissed the tip of her nose. "I don't want to say goodbye. I'd rather we parted with good morning. Every morning."

Her smile released the tension in his arms. Her kiss stoked the fire burning him from the inside out. He glanced at his phone. He was already late. What was one more hour?

&#8282;&#8272;

Whistling, he eased the apartment door closed and jogged down the stairs. Sunbeams danced across the stairwell as he turned the corner of the building. Mrs. Foloosy's eyes widened. "Well, look who's a naughty boy." She propped a broom against a large, concrete flower pot. "Sneaking out before the kid wakes up?"

Ray stumbled at her malicious smile. No doubt she'd create trouble for Cindy. It was time to pour on the charm. "Good morning, ma'am. Here, let me help you with that." Ray hurried over and muscled the flower pot to the side while the floozy swept the loose dirt around it. He replaced it and stood.

Her eyes skimmed over him and her lips curled. "I like to change things every now and then. Could you move it over there?"

She tilted her head and Ray had the urge to hide. He felt like a fly courting a frog, but he smiled his flirty smile and moved the heavy pot where she indicated.

Her calloused hand rubbed his arm and squeezed his bicep. "Thanks, I've needed to do that for quite some time."

He fought the urge to snatch away and held his smile in place. "You're welcome."

"Uncle Ray?" The Twin Terrors wore matching pajamas. "Whatcha doing here?"

"James." Ray's muscles tensed as his mind swirled, and his mouth spit out the first thing it landed on. "I'm planting flowers."

A hand on each of the twins steered them toward the stairs. "Come on, boys. What Uncle Ray does isn't our business." The look James shot over his shoulder said otherwise.

Ray hurried to his truck and raced to the jobsite. James would be here any minute. "Doug! My office now!"

His job lead-man turned red, stumbled up the trailer steps, and hurried to match Ray's long strides. "Shut the door." Ray didn't have much time. In his office, he pinned his lead-man with a hefty stare. "If for any reason, I get canned today?" Ray blew out a breath. "I want you to finish this job, and make sure it's done right."

The trailer rocked with the slamming door. James's voice shook the building. "Ray!"

"And Doug? Whatever you overhear, my personal life isn't to be discussed with the crew."

Doug grinned from ear to ear. "Yes, sir. I won't say anything about the feminine giggles coming from your phone this morning."

James burst through the office door. "What were you doing with her?"

Doug ducked his head and escaped into the hall. The crew knew James was the main contractor for this job. They knew he was the number one boss. His jaw was clenched and his face red. "Answer me, Ray!"

He'd been busted. Caught red handed coming from Cindy's apartment complex. He had no defense, but what about Cindy? "Did you yell at her? James, I swear you'd better not have said one word to—"

"Who? Her husband?"

"What?"

"Don't pretend like you didn't know she was married! Her daughter sometimes babysits Trevor. That's how you met her. Isn't it?"

Ray leaned back in his chair and grinned. He'd been in Mrs. Foloosy's doorway when James and the boys saw him. James thought he was sleeping with the old woman.

"Answer me!"

This was a good thing. He could take the heat from James's overt righteous sermons, and protect Cindy. "What can I say? I've never met the man."

"You disgust me. You're gonna get yourself killed. What if Mr. Foloosy would've caught you sneaking out of his house?"

"I wasn't sneaking."

"You should've been." James scrubbed a hand down his face. "You shouldn't have been there. At all!"

"Why are you so upset? My personal life has never received this kind of reaction. Why do you care what I do?"

"Because of Cindy."

Ray's feet hit the floor. "Leave her out of this."

"She likes you. You've flirted and cajoled your way into her pew. What would she think if she had seen you?"

Ray stood and rounded the desk. "You've got it all wrong."

"Stay away from Cole's wife!"

"No! She doesn't have anything to do with this!"

"Ray! I'm warning you!"

"She isn't your concern!"

Toe to toe they stood. Ray's fists clenched at his side. He caught his breath. This was stupid. James had no clue what he was talking about. "I would never hurt Cindy. She's precious to me."

"Then stop messing with her head." James stomped out of the office. Heavy boots clomped up the hall, and the door slammed again.

Ray stared at the empty spot where he'd been. James thought he was seeing the neighbor. Ray tilted his head back and laughed.

He strode out of his office to check on the job's progress. Most of his crew hung around the coffee pot. No doubt his screaming match with the project manager hailed some red flags. Doug shoved off the wall. "Are we fired?"

Ray grinned at his crew. They were all loyal men. Hard workers. "No." And they all had families to feed. "But let's finish this thing." Before James learned the truth. Then all hell was sure to break loose.

ဢၘ

Cindy had forgotten she'd agreed to watch the twins today while Joni went to the obstetrician. When James appeared at her door so soon after Ray left, she'd panicked. But though James appeared aggravated, he'd said nothing. Ray must have barely missed him.

Until she overheard the twins and Trevor's conversation.

"Uncle Ray planted flowers for the crazy lady."

Trevor glared at the twin. "No, he didn't."

"Yes, huh. We see'd him."

"Boys." Cindy's heart sunk in her chest. "Don't gossip. Where Uncle Ray goes and what he does isn't something we should talk about."

Trevor didn't silence easy. "He comes here."

One of the twins shoved him. "No, he doesn't."

Cindy stepped in between them. "Enough! Play nice or you'll find yourself in timeout."

Three heads hung with guilt. "Yes, ma'am." And then they trotted off to Trevor's room.

Why hadn't James said anything to her? If he'd seen Ray it didn't make sense. Oh! Maybe he told Joni to ask her when she picked up the twins? Cindy's stomach flipped. She couldn't wait until this afternoon. She grabbed her phone.

"Hello, my sweetness."

"The twins saw you this morning. What happened?"

His laughter relieved her fear. "You'll never believe it. Mrs. Foloosy caught me coming down the stairs. I was trying to convince her to keep quiet when James saw me standing on her stoop. He thinks I'm cheating on you."

"With her?"

His laughter rumbled through the ear piece. "Yeah, crazy right?"

She released a breath. "Ah, thank you, Jesus."

"You do know what this means? Other than James isn't speaking to me?"

"What?"

"If someone was to see my truck at your place, they'd assume I was visiting her."

She loved his playful tone. "I find that very convenient. Maybe you should visit her again tonight."

"Leave the door unlocked."

*Chapter Eleven*

Rain pinged against the roof. Ray rolled over and reached across the bed intending to snuggle and sleep in through the rainout, but the other side of his bed was empty. For the first time in days, he'd slept alone. Ray flopped on his back and stared at the ceiling.

Yesterday afternoon, Cindy texted him, and politely asked him not to come over. Something had come up. Something she couldn't control.

He missed her.

Darkness hid the predawn light as a gust of wind howled. He should drop the awning before leaving for the jobsite.

Work couldn't be performed, but he'd have to make a formal decision. Rainout. Normally the delay would put him in a bad mood. Time was money when you were under contract and every delay counted. But the weather freed him to be with Cindy and Trevor today. Ray had found a new Lego pattern on line that he wanted to try.

The alarm sounded. He slapped the off button and surged out of bed. He whistled through his shower. If he hurried, he could be on their doorstep before they woke. On his way out the door, he retraced his steps and stuffed a small duffle bag with extra clothes.

At the jobsite, his boots sloshed through the thick mud the short distance to the construction trailer. In three strides, he grabbed his clipboard from his office desk, and checked off the names of the crewmembers who loitered near the coffee pot. Job rules were clear. If you showed up for a rainout you earned four hours pay.

"Good morning," Ray said the words with a smile.

"You parked kind of close to the trailer today." Doug stepped near. "You in a hurry?"

"Yes." A clap of thunder shook the small building. "I plan to take advantage of Mother Nature's liquid sunshine."

"Ah boss, I love this new woman of yours." Doug lifted his mug to the crew.

The teasing tone piqued Ray's curiosity as yeahs surrounded them. He played along. "Why? Cindy didn't make it rain."

"No, but with her around, we won't be checking the tool room or servicing the equipment."

Ray took their good natured ribbing with a grin. He lifted the clipboard. "You heard the man. Sign the sheet and get out of here. My lady is waiting."

Thirty minutes later, Ray unlocked her door with the key she'd given him. He didn't want to wake Trevor. Movement shuffled from the hall. Cindy rubbed sleepy eyes and finger combed her hair. "Ray, it's not yet seven. What are you doing here?" The hem of her tank tee rose several inches as she stretched her arms and hugged him. She stepped back. "You're wet."

"It's raining. No work today."

Droopy eyes smiled. "Good. Let's go back to bed."

Exactly the words he wanted to hear. He locked the door and toed off his muddy boots. In her bedroom, her hair fanned across the pillow. "You didn't wait for me."

Her lips curled but her eyes remained closed. "You should know your way to my bed by now."

The fingers working on his shirt buttons slowed at her next words.

"I hope you're tired, because sleep is the only option Mother Nature is giving us this week."

Not the words he wanted to hear. Is this why she'd called yesterday and told him not to come over? Was this the something she couldn't control? Normally that would be his cue to leave. Yet, he hadn't planned on an intimate encounter when Trevor could wake any minute. He shed his shirt and stripped out of his jeans.

"Ray? Do you understand what I said?" She bit her bottom lip and stared at his chest.

"Yes." He slipped under the covers. "And if you throw me out, I'll know you're only interested in my body."

She laughed behind him and snuggled against his back. He

closed his eyes and inhaled the clean linens. A gentle hand stroked his arm. The simple rhythm of her touch soothed him.

He'd seen her rub Trevor's back when he had trouble sleeping. "Sing for me. Like you sometimes do for Trevor when you tuck him in bed."

"Ray, I sound horrible."

"Not to us you don't."

A kiss landed behind his ear. The struggles of the job dissipated with her first words. Her voice was low. Her breath tickled his ear as she sang the lullaby.

Ray drifted between the land of dreams and the reality of the woman holding him. The last word hung in the air. This is where she'd say, I love you, sweetie. Her lips moved against his temple. But the words didn't sound. Not for Ray. But with her warmth wrapped around him, he drifted into a peaceful sleep.

&#8286;

"Uncle Ray?" Soft fingers pried his eyelids open. "Are you awake?"

He blinked at the blurred face inches from his own. "Almost."

Little elbows poked into Ray's chest as Trevor propped his chin in his hand. "Momma said we hafta wait until you wake up."

"She did huh?" He yawned and his chest rose and fell.

The little boy sprawled on top of the covers giggled. Ray lowered his arms and captured the wiggling mass. "Oh, no. you've woken the tickle machine. Ray goosed the little boy's ribs as Trevor laughed and flailed.

A pinch landed under Ray's arm as Trevor tried to retaliate. Laughter burst forth from Ray like a dam. He laughed until he could no longer breathe. Panting, he let go of Trevor and held out his hands. "I give up."

"Yay! I win!" Trevor's victory smile faded. He stared at something or someone over Ray's shoulder. "Uh-oh." Little fists shoved handfuls of feathers under the pillow.

Ray flopped on his back and faced the bedroom doorway. Arms folded across her chest, Cindy blocked the exit. Merriment danced in her eyes. "What's going on in here?" Her gaze moved from Ray to Trevor. "Did you wake Ray?"

Trevor scooted close. "No ma'am, I waited for his eyes to open. Just like you said."

Ray intervened. "Come here. I want to show you what Trevor found."

Her head tilted. "I've been warned against your tricks."

"Okay then." Ray propped on the headboard and bent his knee. "But you'll never know what you missed."

"Yeah, momma." Trevor mimicked Ray's movement and crawled next to the headboard. He leaned his head against Ray's side, knees bent. Ray draped his arm on the sleigh headboard above the little boy. With his other hand, he lifted a goose feather and blew it out of his palm toward Cindy, hoping she'd come closer.

Ray smiled as she moved from the doorway and lifted a feather from the foot of the bed. Trevor imitated Ray's movements, his feather fell inches from his leg.

"Like this, Trev." Ray blew again. The feather sailed across the bedspread. Trevor's second attempt reached the middle of the mattress.

Cindy paused near the footboard and gathered several feathers. "Look at this mess."

Just a few inches more and he'd have her. Ray flexed his leg, waving a feather a little bit closer. Cindy reached for it and Ray struck. He grabbed her and yanked her onto the bed. "The tickle machine." She squealed as he and Trevor goosed her without mercy.

She gulped for air in between giggles. "Ray. Stop. Please. I need to tell you something."

He pinned her on the bed with her hands above her head. Trevor climbed on his back and peeked over his shoulder.

Her chest rose and fell. Diamonds sparkled in her eyes.

She was so beautiful.

So real.

So perfect.

"I love you." He swallowed his shock at the declaration he'd not intended to make. The longing in his heart had manifested the words, but they were true. Oh so true.

He loved her.

Surprise widened her eyes. Her hand lifted and lit a fire across his jaw. "Ray." Slowly, her lips curled and her smile had never appeared more brilliant. A similar emotion answered from the depths of her eyes.

He spoke the words again. Making sure she knew that he meant them. "I love you, Cindy." He dipped his head needing the reassurance of her kiss.

Trevor slid off Ray's back and wiggled between them. "Me too. Love me too."

The little boy needed a father's love. Ray was more than happy to lend it to him. He included Trevor in his embrace. "You too, Trevor. I love you."

"I love you, Uncle Ray." The little boy reared back and smiled.

Ray kissed his forehead and ruffled his hair. Cindy hadn't declared her feelings. Why?

Her gaze landed on something over his shoulder. "Ray, I want to introduce you to Zack."

"Who?" Ray rolled in the tangled sheets and blinked at the business man blocking the bedroom door.

Trevor squirmed off the bed and dashed to the man. "Uncle Ray waked up."

One brow was raised as the man looked at Cindy pinned beneath Ray. "I see."

Ray's stomach clenched as the man lifted Trevor in his arms and disappeared from the doorway.

Cindy's touch turned his head. Her smile confused him more. "Zack's my brother. He has some questions about your design for the new facility, but I wouldn't let him wake you."

"Your brother? Why'd you let me sleep?" Ray leapt out of bed and searched for his clothes. "He must think I'm a lazy bum."

"No, he doesn't. And you looked…" Cindy's hungry eyes roamed over his body. "…peaceful. I dried your jeans and shirt. They're on the dresser."

Ray tugged on his jeans and grabbed his shirt. He dove on the bed and kissed her hard. "When he's gone, you're in big trouble."

ଡ଼ଔ

The bedroom door closed out Ray's voice. He loved her? Really? Or was that something that men said to get what they wanted?

Cindy hid under the covers. As a little girl, she'd prayed that her father would love her. He didn't. Zack protected her but he'd abandoned her too. And Cole? Had he really loved her? Or had he married her out of pity? Ugh. Why did Ray have to confuse her?

Love was supposed to stay with you.

Ray was leaving.

She couldn't forget that she'd be alone again while he moved on to the next girl in the next city. She couldn't afford to believe he cared. Or let him guess at her feelings.

The tick of the clock mocked her.

Never let 'em see you cry. The words her granny had spoken long years ago flittered through her mind. Ray could never know she loved him. If knowledge was power, Ray just might destroy her. She wouldn't beg him to stay. She'd be strong and let him go.

Then she'd turn her life back to God.

Everything would go back like it was. She'd been content before Ray. She could be content after he left.

છાભ

Ray sat at the table with Cindy's brother and suppressed a yawn. How long had the man waited?

Zack had introduced the beefy man on the couch as his personal assistant and the young woman as his secretary, but Ray wasn't fooled. The bodyguard stood close by. Ray turned away from the mistress's seductive smile.

"Your design passed the historical society's ridiculous demands, but the lot is in a flood zone. Why build a basement? Won't it leak?"

"Not if it's built right. Cindy wants to house the ladies who have no place to live. The bottom floor is theirs."

Cindy's arms looped around his shoulders, and a tall glass of orange juice slid in front of him. He turned and kissed her cheek. "Thanks, sweetness."

"You're welcome."

Her brother had already caught him in her bed. There was no sense hiding his feelings now.

"Why a third floor? It'll be less expensive if you compacted everything into two."

Ray tapped the paper. "This is how Cindy wants it."

Her brother shook his head and then asked, "Does she get everything she wants?"

"If it's within my power to give it to her? Then, yes."

She hugged his chest from behind. "Thank you, Ray."

He lifted his orange juice with one hand, and pulled Cindy around to his lap with the other. "You're welcome."

Zack cleared his throat and faced Cindy. "Are you sure you trust this guy? Giving him the authority to build the new facility? Putting him in charge of the demolition and the new construction?"

Her arm flexed on Ray's shoulders. "Yes."

Zack scraped his chair back. "Then I'll make the funds available. But I'm keeping an eye on him."

The intruders packed their briefcases and stood. Zack glared at Ray. "I like the sound of Lulu's laughter. Don't screw it up."

&#8500;)&#8500;&#8500;

Despite the rain, the day couldn't have been better. After brunch at The Pancake House, they'd driven to his RV near his grandmother's. Cindy and Trevor had stayed in the dry cab while Ray dashed through the rain and thrown several crab baskets in the back of the truck.

By the time they'd arrived at a large sporting goods store, a gentle mist fell. Ray braked in the pedestrian walkway. "Wait under the awning while I park. I don't want you to get wet."

Cindy leaned over and accepted his kiss. "Come on, Trevor." She reached over the seat and unbuckled him. She opened the passenger door and then the back for Trevor. Hand and hand they darted toward the false log front of the building.

The fish swimming in the man-made stream kept Trevor occupied until Ray swung him into his arms. His other hand trailed down her arm and linked their fingers together. "Come on, sweetness. Let's find some string and start our next adventure."

As they entered the store, she answered Joni's call.

"James rained out today. We're driving to the country, and wondered if you and Trevor would like to go. A change of scenery might do us all some good."

Ray tugged her down the aisle as she replied, "Sorry. Ray's taking us crabbing."

"Oh, I guess he rained out too."

"Yes, but thank you for the invitation. You know I love James's country relatives. Maybe next time." When Ray was gone and she needed to fill the void he would leave behind.

෫෬

He knew the moment Cindy said the word crabbing that James would call and invite himself and the twins to join them. Ray didn't want intruders with his time with Cindy and Trevor, but he hadn't known how to tell his friend no.

How would James react to seeing him with Cindy? Ray hadn't talked to James since their argument in the construction trailer. He stood in the aisle of the fishing section and studied the different types of twine. He needed about a hundred foot per basket. James would just have to deal with the situation.

Hand-in-hand, Cindy and Trevor waited for Ray to gather the necessary supplies. He wished he could erase the worry on her face.

"I don't know about this. What if Trevor falls over the rail? How deep is the water at the end of the pier?"

"It'll be fine. I'll be there right beside him."

"But what if—"

His kiss stopped her words. "Sweetness, I promise. No matter what happens, I'll get him."

Trevor hugged Cindy's leg. "I won't fall, momma."

"See." Ray kissed her fingertips and turned back to his selection.

"We'll be right back." Cindy led Trevor down the aisle and rounded the end.

෫෬

Child-sized wet suits and life vests filled an entire row. Masks, snorkels, and fins were on the opposite side.

"The summer season is nearly over. Everything here is half off."

"Thank you." Her words were meant to dismiss the salesman, but he hovered near. She stepped away placing some distance between them and flipped through the vests. Most had cartoon characters on them. "Which one, Trevor?" She held out one with a caped superhero on the front. "This one?"

"No. I want a truck."

She searched the racks and kept the salesman at arm's length.

Finally, she found a vest in Trevor's size with a huge crane imprinted on the front. "Ah ha."

Trevor nodded his head and reached his arms out. Cindy slipped the vest on her son and zipped the front. She fumbled with the strap adjustment buckle.

"Look, Uncle Ray." Trevor's little hands patted his chest. "I won't sink."

"He doesn't need that thing. We're not going in a boat." Ray's frown sent the salesman scrambling.

Cindy wrapped her arms around Ray's waist. She couldn't bring herself to admit her weakness. How could she keep Trevor safe? She could barely keep herself afloat. Knowing her limitations as a swimmer, Cole always made her wear a life vest when they sailed on the *Lulu*.

She lifted her face and kissed Ray's chin. "I know it's irrational, but with the lifejacket, I won't worry. And if he does fall..." She suppressed a shudder, but Ray's hands pulled her close. "It will keep him afloat until you reach him."

ઝૉૹ

The Port City skyline was beautiful, but not nearly as beautiful as Cindy. She faced the end of the pier and stared across the bay to the cityscape of Mobile. The setting sun danced like flames in her hair as she watched a sailboat bob in the water. Her arms spread like wings. She leaned her head back and stared into the clouds.

A little hand tugged on the hem of Ray's cargo shorts. "What next?"

"We need to secure the bait." Ray tied raw chicken legs in the center of the baskets as Cindy lowered her arms and shuffled around the cut out center of the pier.

She unfolded the chair he'd bought her. "Ray, do you own a boat?"

"Sorry, babe. I prefer my vehicles to stay grounded."

"Oh." Disappointment flashed across her face, and then vanished behind her smile. Once again, she stared at the sailboat.

Was she thinking of Cole? Ray had chosen this pier even though it was shorter than the one in Fairhope because only a handful of locals knew the trail that led out here. He didn't want the crowds to impose on their time together, but how did he compete with a ghost? "Come on, Trev. Let's find the best spot before James and The Terrors get here."

Using the cotton twine, Ray tied one end to the crab net. He eased the trap into the murky bay waters. Trevor climbed on the bottom rail and leaned over. The warning to back off died in Ray's throat. With the lifejacket, Trevor was free to watch.

"Trevor, get down." Cindy's voice trembled.

"But momma, I gotta watch it."

Ray patted the little boy's head. "Go look in the tackle box and bring me my knife, but be careful. It's open."

"Yes, sir." Trevor jumped off the rail and ran the ten feet to the other side of the pier. Holding the knife by the handle like Ray had taught him the first day they'd met, he crossed the wood planks. Ray cut the twine and tied the string to a piling.

"Hey you guys! Wait for us!" The Twin Terrors raced toward them. James and Joni trailed behind.

Ray closed the knife and checked Trevor's vest. He tightened the side straps and tugged the zipper to his chin just as the chaos reached them.

James dropped his arm load of tackle. "Why's he wearing that?"

Cindy stood from her folding chair. "You watch your own children and let me worry about Trevor."

"Sorry, didn't mean to offend. It's just that…"

Ray shook his head signaling for his friend to back off.

James shrugged. "My bad." He opened two chairs as the three boys "helped" Ray tie off the other two baskets.

James had brought another one which gave the group a total of four. A twin tripped and got tangled in the string. James howled and pointed to the chair. "Boys, settle down."

Joni sank in the seat beside Cindy's. "The night sky is so clear after that thunderstorm. Thank ya'll for inviting us."

Cindy smiled at Ray and answered her friend. "You're welcome. It's nice to spend time with friends."

Joni tilted her head toward heaven. "On nights like this, I wonder about Isaac."

Ray wondered about the little boy, too. Cindy asked the

question for him. "Still haven't heard anything from Sam?"

He listened in for Joni's answer. "He hasn't answered our emails for months."

"A twin pulled on his shirt. "Can we pull them up now?"

"Not yet. Let them fish for a while." Ray put away his knife and the leftover twine.

The other twin leaned close. "Can I tug the rope?"

Ray needed a diversion. "Sweetness, are you thirsty?"

Cindy bit her lip. "The cooler is in your truck."

He knew that. "That's not what I asked. Are you thirsty?"

Her smile peeked out. "A little bit."

He winked and turned to the three boys. "Come on guys, I may need some help."

ෂ෮ଓ

"So, you and Ray seem cozy." James had never learned to mind his own business. "Trevor seems to like him."

"What's your point?" Might as well get everything out in the open.

"No point. I'm just saying. Ray…he likes a lot of women."

"Is Ray seeing someone else?" Cindy leaned forward in her chair. She knew James thought Ray was cheating on her with Mrs. Foloosy. Would he tell on his best friend? "Is he?"

James bit his lip and shook his head. "No. Not that I know of."

He lied. James flat out lied for Ray. So if Ray ever did cheat, James would never tell. Figures. Ugh. Men.

Cindy relaxed into the chair. "Ray and I are fine." She looked out into the water. "We're both adults, James. It's nothing to be concerned about."

"I'm just…me and Joni…we care about you both. And well… Ray's never been in a monogamous relationship."

Okay, so maybe James would never tell on Ray, but he sure was giving some heavy hints. In his own weird way, James was a good friend. He felt obligated to her and Trevor because of Cole. "Thank you, but your concern isn't necessary." James was Cole's best friend. As an afterthought, she added, "Did you know that Cole was sick?"

"I—uh." He rubbed the back of his neck and adverted his eyes. "I didn't think he told you."

She stilled her face to mask the pain. "He didn't. Rachel did. I didn't believe her, but…" Mentally shaking off the numbness, she lifted her eyes and faced the sympathy in James's expression. "What was wrong with him? Cancer?"

"No. He had a brain aneurysm. There wasn't anything they could do about it. He didn't want you or his parents to worry. The doctor said he could live two months or twenty years."

"So Mr. Maxwell doesn't know either," She folded the hem of her shirt and traced a finger down the stitches. "Then why did Cole confide in Rachel?" New pain sliced through her heart. Was Rachel right? Had Cole thought of her as a stray puppy needing to be saved? Had he loved her at all?

The fabric on James's chair popped as it opened and clunked against the wood pier. "Hey." Hard lines crossed his face. "I don't know what's going on between you and Rachel, but Cole married you. I don't know how she found out, but you can bet that he's not the one that told her."

Hope fluttered in her stomach. "Maybe he told her before he met me."

James grimaced and rubbed a hand down his face.

"What aren't you saying?"

He rolled his shoulders and straightened the chair. "Cole got the final test results the day before he met you."

The wood planks rumbled beneath her.

"Don't run!" Ray's voice preceded the pounding of feet.

The three boys dragged an empty cooler past her chair and collapsed in heaps. "We beat him."

Cindy shook her head at James. She didn't want to continue this conversation in front of Ray. Taking the hint, James called the boys to his side, and let one of them pull the string. A kiss landed on Cindy's neck. She turned and pulled Ray's lips down to hers. His kiss steadied her tilting world. She didn't care that James and Joni gawked at them. "Thank you, Ray." She accepted the drink from his hand.

His lips grazed her cheek as he whispered near her ear. "Want to catch my crabs?"

Laughter burst out from her heart. "Sure, why not?"

## Chapter Twelve

Ray worked through lunch to tie the loose ends of the finished job. He had the whole weekend to spend with Cindy and Trevor. That is…if he could get her away from Mawmaw.

Judging by the excitement in her eyes last night while she'd told him of all the work they'd done, he'd say she would make a great farmer's wife.

Too bad he wasn't a farmer. But for the first time in his life, he wasn't ready to move on. He didn't want a new job in a new town. And he didn't want a new girl. He wanted Cindy.

He found her standing at his mawmaw's sink. He slipped behind her. Her neck was open as her hair was pulled into a ponytail. He pressed his lips against the sensitive part of her nape as his hands landed on her waist. She whimpered and leaned her head back against him. He covered her skin with kisses.

"Mmmm. I was just thinking about this."

Ray turned her into his arms and claimed her lips. The thought of leaving her in two days added a measure of desperation to his kiss. Her arms clung to him. Her reaction just as volatile as his. She was putty in his hands.

"Rayford Eugene Simmons!"

He cringed at his mawmaw's voice.

Cindy's forehead fell against his shoulder and her giggle shivered through him.

His grandmother reached around them, and refilled her dishpan with the pears that were soaking in the sink. "I can't believe you are carrying on so in my house. You should have more respect." She wacked him in the back of the head and turned away, headed for the back porch.

"I—" The slam of the back screen door stole his words. His

grandmother spoke to someone on the back porch and laughter sounded. He couldn't believe he'd been caught. But it was just a kiss.

A sweet feminine giggle turned his head. Mischief sparkled in her blue eyes. "Rayford Eugene Simmons, I do believe you're blushing."

℘℘

Cindy forced herself to walk out on the screened in porch. Ray's kiss had burned a path to her soul. How could she have forgotten that she was a guest in his grandmother's house? His body heat steamed behind her.

The porch was filled with his female cousins. All with dishpans of pear slices in their laps.

She had learned how to peel the hard fruit with the small knife, but Cindy wasn't as fast as the other women. She was beginning her second pan while the ladies were on their third.

Cindy reclaimed her seat in a double, wooden rocker and resumed peeling. Through the screen walls around the porch, Trevor ran around the backyard with the other children.

Shelia—one of the cousins that hadn't been at the family dinner—hugged Ray's neck. "How long are you in town?"

"Not long."

Cindy blinked. Ray's job ended today. He would leave Monday morning, but she wasn't ready to say goodbye.

Ray claimed the seat beside her and reached in her pan for a slice of fruit. "Are you having fun?"

"Yes, but my fingers are numb."

He reached for her hands and pressed his lips against her fingers.

She didn't dare look at him, because her yearning would be seen by everyone on the patio, yet she couldn't stop her smile or the warmth the flowed with his simple touch. "I've learned a lot about canning, but I didn't realize how much room is needed for a garden. I don't think the other lot will be large enough."

"No problem. I've got nine acres. Next year, I'll borrow Uncle Tony's tractor and build you a garden by the road."

Except she would no longer be around then. Ray would move on to the next girl. "That's not possible."

"Why not? We have plenty of room." He stood and brushed

a kiss across her cheek. "You can even plant some broccoli and asparagus."

The women in his family stared with curious expressions.

His grandmother chimed in. "There's no need for a separate garden. You're welcome to join us. Each person receives a share of the harvest."

Trevor cried and threw a plastic baseball bat across the backyard. "I ain't playing no more." He tilted his head back. "Never!" He collapsed on the ground in tears.

Ray frowned. "What's wrong with my little buddy?"

Trevor always got grouchy when he was tired. She'd finish this pan and go home. "He missed his nap."

"Why?"

A trio of children whooped through the house and out the patio. The squeals and yells preceded the slam of the screen door.

She started to rise.

"I'll get him. You should've taken him to the trailer."

She'd thought about it, but she didn't want to intrude on Ray's private sanctuary. He opened the screen door and stepped into the backyard. "Trevor."

His head lifted with the first sound of Ray's voice. "Uncle Ray, you comed here." He ran into Ray's arms and Ray swung him around his back, and then tossed him high in the air. Cindy held her breath until Trevor landed safely.

"Ugh! Why does he do that? He knows it gives me heart failure." She didn't realize she'd spoke out loud until Ray's cousin patted her hand.

"Honey, men are like that with their boys. They say it toughens them up."

"Bruce did drop Mack once. Straight on his head. But the little fellow got up and said throw me again, Daddy."

Cindy laughed. "Thank you, that's so reassuring."

Laughter sounded through the women as Ray opened the screen door with one hand and carried Trevor with the other. Little eyes drooped and his head rested on Ray's shoulder.

Ray winked as he slipped through the porch into the house carrying her sleepy son.

"Ray's good with him." Mawmaw's eyes twinkled. "Reminds me of Tony and Ray when he was little."

The shame of her own horrific childhood had prevented her from asking about Ray's. He'd never mentioned his mother again. Curiosity rose within her. What about his father? She wanted to know everything about him.

As if her thoughts conjured him up, Ray appeared at her side. "Trevor's asleep in my old room. I have a ton of things to do before Monday. When you're done, drive to the trailer and we'll go out to dinner." His kiss didn't give her time to answer.

He walked out the porch door into the backyard. He faced the group of giggling girls. "Trev's asleep. If you wake him up, I'll make you clean out the barn."

The girls' eyes rounded. "Yes, sir. We'll be quiet."

೫೦೧೪

He lay the screwdriver on the concrete when her car sounded outside the shed. Ray wiped his hands on a rag and came to his feet beside the quad he was working on as Cindy strode through the open garage door.

He stepped forward and took the heavy box out of her arms. Inside was filled with quart-sized bags. "What's this?"

"Yours. The women divided up this year's harvest, and Mawmaw insisted I take my share. When I refused, she said to bring them to you."

"But you worked so hard for this."

"It doesn't matter. I can buy the same stuff at the grocery chain."

"No, babe. Nothing taste as good as freshly picked vegetables."

Her smile appeared and he leaned down into her kiss. Placing the box on the floor, he pulled her into his arms and kissed her like he wanted to since he'd seen her standing at his mawmaw's sink.

She stepped back and shook her head. "Your Uncle Tony is right outside."

"No, I'm not." Uncle Tony grinned and held out another box. "Here, son. Looks like you need something to occupy your hands."

Cindy shoved at his chest as her face flamed. Ray kept one arm locked on her hip and opened the chest freezer with the other. "Put 'em in here."

"Boy, look at all this food." Uncle Tony frowned. "Going to waste."

Ray had no choice but to release Cindy and help his uncle stack the fruit among the deer, beef, and fish in his freezer. "It's not wasting. Mawmaw cooks out of here, too. She knows I'm out of town most weeks."

"Well, this is Cindy's." Uncle Tony waved his hand over the contents and then faced her. "You might as well take all this too. God knows this boy ain't gonna cook. Take it to them street kids of yours."

Her eyes twinkled with mischief. "Thank you, Uncle Tony. As soon as my dining room is finished, I'll take it all."

Ray gawked as Uncle Tony shut the freezer and continued, "If this ain't enough, we'll round you up some more."

Uncle Tony nodded at Cindy and ambled toward the door. "See you back at the house. Mawmaw'll have supper on the table in an hour." A truck fired up and faded in the distance.

Ray reached above the freezer and removed a set of keys from a nail. He offered them to Cindy. "Here. In case you need in here while I'm gone."

She shook her head. "Ray, I can't."

He folded the keys in her palm. "One is for the gate. The other is for the shed." Lifting her hand he brushed a kiss across her knuckles. "Take whatever you need."

80CR

From the outside, most trailers looked the same, but when Cindy stepped inside Ray's, memories assailed her. "I've been here before."

Ray crossed to the kitchen island, and placed a dirty plate into the sink. "I don't think so." His grin was priceless. "I'd have remembered."

She slapped him playfully and then sat on a barstool. "Not with you. With Cole."

Ray's hands fell limp at his sides. His jaw slacked. He blinked twice. "What? In here?"

Her laughter escaped into the room. Ray was so paranoid when it came to her memories of Cole. She needed to reassure him. "We weren't married then." His brow rose. That answer didn't satisfy him. Ray would never understand Cole's morale convictions. "Cole didn't sleep in here. I stayed with Joni and Andrea. Well, Joni was expecting the twins and James made her sleep in the farmhouse. Shortly after midnight, Andrea snuck off to find Derick."

"You stayed here by yourself? Why?"

"It was the night before my wedding. You had parked the trailer at James's family farm. I think Joni said you were in California."

"I remember. Sometimes, it's cheaper to fly and rent a hotel than to drive and pull the trailer. Joni asked about a bachelorette party."

Under the front window, the couch was built into the wall. "I slept over there." Memories washed over her. "I changed my mind at least fifty times that night."

His brow arched. "You didn't want to marry him."

"Oh I wanted to, but I knew I wouldn't measure up to the Maxwell's expectations."

He blinked and lifted her hand. The sweetest kiss heated her skin. "Come outside with me. There's something I want to show you." Ray grabbed a rolled paper she recognized as a blueprint of some sort.

"Where are we going?"

"You'll see." He claimed her hand and led her outside. The wind blew a whiff of his cologne as they rounded the trailer and strolled up a grassy knoll to stand under a grove of pecan trees. He turned her by the shoulders to look toward the trailer. The country road wound around his uncle's fields and disappeared into a forest of trees. He paused and squeezed her hand. "What do you think?"

The wind ruffled the few leaves on the trees above them. In the heat of the summer, the trees would provide a thick shade. Twenty minutes from town and secluded on the country road, the place was private. A barbed wire fence separated his land from his uncle's. The roof of Mawmaw's house rose above the trees. "I love it. How much land did you say you own?"

His laughter floated away on the breeze. "Nine acres. The fence is the landline. Someday, I'll live here."

"It's beautiful. Why haven't you built before now?"

He held her close. "I was waiting to meet my princess."

She wound her arms around his neck and played along. "What will you do when you find her?"

Ray claimed her hand and brought it to his lips. "I'll build her a castle." He released her and unrolled the blueprint of a magnificent house.

Her heart raced as she leaned near. The floorplan tugged at a foggy memory. "You were working on this at the apartment. The day you got me drunk."

He turned toward her and smiled. "You remember?"

She frowned and slapped him playfully on the shoulder. "Vaguely, but it's coming back to me."

His kiss landed on her cheek. "Our relationship hasn't followed the pattern that your church approves." His gaze captured hers. "And I'll never be like those men in your bible, but I do love you, and I'm in this for the long haul. Whenever you're ready…I'm here waiting."

What was he saying? "I think you have that backward. You're leaving Monday. I'll be the one waiting."

His eyes flickered shut and his shoulders relaxed. A flash of his grin teased her senses, and then his kiss erased all thought. His lips lingered and a haze of desire hovered. Whispered words tempted, "Come with me? You and Trevor. We'll pull the trailer. Say yes."

℘ℂ

"You miss him." Maria paused inside the doorway to Cindy's office. Her words were absolute.

Caught staring off into space, Cindy didn't bother to deny them. "It doesn't matter. I knew when I first met him that he would leave."

Her sister came around the beat-up metal desk and wrapped Cindy in a brief hug. "But you didn't know he'd take a piece of your heart with him. Did you? It's okay. You can cry if you want to. No one's looking."

Cindy laughed. "Maria, stop it. I'm fine." She forced a bright smile. "See."

Maria sighed and released her. She strode around the desk, and plunked down in the vinyl covered chair. "I can't believe he just up and left. I thought the guy cared about you."

Cindy couldn't let Maria think bad about Ray. "He didn't. I'm mean..." She wet her lips. "He didn't just up and leave. He asked me to go with him."

"What?" Maria's jaw dropped as she leaned forward. "A fine hunk of man like that invites you in his life and you didn't go?"

Cindy ran a hand through her hair. "I have obligations and responsibilities. Trevor. This place. Sunday School."

"Hey, I got this. The walls didn't cave in while you were off playing farm girl. And I'm sure one of those churchies would love to take over your classroom. As for Trevor...he likes Ray. And it did him good to have a man's influence."

Cindy wished she could've gone with Ray. But it was too late. "It doesn't matter. Ray's gone."

Later that afternoon, Cindy and Trevor waited in line at the ice cream truck. Mr. Carmichael held out their usual frozen yogurt bars.

Trevor reared back and cringed. "Real men don't eat fluff."

The old man laughed and looked to Cindy. She waved her hand through Trevor's hair and nodded. "Give him whatever Ray buys."

He handed Trevor a huge ice cream bar with a smile. "And for you, miss? Do you want the fluff?"

Nothing compared to the smell of chocolate ice cream. "No. Ray's upset our whole schedule. Might as well enjoy it."

Mr. Carmichael's wrinkled face bunched. "A good man will do that. Maybe you should keep him around."

"He's gone." Trevor smeared ice cream on his chin.

Her heart ached. "Thanks." She paid him. "I'll remember that."

The afternoon sun melted the ice cream and a white streak ran down Trevor's arm. Ray had called every night, but she couldn't help but wonder what he was doing when he disconnected. Or who he was doing it with? She blew her bangs out of her eyes. This is why she preferred the yogurt. No mess. "Let's eat in the stairwell. It's cooler there and we don't want to drip ice cream inside."

And it was where she met Ray.

"Okay, momma."

Trevor led the way and soon they were seated on the bottom step. A small cloud dotted the patch of sky visible through the stairwell opening. Cindy sunk her teeth into the heavenly concoction of milk and sugar, and wondered how far the clouds were.

"Where'd he go?"

She smiled and wiped chocolate off Trevor's chin. "Ray's at work, baby."

"Can he come over and build blocks?"

"No. His job is in another city."

"Oh." Trevor gobbled another bite and a chocolate avalanche slid onto his fingers.

Despite the beautiful nights they'd spent together, it was probably a good thing that Ray was gone. Trevor had gotten attached to him.

A sweet face peered up at her. "Does he miss me?"

"I miss you like crazy." Ray grinned in the afternoon sun.

"Uncle Ray!" Trevor vaulted off the step.

Cindy swallowed a stubborn bite of ice cream. Ray dropped his leather knapsack and swooped Trevor in his arms.

He was here, but he shouldn't be.

She stood on the step, her feet paralyzed. Trevor covered Ray's face with sticky kisses. Ray smacked a big kiss on Trevor's forehead and set the boy on his feet.

Like so many times in her dreams, Ray captured her gaze and stalked toward her. Her heartbeat increased its tempo with each of his steps. He stopped in front of her at eye level. "Did *you* miss me, sweetness? Even just a little?"

Words couldn't convey her feelings. She wrapped her arms around his neck and kissed him with all the emotions she wouldn't name. The world faded and she leaned into him forgetting all the past with no worries for the future.

"Momma." Trevor frowned at them and huffed. "You broke the ice cream."

True enough, her treat was now a glob of gooey mess on the stairs. Ray laughed and kissed her again. He rested his forehead against hers. "So, you did miss me?"

"A little."

His lips curled. "Then maybe I should've waited and stopped on my way back from Orlando."

She gripped his shirt. "You're not going anywhere. Except upstairs to wash this ice cream off of me."

"I wouldn't miss it." He stepped back and lifted Trevor and his knapsack while she cleaned their mess and tossed the paper in the trash.

&#8359;&#8278;

Four days later, on the return flight, Ray thumbed through his phone gallery. Cindy's hair lit up like fire in the sunshine and Trevor's smile was more precious than any he'd ever seen.

The pastor beside him smiled. "Nice family. You must miss them a lot. How long have you been gone?"

The old man was nice. Ray had found his comments about Jesus and the bible interesting. "They're not my family. Trevor's dad died before he was born." Ray shrugged.

"But you love him and his mom anyway."

He'd never known love could hurt this much. But then again, maybe it was normal, because he'd never known love at all. He flipped to Cindy's picture. "Yeah, I do."

"She's beautiful."

Ray traced her face with his thumb. "Yes, she is."

Over the loud speaker, the captain announced a twenty minute landing and apologized for the two hour delay.

"Sounds like you'll see them soon."

Ray pocketed his phone. Although he racked up frequent flyer miles with his job, he'd never had anyone greet him at the airport. He hadn't realized how much he wanted to see Cindy's sweet face at the terminal until the flight was delayed. "It's late. Past Trevor's bedtime. I'll see him in the morning."

"There was love in that photo. She'll be waiting at the gate. You'll see."

Ray knew better. Cindy may be waiting, but it wouldn't be at the airport. He helped the pastor with his carry on in the overhead compartment, and waited until the last passenger disembarked. Although he wanted to rush to Cindy's apartment, he'd rather not witness the greetings of loved ones. Regardless of what the preacher said, Cindy wouldn't break Trevor's bedtime for anything. He hung back as the preacher turned the corner. The duffle bag slid off

Ray's shoulder as he rounded the wall. He repositioned it and kept walking. Two hundred feet ahead, muffled excitement traveled from the security barrier.

The crowd thinned quickly.

He was about fifty feet away when a little boy with strawberry hair waved with abandon. "Uncle Ray!"

Cindy grabbed Trevor by the shirttail to keep him from running past the TSA agent. Ray quickened his steps. His long legs passed the slow trod of the preacher. The duffle bag slipped from his shoulder and he let it fall. He lifted Trevor and brought Cindy into his arms. Her soft hair smelled of vanilla. He loved vanilla.

He closed his eyes and hugged her tight while breathing her in. Little arms choked his neck. Ray stepped back, and looked at the little boy in his arms.

"Momma made me eat fluff."

Ray laughed at the expression on Trevor's face. "No more fluff now that I'm here."

"Ray—" His quick kiss ended Cindy's protest.

He lifted his head and answered her smile with one of his own. "It's past Trevor's bedtime."

Cindy shrugged delicate shoulders. "It's a special occasion."

"Yes, it is." He hitched Trevor in his arms, and lifted his bag. Though full, his left hand felt empty without her. To his delight, she looped her arm through his and snuggled close. On the ride down the escalator, Ray couldn't take his eyes off her. Was it possible that Cindy had feelings for him like the Preacher suggested? If so, why wouldn't she admit them? Her lips curled into a satisfied smile as Trevor chatted in his arms.

At the baggage claim, he set Trevor on his feet and claimed his toolbox. Hopefully, all his tools passed inspection and weren't confiscated. Cindy grabbed the duffle as he lifted the toolbox on his shoulder.

"Good grief, what do you have in here?"

It was too heavy for her to carry to the parking lot. Ray lowered his gangbox on a luggage cart and relieved her of his bag.

Cindy smiled at someone behind him. "Hello, Brother Rodger's."

"Hello." The preacher stepped around Ray and shook Cindy's hand. "I thought you looked familiar. Where do I know you from?"

"My husband's secretary, Mrs. Beven goes to your church. I met you during a revival last April."

"Yes, you did. It's nice to see you again." He turned to Ray with his hand extended. "Isn't God wonderful?"

Ray shook the wrinkled hand. "Yes, sir. He is."

"I'll be praying for you, son. And I expect to see you in church before I retire."

"You might do that." Ray waited until after the pastor had gone, and lifted Trevor on top of the tool box." And then he turned to Cindy. "I'm following you home."

She looped her arm around his waist. "Actually, we're riding with you. We caught a cab here." Her smile teased as her thumb brushed under his t-shirt and heated his skin.

Hours later, a teddy bear focused out of the dark corners of Cindy's room.

Ray blinked sleep from his eyes as Trevor materialized beside the bed. Ray had bought pajama pants for just this reason.

Trevor's little face scrunched in a frown.

"What's wrong buddy?"

"Momma lets me sleep here when I'm scared." Trevor's little hand patted Ray's cheek. His trembling voice asked, "Did you have a bad dream, too?"

So that was it. Trevor was afraid. Ray remembered being afraid to hang his foot off the bed when he was a boy. "There's no need to be scared. Dreams aren't real."

Cindy poked him in the back and whispered, "Say yes, Ray. He's trying to reason out why you're in the bed. He thinks you've had a nightmare."

"What?" He rolled toward Cindy. "I'm not gonna let him think I'm a coward." He turned to Trevor. "But sometimes, it's better not to sleep alone. Then you're not ever afraid. Except for when…" Ray swallowed and searched for the right words. "…you're faced with something awkward. And unknown. And you don't know what to do. Or what to say."

"Like now?" Trevor reached for the mattress.

Ray pulled the little boy across his chest and into his mother's line of view.

"Momma, we got bad dreams. Me and Uncle Ray's scared."

Cindy lifted the covers. "Scoot in."

This was all wrong. Ray rolled toward the middle and faced Trevor. "I don't have nightmares. I'm not afraid of the dark."

A little hand patted his cheek. "Momma will save us."

Cindy laughed and Ray set the record straight. "No, Trevor. The man keeps the woman and children safe. Not the other way around. I chase away the boogie men, and kill the monsters in the closet."

Trevor pressed close. "There's monsters in the closet?"

"No." Ack, he didn't intend to scare the little tyke. "But if there were, I'd be the one to squash them. Me. Not your mother."

A little elbow propped on Ray's pillow. "Can you save me from the big trucks?"

With his eyes now accustomed to the dark, Ray brushed Trevor's bangs away from his face. "What trucks?"

"The ones that ranned me over."

The worry in the little eyes was real. "No problem, Trev. I'll shoot out their tires and then they'll be stuck. They won't be going anywhere."

"Thank you, Uncle Ray." Trevor yawned against his chest and the little limbs relaxed. "'night."

Cindy smiled over the top of the covers. "Are you happy now?"

Ray reached over Trevor and caressed her soft cheek. "Yeah. I am."

*Chapter Thirteen*

Why did she let Trevor go with the Maxwell's this morning? Cindy yawned and reached for the loaves of bread. Ray felt guilty about stealing the Maxwell's Sunday visits, but Atlanta was 328 miles away, and Trevor would be gone for five nights.

She missed him already.

Maria swiped mayonnaise on the slices of bread. "Tomorrow's the big day huh?"

"Yes. I wish Trevor was here. And Ray." He was in Montgomery. Whatever a shutdown was, he'd been gone for two days and wouldn't be back for four more. "This was his idea of giving away the old building. And it's saving Lulu's Place a ton of money in demolition costs. Thankfully, he's coordinating everything by phone."

According to Ray, the city of Mobile had awarded them a permit to move the house she'd bought, but in order to avoid traffic disruption, the timeframe was limited to early morning hours. Yesterday, the workmen had disconnected all pipes and electric lines. Today, they loaded the house onto a frame and hooked it to an eighteen wheeler. Tomorrow morning, the truck would pull the house away.

Cindy wrapped the sandwich Maria had made in plastic wrap and looked around her childhood home. "But this house has too many ghosts. When the time comes, I want it demolished."

"Me too." Maria's hand paused mid-air. "I'm glad Ray has given you the courage to move on."

"What?"

Maria resume sandwich making. "Every day for five years, you've forced yourself to walk through that door, just to make a dead man proud. It's time you were free from this place."

"Maria!"

"You know it's true. And Cole wouldn't want you to make yourself miserable here. I don't understand why he used this location to start with."

Childhood nightmares flashed before her mind. "He didn't know about the cellar. He carpeted over the secret door."

"You should've told him."

"Cole was the one person I could turn to and forget the past. I didn't want him tainted by our childhood. He knew enough as it was. Anyway, he…he lied to me. He may not have been the man I thought he was."

"Mrs. Maxwell?" Holding a small duffle bag, the hunter she'd sold the house to stood just inside the open door. "We have a problem."

He couldn't back out on her now. The construction on the new building couldn't begin until the old house was moved. "What's wrong?"

"I found this. Someone has been squatting in the old place. And from the size of his clothes, I'd say he's about ten years old."

Cindy fed many children. She knew most of them slept away from home at night to avoid abusive parents. Much like she had when she and her sister lived with their father. The kind hearted trapper had no idea the hell some children faced.

She took the designer bag and frowned. It must be stolen. "It isn't uncommon to find children sleeping on the streets, but double check the house before you start in the morning."

"We'll do ma'am." He turned to go.

"Wait." She added a sandwich to the bag. "Put this back where you found it. Someone will come back for it tonight."

"Shouldn't we call the police or child services?"

She smiled at his ignorance. "It wouldn't do any good. The child will disappear at the first sign of authority."

He didn't look so sure. "If you say so."

Later that day while passing out sack lunches, Cindy encountered familiar brown eyes. The color of his hair might have been lighter if it wasn't for the grease buildup. The bag on his shoulder matched the one found in the old house. She wanted to help, but didn't want to scare the kid away. When the house was gone, where would he sleep? Under the bridge with the homeless? Tent city down by the creek? Or behind the library?

"Hi." She smiled as he stood before her. "I'm Cindy. You're new here?"

"Yes, ma'am." His empty hand retracted. "Is that okay? Dez said you didn't ask questions and fed people."

She pressed two lunches in his hand. "He's right." She swallowed. "I won't ask questions."

He glanced behind her. "Do men work here? Or just ladies?"

Was he looking for a job? "Sometimes the men in my church fix things, but we're building a new facility. A lot of men will be around then."

The relief was evident in his smile. "Good."

"What's your name?"

He looked uncertain. "Jamey."

"Hey! Hurry up the line. We hungry too!"

Cindy recognized the neighborhood bully. Jamey's eyes widened and he hurried out the door.

&#8359;&#8278;

"...and the frog jumped through the lily pads and lived happily ever after."

Trevor's giggle echoed in Ray's ear. "That's funny, Uncle Ray. Can I tell Papa?"

"I don't know Trev. He might not like my stories."

The giggle morphed into full blown laughter. "Too late. He heared it now."

Mr. Maxwell's laughed joined Trevor's. "Someone can't keep a secret."

Ray'd been surprised when Cole's father called. Trevor had insisted on his nightly bedtime story, and had shown his grandfather the number Ray had added in Trevor's shoe. Ray should've known the older man would listen in. "Goodnight, Trev. Be good and go to sleep. Okay?"

"'kay." A little yawn sounded. "I love you, Uncle Ray."

"I love you too, Trev."

The phone muffled and Mr. Maxwell came on the line. "Goodnight, Ray."

"Goodnight, sir."

The call ended.

It was the highlight of his sad existence. Tucking Trevor in over the phone and then hearing Cindy's voice. He was tired of being away from them. He was tired of sleeping alone. With Trevor in Atlanta, what was stopping Cindy from coming to see him?

She answered after the first ring. "Ray, I don't mean to nag, but when will I see you again?"

Just the words he wanted to hear. "Three hours or less. If you drive up here for a few days."

Silence echoed. "I couldn't do that. You have to work."

"Just during the day. I'll keep you warm at night."

He could almost hear her smile. "That sounds lovely, but I've never driven anywhere outside Mobile or Baldwin counties. I'd get lost."

Ray laughed. "That's what a GPS is for, babe. My hotel is easy to find. The White Knight on Exit 53 behind the service station. It's on the South side so you won't have to drive through traffic."

"Ray, I can't."

"I know, but a guy can dream, can't he? If you change your mind, the crew knocks off at six."

"Thanks, Ray."

"What for?"

"For making me smile and taking away the loneliness."

Was she alright without Trevor? "Are you okay?"

"I'm fine now."

"I'll see you next week. Until then feel free to miss me as much as you want." Ray was tired of emptiness. The emptiness in his arms. The emptiness in his heart. Emptiness in his soul. He wanted to see her. He needed to see her, but she wouldn't leave Cole's memory. "I love you, Cindy."

"I know."

She'd never said it back. Not once. His frustration couldn't be contained as he lowered the phone, and blew out a long breath before lifting the contraption once more to his ear. "I'll see you next week."

"I'm counting down the hours."

Ray disconnected and tossed the phone on the hotel bed. She didn't love him. She loved Cole. Could Ray accept that as a permanent situation? Could he love her without receiving her love in return?

80CR

Cindy rounded the back of the green house, and slung the bag of trash in the dumpster. A blur of blue leapt from behind the bin and ran.

"Wait!"

A boy skidded to a stop.

"Jamey?"

He faced her and lifted his chin. Dirt smeared his cheeks.

There was something about the boy that disturbed her. He looked so familiar. Cindy padded toward the filthy boy.

Wariness flashed in his eyes.

"Don't go. I want to help you."

He looked hungry. Was he waiting around for Lulu's Place to open? It would be hours before lunch was served.

"Let me make you a sandwich." She hurried through the house and grabbed a bag from the counter. When she returned, the skittish boy looked ready to run. She held out her offering.

Shaky hands accepted the bag. "Thank you." His manners forgotten, he devoured the sandwich.

Cindy couldn't abandon the little boy to the streets. "Do you have a place to stay?"

Sadness clouded his eyes. "I have a house."

"Is there anything else I can do to help you?"

His eyes surveyed the yard around them and then his shoulders relaxed. "Am I in the right place?" Jamey reached in his pocket and slid out a crumbled photo.

It was a picture of Lulu's Place, but it was taken before Cindy had made renovations. The screen around the porch let her know it was sometime after her father went to prison, but before the cops raided the place and she went to jail for dealing. Long before she'd met Cole.

"I'm looking for my daddy. My aunt said he used to come here a lot."

Cindy's heart broke for the boy. She didn't know how to tell him that if his father visited here during that time, he wasn't worth finding. "This house was a place for people to buy drugs. A place for people to do bad things."

He shook his head. "She told me he was a bad person, but I don't believe her. I remember what he said. I need to find him."

"Maybe I can help you find him. What's his name?"

"I can't remember." His shoulders slumped and then rose with determination. "She wouldn't tell me. And all I remember calling him is daddy. But I know he loves me, and I will find him." Without another word, the boy ran through the hole in the back fence. "Thanks for the sandwich."

She'd tell Maria to look out for him.

Sleep hadn't come easy last night. She'd arrived early, watched the house be trucked away, and caught up on paperwork. By the time Maria arrived, everything was in order. Cindy yawned and straightened the rows of brown bags lined up on the stainless steel counter. They would serve in fifteen minutes. She turned away from the clock and yawned again.

Maria returned from putting away the broom and grinned. "You look tired. Rough night with that fine hunk of man of yours?"

"Maria!" Cindy gasped. "I can't believe you'd think—"

"Yeah right. You can fool the gullible religious freaks, but I live in the real world. I know why my big sister is dating a guy her church friends warned her about."

Cindy sucked in a quick breath.

"Don't panic. I won't tattle to the preacher. *If* you tell me all the delicious details." Maria leaned her hip against the counter.

Heat climbed Cindy's neck and flamed her face. "I—" Cindy had witnessed to Maria for years, but now her words fell on hard ground. How could one mistake wipe out all the good she'd done? "There's nothing to tell."

Maria smirked. "Yeah, I bet. Where is Ray? With Trevor in Atlanta, your sheets must be smoking."

"You're wrong." Cindy swallowed and admitted the truth. "Ray's working in Montgomery."

"Empty bed and lonely nights?"

Her mind wandered to the strength in Ray's arms. She didn't want to face another sleepless night. Her sister's knowing eyes twinkled. Cindy blurted, "Ray asked me to come up there."

Maria's brows arched with her smile. "Of course he did. What time are you pulling out?"

"I can't go. What if people found out?"

"They'll think you went with the Maxwell's. Or you can always say you stayed with Zack."

Cindy shook her head. It was too risky.

Maria's hand landed on her shoulder. "For once in your life, have some fun. You may never have another opportunity."

Could she do it? Could she drive to Montgomery?

"Go."

Later that afternoon when she entered her empty apartment, Cole's old suitcase in the top of her closet beckoned. Cindy threw in some clothes. Not sure if she could go through with it, she filled the BMW's gas tank and drove.

Just north of Evergreen, an eighteen wheeler swerved into her lane. Cindy slammed on the brakes. Through the rearview mirror, a hatchback nosed close to her rear bumper.

Her heartbeat tattooed against her ribs as a horn blared and the traffic regained speed. She inhaled deep keeping a wary eye on the vehicles around her. If she died, would her relationship with Ray keep her from seeing Cole again?

She shook the paranoia out of her head and continued up this road. She had plenty of time to pray for forgiveness later. Right now, she wanted to spend time with Ray.

An hour later, Cindy inhaled as she exited. The GPS programmed with Ray's hotel directed her to a group of dumpy white buildings behind a convenience store. She parked near the entrance and checked the time. Six thirty-seven. Did Ray park around back? Or was he still at work?

Cindy stepped out of her car on shaky legs. A gentle breeze blew the trash around the pavement as she walked toward the office. The heavy door opened with a screech. Behind the desk, a pretty brunette a few years older than Cindy texted on a phone.

"Excuse me."

Black nails flashed as the clerk held up a hand. "One minute."

Cindy kept one eye on the glass and steel door. She didn't want to miss Ray. She could call him, but that would take away the element of surprise.

The girl—Amanda by her nametag—put the phone down and smiled. "Can I help you?"

Cindy leaned against the counter. "I hope so. I've never done this kind of thing before. You see, I want to surprise my friend with a visit. Can you tell me what room he's in?"

The girl frowned. "Well, we're not supposed to give out guest numbers. Jealous wives and all that, but—"

"We're not married." Cindy's face flamed. "What I mean is…I'm not his wife. Not that he has a wife." She pressed her lips together to keep from babbling.

The girl laughed. "Believe me, I understand." Hands on the keyboard, she asked, "What's your friend's name?"

Cindy swallowed her embarrassment. "Ray Simmons."

"Oh." The girl faltered. "He's not registered."

The girl hadn't looked. Cindy shook her head. "He has to be. Can you check again?"

"Maybe you're at the wrong place."

Was she? Cindy didn't think so. "No, this is the name he gave me."

The girl smirked and shrugged her shoulders. "Maybe, he didn't want you to visit. Maybe, he deliberately gave you the wrong hotel name."

Cindy turned her back on the girl, and fished her phone out of her purse.

Ray answered on the second ring. "Hi, sweetness. Are you still missing me?"

"Did you give me the wrong hotel name?"

"No." Silence echoed. "What's wrong?"

"I sent you a surprise." Cindy glared at the girl frowning behind the desk. "But there're telling me you're not registered."

Ray laughed. "Privacy laws, babe. Don't worry about it. Call them back and tell them to leave it at the front desk. I'll pick it up in three minutes."

Her frustration vanished. "Okay."

"Will I like this surprise?"

She smiled into the phone. "I hope so. You can tell me what you think, as soon as you get it."

"Let me guess, chocolate chip cookies?"

She laughed. "No. It's not food."

"How big is this surprise?"

Cindy looked down at herself. "Big enough."

"What color?"

"Yellow."

He hesitated. "Oh."

"You don't like yellow?" Did she have time to change her shirt?

"It's a girl color."

His blue dodge stopped outside the glass door. Too late to change her mind now. She held her breath and dropped her phone in her purse.

Ray grinned when his eyes met hers. He strode across the floor and swept her into his arms. Cindy inhaled his strength and wound her hands around his neck. His cologne was absent and he smelled like burnt metal, but in his arms she was safe.

He buried his face in her nape. "I love yellow. Love it." His first kiss left no doubt as to her welcome. She held on tight as his second sent her mind soaring.

"Excuse me." The desk clerk knocked on the counter. "We have rooms for that."

No one knew her in this city, but Cindy's face flamed.

Ray lifted his head and smiled. "Yes, I do." Ray lifted her at the knees, carried her across the room, and sat her next to the registration desk. His arm anchored her to his side. "Amanda, this is Cindy. She needs a room key."

A huff sounded at Cindy's back. "Separate room?"

The gleam in Ray's eyes sparkled with all their secrets. "Oh no. This is my lady. She's with me."

"If I rekey the lock, your card will no longer work."

Ray reached into his back pocket and slipped a card out of his wallet. As the plastic cardkey slapped against the counter, he frowned into his billfold and his smile vanished. His frantic thumbs searched through the fan of money. Biting his lip, he snapped his wallet shut, and gave her an indiscernible look. Regret shadowed his smile. "Just my luck."

Her heart fell when he stepped away from her. Their fingers didn't touch as he collected two keys from the desk clerk, and held one out to her. "Ray?"

He kissed her forehead. Without a word, he led her by the hand out the door. "Where'd you park?"

She pointed to the BMW. What was wrong with him? Didn't he want her here?

"It should be safe in front of the office. We'll leave it there." He opened the passenger door and stuffed a white hard hat, gloves and some kind of gadget behind the seat. "Sorry about the mess." He kissed her forehead again and ran around to the driver's side. He braked by her car and got her suitcase. "I'm not exactly..." He rubbed the back of his neck. "I'm not prepared for your visit. I wish you would've told me you were coming."

His words slapped reality in her face. He didn't want her here. "I can stay somewhere else if—"

"No, babe." He helped her from the truck. "That's not what I meant. Of course, you're staying with me." Muscled arms had no trouble swinging her heavy bag from the bed of the truck. She followed him up the outside stairs and down a concrete sidewalk. He swiped the key and held the door.

She'd lived in worse places.

Ray kicked his boots under a small table. Between the king size bed and the kitchenette, an alarm clock blinked on a lampstand. He placed her plain, black suitcase on the dresser, and winked from across the room, but made no move to kiss her. "Make yourself at home while I shower." He glanced at her suitcase. "But don't get too comfortable. I need to run an errand and take care of some business before we um..."

She'd made a mistake coming here. Joni said that he had a different girl in every city. Cindy should've listened.

Did he have a date? She searched for something clever to say. "Just—" Her voice broke. "Go take a shower." She fell back on the bed and closed her eyes.

His footsteps sounded closer.

The bed creaked beside her.

"Go away." If he kissed her forehead again, she would scream.

"Cindy?" His touch trailed down her cheek. "Sweetness?" The emotion flickering in his eyes gave her goose bumps. Leaning close to her neck, his breath shivered down her spine. "I do want you." His mouth blazed a trail to her lips. "But I'm trying to be responsible." He nibbled her bottom lip. "I don't have any protection. We used the last ones the morning before I came here. I planned to stop by the store on the way home but…you're here now." He finally kissed her full on the mouth.

This is what she drove three hours for. This kiss. His kiss that erased the world of hurt she'd been living in since Cole's death. Since her mother abandoned her with an addict father. Since she found out Cole had lied.

His mouth hovered above hers. "Tell me to stop."

## *Chapter Fourteen*

Through the slit in the linen curtain, two girls stopped outside Ray's room. The expected knock followed. Now what? Should she open the door? Or pretend no one was in here? Cindy didn't want to meet any of Ray's groupies. A giggle preceded the second knock. She straightened her denim skirt, inhaled a fortifying breath, and then opened the door.

Two smiling faces greeted her. "Hi. You must be Cindy."

How did they know her name? "Um, Ray's not here."

"Of course he's not. I'm Felicia, this is Peg. Our husbands work for Ray."

Cindy widened the door's opening. They weren't groupies. "Nice to meet you. Come in."

"No thanks. We're going to the flea market. Do you want to come with us?"

"There's a flea market here?" She grabbed her purse, and followed her new friends to an older model sedan. She brushed crumbs off the backseat, and slid in.

The scenery flew by, and she muttered a prayer under her breath as Felicia sped through yet another yellow light.

Peg fluffed her hair. "So, tell us. How did you meet Ray?"

"He brought my son home from a mutual friend's."

Felicia swerved into another lane. "Oh, you're divorced?"

"No." The picture of Cole in her mind wouldn't focus.

Peg turned in her seat. "The jerk never married you?"

Cindy sucked in a breath. "Cole died five years ago."

Sympathy entered Peg's eyes. "Oh honey, I'm so sorry."

Felicia slowed for a red light. "We didn't know."

Cindy kept silent. She never knew how to respond to other wives sympathy.

She changed the subject. "How long have your husbands worked for Ray?"

"Years." The signal changed and the race began again. "It's great to meet his lady. All the crew is talking about you."

"Me? Why?"

"Ray's changed. Since we've been here, he's turned down several maids and the desk clerk twice."

A warm tingle inched its way up the base of her neck. "I hoped people exaggerated about his previous girlfriends. Evidently not."

Felicia added, "Not girlfriends. Girls. And any girl would do."

Peg laughed. "But he never invited them to stay. I heard him tell one that she couldn't stay overnight because his sleep was personal. Yet, here you are."

The warmth spread to her cheeks and ignited a bonfire. Cindy ducked her head. Evidently, Joni hadn't exaggerated.

Peg popped her gum. "Oh, look. She's blushing."

Cindy's phone chimed in her purse. Grateful for the escape, she answered without checking the screen.

"Still missing me?" Ray's voice flamed the fire on her face.

Felicia turned a curve and Cindy gripped the edge of the seat. "Not at the moment." She waited for his laughter to fade. "I'm going shopping."

"Good. Buy yourself a pair of steeled toed boots, and I'll give you a tour of the jobsite tomorrow."

"Steeled toed boots? Where would I find such a thing?"

Peg turned from the front seat. "That must be Ray, tell him we'll help you find a pair."

"Who's with you?" Ray sounded irritated.

"Um, I believe they're friends of yours. I met them at the hotel. The girls know where to find the boots."

She remembered the way the desk clerk wouldn't help her, and that Ray knew her by name. Turned her down twice did he? What would have happened if she'd asked the third time? Cindy had never been jealous with Cole, not even of Rachel. But Ray had more than one girl after him. The way Peg described it, Ray was first come, first served.

Felicia pulled into a large parking lot.

Cindy didn't want to be just another number. "I'll see you this afternoon."

The girls got out of the car. Cindy had a great time hunting for bargains in the open air pavilion, but she wanted a shower before Ray got back to the room. Her phone rang as they left the parking lot. "Ray?"

"Where are you? Your car's here but you're not. Are you hurt? Lost?"

Cindy blew out a breath. Ray had never been this clingy. What was wrong with him? "I'm fine. Peg, Felicia, and I are on our way back."

"You're with Scott's and Doug's wives?" An audible sigh burst through the earpiece.

She lowered her voice. "Are you okay?"

"I wanted to see you. I thought you'd be here."

"I miss you too." She glanced out the window looking for familiar landmarks. "I don't think we're far away."

"Don't tell Felicia to hurry. She drives too fast as it is."

Cindy laughed into the phone. It was nice to have someone care about her safety. She dropped her phone in her purse and met Peg's smile, who had turned around in her seat as they waited at a red light.

"What are the guys doing off work? It's not even five o'clock?"

"I don't know. Ray didn't say they were early."

Felicia's phone trickled gypsy music. "It's Doug." She slid her finger across the screen. "We'll be there in five minutes. Ray's already called Cindy." A pause lingered. Then she laughed. "Well, he should've told us ya'll were knocking off early. How were we supposed to know? It's not raining." Another pause. "Whatever. We're pulling into the parking lot now. Come help us unload."

The car rounded the building. Ray and two of the men she'd seen with him yesterday stepped toward the car. One of the men approached Peg, "What were you thinking taking the boss's lady out?"

"What was she supposed to do? Lock herself in their room and wait for prince charming to knock on her door?" Sarcasm dripped off Felicia's words.

Ray extended his hand toward Cindy in the backseat. "Did you buy them?"

She passed the bag holding the boots out the door and stood. "They are the ugliest shoes I own."

Strong arms wrapped around her. "They're not supposed to be pretty." A kiss brushed her cheek.

Felicia and her husband continued to argue about the girls taking Cindy shopping.

"Excuse me." Cindy butted in. "Thank you for today. It was fun. Let's do it again tomorrow."

"You can't go." Ray's voice hushed all protests.

"Ray." Cindy jabbed her elbow in his side. "What are you doing?"

He held the boots and grinned. "I'm hiring you in, babe."

The men laughed around them confusing her further.

She'd never had a job before. No one would hire her after her arrests. Cole hadn't wanted her to work and when Trevor was born, she hadn't wanted to leave him. "You're giving me a job?" At his nod, she flung her arms around him. "Oh, Ray. Thank you. But, I don't know anything about construction."

He whispered in her ear, "Just keep the boss happy."

&#8359;&#8359;

Ray gripped the clipboard in his hand and scanned his men. He didn't need another firewatcher. He'd hired Cindy because he wanted her with him during the day. He hadn't expected her exuberance. Or her lack of job skills. She'd taken one look at the W4 and called her brother for instructions on how to fill it out.

The crewmen stared as she clicked the pen in concentration while holding the phone to her ear. Some with open admiration, some with mild lust, but most with curious glances. Her glorious hair waved from under the blue hardhat and curled down her back. He needed to think of something quick. Most of the guys were harmless, but he had a few loose cannons that needed to respect Cindy and keep their distance.

At the metal table, she frowned. "No, I'm not."

The anger in her voice pulled Ray toward her. He stopped just shy of touching her.

"But I'm not single." Cindy's back straightened. "I'm a qualifying widow. I'm not checking that box, Zack. I don't care what the stupid law says."

Over her shoulder, the form was completed with the exception of a claimed exemption. The choices were clear. Married or Single. If she considered herself a married woman then they both were guilty of adultery. That was one sin Ray was innocent of. He cleared his throat. "Can I help?"

She disconnected the call and held out the incomplete form. "Zack said, give this to you and let you finish it. I'm done."

He checked the box beside "single" and then clipped the form underneath the others. He reached for her as she stepped toward the crew. "Where're you going?"

Her lips pressed together as she cut her eyes to the crew. She whispered, "With the other workers, I don't want special treatment."

Laughter burst from his heart. She frowned and he leaned near her ear. "You didn't complain about my special treatment last night."

A dainty hand slapped his chest and her cheeks reddened. "Stop it. Everyone's staring at me."

"Because you're beautiful." He anchored her in the circle of his arms, and checked the names off his list. Someone was missing. "Where's Hank?"

A journeyman in the back swung his arm. An oomph sounded as Hank straightened from the wall caught asleep on his feet. "Right here, boss."

"If you can't handle the early hours, lay off the drinking." Ray held the young man's stare until the boy blinked.

"Yes, sir."

Cindy's arm brushed Ray's as she removed her hard hat and combed her fingers through her hair.

Hank's eyes rounded and a leer crossed his face.

Ray whispered through clenched teeth. "Put your hat on."

She cut her eyes at him and then his crew. When her eyes rested on him again she whispered, "It stinks and I don't know whose head it's been on."

He was already twelve minutes late getting started, but her safety came first. "Hold this." He handed her the clipboard and removed the hat from her hand. The band was the color of rust, and the musty smell of sweat clung to the interior. "I'll find you another one."

She stretched on her toes, claimed his hat, and plunked it on her head. Snickers and laughs sounded from the men.

She blinked in innocence. "What? Yours is clean."

She wasn't aware of the significance of wearing his hat. Instant respect. He winked at her puzzled look, and placed the blue one on his own head. The lingering moans and groans subsided as Ray faced the crew. "If anyone's got a problem with my lady wearing the white hat, speak now or forever hold your peace."

Silence descended.

"Yeah. And just so you know—if I have to choose—she wins every time. And I don't mind loading your box. Got it?" Satisfied that Cindy would be safe from unwanted advances, he assigned each man a specific task. "Now, get busy."

The crew turned toward the door, but Cindy's voice slowed their progress. "What about me? This is my first real job. What do I do?"

His hat was skewed sideways on her head. Aware of the men eavesdropping, he kissed her. "You're wearing the white hat, babe. That *is* your job."

She rolled her eyes. "I know what color the hat is."

He grinned down at her. "Only the boss wears white. You are now in charge of this operation. And if this machine isn't up and working in four days…Cecil will fire me."

Her eyes rounded into an o. "I can't." Dainty hands flew to her head.

He laughed and held the hat in place. "Don't worry about it. I have another one in my office. We'll work together."

Her hands gripped his wrists. "What do I do?"

He shrugged. He knew better than to say "stand there and look beautiful." She wanted to feel useful. "Fire everyone you find goofing off." The last of his crewmen groaned their way out the door as he focused on her safety. "But keep the hat on at all times. Don't touch anything, and watch your step. There aren't any sidewalks out here."

"I'll be careful." After a quick kiss, she walked to the door.

"Cindy?" Her smile turned his heart. "Have fun."

ഇരു

Two days later, he carried their lunch cooler through his office door. Cindy lifted her head from his metal desk. "Wake me up when our lunch break is over." Her head lowered onto her folded arms.

"You should eat something first."

"Uh-uh." Her voice was muffled and slow.

He abandoned the lunch cooler and rounded the desk. He swept the papers covering the old couch to the floor. His hands beat the dust from the cushions. Gently, he carried her to the make shift bed. She didn't protest. Instead, she scooted toward the back issuing him an invitation. He shook his head, remembering her lack of sleep since she'd gotten here. Last night included. "I think that's the problem. You don't sleep much in my bed."

A yawn interrupted her Cheshire smile. "That's why I'm taking a nap. Tonight, I won't have to worry about something so inconsequential as sleep."

He crouched down and tucked a strand of her hair behind an ear. "Then rest today, but make sure you eat something when you wake. I've got a feeling you're gonna need your strength." He kissed her soft cheek. "Sleep, my sweetness."

ഇരു

"So the rumors are true?" An unfamiliar male voice intruded on her dreams. She held still and listened as papers shuffled.

"Rumors?" Ray answered the question.

"That you're in love. Are you leaving the company when you settle down?"

Feigning sleep, Cindy didn't know if she wanted to hear the answer. Sure, he'd told her he loved her, but maybe he said that to all his girls.

"I don't know. We haven't talked about a future, but she means more to me than anything. I guess that includes the job. And yes, sir." She heard his smile. "I do love her."

Chair legs screeched across the floor. "You deserve a nice family, son. But you have to provide for her. Remember that before you drag up."

Ray's laughter stirred a longing inside her. "Don't worry, sir. She may not decide to keep me."

"She'll figure out you're a keeper sooner or later. Now, bring me up to speed. Rumors also say that your lady has us ahead of schedule."

## Chapter Fifteen

The snap of his clipboard failed to divert the crew's attention away from Cindy. Ray cleared his throat and stabbed each crew member with his best disapproving frown. "If we can finish tomorrow, there'll be bonuses for everyone."

Cheers erupted.

Cindy yawned and snuggled into his side. These last few days had been pure bliss with her. No sadness. No clouds in her eyes.

"Uh, boss." His lead-man smirked. "You were saying."

Cindy laughed and plucked the clipboard from his hands. "I've watched you enough. I know how to do this." She raised her voice and addressed the crew. "You guys did a great job today, but I'm sure Ray found one area that could've been better. You probably know what it is since I heard him yelling around two o'clock. Go home, rest, and be back here in the morning ready to finish this thing." Snickers sounded and she tilted her head up at him. "How did I do?"

She was awesome. "Pretty good." He turned to the crew. "You heard my lady. Get out of here."

Cindy's phone rang as the crew dispersed. "Trevor? Baby, don't cry. Momma's right here." Her face did that I-told-you-so expression. "Trevor, I can't come get you. Remember the cool airplane ride."

Trevor's cries reached Ray. He claimed the phone. "Hey bud, what's going on?"

A sniff sounded. "I'm dragging up."

Ray smiled at the construction lingo. Atlanta might be a six hour drive from Mobile, but from Montgomery, they could make it in three. "Alright. Pack your stuff. I'm on my way."

Cindy touched his arm. "Ray, what are we doing? What will the Maxwell's think?"

He lowered the phone. "I don't care about the Maxwells. I care about Trevor."

"Drive super fast, Daddy."

Ray's heart tripped at the word. Did Trevor know what he'd said? Ray swallowed the lump in his throat. Trev was a kid. He repeated everything he heard. Good thing Cindy didn't hear him. "I'll be there before bedtime."

"Papa said, that's fine."

Though she kept giving him worried glances on the drive, Cindy curled in the seat and fell asleep. Ray tuned into a country station to keep himself awake. One thing was certain. They both needed more rest. Before she'd conked out, Cindy had placed the Maxwell's address into the GPS.

Ray followed the automated voice to Buckhead. The mansions lining the street weren't a surprise given the Maxwell estate in Fairhope, but Ray felt a moment's panic at the iron gated entrance. He curved his forefinger and caressed Cindy's cheek. "Wake up, sweetness."

She stirred and lifted her head from his lap. "We're here?"

"Yeah. How do we get in this museum?"

She blinked and folded her knees under her. "Roll down the window." While he did as she asked, she brushed her hands through her hair. Leaning over him, she pressed a button. "I've been here once, but I don't remember the code."

A male voice answered. "May I help you?"

"Cindy Maxwell, I'm here for Trevor."

A buzz sounded, and the gate retracted.

"Drive to the front of the house. And don't accept their invitation to stay. They'll ask because it's polite."

"I can't imagine Mr. Maxwell being rude."

"It's not him. It's his crazy brother." Cindy dusted her jeans and then flipped the mirror to straighten her hair. She pulled it back and let it fall.

Maybe they should have gone to the hotel and showered before they made the drive, but he'd been so worried about Trevor he hadn't thought of anything but relieving the little guy's fears. "You're beautiful. Just the way you are."

Her smile was weak. "Beauty has nothing to do with it." Her shoulders rose as she sucked in a breath. Eyes fluttered shut as she exhaled. "I'm ready. Let's go."

The chandelier on the porch spotlighted his scruffy work boots. "Marble?"

Cindy squeezed his hand. "From the Georgia quarries northwest of Atlanta."

The door opened and Trevor flew down the steps into Cindy's arms. "Momma. I knew you'd come. Grandmother said nonsense, but Papa said you never know dear, that Ray's a pretty determined fellow."

Ray smiled at Trevor's impression. Mr. Maxwell stepped onto the porch and held out his hand. "Come in. You must be tired from the long drive."

Ray looked at Cindy who answered. "We can't stay." She pushed passed them into the house like she owned the place. "Come on sweetie, let's gather your things together."

Ray followed Mr. Maxwell into a massive foyer. He hesitated to wipe his muddy boots on the expensive looking rug. Cindy paused halfway up a wide staircase and sniffed the top of Trevor's head. "Your hair stinks."

The little boy clung to his mother. "Papa cleaned it." Trevor's eyes landed on Ray. "Daddy!" He wiggled until Cindy released him. Little feet ran down the stairs away from his slack jawed mother.

Ray tossed him toward the high ceiling, and then caught him in his arms. "I've got him. Pack his stuff, we'll wait down here."

Mr. Maxwell waved a hand. "Come on in."

Ray stood his ground. "I'm good, sir."

Mr. Maxwell nodded. "You made excellent time. There's no way you could have driven from Fairhope in three hours."

Ray faced the inquisition. "No, sir. I'm working in Montgomery."

"I see. And Cindy?"

"She's the newest member of my crew."

"Of course." Disbelief expelled with the older man's sagging shoulders. He didn't believe a word Ray was saying. Not that Ray blamed him, but he couldn't speak the truth.

Trevor laid his head against Ray's and sighed.

Mr. Maxwell continued. "Trevor caught me off guard when he insisted his daddy would come get him. I should've known he meant you. It must be difficult to be his father without a commitment to his mother."

Was that what was bothering Cole's father?

"Until tonight, I've always been Uncle Ray. I don't know why he thinks that's different." Ray wasn't sure how to answer Mr. Maxwell and he didn't know why Trevor had called him daddy. "But I love him and his mother. That won't change anytime in the future." Little hands propped on Ray's head and a sweet kiss fluttered against his temple. Ray looked into the precious face. "I wouldn't let anyone hurt them."

"That's good to hear." Relief flashed across Mr. Maxwell's face. "Before Cole died, he signed everything he owned to Cindy, but Trevor is the heir to the Maxwell estate. If you and Cindy legalized your relationship, there are things you need to know."

Ray shifted his weight from one boot to the other. "Sir, I'm not interested in Trevor's money. If it ever came down to it…I'd sign a prenup or something."

"Never do that. Promise me that you'll protect his inheritance."

If Trevor was the heir, why did he need protection and from whom? Footsteps sounded behind him and Ray turned. Rachel posed inside an open doorway. She smiled, and then waved. Trevor tightened his grip on Ray's neck.

Mr. Maxwell closed a door, shutting out the sight of the woman in a tight fitting dress standing beside a middle-aged man in a wheelchair. Why was Rachel at the Maxwell family gathering? Was this the threat whom Trevor needed protecting?

Cindy rushed down the stairs carrying a small suitcase in one hand and Trevor's booster seat in the other. "Let's go."

Mrs. Maxwell glided behind her. "There's no need to rush off, dear. I could ready rooms for you and your friend."

"No thanks." Cindy nodded toward the door. Ray opened it and they descended the steps. Mr. Maxwell followed them into the brisk night air. At the truck, she buckled the chair in the backseat.

Ray passed Trevor to Cindy and turned to the man. "Thank you for allowing him to call, sir."

Mr. Maxwell laughed. "And thank you for the nightly entertainment. If you ever run out of your own stories, you might want to read some from the Bible."

Cindy reached around and hugged Cole's father. "I'm sorry to cut your visit short."

"It was for the best given the circumstances." Mr. Maxwell hugged her, and then stepped back while Cindy slid into the passenger seat. Ray closed her door and turned.

He held out his hand. "Goodnight, sir."

The man's grip was solid. "Drive careful, son."

Ray rounded the hood. "Yes, sir."

When they drove out the gate, Trevor whooped, "Freedom!"

Cindy's laughter mingled with Ray's. "Was it that bad?"

"The looking lady creeped me."

Cindy frown toward her son. "Who?"

Trevor must have meant Rachel. Ray glanced toward the backseat. "Do you mean the good-looking lady?"

"No. She looks at me all times."

His mother turned in her seat. "Who, Trevor? What was her name? Aunt Dolly?"

"Nope."

Ray waited at a red light. He faced Cindy. "Rachel was there. I saw her down the hall." In the city lights, Cindy's blue eyes turned to ice as he filled her in to all he'd seen. "Who was the man in the wheelchair?"

"Kyle. Mr. Maxwell's invalid brother." Lips pressed into a tight line, her chest heaved. "What was Rachel doing at a Maxwell reunion? I don't want her anywhere near Trevor." She glanced in the back. "Did she hurt you?"

"She washed my hair. Papa cried."

Beside Ray, Cindy gasped and her gaze flew to his. He reached for her hand. A strange woman had given her son a bath. The horrors of her childhood shown on her face. Ray asked the question in her eyes. "Did anything else happen that scared you, Trev?"

"Papa yelled. Grandmother couldn't believe her eyes." Through the rearview mirror, Trevor yawned and blinked.

Cindy's grip tightened in Ray's. "Did you know she'd be there when you said Trevor should go?"

"I had no idea. And judging by his actions, I'd say Mr. Maxwell hadn't expected her either."

"You said good looking. You think she's pretty?"

"No, sweetness. I don't think of her at all. I was translating Trevor-speak."

"Don't fuss at my daddy."

An awkward silence fell.

The light turned green and Ray drove through as Cindy turned sideways. She used her momma-knows-best tone. "Trevor, Ray isn't your daddy. As a matter of fact, he isn't your uncle. He's our friend."

Trevor's feet pushed against the seat. "The looking lady says wait and see. Grandmother said not over her dead azaleas, but me and Papa prayed about it."

Cindy groaned and faced the front. "Lord, help us. He's like a voice recorder. What did he tell the Maxwell's about us?"

"I telled 'em you kissed."

"Trevor!" Cindy gawked into the backseat.

Ray linked his hand with hers. "He could've said worse."

"Uncle Ray, are you my daddy?"

"Trevo—" A squeeze of Ray's hand interrupted Cindy.

He sucked in a breath. He couldn't afford to mess this up. Uncle Tony had done his best, but Ray remembered how a boy needed a dad. And how disappointing it was when you didn't get one. "Trev, your father was a super-cool dude. I bet he's proud you're his son."

Aw entered Trevor's voice. "You knowed him?"

"A little. Being a dad's a special job. And I don't know how to be one. I'm honored that you want me, but we don't get to choose. Maybe later things will change, but for now, I'll just be Uncle Ray and you can be my favorite bud. Okay?"

Trevor's voice lowered. "'kay."

Cindy snuggled into Ray's side. "Thank you."

Ray leaned over and accepted her kiss. "You're welcome."

"You kissed again."

Cindy turned and used her mom voice. "Yes, I like kissing Ray, but I don't want the whole world to know."

"Can I pray about it?"

Cindy huffed the hair from her forehead. "Yes, Trevor. Pray all you want."

As Ray exited onto I85, a soft voice whispered across the backseat. "Dear Jesus. Please make Uncle Ray a daddy. And please hurry. Amen."

Cindy wiped a finger under her eye. Ray lifted their joined hands and kissed her wet knuckle. After spending the past few days in her heavenly arms, he wanted to amen Trevor's prayer. But Ray wasn't waiting on God. He was waiting on Cindy. He glanced into the rearview mirror. "Are you hungry?"

"For chocolate."

"Chocolate it is."

"Ray, he'll be up all night."

He winked to lighten the mood. "Good, he can keep me awake. Someone bailed on the drive up here."

Her head tilted. "I'm sorry. And it'll be after midnight before we reach the hotel. Tomorrow you'll be exhausted."

"With Trevor sharing our bed, I'll rest more than any night this week."

"Ray!" She glanced into the backseat. "He can hear you."

&Oslash;&OElig;&alpha;

Cindy snuggled her back against Ray's chest as his arms reached around her and included Trevor in his embrace. They smiled for the camera. A flash blinded her and she blinked as Ray accepted the ticket from the photographer.

"Your photo is available for purchase in the gift shop." The young man moved on to the next group.

Laughing, they chased Trevor from one exhibit to another in the Montgomery zoo.

As Trevor waved from the saddle of an elephant, his smile reminded her so much of Cole. Would the Maxwell's sue for custody? Why was Rachel there? Ray's arms came around her and his boot landed on the railing. She folded her arms on top of his. "It doesn't make sense."

His lips tickled the sensitive part of her neck just below her ear. "What, sweetness?"

"The Maxwells. They've always helped me, never asking

anything in return. I wasn't Beverly's first choice for a daughter-in-law, Rachel was. But when I lost Lulu and then later when Cole…" She closed her eyes against the fresh wave of pain.

Trevor's elephant made another pass.

Ray's arms tightened around her. "They love Trevor. Maybe they just want to see him."

"But they do, Ray. Or they did, every Sunday. And you were the one who talked me into letting him go to Atlanta."

A kiss landed in her hair. "When you love someone, a few visits here and there isn't enough."

∞Ⴀ

Ray purchased lunch and fought his way to the picnic table where Cindy and Trevor waited.

A little boy darted in front of him, and chased after a girl with cotton candy. "Mom, Susie won't share!"

Ray sidestepped around the bickering children in time to see Cindy shake her head at three guys to her left. One of them smiled and said something Ray couldn't hear. Keeping his eyes on Cindy, Ray hurried to the table. She narrowed her eyes at the group and pulled Trevor close.

Ray dropped the tray and glared at the teenagers. He wanted to knock a few heads together, but the boys couldn't be more than fourteen or fifteen. "Sorry guys. She's taken." He plopped down beside her and kissed her as the gawking boys scrambled away from the table.

Trevor reached for a chicken nugget. "They were weird."

Cindy's face glowed. "They were kids, Ray."

He winked. "I know." He leaned in for another kiss. "But, I'm never leaving your side again."

She swallowed and licked her lips. "Kind of hard to do since you're leaving for Memphis in two weeks and I'll be stuck in Alabama."

"There's an easy solution to that problem, sweetness." Ray offered her a strawberry milkshake. "You and Trevor come with me."

Her mouth fell open. "Ray, we can't."

"Can we momma, please?" Trevor bounced on the picnic table.

Cindy speared Ray with her ice blue eyes. "See what you've

done?" She smoothed Trevor's hair. "Sweetie, we can't go, but Ray can stay with us until he leaves."

෨෬

Trevor snuggled in Ray's lap and huffed as a commercial came on about camping gear. "Momma says no."

Since his trip to Atlanta, Cindy hadn't let Trevor out of her sight. Not that the kid had the opportunity to go anywhere yet. Yesterday they'd lounged around the apartment. Ray needed some fresh air. "What do you want to do, Trev?"

"Camp with the Terrors."

Cindy walked into the living room carrying a basket of clean laundry and settled on the couch. "What?"

Ray reached for a towel and folded it down the middle. "Why won't you let him go camping?"

She sighed and rolled her eyes. "James has his hands full with his boys. Mr. Maxwell never stays the night. There is no one to watch Trevor."

Ray liked camping with his Uncle Tony when he was a boy. "What if I go with him? When is it?"

"I doubt you'll be interested. It's a church thing."

Ray shrugged. Church was a bonus. "I can handle it."

Cindy perched on the edge of the cushions. "We just got home. You're here for two weeks. I don't want to share you."

"Please, please, momma," Trevor begged. "I never do nothing."

Ray was torn between his desire to please Trevor and spending time with Cindy. "How long is the campout?"

"They leave at three this afternoon, but they stay all day tomorrow."

He stood and left Trevor in the recliner. Gathering Cindy in his arms, he kissed the ticklish spot on her neck. She giggled and he growled against her sensitive skin.

"Ray, stop it."

"Come on, sweetness. We men need to bond with nature. Go all primitive, and spit and stuff."

Her arms wrapped around his neck. "Really? What kind of stuff?"

"At a camp out with the church? We'll go wild and crazy. Eat hotdogs and marshmallows until we puke."

"Ray, that's disgusting."

"It's fun, momma."

Tears clouded her eyes. "Fine. Go. I have somewhere I need to be this afternoon anyway."

Her tears surprised him. Could she love him after all? "Don't cry. We'll stay here."

"No." She sniffed and wiped her eyes. "You guys go ahead. I'll be fine. Andrea is hosting a girl's sleepover."

"You sure?"

&#8359;&#8359;

Cindy stopped by the florist after dropping Ray and Trevor off at the church. They would ride with James to the campsite. She'd heard his surprise when Ray had called earlier. Trevor should be with her, but he didn't remember the significance of this day. Unfortunately, Cindy couldn't forget.

Her phone pinged on the seat beside her. Delaying the inevitable, she flipped through the screens and winced.

Rachel! She'd posted on Cole's wall again. *It's been 5 years today since I lost my best friend. Oh how I miss him.*

Cindy deleted the post, and tossed the offensive phone on the front seat. Stepping out of the car, she walked down the path until she came to the Maxwell's plot. She knelt and traced the engraved headstone. *Coleman Alexander Maxwell. November 11, 1984 to September 9, 2013. Loving Husband and Son.*

"Cole. If you were here, I wouldn't be in this mess." She'd give anything to hear his voice again.

Like she'd done hundreds of times before, she lay on the marble slab and stared into the heavens. It wasn't like the boat. She couldn't imagine herself in the clouds with Cole and Lulu, but she pretended his arms held her tight. Cole always knew what to say. He always knew what she needed to hear.

"I didn't give my heart away. Ray burst into my life and stole it." Could Cole see them from heaven? "He's good to Trevor and me." She wiped her eyes and breathed. "I miss you. Oh, why did you leave me? Why didn't you tell me you were sick?" A sob escaped and she bit her fist. She turned and curled in a ball whispering the truth to the one who understood. "I know I shouldn't love Ray, but it's so lonely without you. I'm scared, Cole. I can't feel God anymore. I've lost my way home."

ଌଠଓଡ଼

Ray suppressed the urge to toss his phone into the lake. Why wasn't she answering? She hadn't replied to his texts either. He should've driven his own truck, then he wouldn't be stranded here with James.

James? The women were all at Andrea's. He surveyed the busy campground. Despite the sun hanging over the trees, Trevor and the rest of the children roasted marshmallows around the fire. James walked down the path carrying two sleeping bags. Ray intercepted him before he reached the campsite. He didn't want everyone to know about his paranoia.

"Hey, man. Cindy's not answering my calls or texts. Will you call Joni and see if they're together?"

Sadness crossed his friend's eyes.

"What? What's wrong?"

James touched his arm and led him further away from the others. "Maybe she forgot her phone in the car?"

James wouldn't meet his stare. "What are you not saying? Where do you think she is?"

"At the cemetery. Today's the anniversary of Cole's death."

His girlfriend had a date with her dead husband, and he thought her tears were because she'd miss him tonight. He turned from James's knowing eyes. His worst suspicions were confirmed. Cindy couldn't love him. She still loved Cole.

"Hey, beautiful." Behind him, James asked Joni to check on Cindy without letting her know Ray was concerned.

ଌଠଓଡ଼

"Cindy." Joni rubbed her hands down her arms. "That is so creepy."

Cindy crossed her legs and leaned on the headstone. "Cole doesn't mind."

"Ray's worried."

"My phone is in the car."

"We figured." Joni plopped down on the green grass beside Cole's grave. "So, what does Cole think of Ray?"

"I have no idea."

"You know? I was reluctant to see you and Ray together, but now… Can you believe that I was worried he'd tempt you out of church with carnal pleasure?" Joni's tinkling laughter stirred the guilt swirling in Cindy's stomach. "He must really love you and Trevor. When the time is right, I want to help plan the wedding."

"That's not gonna happen." Cindy twisted the gold band on her finger. "I can't imagine being married to anyone but Cole."

"Yeah, well…" Joni laughed again. "Mrs. Maxwell couldn't see Cole married to anyone but Rachel. God—however—had someone different in mind."

Joni didn't understand and Cindy couldn't tell her the truth.

A gentle touch squeezed warmth into her cold hand. "God wouldn't have created Eve if he wanted Adam to be alone."

Cindy sucked in the hurt. "I miss Cole so much." And because of her sin, she may never see him again. She curled into her friend's hug and accepted the comfort offered. She ached for the life they could've had. She ached for the great father Cole would've been. She longed for Cole's gentle embrace, yet she craved Ray's fiery touch.

How could she love two very different men?

It wasn't fair. It wasn't fair to Cole's memory. It wasn't fair to her, and it wasn't fair to Trevor.

It wasn't fair to Ray.

## Chapter Sixteen

"If you don't have it, you can't lose it." Mr. Maxwell stood in front of the group of young boys and men. Hands behind his back, he paced near the fire.

"I lost my son five years ago today, but I thank God for the years I was given. There are people who can't have children. Yet, God gave me a son to be proud of, and through him a grandson." Trevor waved at Mr. Maxwell from Ray's lap. "He blessed me with a beautiful daughter-in-law, whose love I didn't deserve, and if he gives me a new son-in-law..." He nodded to Ray. "I'll take him, but if he doesn't..." he shrugged. "I'm fine with that too."

Laughter flowed across the campfire. Did Cole's father anticipate Ray's marriage to Cindy? Expect it? Why wouldn't he? That was the church rules, and she trusted him with Trevor when she didn't trust anyone else. He could see himself waking next to Cindy's beautiful face every morning. But could she?

The testimonies ended and prayer requests started going around the campfire. He wasn't one to let the skeletons out of his toolbox, but if prayer worked, he knew someone who needed it tonight. "Cindy."

All eyes focused on him. He didn't elaborate. Unfortunately, Trevor did. "Momma cried."

Ray shushed Trevor and met Mr. Maxwell's gaze across the fire. A single tear lingered on the man's lashes. Ray felt like an intruder. He shouldn't be with Cindy. He shouldn't be with Trevor. Everyone wanted Cole.

৪০৪

"Ray, this is weird." Cindy looped his tie and pulled the silky tail through.

He straightened the knot she'd made. "What? If I hadn't

promised Mr. Maxwell I'd come to the men's breakfast thing, we'd stay here."

She fell on the bed and tucked her bathrobe under her knee. "No. Not you staying here. Us going to church."

He frowned through the mirror. "But you always go to church on Sunday morning?"

How could she make him understand? "I can't do both. Either I'm with you, or I'm in church." She fell back against the mattress and groaned. How did her life come to this? "I don't want to be a hypocrite, Ray. I can't. I hate hypocrites."

"Then don't be one." He pulled her close. "Forget about other people's opinions, and enjoy life to the fullest."

She leaned back in his arms and frowned. "Next week you'll leave. Again." Somehow she'd pick up the pieces of her fragile heart.

Steel arms encircled her and she nestled against his chest. His heartbeat soothed the turmoil inside her. "Did you forget that I love you?" His words gave her hope. "My love isn't affected by my location on this planet." He leaned back and caressed her jaw. "Next week, I'll leave for Memphis. But I'll be back in six weeks. Then south Florida for a month. After that I'm yours. We'll spend Christmas together. Just you, me, and Trevor."

"Ray, I don't know." Could she do it? Could she wait for him to return? Could she loan him out to a different place, a different girl and then welcome him back with open arms? She stepped away from him and sunk into the mattress. This last week would be memorable. Special. Their time was short, but she'd make sure he never forgot her.

The bed dipped. Ray's touch soothed her frazzled nerves. She opened her eyes and found him hovering close.

"Will you wait for me?"

She ran her hand across the short bristles of his hair. Loving Ray would keep her out of heaven, and she'd never see Cole again. She shut her eyes and pictured the clouds. When Ray left, she'd let him go for good. "You'll be gone for over two months. How can you ask me—? That's not fair."

The mattress creaked as he stood. "Life's not fair, Cindy. Deal with it." The bedroom door slammed.

She cringed and then pushed off the bed. With a heavy heart, she dressed and readied Trevor for Sunday school.

When they arrived at his classroom, Rachel beamed from the doorway. "Oh Trevor, you look just like Cole in that suit."

Little hands clung to Cindy's legs. She reached down and lifted her son and then addressed the threat. "What are you doing in here? Where is Sara?"

Rachel tilted her head and ran her hand through Trevor's hair. "She and Mark went to the mountains on vacation. I volunteered to fill in today." Trevor clung to Cindy as Rachel's hand made another pass. "His hair his so soft. Just like Cole's."

Cindy grabbed Rachel's wrist and flung her hand away from Trevor. "Don't touch him, again." Without explanation, Cindy walked past the other parents to her own classroom. No way would she leave Trevor with Rachel.

The twins smiled from the table. "Good morning, Miss Cindy."

They were so cute when they were behaving. "Good morning boys." She dropped Trevor into the empty chair between them.

Andrea's daughter Chloe walked in and pointed. "What's he doing here?"

Head bowed, Trevor colored on a page that Cindy had arranged around the table. "The looking-lady scares me."

One of the twins scooted next to Trevor. "Don't be scared."

The other twin leaned his head close. "Jesus watches us."

Cindy forced herself to concentrate on the lesson. Why was Rachel clinging to Trevor? Because he was Cole's? Was she that unstable? All because she couldn't have kids and she had a failed marriage? Something happened in Atlanta. What? And why was Trevor scared of her?

She pushed aside the unimaginable and concentrated on the bible story. Soon the bell rang ending the class. Children scrambled from their seats. She needed to clean the mess. "Trevor, go straight to Ray. Don't talk to anyone."

"Okay, momma."

"We'll go with you." Each twin held one of Trevor's hands and escorted him out the door. They were such good protectors–unless they were fighting.

She texted Ray to watch out for Trevor and hurried through the cleanup. Minutes later, as she slipped into the sanctuary, a few heads turned her way.

With the congregation standing, Pastor read the story of Samson and Delilah.

Ray stepped into the aisle and allowed Cindy to enter the pew. His arm stole around her and his hand cupped her shoulder. "I'm sorry about this morning." His whispered words calmed her panicked heart as everyone was seated.

After seeing Rachel in Trevor's class, Cindy had forgotten about their argument. Needing a hug, she pressed against Ray's side. The arm around her tightened and a kiss landed on the top of her head.

Two pews in front of them, Rachel turned and gave a little wave. What was she doing on Cindy's side of the church?

"Ignore her." Ray's whisper tickled Cindy's ear.

Rachel's eyes narrowed, and then she faced the front once again. Cindy tuned out pastor's retelling of Paul's testimony before King Agrippa and Festus. The drum stool was empty.

If Cole were here, he'd make Rachel leave Trevor alone.

Cindy blinked, and then peeked at Ray. He winked and his lips quirked in a brief smile.

She was tired of hurting. She was tired of being alone. But what could she do? Next week, Ray would leave. She'd sleep alone again. Alone with the nightmares of the past.

A high pitched voice gave a message in tongues. The hairs stood on the back of Cindy's neck, and her heart raced out of control.

Ray's grip tightened.

The pastor interpreted. "Run to me saith the Lord. For my arms are open wide. Yay, I say unto you. I have heard your cries. I have seen your tears. Yet you come not to the one who can heal you. Run to me saith the Lord. And I will remove all fear."

Cindy couldn't breathe. Her chest burned and her body trembled. The pastor spoke something and people flooded the altars. She gripped the back of the pew in front of her.

"Sweetness, are you okay? What was that about? What just happened? Are you sick?"

"Ray." She gripped his arm like a lifeline. "Get me out of here."

෨෬

The construction of the new Lulu's Place was on schedule. Ray talked with the foreman and inspected the site. This company did good work, but even the best workers needed accountability, like the good steward he'd read about in Cole's bible. Ray shook the foreman's hand and went in search of Cindy.

Derick was frying the fish they'd caught the previous weekend. Ray was looking forward to it. James and a few other families would be there as well.

Cindy's mood had improved since they'd skipped church Sunday evening. She didn't want to go Wednesday night either. He missed seeing the guys, but this week with Cindy and Trevor had been life changing. They'd spent most of their time at his place, cleaning off the spot where he'd build.

He stepped into the kitchen at Lulu's Place and the commotion halted. Ladies whispered as they packed the lunches. Appraising eyes followed him to Cindy's side.

One corner of her lip curled. "I should be jealous, but I like it that I've got something others want."

He laughed at her thought process. "How can I help?"

She stretched on tiptoe and kissed him. "The sink is leaking again."

He winked and walked around the corner. Since he'd been here, he'd fixed the bathroom, the freezer and now the sink. The way things kept falling apart, if the new building wasn't finished soon, they'd be serving lunch from a tent.

He got filthy working on the plumbing, and they stopped by her apartment so he could change.

He opened his closet. Most of it was empty as she'd donated Cole's things to Goodwill during the church campout. A few of Ray's things hung on the rack, but he didn't get his hopes up for moving in permanently. The church people couldn't find out where he was staying. Of course, he'd soon be in Memphis, and they wouldn't have to worry about that.

"Hurry, Uncle Ray. I'm ready to whip some tail." Trevor stood in the bedroom door with a football tucked under his arm.

The front door slammed and Cindy rushed in waving her

phone. Her face was pale as death. She croaked out his name.

He hurried to her side. "What's wrong, sweetness?" He glanced at the screen shoved in his face. A social media photo dominated the screen. An ugly yellow stone covered a woman's finger from knuckle to knuckle. The page belonged to Rachel. The tag read, "Guess who's engaged?"

Cindy sent Trevor to his room to play, and then huffed out a frustrated growl beside Ray.

He rubbed her stiff back with one hand and held the phone with the other. "I'm not sure I see the problem, babe. If she's found someone else, then maybe she'll leave you and Trevor alone."

Cindy's long stiff finger poked the screen. "That's my ring! Cole bought it for me." She spun on her heel and her hands grabbed her head. "Well, Zack gave it to me. But I pawned it. And then Cole bought it back." Her knuckles whitened. "Why? Why would she steal my ring?"

Ray glanced down the hall. "How did she get in here?"

Cindy's head jerked toward him. "She didn't. I wouldn't keep an eighty thousand dollar ring here. It's supposed to be locked in the Maxwell safe." She snatched the phone. "I'm calling Cole's father."

Ray stared at his empty hand. "Eighty thousand dollars? For a ring?"

She pivoted on her heel and caught his gaze as her fingers paused on the screen. "That's why I don't wear it. I didn't know its value until I found the appraisal papers after Cole died. What's wrong?"

"Eighty thousand dollars?" He was an idiot. "And I offered to loan you a couple hundred when we met?" Both mansions must be worth millions! Ray blinked and sucked in a breath. "How much money did Cole leave you?"

She shook her head and shrugged. "I don't know exactly. Most of it was stocks and stuff. And a bunch of land. Zack keeps up with it." Cindy's arm locked around his waist. Her cheek nestled against his chest. "Does it matter?"

Uh! Yeah! He swallowed the panic crawling up his throat and lied. "No. I just—I didn't realize—"

She jerked away and spoke into the phone. "Mr. Maxwell, I

think Rachel broke into the safe." She paced across the living room as she relayed the information.

Ray couldn't move. He had a hard time competing with Cole's marred memory. He couldn't begin to compete with the man's riches. Sure, Ray had a nice portfolio growing for his retirement. And he had a nice nest egg to invest in his new house, but he'd never be able to give Cindy the treasures she deserved. No wonder she couldn't love him.

"My ring is still there. Mr. Maxwell thinks I'm overreacting, but I know that's my ring in this picture. I told him to send it to Zack. Why would Rachel steal it, take a picture, and then put it back? And who does she think will marry her?" Cindy peered up at him as she chewed on her bottom lip. "Ray, are you okay?"

He draped his arms around her. "I'm fine, babe. Just surprised that ugly stone is a diamond."

Her hands locked around his waist. Sharp blue eyes gazed into his. She wet her lips. "Being with you makes me happy. I don't need fancy diamonds or shares of stock."

Desperation drove his kiss. If he could, he'd erase all her memories of the past. He stoked the fire burning inside them both until the blaze took effort to control. He broke the kiss. Yet his lips hovered a breath away from hers.

Worry and desire clouded her eyes. "Don't leave me, Ray. I don't care about the money."

"Ah, sweetness." He pushed aside his doubt and pulled her tight against him. "I couldn't leave you and Trevor if I wanted to. It'd be like cutting out part of my soul."

By the time they arrived, everyone else was at the party. Luckily, the guests didn't include Rachel.

James manned the gas cooker as the men stood around talking. The kids tossed around a football. The twins ran to him and Trevor. "Uncle Ray, will you be on our team?"

Using both hands he bumped knuckles with the twins. "I don't know. We'll see."

"It's not fair. You always play with him."

"You're our uncle. Not his."

Trevor huffed, "He loves me."

"Boys. Play nice." Ray stepped around the bickering boys.

James looped the dipper along a protruding nail. "A little friendly competition?"

"I guess." Ray kept an eye on the boys. The Twin Terrors were bullies, but he wouldn't let them gang up on Trevor.

"He's *our* uncle."

Trevor stomped his foot. "He's gonna be my daddy."

James choked and sputtered on his iced tea as the boys continued their argument over who Ray loved the most. Judging by the men's expressions, he'd say they weren't pleased either.

James wiped the front of his shirt as he hissed. "Do you see what you've done? This is why I didn't want you dating Cindy. You're messing with Trevor's head. He's given you Cole's rightful place. And when you leave, he'll think that's what fathers do."

Trevor's chin lifted as he turned on James. "He won't leave me. I prayed about it."

Ray stepped toward the angry little boy.

One twin pushed Trevor's chest. "Dummy, he ain't your daddy."

Trevor shoved back. "Is so."

"Is not."

"Is so."

The other twin stepped beside his brother. "You don't know what daddies do."

"They live at your house."

"They teach you stuff."

"And they sleep with your momma."

Trevor's eyes rounded and little lips formed an o as he stared at Ray.

"Boys!" James's gruff command halted the argument.

A heavy weight compressed Ray's lungs as if a drill press had lined up on his shoulders. He needed a diversion. "Trev, throw me the ball. We'll play a quick game until it's time to eat."

"Yeah." A twin snatched the ball from Trevor's slack hands and tossed it to his brother. "Stupid."

James reentered the conversation. "Boys, we don't call our friends names. Apologize."

Trevor tilted his head as he blinked at Ray.

He could see the wheels in his little mind turn, but he could also feel James's hostile eyes boring a hole in his back. He swooped Trevor in his arms intending to remove the intelligent boy from the men's hearing before he reached the obvious conclusion.

Little arms curled around his neck. "Mr. James teached me stuff."

Ray's steps faltered at the conviction in the small voice. "Yeah, but I taught you how to fish, how to catch the ball, and how to build blocks."

Little brows furrowed as Trevor leaned back against Ray's forearm and smiled. "Yeah. And you sleep wif momma."

A hiss sounded behind him and Ray cringed. Trevor had no idea what he'd said.

Soft hands cupped Ray's cheeks as Trevor rested his forehead against Ray's. Eye to eye. Nose to nose. "I love you, daddy."

Ray sucked in a breath and shielded the little boy as the men's conversation silenced. All ears were tuned in.

"I love you too, Trev, but we'll talk later. Right now, I need to talk to Mr. James."

"Okay, daddy." Another kiss fluttered against his cheek.

Ray set Trevor on his feet and the little boy ran toward the swings, innocent of the chaos he'd left in his wake. Like a bad dream, the men's voices echoed in Ray's ear.

"Crap!"

"Don't swear."

"A little profanity is excusable in a situation like this!"

"James, calm down."

The heavy breaths behind him made Ray cringe. It was time to man up. He turned and faced James's wrath. "I love her."

His face exploded in pain.

## Chapter Seventeen

Ray staggered back and regained his footing as Derick and Mark each grabbed one of James's arms. "All this time! The morning I saw you? It was her apartment."

"James, it's not as bad as you think."

"Trevor knows where you sleep. What kind of sicko are you?"

"It's not like that. One night Trevor got scared and—"

"One night? How many nights are there?" James slung off the men holding him. "Never mind. I don't want to hear it. I trusted you. You have no idea what you've done. This is not a game. You've ruined her!"

Mark held up a hand. "The Lord can work this out."

Derick moved in between James and Ray. "Unfortunately, these kind of things happen when you leave God out of a relationship."

Ray wiped the blood from his lip. "I love her, and I love Trevor. We're both adults. What we do shouldn't concern you."

"Not concern me?" James slapped the patio table. "My boy's Sunday school teacher is shacking with my best friend."

"Enough!" Blood rushed to Ray's head. "Cindy's innocent."

ഇൗരു

"We missed you at church Wednesday night." Andrea passed Cindy a glass of iced tea.

She looked out the window, but couldn't find Trevor. "Ray's leaving soon. I wanted to spend time with him."

Joni propped her chin in her hand at the table. "You should've brought him with you. James said Ray was curious about the devotions at the campout. You never know. I think the Lord is reeling him in."

"Wouldn't that be a wonderful blessing for—" The backdoor banged open ending Sara's words.

James hollered from across the lawn. "Did you think no one would find out!"

Trevor rushed through the door and flung himself at Cindy. She couldn't understand what he was saying because of his sobs.

The girls followed him in the room. "He started a fight."

Andrea was quick to scold. "Girls, hush."

"Well he did, mom. He thinks Mr. Ray is his dad. Because Mr. Ray sleeps with Miss Cindy."

Trevor leaned back in Cindy's slack arm. "He bleeded."

James's outrage reached the women, "What if Trevor had made his little announcement to Mr. Maxwell around the campfire? Or God forbid to the pastor after church?"

Andrea's gasp echoed through the sunny kitchen as a wave of dizziness threatened to overtake Cindy.

Joni wasn't so subtle. "You're sleeping with Ray?"

Cindy swallowed and tried to focus on her son. "Don't cry, Trevor. Ray will be fine."

All eyes were on her.

Pandemonium broke out in a kid version of he said, she said. Cindy wanted to sink under the table.

"Girls, go to your room. Take the twins with you."

"But mom…"

"Go!"

"Cindy?" Joni didn't give up. "Somebody's got some explaining to do."

What could she say? This was her worst nightmare come true. She shut her eyes and tried to pray, but words eluded her.

"Trevor." Ray's voice calmed the storm. He crouched in the open door and held out his arms. Blood trickled from his busted lip. "Come here, bud. I think I've got an answer to your questions."

Trevor wiggled out of Cindy's slack arms and raced to Ray who lifted him and wiped his tears. Ray met Cindy's gaze. The support she found gave her courage to lift her chin against the condemnation in Joni's frown. His words gave her hope. "Do you need my help?"

She suppressed her smile knowing Joni and Andrea were both gawking at them. "I can explain in here, if you'll take care of Trevor."

He winked and sent her heart soaring. "Don't worry about it.

Trevor and I will be fine."

Trevor held on to Ray's neck. "Yeah, momma. Me and daddy will be fine."

Ray kissed his cheek and turned for the door. "Come on Trevor. Let's get out of here. We've caused enough trouble."

The door closed and she wanted to rush after them. But Joni had demanded an explanation, and Cindy's friends deserved to hear the truth. "I'm sorry you found out this way."

"Please tell me it was just a onetime thing, and you've since prayed through to forgiveness."

Cindy met Joni's frown. "Ray's staying at the apartment."

Joni continued, "Do you realize what'll happen when everyone in church finds out? James and I have been married for six years, but…People never forget your past sins. Never."

Cindy swirled the ice in her glass.

"I'm not mad, and I'm not judging but…What were you thinking?"

Cindy swallowed the knot in her throat and lifted her head. "I wasn't thinking. I didn't plan it. It just happened."

Joni parked one hand on her hip. The other on her head. "How much worse can it get?"

Andrea intervened. "Joni, don't work yourself into a frazzle. I'm sure Cindy didn't plan any of this."

"Why Ray? He's not a forever kind of guy and he isn't saved— obviously or we wouldn't be having this conversation. What about God? What about your salvation? Doesn't seeing Cole again in heaven mean anything?"

"Stop." Cindy was tired of everyone manipulating her life. "When I'm with Ray, I feel loved and cherished. Cole knew he was dying, yet he didn't bother to tell anyone except James and Rachel. Not me. Not even his father. And what about God? If he didn't want me with Ray, he shouldn't have taken Cole."

Silence bounced off the walls.

"Cindy, I'm sorry." Joni hugged her. "I had no idea you were bitter. I wish you would've told me."

She disentangled herself from the awkward hug. "I'm not bitter. I'm grateful for the life I had with Cole as short as it was. I'm thankful for Trevor. Ray has nothing to do with my relationship with God. Jesus set me free from a life of addiction and I will serve him faithfully, but Ray replaces the lonely nights. He fills my days with joy and love." She eyed both of her friends. "God has nothing to do with it."

The back door opened and Ray crossed the room ignoring the other women. Worry framed his eyes. "Unless you're having a rip-roaring good time in here, we'd better go before James starts shooting."

"Where's Trevor?"

"In the truck." Arms tightened around her and she rested her head on his chest. A kiss landed on the top of her head. "Let's go."

Andrea stood in their path. "I don't approve of your living arrangements, but you guys are my friends. Stay."

Ray answered, "Thanks for the offer, but James wasn't kidding about the shotgun."

&#8477;&#8478;

The next day, Ray closed the apartment pantry and walked toward the living room as the doorbell rang. Trevor opened the door and the twins rushed in.

"Yeah!" The boys whooped down the hall toward Trevor's room.

A cold silence remained.

James stood just inside the door.

Despite the bravo she'd shone at Derick and Andrea's, Cindy had cried most of the night. Yesterday, James had threatened to tell the preacher if Ray didn't move out, but Ray couldn't leave Cindy when she needed him most.

James scrubbed a hand down his face. "Are you gonna invite me in? Or do I barge in like the boys?"

"Sure." Ray stepped back and closed the door behind James. "Cindy went to the spa with Andrea."

"I know. Joni's with them. I came to see you."

Ray clapped his hands together. "Have a seat. You want something to drink?"

"I'm good."

Ray didn't want to lose James as a friend, but he wasn't willing to give up Cindy and Trevor either. "The game's on."

James smiled. "Sounds good."

Ray claimed the couch and unpaused the television.

From the recliner, James said, "I'm sorry for losing my temper. I shouldn't have punched you."

Ray kept his eyes on the screen. He didn't want to fight with James again. "I deserved it."

"You did." Resting his elbows on his knees James leaned forward. "But Jesus wouldn't have hit you. And I am sorry I did."

Ray stood and escaped into the kitchen. He fixed two cokes and added a shot of whiskey to his. He sensed an inquisition coming on.

James accepted the glass, but set it on a coaster on the coffee table. "If you love her, you should marry her."

Ah, here it comes. The strings attached to his forgiveness. "Cole was her husband. I want to be more." Ray paused the gameplay. "And I don't care about church rules."

"There is no greater pinnacle in a relationship than becoming the Godly head of a household. And church rules exist for your protection."

"I don't need protecting from Cindy." Did she need to be shielded from the hypocrites? "But even if I did propose, she wouldn't say yes."

James shook his head and huffed. "If she doesn't want to marry you, then why does she keep you around?"

Ray grinned. "Must be my mad bedroom skills?"

"Hey!" A chuck of ice bounced off his cheek. "Don't make me hit you again. Now, what are you going to do?"

Ray stretched his arm along the back of the empty sofa. "I leave for Memphis Tuesday. I asked her to come with me, but she turned me down. Just my luck. I found the woman I want, and *she's* scared of commitment." Ray grimaced and toasted James with his glass. "What's that old saying about karma coming around to bite you?"

James chuckled. "Karma has nothing to do with God's plan for your life."

"Maybe, he's punishing me. You know *Vengeance is mine and I will repay.*"

"Of all the verses to memorize, you choose that scripture. How about a father to the fatherless?" James swirled the ice in his glass.

"When I found out that Isaac…when the paternity test came in—I know what it's like to love another man's son. And when I met Joni, I wasn't exactly a saint. I don't blame you for loving them. But you could've waited on the physical demonstration."

෨෦෬

"I'm sorry miss." The young college girl tapped her forefinger against the pad of the computer keyboard and gave Cindy an apologetic smile. "Someone scheduled your appointment incorrectly. I have you down for the facial, and the foot and hand treatments. Normally you have the hot stone, full-body massage."

"It's not a mistake." Cindy's cheeks heated as she remembered how Ray declared parts of her body off limits to everyone but him. "I wanted to try out some other options."

Joni whirled around in front of her. "Because of Ray?"

Cindy ignored Joni's comment and Andrea's raised brows as they followed the girl into a treatment room.

She tuned out Andrea and Joni as an attendant helped her step into the foot bath and position her hands into the bowls. Leaning back against the chair, she waited for her facial to begin.

"Tom needs a wife." Joni wouldn't leave that subject alone.

Andrea tried to defend Cindy. "He has too much baggage, but Phillip isn't as reckless as he used to be."

A soothing gel-pack covered Cindy's eyes.

Joni didn't give up. "There are plenty of good men in the church. Cindy didn't have to settle for Ray."

She was tired of her friend's meddling. "What I do with Ray is definitely *not* settling."

Joni gasped. "No, you didn't."

"Yes, I have. Several times in fact. You and James should try it sometimes. I hear it makes a person less grouchy."

"Cindy!" Andrea scolding from her other side. "Quit goading her. Joni quit being judgmental. Today is for relaxing."

"Well, I can't believe you'd hide this from us. James wanted to go to the deacon board, but since you're our friend, he said if you resign your Sunday class, he won't tell."

"How nice of him."

The vinyl beside her squeaked, and Cindy pictured Joni sitting up. "Why didn't you come to me before it got out of hand? We could've prayed away the temptation. That's what fellow sisters in Christ are for."

Cindy flexed her toes in the soothing water. "I did."

"No, you didn't."

"Weeks ago. After I first met him. And you laughed in my face. I think you're exact words were. Only a fool would date Ray. I guess I'm worse than a fool, because I live with him. And yes, you've told me all about his other girls. Multiple times. But I don't care. They were before he met me and when he leaves Tuesday, I won't be sorry for loving him." She sucked in a breath. "So leave it alone, Joni. I'm sure I'll suffer enough pain when he breaks my heart."

The thought of Ray leaving crushed her. Struggling to breathe, she sat up and the gel-pack fell from her face.

Rachel walked through the beaded curtain, and claimed the empty chair. "Hi, ladies."

Cindy cut her eyes at Joni. This was the last thing she needed. She was in no mood to deal with the pest in a public place. She'd rather drag her into the alleyway, and beat the snot out of the trouble maker.

Joni winced as she peeked out of her heated towel. "Rachel? When you asked me to recommend a spa, I had no idea you intended to join us."

Wrapping a warming towel around her head, Cindy ignored the awkward conversation. From now on she'd schedule her spa days without Joni.

"Where's Trevor?"

*None of your business.* Cindy bit her lip and counted to four.

Rachel rephrased the question. "Is he with Mrs. Beven? Oh, how Cole loved that woman. It's understandable why Trevor is so taken with her. Why just the other morning—"

"He's with Ray."

An exaggerated gasp echoed through the small room. "You left Cole's son with another man? How could you? Why, Cole must be roaring from heaven."

Joni attempted to intervene. "Ray's a very nice man. He and Trevor get along wonderfully."

Cindy sat up straight in the chair. The towel plopped into the heated water at her feet. "Ray is none of your business. And neither is Trevor." Cindy pointed a finger at Rachel's too innocent face. "Stay away from my son."

Tears puddled in her eyes. "If Cole were here, he'd be appalled at your behavior of late. And poor Trevor…exposed to his mother's loose morals."

Andrea intervened. "Rachel, that isn't necessary."

Cindy couldn't take anymore. "I'll say this once." She stepped out of the water and wiped her hands on the towel. "Cole married *me*. *I* gave birth to his son. Not you. You are *not* a Maxwell, and you never will be. Get over this little fantasy you're living. And leave my family alone." She slipped into her sandals.

As she passed Rachel's chair, the idiot smirked. "Would you like to see pictures of *my* family reunion?" She shoved her phone at Cindy.

In the photo taken at the mansion, a child-sized Cole had his arms crossed and a frown aimed at the photographer. Cindy blinked. Wait a minute. It wasn't Cole. It was Trevor. What happened to his red hair? It was an unnatural dark shade in the picture. Trevor's description of the reunion washed over her in hot waves of anger.

*The looking-lady washed my hair…*

*Papa cried…*

*Grandmother couldn't believe her eyes…*

*Papa yelled…*

Cindy sucked in a breath at the blow she'd taken. The smell of peroxide and ammonia rose to her memory. "You dyed Trevor's hair?"

"What!" Andrea sprang to her feet.

"Let me see." Joni snatched the phone. "How could you do that to Trevor?"

Rachel's voice reeled Cindy back to the present. "Unlike you traitors, I cherish his father's memory. Cole belonged to me and soon, so will his son."

A red haze flashed. Someone screamed as water splashed.

"No! Cindy! Stop!" Joni's voice sounded and the fog lifted from Cindy's mind. Her hands were locked around Rachel's throat.

The owner ran in and yelled, "Call the police!"

Cindy released the purple-faced troublemaker. "You will never get your hands on Trevor. I will kill you first."

Sirens sounded as she hurried out the door. Her long legs ate up the pavement. Thunder cracked and dark clouds gathered above. Light rain covered her as she sought out a place of refuge.

෨෮

The doorbell rang.

Ray paused the final seconds of the fourth quarter and turned to James. "Thank God for the DVR."

Before either man moved, Joni opened the door and stepped in. "Cindy?"

Ray's heartbeat stalled. "Why isn't she with you?"

Joni burst into tears. "Oh, Ray. I had no idea Rachel was that unstable. I felt sorry for her because of Blaine's abuse and everything." Her voice cracked and became undecipherable.

James leapt out of his chair and wrapped his arms around his sobbing wife. "It's okay, beautiful. You tried to help."

Ray didn't give a spud wrench about Joni's feelings. He stood. "Where? Is Cindy?"

A shaky hand wiped her cheeks. "We don't know. Andrea is driving around looking for her. I was hoping she'd be here. Rachel showed up at the spa and accused Cindy of loose morals. Okay, I get that. A little tacky but…you do live here."

"Did Rachel hurt her?"

"No." Joni leaned back against James's chest. "If I hadn't seen it with my own eyes, I would have never believed it. Rachel threatened to take Trevor."

Ray looked down the hall, but Joni's voice reclaimed his attention.

"Rachel had a picture. One she took in Atlanta of Trevor. His hair was dyed black. Like Cole's. Cindy grabbed her by the throat. And oh good grief. I thought she would kill Rachel. But then the manager came in and Cindy left. She just walked out the door. The manager—being Cindy's friend—tossed Rachel out into the rain. Rachel threatened to sue and by that time, I couldn't find Cindy anywhere. I was hoping she'd somehow made it back home."

Ray checked his phone. "Why didn't she call me?"

Joni held out her hand. Cindy's phone rested in her palm. "She stormed out and forgot this. I'm worried."

Ray looked at James. "Will you stay here and protect Trevor?" His friend nodded his consent, and Ray reached for his keys. "Don't let anyone in here. Not even the Maxwells."

"You got it." James followed him to the door. "Call me when you find her."

A fine mist covered the stair rails. Ray ran through the rain toward his truck. Cindy must be soaked by now. There was one place he knew to look. He accelerated out of the apartment complex and raced across town. The cemetery was huge, but through the rain, Ray spotted a lone figure resting on a slab. He parked the truck and jogged through the puddles. His steps slowed as he approached.

Cindy leaned against Cole's headstone and shot Ray a watery smiled. "I knew you'd find me. Where's Trevor?"

"Safe. With James. Everyone is worried about you."

Her head bent. "I would've called, but I lost my phone."

"Joni found it at the spa."

"Good." Her hand splashed in the small puddle on Cole's slab. "I guess you think I'm weird for coming here."

Raindrops continued to soak him. "Someone threatened your son. It's natural you'd tell his father."

"But why, Ray?" She bent her knees. "I mean. Come on. You hear those stories about loved ones watching from heaven and guardian angels, but it isn't true. When people die, they're gone. No doubt Cole's in heaven, but how does that help us here? How does that keep Trevor safe from Cole's crazy friend?"

The heavens opened and Ray raised his voice against the sound. "I'll protect you."

Cindy lifted her chin and spoke above the downpour. "I'm counting on you to take care of Trevor if I go to jail for attempted murder."

Ray wiped the cascading water from his face and nodded to the headstone. "And what does Cole say?"

Cindy laughed. "He hasn't spoken to me in five years. I guess I'm on my own."

"As long as I'm breathing, you or Trevor will never be alone. And you're not going to jail. Come on, sweetness." Ray held out his hand and pulled Cindy to her feet. He leaned down and kissed her. "Let's go home." Ray glanced at the headstone. He wanted to reassure Cole of his love for Cindy and Trevor, but talking to the dead was beyond him.

She looped her arm in his and they walked through the rain toward the warmth of his truck. Cindy shivered as she climbed in the front seat.

Ray raced to the driver's side and dove out of the rain. He wiped the water from his face. "You cold?"

Her smile brightened the dreary day. "Are you kidding? With this rain shower and you at my side, I have a natural sauna."

"Don't you forget it." Ray seared her lips with a kiss. Cindy snuggled against his side and steam rose between them.

Her phone rang from the cup holder. She ended their contact and answered, "Hello?"

Ray heard a female voice on the line.

"No ma'am, you're not bothering me at all. How are you?" Water trailed down her slender neck and disappeared under her shirt. Ray turned the defogger on high and waited for the windshield to clear.

"I would love too. And Ray wants to measure off the foundation for the house. What time should we come over?" She turned to Ray and lifted one brow. "Great. I'll see you in the morning." Cindy disconnected and rubbed her hands in front of the vent. "Mawmaw's teaching me to cook jelly."

He turned into her apartment complex. "Good. Maybe, she'll keep you from contemplating murder. But, I promised James, that Trevor and I would keep him and the boys company tomorrow."

Her hand stilled on the door handle. "I don't want Trevor with anyone else but us."

Ray pulled her from the truck and into his arms. "He won't leave my sight." He tasted the rain on her lips. "Let's go. Before I forget James and Joni are waiting."

Together, they climbed the stairs. Ray claimed one more kiss and then opened the door to find Joni pacing the floor.

"Oh, my goodness. Cindy, you're soaked. Are you okay?"

Ray nodded at James as Cindy hurried down the hall. Trevor squealed. "Momma, you wetting me."

Cindy laughed. "Sorry, sweetie."

Ray met her in the hall. In the air-conditioned apartment, chill bumps covered her arms. Ray hustled her into their room and toward the shower.

"But Ray. I can't. We have guests."

He turned on the hot water. "You need to warm up, and since we do have guests…I suggest you choose the tub."

Color flooded her cheeks. "Ray."

"What's it gonna be?" He winked.

Her smile was laced with their secrets. "I'll be out in a minute."

Ray snagged a towel, shut the bathroom door, and changed into dry clothes. Back in the living room, he invited James and Joni for supper. Then he ordered pizzas. "You guys want a drink."

"Yeah. What do you have?" James followed Ray into the kitchen.

He opened the fridge. "Coke, tea, juice, milk?"

Joni yelled from the living room. "Coke."

Ray opened the cabinet and selected three glasses. He fixed three cokes. While James carried Joni's in to her, Ray got placed a mug of water into the microwave.

Cindy hurried in the kitchen. "Do you need me?" Her jeans hugged her long legs.

"Not like you're offering."

She pressed her lips together and tilted her head toward the living room.

A beep sounded. He winked, stirred a pack of cocoa in the now steaming water, and grabbed the whipped cream out of the refrigerator. He topped off the mug and held it out to her. "A sweet for my sweetness. I have no idea why you drink the tea you abhor."

She reached for the mug and sipped. "Mmm. This is delicious."

A creamy mustache lined her mouth. He leaned in for a nip and then smacked his lips. "Yummy, I believe I'll have another taste." He nibbled her bottom lip.

"Oh!" Joni blushed and pivoted in the doorway. "Excuse me."

Ray claimed another quick kiss and led Cindy into the living area. He wanted to forget the Rachel debacle for a while, but Joni insisted on broaching the subject. "She's always been jealous of you, but I don't understand why she's waited until now to go all kinds of crazy?"

James pointed his slice of pizza at Ray. "That's an easy one. She can't stand to think of anyone taking Cole's place."

The glass halfway to Cindy's mouth paused.

Ray cleared his throat. "I don't want to take his place. But I do love Cindy and Trevor, and no psycho woman is gonna run me off." The game he'd waited for all day was scheduled to start in five minutes. He grabbed the remote and tuned into the pregame show. A kiss landed on his jaw and the women vacated toward the sunroom.

Seconds before kickoff Trevor yelled, "Momma!" Cindy rushed in as Trevor ran up the hall. "I want a shirt like the Terrors."

Her shoulders sagged as she fluffed his hair. "Mr. James bought you a jersey last year. Remember?"

James perked up. "Yeah Trev, go put it on and show your new daddy your favorite team's colors."

Trevor jumped off the couch and ran down the hall.

The football rivalry in Alabama was as strong as his and James's friendship. He caught Cindy's gaze. "He's not wearing crimson and white."

Cindy frowned and shook her head. "Cole didn't go to the same school as James. His school color was orange."

"Oh." Ray relaxed against the couch as Cindy followed Trevor to his room.

James grinned from the recliner with a sadistic twinkle in his eye.

"What?"

His friend shrugged.

Trevor ran through the hall in an orange and white jersey. "Tada."

"No way." Ray wasn't having it.

James howled with laughter. "One cow college is as good as another."

Silence thundered in the room as Trevor stood poised for Ray's acceptance. But some things he couldn't tolerate. "You look great, Trev. But that color is a little pale. Let's go look and see what I have in my closet." He led the little boy down the hall, found the shirt he was looking for, and slipped it over Trevor's head. Using his pocket knife, Ray cut off the excess shirttail. "Don't move." He walked into the bathroom and dug through the drawers. Returning to Trevor's side, he tied each sleeve up with one of Cindy's hair things. Leaning back on his heels, he smiled. "That's your daddy's favorite team."

Trevor whooped and ran up the hall. Ray followed at a slower pace. When he reached the living room, James was choking on his laughter.

Cindy's lips disappeared into a fine line. "Really Ray? All this for a football team?"

"Some things are sacred, babe. No son of mine is wearing a Longhorn jersey."

James snickered and said, "Really Ray. It's just a shirt."

"Shut up."

"Oooh, Uncle Ray said a bad word." One of the terrors ran down the hall.

Joni gasped out loud.

"Sorry, it slipped out." Ray turned toward Joni's pale face. Her phone was in her hand. "What?"

"Rachel's social update."

James glanced at the screen and flinched.

Cindy leaned over James' shoulder. Her mouth opened and her eyes blinked. One palm flashed as she swayed on her feet.

Ray leapt off the couch and caught her in his arms. "Sweetness? What?"

"No!" She swatted Joni's phone from his line of view. "Don't look!" Tears pooled in her wild eyes. "Please, Ray!"

The frantic shake of her head scared him. He wanted to see what shook her calm façade to the point where her lips trembled, and her grip clenched his bicep. "Tell me. What is it? I won't let anything hurt you."

Her lips pressed into a fine line as she shook her head. "Not until you promise."

"I won't look. Tell me."

Her wild eyes blinked and her chest heaved with each breath. A dark shadow passed through her eyes before she closed the window to her soul. "It's a picture. I never want you to see it." She hid her face in his shoulder. "It's my mug shot from years ago. The first one. Before I cleaned up. It's awful."

His arms tightened around her and her heartbeat knocked against his chest. There were things in his past that he never wanted her to know. Like his involvement in her initial arrest. Inside his gut, curiosity swarmed like bees protecting their hive. But, he wouldn't betray Cindy's trust. "It's okay, sweetness. It wouldn't change how I feel about you, but if it means that much, I won't look."

Joni pinched James's side. "We better go. Thanks for dinner."

Cindy snapped her head up and blinked. "Message me a copy. I'm gonna report it to the authorities. I doubt they'll do anything, but…"

Joni's fingers ticked over her phone. Ray kept his focus on Cindy, but breathed a sigh of relief as James and Joni wrangled the twins and said goodnight. Cindy disappeared into the kitchen as Ray saw their friends out. He shut the door and went to help clean up.

She turned and faced him. "This is too hard, Ray. I can't do this anymore."

He didn't care about her past. And he wouldn't leave her. "What can't you do? I'll help you."

"This." She waved her hand in frustration. "Us." She stopped and whirled on him. "Loving Cole was easy, but loving you is like… it's like going to the dentist. You're high on laughing gas one minute, and writhing in pain the next." She ended with a sigh.

She loved him. His heart grew wings. That's why she was scared. He shoved away from the sink and toward her.

"Everything is crazy." She stopped and stared. "Rachel. The Maxwells. And I can't take another sermon from Joni. Why are you smiling?"

"Because loving me is hard." He advanced and backed her into the corner.

"Yes. Loving you…" Her gasp cut her off. Her eyes widened and her shoulders rose.

He trailed her arm and captured her hands. Claiming them, he brushed his lips over her cold knuckles.

Her chin lifted. "Quit distracting me, Ray. I'm breaking up with you." Though her words were harsh, love shimmered in her eyes.

"Not in this lifetime, babe. Now, tell me. I need to hear the words."

She melted against his chest and lifted her face toward him. "I love you, Ray."

He closed his eyes, breathed, and then he captured the love in her gaze. His lips brushed hers. "Don't ever forget, Cindy, and don't forget that I love you, too."

*Chapter Eighteen*

Ray secured Trevor's booster in the backseat of James's truck. The twins were buckled on his other side. James turned. "Hey, Trevor, my man. How ya been?"

"Fine." Trevor lifted his arms and Ray buckled him in. "Daddy, I'm thirsty."

Ray groaned. "I asked you if you wanted something a while ago in the apartment. You said no."

One little foot kicked in time with the Christian music coming from the speakers. "My mind changed."

"I'm thirsty too."

"Me too, Uncle Ray."

Ray ran a hand down the back of his neck and met James's frown. "Cindy has some of those juice box things. I'll go grab three."

He ran through the stairwell, without bothering to acknowledge Mrs. Foloosy. He fumbled with his key and hurried to the refrigerator. The package was half full. He grabbed the whole thing, locked the door, and raced down the steps.

In the truck, he slid in the passenger seat and James reversed into the street. Ray stabbed a straw in the cardboard and passed it to Trevor. Repeating his actions twice, he doled out drinks to the Twin Terrors.

There were two drinks left. Ray grinned at James. All that running had stirred his own thirst. He opened another and slurped half the contents down in one gulp. "This stuff is pretty good."

James glanced over. "I can't believe you're drinking juice."

"It's not my beverage of choice, but..." Ray stretched out his legs. "You want one?"

James shrugged. "Why not?"

Ray opened the last container and passed it to James.

Slurps and sips sounded all around the cab. He tapped his palm on his knee. "This reminds me of the night we set Trent and Kathy up to be busted." Ray laughed. "Except this time we have witnesses. So let's not involve the cops."

James turned eastbound onto I-10. "That was for Kathy's benefit. She's no longer in the picture."

Ray crushed the juice box and searched for a trash bag. "Who is?"

"The message from the private investigator Mr. Maxwell recommended said he traced Sam and Anna to Pensacola. It also said he had additional information he'd share in his office, Monday. I can't wait that long. I can't believe Isaac's been less than an hour away this whole time."

"Me either. So, what are we doing?"

"I have the address. Joni doesn't know so watch what you say around the blabbermouths. Basically, we are enjoying an afternoon ride. We'll drive by with no contact. Reassure my nerves all is well and we are home again, home again."

Trevor piped up from the back. "Just like the little piggies."

Ray turned. "Yeah, except we're not lost, and we know our way home." He blew out a breath. This could be tricky. "You're not the only one with a blabbermouth. You never know what he's gonna say next."

James laughed. "I know, man. Believe me, I know. But I just want to see him. I need to know he's okay."

"Why are you looking for another boy? Are you gonna trade us in?" One of the twins asked the question, but three pairs of ears leaned forward.

James stuttered, "Um, We're...well."

The story Ray had read about the little lost lamb flashed through his mind. He turned in his seat and grinned at the boys in the back. "I thought you guys went to Sunday school. Didn't they teach you about the lamb that got lost?"

Trevor turned toward the twin on the right. "Daddy told me this yesterday."

Ray continued the tale of a poor little lamb stuck in a ditch crying for help. He added super hero qualities to the shepherd and a rabid wolf on the prowl. When the story was done, the boys where oohing and aahing.

James had that I-see-you look in his eye.

Ray slurped through the empty straw. "What?"

"Nice story. Where did you hear it?"

He lowered his voice. "I read it in Cole's bible. Pretty freaky, right?"

"No." James's grin widened. "Given your relationship with his wife, I'd say Cole smiles in heaven every time you open the book."

Ray laughed. "Yeah, I'm sure he's roaring from his grave."

"Hallelujah!" James slapped the steering wheel. "I do believe God is drawing you. And if I know Cole, he's rooting for you to give in."

Ray squirmed in his seat. "I doubt it."

"That's how it started with Joni. Her hunger for God's word terrified me. But there was nothing I could do about it. Believe me, I tried."

"You didn't want her reading the bible? Why?"

"Because I knew she couldn't love me *and* Jesus. At least not like I wanted her to love me."

Was that why Cindy didn't encourage Ray to attend church? He liked hanging out with the Christian men. And why did James think she couldn't love Ray and Jesus? Sure, they'd broken a few church rules, but who hadn't?

"While you're reading, check out Hebrews twelve. I bet Cole is in the middle of your cloud of witnesses."

Ray needed to end this conversation. "Christians shouldn't gamble."

The female voice from the GPS broke the awkward silence. James took the first Florida exit and followed the automated directions. Ray turned to find all three boys asleep in the backseat. "The boys are out."

"Good. They can't tell what they don't know."

The computerized voice interrupted. "Right turn, one hundred yards."

"This is just a drive by. I promised Sam years ago, I wouldn't interfere. I want to know Isaac is ok—" James's words ended abruptly. "Kathy." He accelerated towards the end of the cul de sac, and then hit the brakes.

Kathy's eyes widened as James slammed into park, and flew out of the truck. Ray's stomach flipped over at the sight of her sunken cheeks. The designer pants suit hung on her skeletal frame. Pale arms contrasted her painted face. Ray opened the door, but stayed near the truck. No one would get near Trevor.

James grabbed Kathy's arm and snatched her around. "What are you doing here? Where's Isaac?"

It was a wonder the bone didn't snap. "Go away. How did you find out?"

"Where is he? God help me if you've hurt him. What are you doing at Sam's house?"

Ray cringed from her sadistic smile. "This is now my home. My sister and her husband died in a car wreck."

James rocked back on his heels. Kathy yanked away. James caught her a few feet on the sidewalk. Ray had no problem hearing their heated conversation. "When? What happened to Isaac?"

"Four months ago." Her smile grew into a snarl. "As his aunt, I'm now his guardian and the overseer of his trust."

"Isaac?" James ran for the steps. "Isaac!" He disappeared into the house.

Kathy turned to Ray. "It's been a long time, but not long enough. I suggest you get your idiot of a friend out of my house before I call the police."

Isaac wasn't in there or else Kathy wouldn't be so smug. "We both know you aren't calling anyone. Where is he?"

"My nephew isn't home at the moment. He's visiting friends." The wrinkles on her face added twenty years to her age. Drugs stole her beauty. Nothing was left except a shriveled shell. She followed James into the house. Ray wasn't worried. If James hadn't killed her six years ago. He wasn't gonna do it now.

Ray turned back to the truck. James had left it running. Across the street, three kids—two girls and a boy—huddled together and whispered. Ray smiled and eased across the street. Taking care not to startle the children, he stopped on the concrete sidewalk. "Hi, I'm Ray. I'm a friend of Isaac's. Do you know where I can find him?"

The oldest girl, probably about eleven answered, "We don't know an Isaac."

"Tricia!" A woman barreled out of the house, and ushered the children toward the porch. "Go inside. Go now."

"Ma'am." Ray smiled and made eye contact. "I can assure you." He gave his little boy shrug. "I'm completely harmless." The hard lines on the woman's round face softened and he stepped forward. "We just heard about the accident. Sam was a good friend. We're worried about his son."

Her shoulders sagged. "Thank God." A shaky hand pointed across the street. James hurried their way. "That woman is evil. Pure evil."

Ray didn't doubt Isaac's biological mother worked for the devil, but it didn't help them find the boy. "How long has it been since you've seen him?"

"This time? A few days ago. He's ran away twice before this." She glanced over her shoulder at her children and then back to Ray. James was silent. "He was adopted. He told Tricia he's looking for his real father."

James hissed in a breath. The lady turned to him. "You're him aren't you? He looks just like you."

Ray wished he could help James, but there was nothing he could do. "How long is he usually gone?"

"Weeks, and then she drags him back, but he never stays with her for long. She's going through the money like water. That poor boy has been through enough. I've called child services. They're checking into it."

James reached for his wallet and pulled out a business card. "If he returns, please call me. Tell him I'm searching for him. I won't give up until I find him."

A large tear trailed James's jaw.

The lady sniffed and wiped multiple tears from her own cheeks. "I'll call as soon as he comes back."

"Thank you. My wife and I could never repay you if you helped us." James returned to the truck.

Ray held out his hand. "Do you mind giving me your number? In case James wants to check on him."

"Sure."

Ray pulled out his phone and added her information. When he reached the truck, James was kneeling in the passenger floorboard. With his face buried in the seat, he squalled like a baby.

80CR

Cindy tucked her son into bed and padded into the living room. "Ray, I can't believe you endangered Trevor."

She steeled herself against his flirty grin. "Sweetness, he wasn't in danger. He and the twins slept the whole time. Except for the ride back." His eyes went wide. "It was the strangest thing."

She didn't want to hear this again. She pasted a smile on her face and counted. One, two, three…it was no use.

"One minute, he was a basket case. I seriously thought he'd have a nervous breakdown. But then…he prayed."

Ray stood and paced the living room. "Not like a blessing before you eat, but the kind of prayer the men do before your church." He waved his arms. "He did that blah-la-blah thing." Ray paused and shook his head. "For over an hour. A solid hour. The boys woke and we left him in the truck while we grabbed a burger. We came back out and he was fine. No sign of tears or distress. Explain that to me. How do you go from complete chaos to—He tilted his head and imitated James—'The Lord said everything's gonna be alright?'" Ray dropped to his knees in front of her recliner. "What happened?"

She shrugged. "The Lord answered his prayer."

He leaned in and she cupped his jaw. His kiss calmed her frantic heartache. "That's what we should do. Let's pray about Rachel's threats." A fire sparked in his eyes. "Let God work it all out. Like James did."

Before she'd fallen into bed with Ray she could have prayed. But Ray was the temptation she couldn't resist. "It doesn't work like that."

He stood. "Yes, it does. I saw it with my own eyes." He turned down the hall.

"Where are you going?"

"To Cole's office. To pray."

## Chapter Nineteen

Cindy gasped and sat straight up in the bed. A welcoming breeze from the air conditioning duct cooled her perspiring brow as dark memories gripped her mind and her heartbeat tattooed inside her tight chest.

She inhaled. Counted to three. And exhaled. Yet the images lingered. She rubbed her forehead with both hands and struggled to breathe. Her lungs slowly inflated, and her heart calmed as the nightmare released its hold.

A greenish-blue glow focused. The smoke detector on the ceiling materialized. "I'm okay. I'm okay". She took comfort in her own whispered words until her breath became normal, and her mind pushed the memories back into the darkness—where they belong.

Rolling on her side, she reached for her pillow. Her cold hand encountered warm flesh. She flinched and snatched her hand to her chest.

Ray smiled. "It's me, babe. You're okay."

Tears of relief sprang to her eyes. "I woke you."

His hand caressed her cheek. "It's kind of hard to sleep when you're being tossed to and fro."

"Sorry." She rolled away, hiding the shame of her childhood. "It was just a dream."

An arm hooked around her waist and tucked her into his body warmth. "I know. This isn't the first time. And you talk in your sleep."

She curled her back into his chest.

A kiss landed on her shoulder. "Your father didn't deserve to live."

Eyes closed, she savored his protection. "Thank you, Ray. That means a lot. Cole, he never—"

His muscles flinched and then relaxed. "Tell me."

She held tight to his forearm. "It isn't pretty."

His breath caressed her temple. "It might help to talk about it."

The dam inside her broke and the words poured out of her. "Cole was all for love and forgiveness, but just once I wished someone would have taken my side." She swallowed the burn in her throat. "I wished I'd had Dinah's brothers."

"Dinah who?"

"In the bible, a man raped her and locked her in his house. But her brothers killed him and set her free. I wished someone would have stood up for me." The should've-beens from her life rose up and choked her. "Where was my rescue? Where was my freedom? Instead, I survived until I saved myself. Just once. I wished someone would've loved me. Not for what I could give them, but because they chose to."

"*I* love you." His soothing words were a balm to her soul. "It's a good thing your father's dead. Or I'd kill him."

"Thank you. Cole never offered." A single tear slid down her cheek. Safe in Ray's embrace, she let it fall. "Why did he lie to me." A second tear followed. "Why didn't he tell me he was sick? He confided in James, Zack, and Rachel. Why would he do that?"

Ray's fingers weaved through her hair. "I don't know, sweetness. Men go stupid when they're in love."

She sniffed and choked on a laugh. "You're not stupid. Yet you claim to love me."

His thumb circled her wrist once. "I do love you." The whisper near her ear soothed. "And..." His leg draped over her hip as one of his arms slid under her pillow.

She curved her body into his and rubbed her cheek against his t-shirt sleeve. Ensconced in his arms, she felt cherished, protected.

He wrapped himself completely around her. "You are now surrounded by six feet, two inches of one hundred ninety pounds of pure muscle." His laugh tickled her neck. "I am an impenetrable fortress, babe. No one can hurt you in my arms."

The tension left her body and her eyelids grew heavy.

His voice lowered and soothed. "You're safe, sweetness. Close your eyes." A kiss brushed her temple. "Sleep."

ഇരു

The next evening, Ray snuck behind Cindy with a bouquet of roses in his hands. He waited a foot behind her back and cleared his throat.

As she turned, her gaze locked on the buds in the vase. Her lip quivered. A trembling hand covered her parted lips. Tears pooled in her eyes. He felt like a fool. The flowers must remind her of Cole. "Ray?"

He pulled the vase toward him. "I'm sorry. I didn't intend for you to be sad. I'll throw them out."

"No!" She snapped out of her stupor and snatched the vase out of his hands. "Don't you dare throw them away." Tears continued to fall, but a brilliant smile emerged.

"Cindy?" Was this about the nightmares?

She turned her back and swiped the back of her hand under her eyes. "I'm not sad, Ray. These are happy tears."

His hand massaged her shoulder. "They are?"

She faced him, holding the roses close to her. "I'm just being silly." She inhaled the petals. "No one has ever given me flowers before."

"No one?" Not even Cole? He didn't add the last part, but he knew she heard the question when she answered.

"Well, Mrs. Maxwell brought a peace lily to the hospital when I lost baby Lulu, but that doesn't count." She laughed and wiped the last of her tears. "Thank you, Ray. I love them." Holding the bouquet with one hand, she cupped his jaw with the other. "And I love you." Her kiss was the sweetest he'd ever tasted.

ഇരു

"We filed for custody."

Joni passed out lunches, but Cindy wished she'd picked a different day to *help*. Since Ray left for Memphis two days ago, she'd gotten very little sleep. Her nightmares had intensified and her fortress was miles away.

"After James and Ray left Pensacola, Kathy reported Isaac as a runaway."

"Joni, no one knows where he is. How can you win custody without a child?"

"God's got His hand on Isaac. He'll work everything out. And this time we're dealing with an aunt not his mother. It's horrible about Sam and Anna though. I wished we had known sooner. Poor Isaac. All alone, and out there looking for James."

"I hope you guys win, and I hope you find him." Alive. She didn't voice this last statement.

Joni changed the subject to the antics of the twins. The nervous chatter grated on Cindy's sanity, so she went to the cabinet for another loaf of bread. The hinge opened soundlessly. "Maria, what did you do to the cabinets?" The shelf was empty. "Did you forget to order the bread?" They used one hundred twenty loaves a week.

Her sister opened the pantry and grabbed two loaves in each hand. "Nope. I moved them. And I changed the delivery from once a week to twice. That way we don't have stale bread on Saturday."

"Oh." Cindy reached into the refrigerator for the tub of shredded lettuce. "That's good."

Maria retreated to the front table where the lunch bags were filled leaving Cindy alone with Joni near the rear counter.

"You're a little snappy aren't you?" Joni lifted her brows and pressed her lips into a fine line.

Cindy was in no mood for a sermon. "I miss Ray. I should have gone to Memphis."

"If you were married..." Joni adjusted the plastic serving gloves on her hands. "I would agree."

Maria returned and collected the sandwiches.

Joni shrugged. "I'm sorry if I sound judgmental. It's just I don't understand your reasoning."

"That's right. You don't understand. Look around you. This is my world. Starving children and drug addicts."

"It *was* your life. Just so you know, I'm praying for you and Ray."

Joni words should've been a comfort, but they sounded more like a threat.

Mrs. Maxwell entered the door and paused. Curiosity prompted Cindy to turn her station over to Joni's college friend, but when the pastor stepped in the door beside her mother-in-law, Cindy approached with caution.

"Hello. What brings you down here?"

The pastor smiled. "This isn't my first visit. I, as well as other congregants, often come and help distribute."

"But this is the first time since…" Cindy searched for the politically correct word. "…I resigned my Sunday class."

Pastor nodded his head. "True enough, and that is why we are here. May we talk?"

"Of course." Cindy led them to her office. "Have a seat." She indicated two chairs opposite her desk.

Pastor steepled his fingers. "As you know, the church contributes to the funding of this facility—although most of the donations can be traced to a handful of donors."

"Yes, the Maxwells, myself included."

Mrs. Maxwell wouldn't meet her eyes as the pastor continued. "This is a Christian charity and its volunteers have signed a morality clause. Correct?"

Cindy waited for the condemnation in his eyes to be manifested into words.

"You are in violation of that clause and are no longer eligible to volunteer. We ask that you vacate the premises immediately."

The jab pierced Cindy's heart. A sharp pain stole her breath. "This is my house. My work! My calling! My money supports it."

"I disagree. When Cole filed for charitable status, you deeded the house to the organization. I'm afraid you are no longer a representative of the gospel. And unless you turn the management over to Mrs. Maxwell and Rachel—who have kindly volunteered to take the reins—Lulu's Place will lose its funding."

Cindy gritted her teeth. This was her dream—to give her friends a safe place to stay after they were clean, and a place to feed the throwaway children of the street. She stood and glared at her mother-in-law. "If Rachel steps one foot in this house, I will burn it to the ground. With her in it!"

Mrs. Maxwell paled. "I'm simply filling in until your life is in order."

"That's the Maxwell way, isn't it? To control everything and everyone around them." Cindy lifted her chin and refused to cry. "Have it your way, Beverly." Cindy waved her hand. "The place is yours, but you, nor Rachel, will ever get my son."

She walked out of her office and into Maria's arms. "Listen, Mrs. Maxwell isn't one to get her hands dirty, so I need you to stay here and take care of the place."

"You got it, Sis."

The hug from her sister didn't help her frazzled nerves. She had to escape. "I gotta go."

"Call me later."

She barely remembered the drive to Trevor's preschool. She parked and stared at the dash. How did this happen? She reached for her phone. Zack answered on the fourth ring. "The church found out about my relationship with Ray. They threw me out of Lulu's Place." She quickly filled her brother in on her chaotic life. "Where do I stand legally? Isn't it my house?"

"Cole wrote the charity's charter. I'm sure he placed a clause protecting you in there somewhere. We just have to find it."

"Thank you."

"And for the record. I like your new addiction a lot better than the previous ones."

His sudden change of topics confused her. "I haven't gotten high in years. What are you talking about?"

"First it was drugs. Then church. Now you risk everything to be with him."

"I'm not addicted to Ray. I love him."

"Hey, I'm not complaining. I like the guy. He's good for you and Trevor."

"A person isn't an addiction." Cindy thought maybe her brother was the one smoking something. "Forget about Ray and find that loophole."

"You got it, Lulu."

Judging by the look on his face when he walked up the preschool hall with his backpack bulging, Trevor's day had been no better than Cindy's. "I'm dragging up this place."

She smiled at the construction lingo. "You can't drag school."

Trevor walked to the nearby garbage can and reached in his pocket. "And I don't eat fluff." A handful of baby carrots and cauliflower landed in the can.

The director hurried their way. "Mrs. Maxwell, a minute if you please."

Ray had turned her perfect angel into an opinionated little boy. Cindy smiled and prepared to defend Trevor's actions. "Yes, ma'am."

"I apologize for not allowing your sister to collect Trevor, but I thought we covered the written permission requirements when Mr. Simmons dropped him off the other morning."

Cindy's heart tattooed a warning. "I just left my sister. She wouldn't have—" Cindy sucked in a breath. "What did this woman look like?"

"Blond. Very pretty. A little bit taller than you. She had a nice smile."

Trevor clung to her hand. His words confirmed her worst fears. "The looking lady camed here."

Panic raged as she faced the daycare director. "That wasn't my sister. If you see her again, call the police. If fact, I insist you call them now."

The lady's eyes rounded. "Oh, my. I'll call them right away. Wait here, Mrs. Maxwell."

After a two hour ordeal of filing the police report, they promised to check into it. Cindy kept a watchful eye in her rearview mirror on the drive home.

She'd underestimated Rachel twice, but never again.

She closed the garage door as soon as she shifted into park. And then hurried Trevor up the stairs. His safety was top priority. With her banned from her own charity, there was only one thing to do. She secured the deadbolt and announced, "Pack up, Trevor. We're going to see Ray."

&#8359;&#8359;

The chink of shot glasses sounded over the ballgame on the big screen. Ray found an empty stool and motioned for the bartender. Maybe a few beers would take his mind off Cindy. He missed sleeping next to her warm body.

His phone chimed as he received a text.

*Heard you were back in town. I've been waiting.*

Ray ignored the message and called Cindy. "Hello, my sweetness." A horn blared in the background. "Are you driving?"

"Traffic's a nightmare. Can I call you back later?"

"Is everything okay? Where's Trevor?"

"We're fine, now. He's in the backseat." Her voice muffled. "Trevor say hi to Ray."

"Hey, daddy!"

"Where are you? Why isn't Trevor in bed? What's wrong?"

"I can't say in front of little ears. We'll talk in an hour. Love you."

"Cindy wait—" She'd disconnected.

A hand slid over his shoulder. "Hello, Ray." A familiar waitress pressed against his arm. "I've missed you."

He thought back to when he was in Memphis last. He'd taken her home, but he couldn't remember her name.

Seductive eyes traveled down his chest. "I didn't think you'd return, but I'm glad you're here. My shift ends at nine."

"Sorry…" What *was* her name? "I'm just here for a drink. I'm not looking for anything else."

Her face paled and anger flashed in her eyes. "Who said I was offering anything else?"

The bartender slid in front of him and speared him with a dangerous look. "Are you bothering Shay?"

Ray finished off his beer and stood. "Nope, I was just leaving." His phone chimed after three steps. And again at the door. He received a third text as he reached his truck. All from the same number.

*Are you working overtime? I don't mind waiting up. My address is the same.*

෨ඥ

The GPS directed Cindy to a graveled RV park hidden behind a five story hotel. People stood around a pavilion as smoke flowed from an open grill. She recognized some of the faces as Ray's crewmen.

"Are we here?" Trevor had slept most of the way, but the city lights had awoken him thirty minutes ago. He was like a live wire. "Where's daddy?"

Cindy spotted Ray's RV four lanes from the pool. She squeezed her car in between his truck and the awning.

Trevor had somehow managed to unbuckle. As Cindy shifted into park, he jumped out of the car and ran to the steps. "Daddy! I'm here!"

Deep feminine laughter flowed from the inside of the trailer. Cindy's stomach heaved.

৪৩

Ray pulled Trevor onto his lap. Little arms strangled Ray's neck and a sweet kiss fluttered against his cheek. "Guess what? We're moving in."

Ray stood. "That's what I'm talking about. How'd you convince your mom to do that?" He carried Trevor outside.

"I dragged up school."

"Oh yeah?" Ray swung the little boy onto his shoulders and walked around the car.

Cindy stood inside the open driver's door. He bent his head and seared her lips with his. Instead of melting in his arms, her body tensed. He lifted his head.

"You kissed." Trevor giggled from his position on Ray's shoulders.

Cindy lifted red-rimmed eyes.

"What's wrong, babe?" Her car was packed to the brim. Boxes crammed against Trevor's carseat in the back. A laundry basket overflowed with foodstuff and full garbage bags lined the floor. "You are moving in."

She wouldn't leave Cole's memories without a reason. "What did I do to deserve this?"

Trevor answered. "The looking lady comed to get me at school."

Ray tightened his grip on Trevor as Cindy glared at his door. "Do you have a woman in there?"

The TV blared through the screen door. So that was why she didn't respond to his kiss. She was jealous. "Sitcom, babe. Now, what happened with Rachel?"

She sagged against his chest and her arms locked around his waist. "She attempted to check Trevor out of daycare."

His fists clenched against her back. "Did they arrest her?"

"No. She claimed I asked her to. It's my word against hers. As usual, the cops can't do anything right."

He tilted her face and searched her shadowed eyes. "You're here. And you're both safe. That's all that matters."

"I know. I'm just…I'm tired, grouchy, and I want to go to bed."

※∞※

Doug had hired two greenhorns and Ray had no patience. All he wanted was a splash of whiskey, and Cindy's arms around him as he parked in front of his trailer.

But the smell of bleach permeated around the RV. The solid door was open, but his hand slipped off the handle of the locked screen door. "Cindy?"

"Hey, daddy." Trevor bounced in front of the door. "Momma locked it. Cause that girl can't wash clothes."

Fumes burned his eyes. He stooped down and retrieved a gallon of bleach from under the steps. "Ask her to let me in." She was protecting Trevor, but locking the door while she was home was taking things a little over-the-top.

Cindy appeared. The lock snapped and she whirled in the opposite direction. Where was his hello kiss?

"Don't bring that crap in here, Ray."

The bleach jug? He shook the bottle and liquid swirled in the bottom.

"Throw it in the trash."

Ray tossed the bottle in the big can tied to a tree. He cautiously entered the trailer. Cindy stood at the sink with her back toward him.

"Sweetness?"

She didn't turn. "Supper will be ready in twenty minutes. You have time for a shower."

What was going on? Did she find Cole's hidden bible? Trevor played with building blocks on the living area floor. Ray slipped behind Cindy and kissed her neck. "I love you."

Her whole body flinched. She turned and he shivered at the ice in her eyes. "I know that Ray. But I'd convinced myself the women Joni kidded about weren't real. But now…I'd like to go somewhere, and *not* have the entire female population volunteer for services not needed."

The bleach? Mirabella ran the laundry at the park. In the past, she'd always washed his clothes and a few times he'd enjoyed her company after hours. Was she the one who had been texting him?

Cindy shook her head. "I see you've figured it out."

"I've said no to every offer since I met you. I swear. You are the only woman I want."

Her frozen expression cracked.

"Sweetness, I'm sorry. I wish I could go back. I wish I could do it all over again." He cupped her cheek and kissed her tenderly. Her breath hitched and he cradled her close to his heart. "How can I fix this?"

"Sorry can't change the past."

"Knock. Knock." Peg's voice called from outside.

Cindy turned toward the door. She poked his side and he stepped back allowing the two women to enter the trailer. "Come in."

Peg popped her gum. "Did you tell him?"

"It doesn't matter. I've dealt with worse."

"Hey." Felicia parked her hand on her hip. "That witch deserves whatever she gets."

"Whoa." Ray shook his head. "Are you talking about Mirabella?" She'd always treated him so nice.

"She attacked Cindy."

His ears popped and he blinked. Fists clenched, he turned to Cindy. "Are you hurt?"

"So, you remembered this one's name?" Icicles shot from Cindy's eyes.

He had no defense. "I love you." Trevor was quiet. Little feet swung in the air.

"He's fine, Ray. We both are. She just caught me off guard when she barged in here today."

He stepped close and brushed her lips with his. "I'll handle it." He moved passed Peg and Felicia. "Keep her company. Here."

"Ray, don't. It doesn't matter."

"It does. You matter to me. And no one will hurt you."

The door slammed behind him. He got in his truck and spun onto the gravel road. The pool house held the laundry facilities. Both places were empty.

He didn't trust the hot-blooded girl to leave Cindy and Trevor alone. But how could he protect them from the jobsite? After searching the campground, he parked in front of his own trailer. Doug and Scott lingered under the awning.

"Hey, boss. Heard you had a little trouble. Can we help?"

He rubbed his hand down the back of his neck. "I'm moving." He liked for his crew to stay together, but it wasn't a job requirement. "You're not obligated to follow but if you know somewhere…?"

"No problem, boss. Peg found this place on the Mississippi River. She wanted to move there to start with, but I talked her into staying with the crew. It's woodsy. You know we are simple country folk."

"Good. Check it out in the morning and see how many places they have available. Did you say on the river?"

Doug nodded.

"Reserve me a waterfront if possible. If it works, we'll knock off early and make an afternoon move."

୫୦୬

Ray had told her to stay close to the RV, but Cindy wasn't going to hide for the weeks they'd be here. Not from Rachel and not from…Mirabella? Wasn't that what Ray called the floozy? She hadn't attacked Cindy, so much as thrown the gallon of bleach in anger. The splash could've blinded Trevor. A mother's instinct kicked in, and she'd dragged the girl by the hair into the lane.

Ray wasn't supposed to find out about the altercation, but Felicia couldn't keep her mouth shut. Cindy watched Trevor fly down the slide and then run toward the merry-go-round.

A shadow fell over her legs. "You were supposed to stay near the trailer."

"Hey, Daddy. Me and momma won't cower down."

Cindy let Trevor answer for her. Ray's frown didn't soften.

"What are you doing here? Shouldn't you be at work?"

He leaned over, kissed her, and then knelt at her feet. "Doug found another park. One I've never stayed at. We're moving."

She was speechless.

His hand massaged her ankles. The love in his eyes humbled her. "This job will last for at least three weeks. I want you to be able to enjoy your day, and I can't concentrate on work while worrying about you and Trevor." He flashed his trademark grin. "It's a done deal, babe. Either you're with me, or you're not." His wink sent her heart fluttering.

Trevor lunged on Ray's back. "I'm with you."

Ray stood and held out his hand. Cindy left the bench and wrapped her arms around his waist. Face tilted, she stretched on her tiptoes and tasted the love in his kiss. "I'm with you, too."

The new campsite was breathtaking. Spanish moss smothered the huge oak trees surrounding the trailer. Their site was on the riverfront and Cindy loved sitting in the shade and watching Trevor dig in the dirt. The park was large, but peaceful and relaxing. Especially since Zack's private investigator followed Rachel to Atlanta.

છાલ્ક

"This has been the best three weeks of my life." Cindy's knife flicked the black seeds from the watermelon Ray'd brought home. Probably the last one of the season.

Juice ran down her wrist and she licked it up. "Mmmm. I've never tasted anything so wonderful." She carved out a second bite. A moan escaped her, but a third bite drowned out the sound. "This is the best watermelon I've ever eaten." The next bite disappeared. "Incredible." Her knife scraped against the rind. "Ugh."

Ray's hand paused in midair.

She snatched the piece of fruit out of his hand and devoured it. "What is it about this fruit? I usually can't stand the stuff. When I was pregnant with Trevor just the smell made me nauseous."

Wait! What? "Did you say pregnant?"

Cindy's eyes widened and her face paled. "Ray?" Her hands ticked off her fingers as she counted. "Ray." She looked down. Swayed. And caught the edge of the bar. Her panicked gaze met his. "Ray!"

Pulse racing, he calculated the time since the night she'd driven to Montgomery. And no visits from Mother Nature since his rainout weeks before then. "It's okay sweetness. I'm not going anywhere."

"But Ray, my body works like a clock." She rubbed her temples and paced the tiny kitchen. "This can't happen."

Trevor swallowed. "What's wrong, momma? Did you get a seed?"

Her palms flattened against her stomach. "I don't know."

Ray stood and gathered her close. He kissed her hair as she trembled in his arms. His heart leapt at the thought of becoming a real father to both Trevor and a newborn. Was this the answer to his secret prayers?

He loosened his grip and caressed her cheek. "I want to show you something." He stepped back and reached above the oven. He knew she didn't want to see what was in the cabinet, but he opened the door anyway.

Three whiskey bottles lined the shelf.

Since he'd met Cindy, he didn't drink as much as he used to, but he wasn't after the bourbon. He slid a bottle to the side, and she gasped in his arms as he brought down a square, velvet box. The one he'd bought before he left for Memphis—after his talk with James. "Don't panic. I just want you to know I have this."

Surprise lined her pale face.

"Let me tell you a story about a handsome prince." He cleared his throat and captured her watery gaze. "You see...the prince traveled from town to town searching for a priceless treasure. He dug through a lot of dirty rocks, but he finally found the precious stone he'd love forever. So, the prince purchased this box and hid the diamond. Now he's waiting until he's sure his princess is ready to receive it."

Tears fell down her face. He wiped them with his thumbs.

"If a little miracle brings that day sooner than he expected, he's okay with that." He dipped his head and tasted salt on her cheek. "I love you, Cindy." He reached around her, and replaced the green box in its hiding place.

"Wait." Her hand clutched his extended arm. "Aren't you going to show me what's inside?"

He slid the whiskey bottles back into place blocking the sight of the box. "Nope."

She huffed. "Ray, that's not fair. I want to see." The hand on his arm dropped to her side. "The box could be empty for all I know."

Cole's gold band shimmered on her finger.

"It's not empty. And lucky for you, I'm a patient man." He kissed her, and then grabbed his keys. "Come on, Trev. Wash the sticky off your hands and let's go."

"Where are you going?" She dried Trevor's hands.

"To buy one of those test things." He kissed her again and followed a bouncing Trevor outside. "No peeking."

Cindy stared at the closed door and pressed a hand to her abdomen. The watermelon in her stomach rode the waves of disaster. They were panicking for nothing. Right? Trevor loved the watermelon, too. Just because she liked the fruit didn't prove anything.

Her gaze drifted to the cabinet above the stove. When had he visited a jewelry store? Ray wouldn't expect her to wear an eighty thousand dollar ring. But what had he chosen?

She stood and tossed their rinds into the trash. The countertop was drenched in sweet juice. As she cleaned the sticky mess, Cole's plain gold band glistened. She touched her fluttering stomach. She'd never thought about having another baby. She'd been on bed rest for the last four weeks of her pregnancy, but she'd had Trevor and raised him in the midst of the church gossips.

When Mrs. Maxwell accepted that Trevor was indeed Cole's child, and therefore her grandson, she'd demanded Cindy move into the mansion. Zack had stood by her side during her fight to raise Trevor.

Alone. Without a father. Without brothers or sisters.

With Cole gone, more babies weren't an option. Were they? She blinked and swayed on her feet.

Ray hadn't panicked at the thought of becoming a father. Was it because of Trevor?

Her eyes strayed to the cabinet once again.

Did he buy a cluster? Or a solitaire? She'd always wanted an emerald cut diamond, and although she could afford to buy it, she couldn't very well purchase one for herself.

If she married Ray, Trevor would have a real father, and maybe, the Maxwells would leave them alone.

Cindy lifted her hand toward the light. How could she think about Ray's ring while wearing Cole's? She twisted the band, but it wouldn't slide over her knuckle. Without thinking, she moved to the sink and reached for the dish soap. Lathering her finger with the slippery gel, she tugged.

The ring pinged into the sink and rolled toward the drain. "No!" Her wedding band disappeared down the black hole.

ဆၢ

Ray heard her sobs before he opened the trailer door. In deference to her feelings, he'd tried to contain his excitement at the thought of a baby. He didn't want Cindy to *have* to marry him. He wanted her to *want* him. Did she think having his baby would be that horrible?

"What's wrong wif momma?" Trevor piled out of the truck and ran toward the trailer.

Ray rushed in. Despite her sobs, Cindy stood at the sink and prodded a twisted metal coat hanger into the drain. Her head turned toward them. Tear stains lined her cheeks from her red eyes to her pale chin.

She sniffed and held out a bare hand. Her finger was coated with soap. The gold band was absent. "Help me, Ray. I can't reach it. Please, it's the only thing Cole ever bought me. I just—I want—" Her cries escalated and he couldn't understand her incoherent babbling.

He dropped the paper sack onto the middle bar and opened his arms.

She leaned into his chest and sobbed.

"Ah, sweetness." He'd pieced the puzzle together. "Let me make sure I understand. Okay?" She lifted her head. "Is your wedding band down the drain?"

Her lips trembled and fresh tears fell. "I'm sorry, Ray but I wanted to keep it. Now, it's gone forever." She collapsed against him again, and he rubbed her back.

She'd taken off Cole's ring. Ray kissed the top of her head and inhaled the sweet fragrance of her hair.

"Momma, don't cry." Trevor wrapped his arm around his mother's leg.

"Dry your tears, sweetness. This is an easy fix."

She gasped and leaned against his forearms. "You can get it?"

He nudged her to the side, and opened the door below the sink. "It's probably in the p-trap."

She wiped her eyes and squinted. "Ahhh."

Her tears had mixed with the soap and suds now covered her cheek. "Don't worry about this. Go rinse your hand and your face." He turned to Trevor. "Find a towel or a bowl to put under here." Using his hand, he loosened the nut around the PVC pipe and separated the u-shaped section.

Cindy slid a cake pan under the pipe. "That's all I found."

Trevor reclined on the couch, playing a game on his electronic tablet. Dirty water splashed into the pan as Ray turned the pipe upside down. A chink sounded. His fingers closed around the ring, and he held it over his shoulder.

Cindy squealed. His fingers emptied, but her arms circled him and kisses covered his head and shoulders. "Oh, thank you, Ray. Thank you. Thank you." She smacked a big kiss on his neck. "Oh, I love you so much."

Ray put the plumbing back together and then ran enough water in the sink to check for leaks. She'd removed Cole's ring before they'd used the pregnancy test.

Why?

With a light heart, he stepped past the bathroom area. Dressed in sleep pants and a tank top, she sat on the end of his bed. He wanted her forever, but not against her will.

He propped in the doorway. "What are you doing?"

Her beautiful smile trembled. "Waiting for the results."

Cindy's emotions had taken enough of a roller coaster ride for one day. He moved toward her. "We don't have to do this tonight."

Her phone beeped and an automated voice said, "Time's up. Time's up."

"Too late." Cindy swiped the screen. Fear laced her wide eyes. "Where is it?"

"On the bathroom counter. One blue line means the test worked. Two blue lines and it's positive."

Ray forced himself not to run. He lifted the plastic pen-shaped device laying on the kit he'd purchased. Two thin lines ran across the results window. He breathed and read the instructions for himself.

The floor moved beneath him. A baby. His baby. He carried the pen with him to the bedroom.

"You have a stupid grin on your face. What does that mean?" She accepted the pen, and then hid her face against his chest.

He stroked her back and tried to contain his happiness. A baby! Trevor would have a brother or sister.

Her face tilted, and he painted a kiss across her lips. Without hesitation, he stepped down into the kitchen. When he'd retrieved the ring, he returned to her side. She scrambled onto her knees in the middle of the bed. He flipped the velvet lid and dropped to one knee.

A trembling hand covered her mouth.

His tongue stuck to the roof of his mouth. He swallowed. "I love you. I'll never leave you. I'll never abandon you. And I'd rather cut out my heart than to hurt you." He sucked in a breath. "Will you marry me, Cindy?"

She sniffed and then offered him her hand. "Yes."

He pushed the emerald cut diamond ring over her knuckle. The pale strip of skin underneath shadowed the platinum band covered with smaller diamonds.

"It's beautiful." She cradled her left hand with her right and he saw Cole's gold band there.

He gathered her close and held on. He'd have the family he wanted, but at what cost?

*Chapter Twenty*

Ray circled the doctor's office parking lot twice before he found an empty space. He lifted Cindy's hand and brushed a kiss along her knuckles. "Before we go in—I want to ask you something." He sucked in a breath. "If the results are negative…if for some reason the first test was wrong…will you still marry me?"

Her head lolled back with her laughter. "I thought you were gonna ask for your ring back."

"No way, babe." He stroked his hand through her silky hair. "Baby or not. I want you forever."

"If the test was wrong, I want one thing." She wet her lips and swallowed. "A longer engagement."

"If you're not ready—"

"No." She cut him off. "I am ready. I think. But the waiting period for a special designed dress can be up to twelve weeks." She snuggled close and toyed with his shirt buttons. "Last time, my wedding happened so quick, I had to settle for whatever we could find."

"Why didn't you wait?"

"I think Cole was scared that I'd change my mind."

He inhaled the scent of her shampoo. "Would you have?"

She shrugged. "Joni and Cole planned the whole thing. We were going to the courthouse, but at the last minute Cole decided I deserved a church ceremony."

Ray tilted the steering wheel, and turned toward her. "Wait. Joni planned your wedding? What did you do?"

"I got married." She snuggled close and he hugged her tight.

Ray didn't like talking about Cole, but it sounded more and more as if the guy was a control freak. He searched her gaze and couldn't decipher what he saw there.

She sighed into his chest. "I wish I had time to plan a real wedding. Like Dawn had. I know I don't deserve it, but I want our day to be special."

He stroked her back. What would it hurt to wait? People we're going to talk if they married today or in six months. They were already talking about their living arrangements. He didn't want to rush her and he wouldn't change his mind. "Let's wait. A scrap of paper won't change how much I love you."

She stiffened against him. "Are you serious?"

He kissed the top of her head. "Yes. I don't want you to regret our wedding. Take your time and plan things the way you want them. As long as we're married before the baby is born."

She leaned back against his forearm and tilted her smiling face. "What if you don't like my ideas? Or the color scheme?"

He reassured her with a kiss. "I don't care about that frilly, girl stuff. Tell me when and where and I'll be there."

Her laughter was a good surprise. "There's no way I'm doing all the work myself. You'll have to share the load."

Her cheeks were soft against his palm. Her lips warm and pliable. Forget the wedding. She belonged to him. Ceremony or none, he'd love her forever. "Let's go see the doc. Before Trevor drives Mawmaw crazy."

Cindy laughed and mimicked the elder lady. "Oh, my dear, that's what grandmothers are for."

ഈൽ

Cindy snapped a picture of her engagement ring and sent her best friends and Maria a private chat message.

*Hope you're free for dinner tomorrow night. Bridal planning session at the apartment. Bring your husbands. Ray has news of his own.*

She pressed send and her phone rang. The display revealed her brother's number. "Hello."

"I found it, Lulu." Zack's voice shouted through the earpiece.

Cindy lowered the bridal magazine to the soft grass. "What did you find?"

"The clause protecting you and your charity. Cole couldn't list you as the owner of a nonprofit, but he did name you as the sole manager until your death, or until you appointed someone in your stead. I took the liberty of faxing a copy to the church. They may withhold funding, but they can't stop you from running the place."

"Oh, good."

"I thought you would be a little more excited."

"I am. I can't wait to throw Mrs. Maxwell out of the place. It's just…" She inhaled deep. "Now that I'm engaged…well…I'm tired of living in the past." Ray crossed her line of vision as he carried downed limbs to the raging fire in the middle of the pecan grove. He was determined to finish the house before the wedding.

"Do you want to shut the place down? Because if so, you need to have Ray halt the new construction."

"No. The kids need a place to eat. I don't want to close the doors. But I don't want to be the one to open them either. These past weeks have been liberating. I want to travel. I want to see more of the world. Anyone can run Lulu's Place. Just not Mrs. Maxwell."

"Then do what Cole suggested. Hire a manager. You could keep an eye on the place from a distance, and if things weren't going the way you want them, we can always pull rank."

Her heart lightened as Trevor sword fought with an imaginary opponent. "I just thought of the perfect person for the job." But her sister didn't have Maxwell money to live on, and Cindy couldn't ask Maria to work for free. "Could we give a small salary to Maria?"

"Sure, if you want to fund it. Cole left you with enough money for two lifetimes. And your new fiancé turned down my offer to finance that fancy castle he's building."

Her heart stalled. "You didn't offer Ray money?"

"I did. He's adding your name to the deed. It's only fair you pay half the construction cost."

"Ray is a proud man. He wouldn't take anything belonging to Cole. Why did you do that?"

"To see if he had dollar signs in his eyes when he looked at you." Zack laughed. "I insulted him. He said he could take care of his family without my help, and to put the money in a trust fund for Trevor."

"Then do it. Call Mr. Maxwell. I trust him to do the right thing with Trevor's inheritance. But Cole would want to take care of Trevor's expenses. So set up something that pays Trevor a stipend."

"Are you sure you don't want me to set something up for you? Once the papers are finalized, if you divorced, you'd be left with nothing."

"I trust Ray to take care of me. And he'd rather do it without Cole's money."

"What about apartment expenses?"

Across the yard, Ray tilted a water bottle to his mouth. Sweat glistened down his muscled arms. "Send Ray the bills. I'm assuming you have his number."

"Okay, Lulu. I'll call him now. But if you ever need me, you know where I am."

Cindy disconnected and stood. A minute passed and Ray raised his phone to his ear. His gaze found hers. He stalked toward her. Had she done the right thing?

His lips curled as he replaced his phone in his pocket.

She lifted her chin as she waited. His arms opened and she fell into them.

"Ah, sweetness. That was the best wedding gift you could have given me."

"Yeah? Well, kiss me quick, because I'm off to kick Mrs. Maxwell out of Lulu's Place."

Only Ray's kiss could erase all thought from her mind. She let him sweep her away on a wave of euphoria. His face focused. The kiss had ended.

"Are you expecting trouble?"

"Where?"

He winked. He knew exactly how his kiss stole her thoughts. "Do you want me to go with you?"

She shook her head clear. "No. But just in case, can Trevor stay here?"

"Sure thing, sweetness." He leaned in for one more kiss and then jogged off toward Trevor.

The commute across the bay was long and tedious. Cindy didn't know how she'd made the drive almost daily for five years. It was time to move on. As she entered the glass doors of Lulu's Place, the cleanup was almost done. She rounded the bar.

Maria lifted Cindy's left hand. "Ooh wee. That's how you know a good diamond. Forget the carats. It's all about the sparkle." Maria wiggled her hips and Cindy couldn't hold back a giggle.

"You are crazy."

"Yeah." She looked around Cindy. "Where is that fine hunk of a man of yours?"

"He's building our house."

"Uh-huh. Wore him slap out. Didn't ya?"

"Maria, stop it."

A clatter sounded from the back porch. Cindy ran to the window.

Maria's voice came from behind her. "I call him Houdini because I have no idea where he disappears to. I leave him an extra sandwich. I know it breaks the rules, but he won't come inside. He's afraid of Turk. The other kids say he's looking for someone. I hope he finds them before it turns cold." She sighed. "I've grown quite attached to the little guy. I hate to see you return."

"Good. I'm not coming back."

"But Zack said…"

"Forget what he said. I have a proposition for you."

෧෬

Trevor needed a nap and the RV wasn't set up, so Ray drove them back to the apartment. They ate marshmallow and peanut butter sandwiches, and then Ray tucked Trevor into bed.

Little eyes drooped. "Building a house is hard work."

Ray kissed Trevor's forehead. "Yes, it is. Rest up, now. We'll work on the house again tomorrow."

With a yawn, Trevor snuggled into the covers.

Ray strode to Cole's office. Zack's call had surprised him. He'd only dreamt that Cindy would trust him as a provider. He wasn't poor, but he couldn't compete with the Maxwell money. Zack had said the apartment expenses were in the bottom right drawer. Curiosity drove him to Cole's desk.

He thumbed through the files. Everything was neat and in order. He could afford the rent. Zack had the bills automatically deducted from Cindy's checking account. Ray scribbled the account number on a post it. Tomorrow he'd deposit enough money to cover next month's expenses.

Ouch. He blinked and reread the statement. The spa days were expensive. He scratched his head and scribbled a higher amount on the slip of paper. He did a more thorough search through the files. He wanted to make sure he provided everything she needed.

When he was satisfied he could support his new family, he reached for the Bible. The book fell open to Matthew.

It was odd how he felt the liberty to read through the pages, including the notations in the margin. The words pulled him in and Ray read several chapters.

Trevor scrambled into Ray's lap. "Whatcha reading?"

Ray smoothed Trevor's bedhead and then wrapped his arms around the wiggly little boy. "Your father's bible." He read a portion out loud.

Though the words intrigued him, Ray's little buddy grew restless, and eyed the drum set in the corner. "Momma says don't."

Why wouldn't Cindy let him experience his father's life? Ray lifted Trevor. "Momma isn't here."

Could people in heaven see what was going on down here on earth? Ray hoped not. Since meeting him, Cindy had stopped praying, she didn't go to church, she'd lost her position because of living in sin, and she'd gotten pregnant before their wedding.

He could almost hear Cole turning over in his grave.

Trevor giggled as Ray settled on the stool. A pouch held a variety of sticks. He passed Trevor two and the little boy slammed the cymbal. Ears ringing, Ray smiled and reached for a stick.

The drums held no appeal to him, and his attention wandered back to the verses he'd read. He stood and planted Trevor on the stool. Ray left him drumming away and returned to the desk.

It was difficult focusing on the verses, as Trevor's chaotic banging merged into a choppy rhythm. Trevor had inherited his father's musical ability. Ray'd talk to Cindy about getting him lessons.

He smiled at the thought of her as he flipped through the book. A folded paper was neatly wedged in the creases. He unfolded the official document and found a yellow, legal pad page tucked inside. Neat, small script had written in between the lines: *How to build a house.* Cole was an attorney. What did he know about carpentry and construction? Ray reclined in the chair and read.

1. *Seek the Father's will.*
2. *Count the cost.*
3. *Draw up a plan.*
4. *Build.*

Maybe Cole knew more than Ray gave him credit for. In the bible, one part of the scripture was highlighted. ... *This man began to build, and was not able to finish it.*

Ray's pulse quickened. His heart threatened to fly out of his chest. What was happening? A trembling hand clutched the pages, while the other placed the book on the desk. He counted his breaths until the weirdness passed. Over his shoulder, Trevor had placed earphones over his ears. Ray swallowed and continued to read.

The drumming halted.

"What's going on in here?" Cindy's chin trembled. "Trevor, you know you're not allowed to play with those."

Ray closed the papers in the Bible and shoved the book near the others stacked on a shelf. He stood.

Misery pooled into little gray eyes. "Sorry, momma."

Ray stepped into the line of fire. "It's okay, Trev. I gave you permission."

Cindy walked around Ray and kissed her son. "There's cookies on the counter. Maria sent them to you."

Trevor ran up the hall and Ray pulled her into his arms. "Don't be upset. The drums are part of his legacy. Trevor kept a steady beat. I'm proud of him."

She rested her forehead against Ray's chest, stiff as a two by four. "He could break them. I know they will one day be his, but right now he's too young to understand their value."

Ray massaged the tense muscles in her upper back and shoulders. "I was here the whole time. He didn't hurt them."

She sniffed. "I hate hormones."

Ray cupped her head and wiped her tears with his thumb. "Good news. They'll start digging out the basement and laying the foundation for the house next week. Hopefully, we'll move in before the ceremony."

She leaned against his arm. "That soon? The wedding is in three months."

"I'm cracking the whip. I want the house before the wedding, and the wedding before the baby."

She curled her arm in his. "If you don't finish it, we'll still have the apartment."

The apartment belonged to Cole. "Sweetness, I love you more than anything, but he isn't moving in with us."

She snatched out of his arms.

"The house has plenty of storage for any keepsakes you want to save. Except for the drums. The way Trevor kept a steady beat...I think we should find someone to give him lessons."

She whirled around. "What makes you think you know what's best for my son?"

Seeing Cole's things must hurt her. She wanted a fight, but he wouldn't give her the satisfaction. His heartbeat raced, contradicting the calm in his voice as he pulled her back into his arms. "I know it's hard, but if we're gonna have a life together, you have to let him go."

Her face tilted upward. "I'm trying."

She had more courage than she knew. He painted a kiss on her lips. "Don't forget I love you."

"I won't." Her smile gave him hope, and her kiss fueled his dreams.

"Gross." Trevor stared from the hallway.

Cindy smacked her lips and chased after the little boy. Ray followed. In the living room, Cindy swung Trevor in her arms and smothered him with kisses.

His giggles erupted and Ray's laughter joined in. Cindy swayed on her feet and Trevor slipped from her grasp. Ray caught him and set him on his feet. While Trevor danced around them, Ray balanced her shoulders "Okay?"

Her palm flattened against her stomach. "Yes, just a little dizzy spell. I think someone is jealous of their brother's attentions."

"Jealousy seems to run in the family."

## Chapter Twenty-One

The orange glow of the setting sun hovered on the horizon. Cindy inhaled the salty breeze as the surf crashed on the beach. The job in Orlando wrapped up yesterday, but they'd taken a few days to relax before returning home.

Trevor's giggles lightened her heart as he and Ray chased the tide. Parallel to the shore, a sailboat skimmed across the surface. The wind whipped fluttering the hem of her sarong wrap. She held her wide brimmed hat on her head, and wished she could swim in the clouds.

Strong arms wrapped around her and she leaned back into Ray's embrace. A kiss landed on her neck.

"I miss that." The sail flapped and then caught with the wind as the captain turned the vessel in the opposite direction.

"What? My kisses?"

"No." She nodded toward the water. "Sailing. Have you ever been? Could we charter a boat for a few hours?"

His muscles flexed. "Sorry, babe. It's not for me, but you and Trevor could join one of those tourist groups while I pack up the trailer tomorrow."

She caressed the visible veins in his arms and tried to hide her disappointment. "That wouldn't be the same." She turned in his arms. Trevor scooped sand with his bare hands and patted it into a mound.

Another gust of wind caught her hat and lifted it. Ray caught it just above her head. "Cole had a boat. If you loved it so much, why did he sell?"

"I don't know." Cindy stepped out of his arms and knelt beside Trevor. She reached for a plastic shovel to help with the sandcastle. "One day I was thankful, I had something of Cole to hold on to, and the next day the District Attorney came and took the boat away. Zack said Harry bought it before Cole died. Evidently, my husband was good at keeping secrets."

Ray filled a bucket with sea water. "That must have been a hard blow."

"It was. I fainted." She glanced at her son playing in the sand. "That's the day I found about Trevor." She ruffled his hair. "He's better than a sailboat."

ഇരൾ

Two days later, she held tight to Trevor's hand and hoped Ray would like what she'd bought. When she married Cole, Cindy hadn't known how to shop at the upscale furniture galleries, and had allowed Mrs. Maxwell's Interior Designer to furnish the apartment.

Years ago, she'd been grateful for the home Cole provided. This time, she knew exactly how she wanted to furnish their house. But would Ray like her decorating ideas?

He answered her call on the third ring. "Hello, my sweetness."

She dropped her voice to a purr determined to sweet talk him into accepting the purchase. "I need a man with big strong muscles."

His laughed tickled her eardrum and sent delicious vibrations to her brain. "Any man? Or do you want one in particular?"

"You. I want you, Ray."

He hissed through the phone and she smiled knowing he was fighting his baser desires. She had him right where she wanted him. "Bring your truck. I bought something big, and I need you to deliver it to the apartment."

"Where are you?"

"Twice Around the Block." Cindy gave Ray directions to the thrift store and reentered the building. She needed a couple of old sheets to protect the wood. And maybe some pillows to pad the mirror. The seven piece antique bedroom suite was a rare find. Someone had splashed white paint over the stained wood and ruined the antique value. But that gave Cindy freedom to sand the piece and distress it to match the master bedroom décor she'd chosen. She draped a sheet over the footboard. Little hands reached to help her. "Hold it tight while I tape it down."

Trevor wore his gameface as she wrapped the duct tape around the sheet, careful not to let it adhere to the wood. The bell over the door jingled and Ray stalked toward them.

He ran a hand down the nine-drawer dresser and then frowned. "Sweetness, there's no way I'm carrying this heavy thing up the apartment stairs." He lifted one end and his muscles bulged.

Her heart fell, but she forced a smile refusing to show her disappointment.

His arm snaked around her waist. "How 'bout we take it to the shed? We'll have more room to work on it there. When the house is finished, it'll be an easy move."

A squeal of delight escaped her. "Really?" At his nod, she threw her arms around his neck. "I love you, Ray."

He accepted her kiss and returned it with one of his own. "While you're in the mood, let's do some more shopping."

"Okay. What are we buying?"

"Cabinets, carpet, tile?" His grin sent her heart soaring.

She bit her thumb nail. "Are you sure you don't want to hire an interior decorator?"

His laugh relieved the last of her doubt. "You're the only woman I want prettying up our home."

&#8500;&#8450;

Life with Cindy and Trevor was a bit of heaven on earth. Judging from the many bridal magazines, his wedding would soon become a reality. Cindy would show him two of something and he'd pick one.

Why then did he feel as if something was missing? Ray closed the pages of the bible and slid the book under his truck seat. He'd worked late, but the contractor and his crew had the house dried in. Now, he longed for Cindy's kiss and Trevor's smile. They were in the trailer waiting for him.

His phone rang and he answered James's call. "Hey, man what's up?"

"God is so good to me."

Ray held the phone away from his ear as James shouted hallelujah.

"Dude, chill."

"Ah, Ray. He's mine. For the first time ever. Isaac is finally, legally my son. Mine and Joni's. Although Sam and Anna changed his name." Laughter flowed through the phone. "To ours. I can't believe it. God's grace amazes me."

Ray's heart smiled for his friend. He'd been there beside James as he went through hell trying to win custody of Isaac. The heartache of his mother's abuse and devastating news of the lack of paternity. A whiskey bottle could only heal so much hurt. "That's great, James. It's unbelievable. Where did you find him?"

"Ah." A beat of silence reigned. "We haven't. But when we do, we can legally take him home. I know you're skeptical, but if God can alter a judge's mind, he can bring Isaac to safety."

Ray drove down the hill and parked next to the shed. The quad Cindy and Trevor had taken to Mawmaw's cooled under the awning. "That's awesome James."

After a few more minutes of James praising God, Ray disconnected and went inside. A sense of déjà vu covered him. "Cindy? Sweetness, what's wrong? Is it the baby? Where's Trevor?"

He caught her in his arms as she lunged for him. "Rachel and Kyle are married. They've filed for visitation rights." Her sobs ripped at his heart. "Please tell me they can't take Trevor."

"Kyle Maxwell? Cole's uncle? The invalid." Ray's heart ached in his chest as she nodded. James had been awarded custody and someone threatened Ray's son. It wasn't fair. God help them. The stiff papers in Cindy's hand scratched his neck. Ray stepped back and claimed them. With one hand around Cindy, he led them to the couch. "Alright. Let's start at the beginning. Where's Trevor?"

"Mawmaw's." She sniffed and curled into his side.

Ray couldn't make head nor tail of the legal gibberish in the document. "I don't understand this."

"I wish Cole were here. He'd know what to do?"

Her words stabbed him, but she was right. "Just give me a minute. I'm not completely stupid."

"Oh Ray, I'm sorry. I know you're not. It's just—"

His kiss cut off her words. "I know. Now be quiet." He scanned the top page. "Kyle and Rachel Maxwell are suing for custodial rights. They want full custody."

Her face lost all color. "Rachel's a Maxwell now. But, I'll never let her have Trevor. Never." She brought out her phone. Trembling hands slid across the screen. Helplessness stole over him as she asked her brother Zack to locate the best child custody attorney in Alabama.

If Cole were here, he could pray like James did in Pensacola. A prayer God was answering. Ray wanted to pray, but he didn't know how. Would God hear if he did? Would God save Trevor?

Cindy held the phone to her ear and sighed. "I'll wait."

Ray kissed her cheek. "I'm going to get Trevor. Are you okay by yourself?"

"I'll be fine." Her smile waivered but held.

He hugged her close and whispered, "I love you." He couldn't help her with the legal stuff, but he wanted Trevor near. He left his truck by the shed and ducked between the fence.

Cutting across the field, he stopped at the pond and studied the calm waters. An alligator floated just beneath the surface. Cindy had been so determined to keep Trevor out of the gulf waters, she couldn't see the threat on land. Ray was powerless to protect Trevor from the Maxwell's and their money. He needed help.

"God, are you listening?" Birds chirped overhead and Ray blew out a breath. "I can't pray. I don't know how. I'm sorry if I'm doing this wrong, but Trevor needs your help. His dad is in heaven with you, and his uncle only wants the money." Ray tossed a pebble into the still water. "Will you help us? James says you still work miracles, and I know you did something in Pensacola. I don't know how you can fix this, but…Can you figure something out, and then somehow tell me what to do?"

Tires crunched on the road and a car disappeared around the curve.

When Ray faced the murky waters of the pond, the alligator was gone.

Trevor was waiting.

## Chapter Twenty-Two

"I need a place to stay."

"Kathy?" Cindy stared at the shell of the woman standing inside the door of Lulu's Place. The designer clothes hung on Kathy's skinny frame. "What are you doing here?"

"James and his little Barbie doll stole everything." Kathy wound her way around the serving counter. She swiveled her jaw and sniffed. "I have no money. No home. No nothing. I need somewhere to crash until I get back on my feet."

Ray would never allow Cindy to bring Kathy home and Cindy wasn't so sure she wanted to, especially with her own custody threat looming. Despite Kathy's obvious usage, Cindy felt sorry for the woman. "You can't stay here, but I think the homeless mission has an open bed."

Kathy's eyes rounded. "I'm not sleeping beside some wacko. Forget it." She turned for the door.

"Wait." Cindy hurried around the counter and blocked the exit. "Ray and James have looked everywhere for Isaac. Do you have any idea where he may be?"

"Seriously! If I knew where he ran off to, don't you think I'd have drug his butt home? Then I wouldn't be in this mess. That kid has no respect. I tried to be a good parent. I did. He's the one who kept running away."

ॐ

Ray removed Cole's bible out of the desk drawer. Cindy was at Lulu's Place teaching Maria how to keep the books, and Trevor was in the living room watching cartoons.

He read about a father giving good gifts, and he vowed to be the best father he could be. But how could he be a godly man without God?

A yellow piece of paper slid from the pages. As it fluttered to the floor, a legal document separated from its midst and landed on Ray's foot. He lifted the document, intending to return it to the book, but an unseen hand squeezed his breath. Ray's heart thundered out of control. He read the bill of sale for a sailboat. The one Cindy wished she still owned? The one Cole sold before he died? Wait. The date was wrong.

Ray wiped his palms on his jean covered thighs and reached for his phone.

James answered on the third ring. "What's up?"

Ray didn't bother with niceties. "When was the campout? Give me the date."

"Uh, September the ninth."

Ray blinked at the paper in his hand with Cole's signature dated the tenth. "Are you positive? Cole died on the ninth?"

"Yeah, man. I was there when the Coastguard hauled in the boat."

"Did you see the body? Are you sure it was Cole they buried?"

"Ray, what's wrong with you?"

"Nothing." Ray laughed. "I'm good. Never better. I'll see you later." Ray disconnected. "Trevor!"

Little feet pounded from the living room. "Sir?"

"Get dressed. We're going on a road trip."

Forty-five minutes later, Ray dusted his boots off as he got out of the truck. Opening the back door, he smiled at Trevor dressed in jeans. "Be extra cute today. Okay?"

The cap on Trevor's head was similar to Ray's. Maybe he should have dressed him in a suit and tie. He didn't want Mr. Maxwell to think he was trying to change his grandson. But, Trev was a kid and a kid should have fun—not worry about getting his clothes dirty. "How 'bout we leave the hats in the truck?"

"What for?"

"Because we want to look good today?"

"My hat looks good."

Ray unbuckled Trevor and carried him to the door of Maxwell, Bedlight, and something or another. He set him on his feet and straightened his shirt. "Ready?"

"This is Papa's desk."

Ray straightened his shoulders and opened the solid oak door. A pretty receptionist glanced over a computer screen. "Good morning. May I help you?"

Ray held tight to Trevor's hand and crossed the polished hardwood floor. He flashed his flirty smile. The one that always got him what he wanted. It was a good thing Cindy wasn't here. She'd be jealous. "Yes. We'd like to see Mr. Maxwell."

The girl blushed. "Do you have an appointment?"

He should've called first. "No, but if he isn't busy, he'll want to see us." Ray smiled down at Trevor. "Well, one of us."

Trevor tugged on Ray's hand. "Come on Daddy, Papa's here."

Ray resisted. "No Trevor. Your papa may be busy."

"Are you Mr. Simmons?" The girl's eyes rounded on Trevor. "And you're the grandson? Mr. Maxwell's secretary can check his schedule. Go on up."

Ray followed Trevor to a wooden staircase. Behind him the girl said. "Kay, young Mr. Maxwell is here to see his grandfather. You're welcome."

"Hurry, Daddy." Trevor clomped up the stairs.

Another reception area hailed from the top. More than one pair of eyes filled the doorways. Mr. Maxwell stepped into the hall and squatted. "Trevor!"

"Papa!" Trevor let go of Ray and ran into his grandfather's arms.

Mr. Maxwell lifted the little boy high and hugged him close. "Oh, how Papa missed you."

Trevor wrapped his arms around his grandfather and grinned from ear to ear. "I seen big fishes in the water. And waves. And beach."

As Trevor continued his chatter, guilt slammed Ray. How long had it been since Trevor'd seen his grandfather? In Atlanta? Weeks ago?

"And daddy told momma to let me swim. We built a snowman in the sand. It was fun."

Mr. Maxwell extended a hand. "Ray, come on in. And thank you for bringing this rascal by." Mr. Maxwell sat behind the desk, but kept Trevor in his lap.

Ray closed the door and shut out the curious glances.

He noted the moisture in the older man's eyes. "I'm sorry for keeping Trevor away for so long. No wonder your brother and Rachel filed for custody."

Mr. Maxwell flinched. "I had nothing to do with that. I'd never separate Trevor and Cindy. And neither would my father. Needless to say, we are fully on Cindy's side."

Choosing his words in front of Trevor, Ray slid the bill of sale across the desk. "I was hoping to file a lawsuit of my own. I think it was forged. Unless he signed it from the grave."

Trevor laid his head on Mr. Maxwell's chest. A hand stroked his little back and Trevor yawned. "I love you, Papa."

"Papa loves you too, Trevor. You know what? Mrs. Beven has some candy in her desk."

Little eyes lit as Mr. Maxwell pressed a button. The lady from the mall materialized in the door.

Once she and Trevor were out of hearing, Mr. Maxwell spoke. "I've often wondered about this. At the time, I was so full of grief I let Zack handle the sale, but we all questioned Cole's motives." He held the document up and squinted. "This is his signature. I'd recognize it anywhere." Unsteady hands lowered the paper to the desk. "After she lost the baby, Cole convinced the DA to drop the charges against Cindy. He said the negotiations were extreme, but I never suspected this. They must have postdated the bill of sale to keep suspicions down."

Ray nodded at the paper. "Since that's illegal, can we get the boat back for her?"

"Probably. Harry isn't in office now. There was a big scandal two years ago. Give me a few days, and I'll get back with you."

"Thank you, sir." Ray relaxed into the seat. "But don't tell Cindy. I'm hoping I can make it a wedding gift."

Cole's father nodded. "I have one request."

Ray gave him his full attention.

"I appreciate the wedding invitation more than you know, but I'd like to see Trevor raised in church."

Ray sighed and relaxed into the chair. "From the notes in his Bible, I'm sure Cole would want Trevor in church, too. But Cindy's at odds with the preacher."

A spark flared in Mr. Maxwell's eyes. "You're reading Cole's bible?"

Ray straightened in the seat. "Yes, sir. But...I haven't quite figured out the concept of prayer."

Mr. Maxwell leaned back in his chair, folded his hands behind his head, and grinned.

Ray's shoulders relaxed. "From what Cindy has told me, Cole was an expert. And I can't pray like the men at church either."

"Cole was afraid of heights. He could never walk a high beam. We're all fallible. That's why we need a savior. To make us better men."

Ray wanted to be a better man. "My life is good. James went through hell before he found religion."

Mr. Maxwell laughed. "You don't have to go through hell to reach heaven. Jesus will lead you if you let him."

Ray's heart throbbed against his ribs. He wiped sweaty palms on his jeans and leaned across the desk. "Will you teach me how to pray?"

## Chapter Twenty Three

The phone in his hand rang. The number was an Atlanta prefix. "Yeah."

"Stop stirring up trouble." Zack sounded angry. "Cindy's memories are already tarnished by crazy Rachel and Cole's secrets. There's no reason for her to know about the boat deal."

Ray leaned against the apartment's kitchen counter. "Are you saying that Cole had underhanded dealings?"

"No." Zack laughed. "Cole was innocent as a newborn."

"Then tell me about the boat. Mr. Maxwell said you handled the sale."

Zack sighed. "Cole felt guilty when Cindy went to jail and lost the baby. He'd tipped the cops off, but didn't know the DA was dirty. He used the boat to buy her freedom."

"He was protecting her."

"Yes, but she won't see it that way. Cole was a naïve but he loved my sister. Everything he did was for her. Everything. I hope you love her half as much."

"I love her more. And this is want I need to do." As Ray outlined his plan, Cindy's brother reluctantly agreed.

The call ended as the oven timer buzzed. Ray tugged on the oven mitts.

A muffled, female giggle floated from the doorway. Ray turned and set the large roaster on a hot pad while Cindy dropped her keys and hung her purse on the rack. A hand covered her mouth and another giggle sounded.

Ray slipped off the flowery mitts and waved a wooden spoon. "Don't laugh. Or we'll send you to bed without any supper."

"You look so…" Her gaze scanned the ruffled apron tied around his waist.

Trevor insisted they wear the matching garments. Cindy's lips curled. "…domesticated." Her shoulders shook with suppressed laughter. "What's in the pan?"

"Stuffed flounder." Ray pulled her close and kissed her until he remembered why he was buttering her up. He grinned and held her head in each hand. Forcing her to meet his gaze. "The Maxwells are coming over."

A fire sparked in her eyes as she snatched out of his arms. "You invited the enemy for dinner?"

"Mr. Maxwell invited us to the mansion, but I thought this would be better."

"We went to Papa's desk."

"Trevor, go wash your hands." Cindy lifted Trevor off the chair and turned him toward the hall.

Ray leaned against the counter waiting for an explosion of tears. She kept her back to him for a minute. And then she turned. He wasn't prepared for the anger in her eyes. "Why Ray? Why? You went behind my back and courted the very ones trying to take Trevor from us."

"No, babe. You got it all wrong. Mr. Maxwell isn't behind the lawsuit." He filled her in on the events of his day. Except for the wedding surprise.

"Thank you for trying to help, but you don't know them like I do. Maybe, Cole's parents aren't behind the custody thing, but they could be. You said yourself Mr. Maxwell missed Trevor." The doorbell rang. "I'm not appropriately dressed. You could've at least warned me about your little party."

He checked his phone for the time. "It's too early for Maxwell's." He headed for the door, but called over his shoulder. "You have time to change if you want."

Trevor ran up the hall, and met Ray at the door as the bell dinged again. A courier handed him a documented legal envelope from Zack Worthington. Ray scribbled his signature and closed the door. "Your brother works fast."

"So do you." Cindy turned toward the bedroom.

He followed her. Maybe his other news would cheer her up. He leaned against the headboard while she raffled through her dresser.

"I prayed today."

"What?" She blinked twice. "Why?"

"I want to be a godly husband and father. Mr. Maxwell helped me."

"When?"

"In his office." He shrugged and grinned. He stood and crossed the room to her side. "It was amazing, why didn't you tell me it could be like this?"

The truth haunted Ray from her eyes. He'd led them down this path of sin, but she didn't blame him. "I don't know."

"I'll pray for you." He swallowed the guilt. "I'll pray for both of us."

The tears he'd anticipated earlier formed in her eyes. She glanced up and then her gaze held his. The emotion disappeared with a blink. "The Maxwells will be here any minute. I can't deal with this right now. We'll talk about it later." She stepped around him and the bathroom lock clicked.

Despite the turmoil from Cindy's reaction, peace lined Ray's soul. He turned back to the dining area, and checked the list on the etiquette app Joni had sent him. All the forks seemed to be in the right place. Trevor was clean and Cindy was moving around in her closet. He was ready.

&⊃⊂ℜ

The doorbell dinged off in the distance. Trevor's voice rang through the apartment. "Grandmother. Papa. You're at my house."

Cindy forced a smile and went to welcome Cole's parents.

Beverly Maxwell stood in the doorway. Gone was the stiff society lady. In her place, Trevor's grandmother smothered him with kisses.

A light sunburn brushed Mr. Maxwell's face. He always forgot sunscreen. He gathered Trevor in his arms and Cindy ached with longing. She hadn't seen Mr. Maxwell in weeks.

He caught her stare and stood. His arms opened and she stepped into them. Cole's father wrapped love around her, and she snuggled up to him like a little girl. She'd failed Cole by loving Ray, but his father hadn't turned his back on her yet. In Mr. Maxwell's arms, she found the missing component for her wedding.

"Will you walk me down the aisle?" His arm flinched and she wished she could recall the hastily spoken words. She'd spoken from the heart, but she'd lived without a father's love for her entire life. She wouldn't beg for it now. "You don't have to. I just thought it would be nice."

Gentle hands held her at arm's length. Moisture had gathered in Mr. Maxwell's eyes. "It would be an honor to give my daughter away in marriage. And that's what you are to me. The first time Cole brought you home, I knew. No matter where God takes you, you will always be part of my family. I love you, sweet girl."

Cindy embraced him again and blinked. "I love you, too."

Mr. Maxwell nudged his wife. Beverly swallowed and turned toward Cindy. "I'm sorry for what Rachel has put you through. I had no idea. What color should I choose for my mother-of-the-bride dress?"

"Silver." She endured the awkward hug from Mrs. Maxwell.

Ray winked from the doorway, "Supper's ready."

Everyone gathered around the beautifully set table. Ray and Mr. Maxwell sat at the ends. Despite her anger, Cindy needed the comfort of Ray's touch. She reached for his hand.

"The table is lovely, dear." Mrs. Maxwell placed a linen napkin in her lap.

"We have Ray and Trevor to thank. I arrived home in time for a quick shower. I was no help at all."

"Me and daddy fixed it."

Mrs. Maxwell cringed. Did hearing Trevor call Ray daddy bother Cole's mother? "Trevor?"

"Yes, grandmother."

"It's Daddy and *I* prepared dinner."

Cindy breathed easy.

Mr. Maxwell cleared his throat. "I spoke with my father. Based on Kyle's mental instability, Dad's petitioned to have Rachel's wedding annulled."

A heavy burden lifted from Cindy's shoulders. "Are you certain?"

"Yes. Rachel's in Atlanta begging him to reconsider, but the papers were filed today. You should never fear your own family.

We're here to help you raise Trevor. Not steal him from you."

"Papa, you can borrow me."

Laughter flowed around the table. To show she didn't intend to exclude the Maxwells Cindy offered, "How about next Friday night?" Now that Rachel was at odds with the Maxwells, Trevor would be safe in their care. She turned to Ray. "James and Joni have invited us out."

Ray nodded his approval and Mrs. Maxwell beamed. "Oh yes. We'd love to borrow him Friday. Send him some clothes and he can stay overnight."

"Beverly, we don't want to over impose."

"Having our only grandson over is hardly an imposition." Mrs. Maxwell's love for Trevor had never been in question.

Cindy was careful to hide her smile. "Ray can pick him up Saturday morning."

Mrs. Maxwell addressed Ray. "I wish you didn't travel with your job. I miss my grandson when you're gallivanting around the country."

Ray lowered his tea glass without taking a drink. "I'm taking a few months off to build our house."

Mr. Maxwell set his fork down. "Don't you have to be a licensed homebuilder?"

Ray grinned. "James and I both were grandfathered in a few years ago. My only concern is hiring an adequate crew. The crewmen I have now are skilled with iron and steel. I need some carpenters, plumbers, and electricians."

"What about the men building the new soup kitchen? Couldn't you hire some of them?"

The buzz of the new house consumed the conversation. The Maxwells were pleased to find the location was in Baldwin County and offered many suggestions to keep Ray working local. Beverly Maxwell offered to hire Ray to build a pantry. A complete waste of money, as Marquetta always resisted the decorating changes at the mansion.

After the Maxwells left, Cindy sent Trevor to put on his pajamas and wound her arms around Ray's neck. "I didn't realize you wanted to stop traveling?"

"I haven't decided for sure, yet. Starting a business in this economy is risky." That seductive grin she loved so much lit his face, but suspicion clouded his eyes. "And now that I have a family to support, I can't take chances."

She wrapped her arms around his neck. "I'm sorry for being grumpy earlier. You surprised me." He resisted her kiss for half a second, and then his arms locked around her waist. He took control and she gave herself to him. Regardless of his prayers, he was still hers.

"Daddy!" Trevor's voice yelled up the hall. "I'm ready for my story."

Ray's hands fell away and he took two steps back. "I'll read to Trevor before I go."

She whirled around. "Go where?"

"To the trailer." Conviction was written all over Ray's face. "Until after the wedding."

It was just as she feared. He already felt convicted over their sleeping arrangements. Why did he pray before their marriage? "We've broken the rules before."

"Yes, but does that give us the right to break them again?"

"You don't have to leave. We're both adults. We can sleep in the same bed without—"

"Daddy!"

"Just a minute, Trev." He turned toward the hall but called over his shoulder. "We'll talk later?"

ℬ∝ℛ

His phone danced across the island countertop in the RV. Ray winced at Cindy's text. *Coward.*

He knew his limits and he'd seen the determination in her eyes. He'd never be able to resist her so he'd slipped out of the apartment while she tucked Trevor in bed.

Why hadn't he thought about their sleeping arrangements before he gave his life to Jesus? That she'd texted and not called spoke volumes.

*I know my weaknesses. It won't kill us to wait 2 months.*

Her reply came quickly. *???? Two months? Love? If you're not here in 30 mins I'll call off the wedding*

Panic tattooed against his ribs. Would she? Jesus, help me. His elbow slipped against Cole's bible. Somehow the book reassured him. In order for God to bless their marriage and help protect Trevor, they must follow the rules. *I love you.*

She didn't respond.

He'd wait a few minutes and call her. The bible seduced him. He settled on the bar stool and opened the pages to the bookmark in John. He blinked as the words leapt from the page. The letters of the words appeared clearer, more crisp. How did this happen? The complicated language translated easily in his mind. He devoured the words and turned the page as God's love wrapped around his heart.

Ray blinked against the burn in his eyes and lifted his phone. One fifteen? He'd never read any book for three hours. It was too late to call Cindy. Was she still mad? She hadn't called. He marked his page and headed for bed.

## Chapter Twenty-Four

"I can't believe Ray moved out." Maria taped the flap of the last cardboard box. "He's still gonna help us move into the new building though? Right?"

Cindy yawned and stretched. "Yeah. He would've been here today, but he went to Orange Beach to work on something for the wedding. I'm meeting him for dinner in a little bit though."

Maria hugged her. "That's great. I'm so happy for you. Oh, by the way, there's someone else sleeping where they're not supposed to. A little someone."

"Jamey?"

"If he has a blue backpack, he'd be the one."

Cindy found Jamey huddled on the back porch, shivering. He looked up as she wrapped a blanket around his shoulders.

"I thought you said you had a house? My sister tells me you've been sleeping here."

He gripped the blanket, but scooted to the edge of the porch. "I do. But I think I saw him riding by the other night. It was too dark to tell."

A clatter sounded from inside. As if Maria dropped something.

The forecast called for overnight freezing temperatures. She couldn't let him stay outside. "Come stay the night with me. It's dark and cold out here. We'll search for your father in the morning."

A shadow passed by the window. Jamey gasped and fell off the porch backward. He landed on his back. He propped on his elbows. The streetlamp illuminated the fear in his eyes. "She's here."

Cindy turned and followed his gaze to the window, but she couldn't see who Maria was arguing with. "Who is it?"

"My real mom." Jamey scrambled to his feet.

Cindy stood and looked through the window.

Kathy pointed an angry finger at Maria. Kathy was Jamey's mother? But that would mean…? Isaac? Jamey was Isaac?

The little boy ducked through the hole in the fence.

"Wait!" Cindy ran after him and peered through the opening toward the new building. "Come back."

Isaac was gone.

&#8287;&#8766;&#8287;

A huge grin splashed across James's face as Ray told how Mr. Maxwell had helped him pray. "I'm sorry for not telling you sooner, but I wanted to tell you in person and you've been in Pensacola looking for Isaac."

Joni squealed across the table. "I'm so glad. I knew you were under conviction. Cindy must be ecstatic."

Ray grunted. "Her response was very emotional."

James grinned. "I bet it was. And so you moved out until the wedding?"

"Yeah." And that was the problem, Cindy didn't want a godly man. Ray was half expecting her not to show up for tonight's dinner date. Except for the text he'd gotten earlier this afternoon asking him to pickup Trevor from Mawmaw's and drop him off at the Maxwell mansion, she wouldn't respond to his messages. "She's threatening to cancel the wedding if I don't move back in. I don't want to be a weekend dad to my baby or Trevor."

James laughed. "I told you God's laws were for your protection."

Joni leaned both arms on the table. "If you married her *before* you got her pregnant, you wouldn't be in this mess."

"I don't need a sermon." Ray smiled to soften the blow, but he wasn't listening to one of Joni's lectures.

Thankfully the waitress returned to the table. "Is everyone ready to order?"

"Give us a few more minutes." James leaned back in his chair. "Are you sure Cindy's coming?"

Joni answered. "Of course she is. I talked to her a few hours ago. She loves eating fresh seafood on the causeway. And she won't cancel the wedding. She knows—"

Ray's ringtone cut her off. It was Cindy. His heart jumped in his throat at her incoherent babbling.

"Calm down, sweetness. I can't understand you. What about Isaac?"

Both James and Joni gasped and leaned in for Cindy's answer. "He's here. Or he was. I didn't know it was him." She sniffed and sobbed again. "Oh, Ray. He's been here for months."

"What! What did she say?" James's voice echoed through the restaurant. "She found Isaac?"

Ray nodded as he stood. "Don't cry, babe. We're on our way. Now tell me what happened?"

James grabbed Joni's hand, and pulled her toward the exit knocking a chair over in the process. People waiting for a table scurried out of their way as they ran into the parking lot.

Ray slid in the backseat of James's truck and asked Cindy for details. "How long has he been gone?"

She huffed and sighed. "Ten minutes? I chased him, but he jumped over a fence and I can't climb it."

Concern for her and the baby added caution to his words. "Go back to Lulu's Place. Wait for me. Do NOT look for him by yourself. It's too dangerous. We'll be there in five minutes."

James didn't slow for the tunnel. Eerie lights flashed by as Ray disconnected.

*Please God, keep her safe.*

An eternity later, James's truck screeched to a halt. He slammed into park and hit the ground running. "Isaac! Isaac where are you? Daddy's here, Isaac. Come out! Daddy's here!"

Ray slid from the back as Cindy and Maria jogged up the dimly lit street. Joni ran around the old green building calling Isaac's name.

Ray ran to Cindy. "I told you to wait for me." She fell into his arms and he hugged her tight. *Thank you, Jesus, for keeping her safe.* He kissed the top of her head. "Let's find Isaac."

"His name is Jamey." Maria shook her head. "But he's gone. We've looked everywhere."

Joni turned the corner of the house. "What about the secret tunnel? Did you check there?"

"What?" Ray and James both asked at the same time.

Cindy ducked her head. "It isn't a tunnel." She then looked to Joni. "And the key word is *secret.*"

Joni's eyes widened. "Isaac's smart. He may have found it." All three women hurried to the dark side of the building.

Ray glanced at James and then they followed. The women were crying over small footprints near a what looked like a crude, root cellar hatch. Ray swung open the hatch. A dark hole greeted him.

"Isaac?" James's phone shined a beam of light. "Isaac, are you down there?"

Ray turned to Cindy. "Stay here."

He ducked and followed James into the dirt floored cave. Neither one of them could stand to their full height. The crudely dug room measured about six feet by eight. The depth slanted to meet the floorboards of the house.

Cindy crowded into the small space and pointed upward toward the floor. "That opens into my closet, but I haven't used it in years."

"Didn't I tell you to wait? The walls could cave in."

"This was my childhood sanctuary. Zack made it for me. I've lived down here for weeks at a time."

Above them, hinges squeaked. Part of the floor joists opened. "Me, too." Maria smiled from the opening in the floor above them. "But it always gave me the creeps."

James turned to Joni standing at the ground entrance. "How did you know about this place?

She turned red and shrugged.

Cindy frowned. "It was how we met. Joni bought a rifle Kathy had pawned me. I think it was your grandfather's. Anyway. Kathy had other ideas for Joni, but I smuggled her out this way." Despite the darkness, Cindy's smile sparkled. "It was the first time anyone told me God loved me. Remember, Joni?"

Ray shook his head. "I bet this is the first time James is hearing this story."

James climbed out of the cellar. "Yes, it is."

Joni slid over to her husband and wrapped her arms around him. "Oh, come on. Did you think Kathy just handed the thing over to me?"

"No, but..." James scrubbed a hand down his face. "Forget it. Let's just concentrate on finding Isaac."

Joni lifted an empty water bottle off the ground. "I can't believe he's been living down here and no one knew."

James glared at Cindy. "Where'd he get the blanket?"

She lifted her chin. "I gave it to him."

"You knew he was here! And you didn't say anything?"

Ray stepped between them and glared at his friend. "Watch what you say, James. And how you talk to her. She didn't know Jamey and Isaac was one and the same."

"But you knew a kid was living on the streets. Did you call the authorities?"

Cindy's arms wrapped around Ray's waist from behind. She peeked around him at James. "There are a lot of kids afraid to go home. Calling the cops would make their lives worse."

Tears pooled in James's eyes. "But Isaac is mine."

Her hands stroked Ray's forearms as she spoke to James. "I'm sorry. If I had any idea it was him…" Her chest rose against his back. "He's looking for you. And he knows Kathy is his real mother."

James ran a hand down his face. "How was he? When you saw him tonight, was he hurt? Was he okay?"

Cindy tilted her head. "He was fine. A little dirty, but…"

"He comes through the line on a regular basis. Has for months now." Maria sniffed. "He'll be back."

Joni cried and fell against James's chest. "How could Kathy do this?"

Cindy stiffened at Ray's back. "Everyone here feels sorry for Isaac because he has an addict mother, but what about the little girl whose mother was a prostitute. The girl whose father looked at her with shame, not love. Doesn't she deserve protection? Doesn't she deserve God's love?"

Joni released James and stepped toward Cindy. "Where is she? I'll do all I can to help."

"That little girl is Kathy. Do any of you know what it feels like to lay in your bed choking on tears and begging for someone to love you? How can you expect her to be a loving mother when she's never had an example? Why help me and not her? What's the difference between us?"

James's jaw ticked in silence.

Ray pulled Cindy in front of him and kissed the tip of her nose. "Don't judge us too quickly, sweetness. We don't know what her life was like. But you are nothing like her. You accepted the mercy God offered. Kathy never did. James tried for months to help her. She didn't want out. You did."

A tear slid down Cindy's cheek.

His thumb wipe it away. "Regardless of what you've done in the past—or the sins we've committed recently—God still loves us."

Her chin lifted. "I don't deserve it."

Ray brushed a kiss on her lips. "That's what's so amazing about grace, sweetness. None of us do."

A few hours later, Ray parked in front of the apartment building. He should walk her to the door, but he didn't trust himself. "Call when you're inside so I don't worry."

She snuggled close and whispered. "You can walk me to the door like a gentleman."

He untangled her arms from his neck. "You know why I can't."

Her smile reminded him of past pleasures. "You prayed once and he forgave you. It's not God's fault the wedding is two months away. You can pray again. In the morning."

"That's ridiculous. I like this feeling. I won't sabotage it."

She snatched away. "I'll tell you what's ridiculous. You. I'm expecting a baby. Yours." She held out her ring finger. "We are engaged. And you are abandoning your pregnant fiancé for a sense of self-righteousness?"

"I'm not abandoning you. It isn't my fault you wanted to order a specially made dress. I'd have married you weeks ago."

A beautiful smile lit up her face. "It was delivered yesterday. I can't wait for you to see it. You'll love it."

"Because you'll be the one wearing it and I love you."

"Come upstairs. I'll model it for you." A cloud smothered the sparkle in her eyes. "I couldn't sleep last night. I need my fortress. I need you to hold me."

Her soft touch trailed his jaw and he shivered. He caught her hand and caressed her ring. "From here on, I want to do things God's way. And you and I both know what will happen if I stay the night."

She snatched her hand, and slammed out of the truck.

He pressed a button and lowered the glass on his side. "Sweetness, call me."

She didn't answer, but instead kept a steady pace around the building. Ugh. He rubbed his palm against the back of his neck and raised the window. He waited ten minutes for a call that never came. *Lord, please let her know we both love her.* Pocketing the keys, he followed the stairs.

She leaned against the outside, apartment door. Her head lolled back. At his footsteps, she straightened.

From the distance between them, he thought he saw tears on her lashes, but when he reached her they were gone.

Clear eyes bored into his. "I forgot my keys."

Of course, she was too hardheaded to call and tell him this fact. What if he hadn't checked on her? The stubborn woman would've probably slept outside. He shook his head as he unlocked the door. The knob turned easily under his hand. He pushed the door inward without stepping inside.

"Ray." Her hand cupped his jaw. "Stay with me."

"Not yet, sweetness." He rested his forehead on hers.

She stiffened in his arms. "Get out."

"Cindy—"

"What's the point in having a man if he doesn't want you?" She shoved him away.

"That's not fair." She looked so venerable standing there. Love washed over him. The need to protect her consumed him. "Pray for me, Cindy. Pray God will mold me into a godly husband and father. Pray, I'll take this love he's given me, and take it to those who believe they are unlovable."

"If you love me, stay."

"You know I can't."

"Then just go!"

&#9765;&#9767;

Pale moonlight shimmered against the silver sash adorning her wedding gown hanging from her dresser mirror. Cindy tossed around on the bed and then flopped on her back. She refused to close her eyes. Images from her childhood waited in the shadows.

Climbing into the black hole tonight resurrected horrible memories. Ray had been shocked she'd called the tunnel a sanctuary. But that was because the alternative was far worse than a damp, dark hole. Her mind's ear heard a little girl cry, and Cindy fought against the sound. She closed her eyes and pretended to fly away. High into the clouds, she'd soar while her body was abused. The attacks hurt less and ended sooner if she didn't fight.

When she first met Cole, she'd wanted to believe in his goodness, but it wasn't until he'd taken her sailing that she believed he was her angel sent by God. Cole taught her how to swim in the clouds, but Cindy wanted to fly. Ray introduced her to new heights, but in doing so she'd lost her ability to swim with Cole.

Her eyes burned as she stared at the white lace adorning her wedding dress. White. Guilt choked her as she pressed her palm flat against her abdomen.

Joni thought she'd added the silver sash to disguise the gentle swell of her belly. Not so. Cindy wasn't ashamed of the child growing inside her. She'd suffered enough shame during her own childhood than to subject her baby to the humiliation of thinking he or she wasn't wanted. The religious crowd may look down their noses at someone conceived in sin, but she loved this child and she'd protect her baby from the prejudices of the world.

Cindy fluffed the body pillow and rolled on her side. God hadn't given her the opportunity to stay pure for her first wedding night. When she married Cole, it hadn't mattered much because she felt reborn, but now…A tear trickled down her cheek. If she'd been given the choice, would she have remained virtuous?

She rolled onto her stomach. If this baby was a girl, she'd make sure no one hurt her. Cindy turned on her back and stared at the green glow of the smoke detector. Her lids grew heavy and drooped.

The ping of her phone jerked her awake. She'd forgotten to turn off her notifications. Her eyes blinked at Rachel's latest post. The caption under the photo of a little boy's dream room read: *Can't wait. Preparing for God's blessings.*

An unseen hand squeezed Cindy's breath. Trevor? The post was tagged *in Atlanta, GA.* She blinked and looked closer. She recognized the room as the one Trevor had stayed in during the family reunion.

Her hand reached for her fortress, but encountered the empty mattress. She needed to be held. And she couldn't wait until morning.

಼ಀಀ಼

The artic spray of the shower did nothing to cool the heat flowing through his veins. When had Cindy climbed in his bed? Why hadn't he awakened? Or had his subconscious refused to reject her?

His hand trembled as he turned up the cold water. Ray's shiver had nothing to do with the water temperature. He'd barely made it out of the bed without giving in.

Who was he kidding? He couldn't have lasted another minute. He leaned his head back in the arctic spray. Don't think about her.

She'd been so soft cuddled next to him. So warm. A groan escaped him.

He beat his head against the shower wall. Don't think.

His arms longed to embrace her. He wanted to feel her mouth on his. Why shouldn't they? She was right. They'd broken the rules before. No doubt people would judge them guilty as soon as they saw her car in his drive.

His hand reached for the cold water knob. He shouldn't. The image of her curled against him etched itself in his mind. He was the stupidest man on the planet. She'd driven in the middle of the night because she needed him. Ray shut the facet off. Throwing a towel around him, he stormed out of the bathroom.

Cindy sat on the bed with Cole's bible in her hand. Her hard gaze cooled the hot blood shooting through Ray's veins. He'd left the book on the built in shelf beside the bed.

Her blue eyes narrowed. "Where did you get this?"

He smiled his flirty smile. "You weren't supposed to see that."

"But I did. This—" She held up the book. "This is why you left me."

"I haven't left you. I never will."

"Yes, you have. You barged into my life with your sweet talk and that stupid sexy grin and made me love you. And then you left me." She stood as her voice raised. "Because of this. Just like Cole left me." Tears poured down her cheeks.

"No, sweetness. I'd never leave you."

"But you have, Ray. And now I know why." She dropped the bible on the ruffled covers and stalked toward him.

He gripped the towel with both hands as she neared. Her hands wiped the beads of water clinging to his skin and he could swear his pores steamed. He swallowed and found his voice. "Don't you want the fulfillment of God's promises?"

Her smile scared him. "He never promised me anything."

His back was against the wall. He sidestepped and crossed the room. The bible caught the corner of his eye. He lifted it and pulled it between them as she pressed against him. "He may not have given you a vision in the sky, but there are countless promises in his Word just for you."

Anger iced over her blue eyes. "No matter how much you pray, or how many sermons you hear, or how many times you read his bible…you will never be like Cole. Never! And I never wanted you to be. I want the man who winks and smiles. I want the man whose touch can comfort or send my soul soaring."

He reached for her.

She flung off his hand. "I do *not* want a man who leaves me for a misguided sense of heaven. I want the old Ray back. The one who loved me!" She spun on her heel.

Her words knifed through him. He charged after her. "Giving my life to God hasn't changed that. If anything it's made me love you more."

"Shut up!" She wretched open the door. "I don't want to hear anymore lies."

Glancing toward heaven, he held tight to the towel and ran out the door after her. "Wait. After the wedding—"

She pivoted on her heel and poked a finger into his chest. "I take it back. You are like Cole. Promising to love and cherish me one minute, and then leaving me the next. I don't need either one of you. I can do fine on my own. The wedding is off."

Ray reeled back from the blow. *Jesus, help me.* What could he do? "Sweetness, wait."

The car door slammed and almost pinched his fingers. He leaned his forehead against the frosted driver's window and prayed for help.

She shoved the key into the ignition. A series of clicks sounded. Ray breathed easy. The car wouldn't crank. Cindy slammed a fist against the dash. Her head fell against the steering wheel. Sobs shook her shoulders.

Ray opened the door and tugged her into his arms. Her hands locked together against the frozen skin of his back just above the towel. She buried her face in his chest.

He stroked her hair and whispered into her ear. "I love you, sweetness. Please don't ever doubt it."

She sniffed and cuddled against him. "God would've healed him, but Cole didn't ask. He chose to swim away in the clouds with our baby rather than stay here with me. He loved her more. Don't leave me, Ray. Don't be like Cole. I don't want to be alone."

He braced himself against her touch as she clung to him. A cold shower and frigid temperatures could only erase so many memories. "I'll never leave you, sweetness. Never." He squeezed his eyes shut and held on.

A tractor rumbled in the field beside them. "Get some clothes on, boy!"

Cindy giggled against his chest and then lifted her head.

Love shimmered up at him. He ignored his uncle's scolding and seared her lips with a kiss. "Stay here while I get dressed. I don't trust myself right now."

Her soft touch caressed the stubble on his jaw. "I love you, Ray."

Her words were balm to his battered soul. "Stop tempting me. After we pick up Trevor, we'll go car shopping."

She glanced heavenward and blew out a breath. "Cole gave me this car."

He untangled himself from her arms. "Cole loved you. If he was here, he'd buy you a new one."

Her lips turned into one hard line. "He didn't love me."

"He did." Ray spun on his bare heel and hurried in the trailer. After yanking on a pair jeans and a long sleeved t-shirt, he slipped into his shoes and stepped outside.

Cindy leaned against the car, arms across her sweater. "You can't force me to do anything. I don't want a new car."

He counted to ten. "Suit yourself." He refused to be baited into another argument. "You can stay here with a car that won't run, or you can get in the truck, and let me show you the surprise I've been saving for your wedding present."

Her eyes zeroed in on him. "Is it a car?"

"Nope." He turned and walked toward his truck. With a deliberate effort, he didn't look over his shoulder but prayed she'd follow. She slid into the passenger seat as he hit the ignition. He backed out of the driveway and reached for her hand. Lifting it he kissed each knuckle, and then rested their joined hands on his knee forcing her to scoot close.

Her head fell against his shoulder, and he placed a kiss in her hair. Not a word was spoken during the short drive to Orange Beach.

Her eyes widened as he turned into the marina. "I thought we were car shopping? What are we doing here?"

"You'll see." Ray parked and turned toward her. He held both of her hands in his and captured her wandering gaze. "I'm sorry for taking Cole's bible without permission."

Her eyes narrowed. "I don't want to talk about it."

"It needs to be said." He sucked in a breath and forged on. "I love you, Cindy. But you've allowed the thoughts and opinions of others to cloud your memories."

Her head tilted. "What?"

"When a man loves a woman, he wants to protect her, provide for her, and—"

"Okay about the car already."

He pulled her into his arms. "I'm not talking about *my* love. I'm talking about Cole's love."

She inhaled and spoke through her teeth. "I don't want to discuss it."

"I don't either." He used his strength and gently forced her to face him. "Cole loved you. So what if he didn't tell you he was sick? A man doesn't like to acknowledge his own weakness."

"But Rachel said—"

"Forget crazy Rachel. That's what's got you confused. That and your guilt from loving me. Open your eyes, Cindy. And look at the evidence around you. The man hated your past, but his love was greater than his prejudices. He didn't understand your childhood, yet he married you in secret without the approval of his mother."

The stricken look on her face spurred him on.

"Let me tell you a story…It all started when I borrowed a pencil from Cole's desk."

"Ray, I don't want to hear this."

"Don't interrupt me, sweetness. This is important." He lifted her hand and kissed the ring on her left hand. "Anyway. As I was finishing my house plan, I found his bible. And it—don't laugh—it called me somehow, but I couldn't understand the words."

"Ray—"

"It's okay, babe. Let me finish. I found something else in there. I didn't realize the significance of the date until later but…I don't know how to tell you."

Her hand trembled beneath his. "What did you find?"

He sucked in a breath and then blew it out slowly. "You were in jail. You thought it was because you helped that kid, but it wasn't. It was because Cole and the district attorney had some kind of rivalry and the DA wanted Cole's boat."

"The Lulu?" She blinked several times and then frowned. "But Cole sold him the boat the day before he died. I never understood. Ray, you're smiling. Tell me."

"Cole broke the rules, babe. *Because* he loved you. The bill of sale is dated September tenth. The day *after* Cole died. At first, I thought his signature was forged but it's real. According to Zack, the day before the hospital released you, Cole postdated a bill of sale for two months. He lost more than a baby that week. He gave up his dreams of Lulu because he loved you. He loved you for you. Not for some childhood fantasy."

One tear slid down her cheek. "Are you sure?"

He wiped it away. "I'm sick of hearing the stories of how he saved you from jail when your stubborn will to feed hungry children put you in danger. And despite the objections of his family, he gave you all his earthly wealth and introduced you to his God and Savior. Cole loved you. Unselfishly. Unconditionally. Accept it and get over it." Ray flipped his sun visor and held out the folded bill of sale. "See for yourself."

She read the legal document and traced the date. "Cole did love me?" Beautiful sparkles shimmered in her eyes.

"Yeah, he did."

"But that means, this is illegal. Cole died on the ninth. I can sue Harry and buy the sailboat back."

"Sorry, babe. That's no longer an option. But. I have a wedding gift for you." He got out of the truck and led her past the security guard down the swaying sidewalk.

Her body stiffened and her feet stuck to the wood planks. She stared over his shoulder at the sailboat he'd had trucked in. *The Lulu*. The boat Cole had forfeited for her freedom.

The boat Ray'd recovered from South Carolina's coast.

"Ray. You found it. Is it mine?" Happiness flooded her eyes and spilled down her cheeks.

"It's all yours, babe. It's all yours."

She released him and ran toward the boat. Ray grabbed the lifeline to steady himself and followed. Her musical laughter was worth all the pain of knowing she preferred her past to their future. He sucked in the hurt.

She was happy.

On the deck, she held her arms wide and twirled. "Rayford Eugene Simmons! This is the best wedding gift you could've given me." She paused mid-twirl. "Get up here so I can kiss you senseless."

"No thanks. Boats really aren't my thing." There was no way he'd admit to seasickness, but he wasn't going to step onboard the floating tilt-a-whirl either.

Her smile vanished and her tears returned full force.

"Sweetness, are you okay?" He dashed up the portable steps and gathered her in his arms.

She collapsed against his chest. Her shoulders trembled and tears soaked his shirt. He held her close and rubbed her back.

Her sobs slowly subsided.

A giggle burst into the air. "Stupid hormones." Her shoulders jerked as she hiccupped. Another giggle sounded. She tilted her head and red-rimmed eyes peeked up at him. "I can't believe you convinced me of another man's love."

He grinned down at her. "Pretty stupid, huh?"

She shoved his chest and he fell back against the bench seat at the back of the boat. She scrambled to her knees and straddled his lap. "Ingenious." Her palms cradled his jawline on either side of his face. "Cole's love was a gentle warmth. Yours—" Tears fell but she smiled. "Yours is a raging fire that consumes me. I was terrified you'd make me forget him. But this…" She waved her hand around them. "This lets me know you understand. Part of me will always love him, but you are the man I want as my husband. I love you, Ray."

Her kiss singed all thoughts from his mind. Except one. "Is there any way to move up the wedding?"

Her giggle tickled his neck. She kissed him again. "Maybe. I have my dress. I'll see what I can do."

He gripped her waist. "I love you, sweetness." He took possession of the kiss and branded her as his. "Don't ever forget it."

A little giggle and an exaggerated grunt sounded from the floating dock. Mr. Maxwell held Trevor's hand who was wearing his lifejacket. "Are we early? Or right on time?"

Cindy squirmed off Ray's lap. "Mr. Maxwell? You knew about the boat?"

Ray couldn't stand. Without Cindy to anchor him, nausea churned in his gut.

Trevor ducked under the lifeline and raced across the deck. "Is this it? Is this me and momma's surprise?"

Mr. Maxwell hugged Cindy in a fatherly embrace. "I questioned Cole's reasons for selling the boat to Harry, but I never had any proof until Ray pointed out the date discrepancy. My role in recovering *The Lulu* was insignificant. Besides Ray swore me to secrecy."

Cindy kissed Mr. Maxwell's cheek. The wind and sunbeams danced with her hair highlighting the strands to a rose gold as she crossed the boat to Ray's side. Her kissed steadied him.

He dropped an arm around her shoulder as she snuggled into him.

Her gaze caught his and he read the love in her misty eyes. "You have no idea what you've given me."

He cupped her jaw as his thumb traced her lips. "As long as you're happy, I don't need to know."

She giggled and turned to her father-in-law. "Let's introduce Ray to Lulu. Take us for a sail."

*Chapter Twenty-Five*

The problem with sitting on the front row at church was you never knew when to stand, or when to sit. Ray stood with the rest of the men as the musicians played. He tugged at his shirt cuffs and straightened his jacket. Unfamiliar with the song lyrics, he listened to the other worshipers.

Beside him, a haggard James lifted his arms in the air. Hoping Isaac would return, he'd slept in Cindy's office the previous night. This afternoon, Ray had helped him post flyers all over both sides of the bay while Cindy and Trevor sailed with Mr. Maxwell.

Ray thanked Jesus that his family was safe. If Trevor was on the streets, he'd stop at nothing until he found him. But James insisted that this men's meeting would give him the strength he needed to continue searching.

Ray rocked on his heels and surveyed his surroundings. He liked the inside of this building even though a few water stains marred the white walls. Naturally finished, wood support beams crossed high above his head. In the baptism room behind the choir loft, a mural of a rushing river calmed the red carpet that flowed from the stage to the door.

Ray turned and looked at the whole room and an image clicked in his mind. It was a picture of Calvary. Christ lifted high on a wooden cross with water and blood flowing below. Is that what James had come for? To sit at Jesus's feet?

Ray stood alone in the pews. He swallowed and popped a knuckle as he lowered next to James.

His friend answered a request for a song. "Sorry, I don't sing without my wife."

Wesley smiled. "I understand." He then nodded to the other side of the sanctuary and another guy walked to the piano. As he sang the men stood yet again. Ray stayed on the pew and fumbled with his new bible. He didn't want to stick out from the other men, and he'd probably forget to sit again.

The song ended and The Street Preacher took the stage. Ray leaned forward and listened to a bible story he'd not heard before. Some men were chopping trees and an axe fell into the water. The preacher in the story had thrown in a stick and the axe swam to the riverbank.

The preacher propped in front of the pulpit as he posed the question. "If you saw a piece of metal flapping across the water toward you, would you have the faith to reach out and claim it? I don't know about you, but that's a little too strange for me."

Ray laughed with the rest of the men. Yeah, it was. Metal objects can't float, can't move, and definitely couldn't swim.

"What happened?" The preacher's fist pounded the desk. "God! He took control of the iron! And when God takes control, miraculous things happen." The man paced the length of the stage. "God took away the weight. He caused the metal to rise out of the murky deep to the surface. And then he gave it wings to propel itself out of danger."

The preacher jumped off the stage and landed on both feet. He pointed a finger and waved it over both sections. "You are a tool of God. When he saved you, he removed the heavy weight of sin. Sometimes, the waves of temptation take us under, but there is more to Christianity than floating through life. God wants you to swim. Miracles never follow nature's laws. That's what makes them miraculous."

Ray could swim, but he wasn't about to toss his tools in a river to watch them sink.

"Most of us don't want to experience strange things. We're scared of the unknown. Afraid to extend our hands to God, because we're not sure what he'll give us."

Ray straightened on the pew. He wasn't a coward. He wasn't afraid. It would take a miracle to find Isaac. Would it take a miracle to protect Trevor from crazy Rachel?

"Don't be reluctant." Music played. "Reach for God. You can hold miracles in your hand."

People moved toward the front. Something propelled Ray to his feet. Beside him, James lifted both hands as tears poured down his face.

Weak men cried, but James was strong. What was going on here? The same heaviness he'd felt as he read the bible pressed against Ray's heart.

The preacher spoke again. "Scientist could've studied the axe head for years, but they never would've understood how it swam. And you can't either. Don't try to understand God's power. Just accept it."

A cloak of unseen mist covered Ray. His whole body hummed with expectation. He closed his eyes and bowed his head. How could he have the power of God? He couldn't even pray in the Spirit.

Shouts surrounded him.

"An ax by itself sinks. But if you surrender your complete self to God. He will do great things. For you. In you. And through you."

A whirlwind rushed beyond Ray, but he felt the hurricane force wind and planted his feet. *Jesus, I want your power, help me find it.* Another powerful gust surged by. Ray caught his balance as something jostled his shoulder. A third wind blew over him and his body shook. Something was hiding in the wind. Something he needed. Something powerful.

The wind moved. Ray needed to feel it. He opened his eyes as men ran past. They were after the power too. The need to possess consumed Ray. The wind teased him again, and he ran. It was beyond his reach. He met James head on. Arms steadied him and then moved passed.

Heat covered him as the wind returned. It beckoned and Ray chased it again all the while knowing he was running a different race than the others. He slowed. Should he turn around?

A voice spoke from the wind. *Don't worry where others are going. There is a unique path for you. Follow me. Build great things for my kingdom.*

Ray's momentum doubled. He had to catch the wind. He needed the blueprint it held. He turned the corner and surged ahead. With one last leap, he landed in a vortex of energy. His core being caught fire. Doubt burned away as molten gold flowed through his veins.

℘℣

Morning sunbeams danced along the choppy bay water. A hallelujah chorus rose in Ray and he burst into song.

Cindy frowned in the passenger seat. "I take it church went well last night?"

Ray lifted her hand to his lips. He wanted to tell her about his new experience. "I've always wondered how Popeye felt when he ate his spinach. Now, I know."

She turned away from him and stared out the window.

He was worried for her soul. Cindy had no desire for anything spiritual. "The first time I went to your church the Holy Ghost scared me, but last night I figured it out." He squeezed her hand.

Her head turned in his direction. Her smile outshone the sun. "Oh really? You figured out God's spirit?"

"Yeah." Ray winked. "He's a magnifying glass. Magnifying everything like love, peace and joy, and letting us see sin and deception for what it is."

Her eyes sparkled and then dimmed. "That's what I thought when I first felt it too."

Was that conviction in her voice? Oh, God. Let it be so. "I want to help you find God again."

"I wouldn't mind finding God. But I refuse to go to church just so people can condemn me. Joni said the rumor mill is churning again. Four different people—people who have no idea what they're talking about—requested prayer for me last Sunday."

"I'm sorry." He'd taken her salvation and replaced it with temporary pleasure.

"It's not your fault. They've always been like this. When Cole married me, they said I was pregnant. Which I wasn't. When I lost baby Lulu so soon, they insisted the rumor was true. When Trevor was born, they questioned his parentage. So thanks for the offer, Ray. But I think I'll pass."

"Last night, at Wesley's new church, the people seemed different. I want us to go there. As a family."

Her hand snatched from his. "I don't know. Let me think about it."

Today was the first day serving from the new dining room

facility. Maria was expecting a big crowd and Cindy and Ray came to help serve. After a few minutes of dishing out food, an eerie feeling crawled his spine as if someone was watching him. He shook off the feeling and glanced over his shoulder.

Maria walked behind Ray with a fresh pan of mashed potatoes. "Mind if I ask you a question?"

He turned. "Go for it."

Maria craned her head and glanced around the room. "Why'd you get religious before the wedding? Didn't you believe in God as a child?"

Ray laughed at the anger in her voice as he scraped the last of the potatoes in his spoon. "When I was a kid, I just wanted a free ticket to Heaven. But it turns out that you can't just recite a prayer. You have to mean what you say."

"So you ditched my sister and gave your heart to Jesus?"

"I didn't ditch your sister. I'm making her my wife. Why all the questions?"

Conviction covered the smirk on her face.

He removed the empty pan and stepped aside. "Do you want to pray?"

"No thanks." Maria harrumphed as she set the hot pan in its place. "Unlike my big sister, I'll keep my heart in my chest."

"Jesus doesn't want just your heart. He wants all of you."

"Whatever." She collected the empty pan and disappeared behind the double swinging doors.

Ray kept his guard up while he served. The crowd in the dining room thickened, and he swore someone was watching him. The suspicious feeling intensified as the minutes passed.

ꟷ

At this rate, they'd be late for service. Cindy didn't mind slipping in the back of the church, but Ray had this obsession with being punctual. She'd changed her dress three times and settled on a floor length maxi. He might appreciate her legs, but for today she wanted to keep the attention away from their physical relationship.

Mawmaw had insisted she and Trevor stay with her at the farmhouse since Ray had moved out. Since her nightmares had returned full force, she'd accepted the offer.

Ray's old room didn't have a full length mirror. Cindy stretched on her toes and smoothed the fabric tight against her flat belly. With Trevor, she hadn't shown until the latter part of her second trimester.

A knock sounded at the bedroom door. "Sweetness, are you ready? We're gonna be late."

She opened the door and turned for her shoes. "Sorry, Trevor got jelly everywhere. I changed his shirt twice." She slipped on her heeled sandals and straightened. "How do I look?"

"Beautiful." He leaned in and kissed her cheek, and then glanced at his phone. "Twenty-four minutes until start."

Trevor bounced into the room. "Mawmaw said we shoulda went wif her and Uncle Tony."

Ray dropped a hand on his small shoulder. "There's no need to go to church, if you can't feel God there."

As Cindy straightened Ray's tie, strong hands rested on her waist. "You're welcome."

His lips covered hers and she breathed him in. He lifted his head and winked. "Let's go, before we're late."

She grabbed her purse and inhaled. Ray's hand pressed against her lower back as he steered her out of the house to his truck. The knots in her stomach tightened with every passing mile. By the time they reached the church, her insides were a jumbled mess.

Ray parked. His hand removed the key from the ignition and he caught her gaze. "Ready?"

No, she wasn't. She didn't want to face the women's hateful, judgmental attitudes. She should've stayed home.

"Cindy?" A calloused hand caressed her cheek. "It'll be fine. I promise. I won't leave your side."

Her lungs had turned to stone. She nodded and concentrated on breathing. It wouldn't do to pass out before they made it to the door.

Ray carried Trevor, and Cindy forced her feet to walk by his side. Thick red carpet covered the foyer.

"Cindy!" Mrs. Bevin raced to her side—a wide smile on her face. "Oh honey, you look lovely in that peach color. I'm so glad Ray decided to attend service with us here."

The welcome in Mrs. Beven's hug gave Cindy the strength to lift her head. Other women introduced themselves and Cindy hoped she gave the correct responses.

An awkward pause pulled her into the present. Ray squeezed her hand. She breathed easy. He'd kept his promise and stayed by her side.

Mrs. Beven smiled at Trevor. "Hello there, sweetie."

Trevor squinted his eyes. "You have scotch candy."

"Butterscotch, yes." Mrs. Beven laughed and dug in her purse. "Promise to wait until after church to eat it?"

One piece landed in Trevor's outstretched palm. "My daddy likes candy, too." His fingers wiggled.

Mrs. Beven's eyes widened. "Why yes, he did." She handed over a second piece.

Trevor gave the treat to Ray.

Dawn rounded the elder lady. Her smile was genuine and Cindy was glad to see a friend. Her hug was welcomed and steadied Cindy's nerves. Mrs. Beven excused herself. Cindy promised to talk to both women after the service, and followed Ray to a middle pew.

Paper crackled. Both Ray's and Trevor's jaws bulged. Cindy tried to frown, but her lips twitched.

Ray sucked on the butterscotch. "What?"

"I love you."

He winked as the worship service began. After the last hymn, Trevor wiggled between them and she missed Ray's reassuring touch.

As the preacher took the platform, comforting arms wrapped around her. She glanced at Ray who was out of her reach and then peered behind her. Two little girls colored on the next aisle. No one was touching Cindy, but she felt the hug and remembered her savior's touch. She closed her eyes and leaned back into Jesus's arms.

"No pedigree required." The preacher's words pierced her heart and her tears flowed. "If you think you're not good enough for the kingdom of God, think again. Jesus chose his twelve disciples from society's rejects."

Cindy faced the front as God's presence surrounded her and she longed for the joy of forgiveness. She wanted to find that secret place and rest at Jesus's feet.

"So if this world rejects you. Rejoice! Jesus *loves* you. Jesus knows where you are. He *chose* you."

Love covered her from the top of her head to the nail on her pinky toe. She closed her eyes and welcomed the touch she'd forgotten. The touch of her Savior.

*Forgive me, Lord.*

A glorious mist evaporated the bad memories and transformed them into a tinkling light. The future didn't matter, as flames engulfed her and burned the hurt, the hatred and the hunger. Warmth filled her belly. A fountain of joy bubbled in her soul and flowed.

*Chapter Twenty-Six*

It still amazed Ray how much difference one heartfelt prayer made. The steel and glass door of Cindy's childhood house had been removed by the demolition crew. The early morning sun highlighted Cindy's hair as she stepped into the middle of the empty living room. She leaned her head back and inhaled. Slowly, her shoulders relaxed.

"Are you sure you want to destroy this place?" Ray slid a hand along her shoulder and squeezed. "It's not too late to change your mind."

"I know." Peace lined her eyes as she met his gaze. "But I don't want to live in the past anymore. This is my way of letting go."

He pulled her into his arms and hugged her close.

She leaned back, and her hand caressed his jaw. "Thank you, Ray."

"For?"

Happiness danced in her eyes. "Making this happen. Building Lulu's New Place." A laugh escaped her. "I kind of threw that on your plate and left it there."

He claimed a kiss. "Building things is what I do best."

"Good." She linked their hands and tugged him toward the back door. "Because I'm ready to build our future."

He let her lead him down the path around the house, until he stumbled. The two by four he'd used to board up the tunnel entrance lay broken at his feet.

"Isaac?" A flicker of understanding passed between them. Ray let go of her hand and lifted the hatch.

"Where's the blanket?" Cindy stepped around him, but he caught her hand.

"Don't go in there." A portion of the dirt wall had collapsed.

The vibrations from the heavy machinery as they were unloaded from the lowboy must have jarred the ground. "It's not stable."

She pointed into the cellar. A blue backpack lay on its side. "That's Jam—Isaac's. He's here." She turned and scanned the roped off area. "Somewhere."

Ray ducked into the small opening and ignored her squeal of outrage. He grabbed the bag and crawled out of the small space.

Her eyes narrowed and her hand landed on her hip. "If it's too dangerous for me, it's too dangerous for you."

He smacked a kiss across her lips. "I'm stronger."

"Strong enough to hold up a whole house?"

Maria and Trevor crossed the yard toward them. Trevor's eyes widened at the sight of the hole. "Can I go in there?"

"No!" Ray and Cindy answered as one.

Ray softened his voice. "The house is ready to fall down. We don't want you hurt. Come on. Let's find Mr. James and give him the good news." Ray gestured with the blue backpack.

Maria gasped. "He's here? Where?"

Cindy shook her head. "We didn't see him. But keep an eye out."

Trevor tugged on her hand. "Momma, can I look at the hole first?"

"No sweetie." Cindy lifted Trevor and stared into the dark earth. "There's nothing down there."

Ray closed the hatch and jammed the hinge with the broken piece of lumber. "Let's clear the perimeter. The demolition foreman looks ready for his final check." He guided his family under the yellow tape, and into the crowded street that had been roped off to protect passing vehicles from debris. Cindy stood with her back toward him as she talked to her sister.

"Trevor?"

A sweet face peered around Cindy's legs. "I'm right here, Daddy."

"Stay close to me or momma. It's crowded out here."

"Yes, sir."

Ray pulled his phone from his pocket and left a voice mail letting James know about the backpack.

Searching for Isaac, he then scanned the few blond heads in the crowd.

*Lord, thank you for the miracle of Cindy's salvation. And thank you for giving her peace about her childhood, but please help us find Isaac. Let him know we care. Let him know he doesn't have to be alone.*

The demolition foreman yelled over the rumble of the backhoe. "Mr. Simmons? We're ready to start."

ೲಚ

Cindy covered her ears as the big yellow machine roared to life and crawled toward the house. Its scoop landed on the roof above the cellar entrance. The outside wall collapsed like a house of cards. No one would ever be trapped in that tiny dirt room ever again.

The arm-like bucket collided with the adjacent wall and then scooped a ton of rubble.

"Trevor?" Ray's cry sent Cindy into panic mode.

Maria circled, her eyes wide with fear. "Where is he?"

Debris crashed into the half shelled semi-trailer. Black smoke piped into the air as the machine turned back toward the remaining structure.

"Trevor!" Ray ducked under the tape and waved his arms in front of the operator. He swiped his hand across his throat signaling to shut down the machinery.

Ears ringing in the silence, Cindy's world tilted at Maria's words. "Trevor's gone. I turned my back for two seconds and…"

Tons of debris blocked the tunnel entrance.

Words attacked her from every side.

"A little boy was in there."

"There's no way he could have survived."

Ray ran toward the rubble.

"Sir, wait! The house isn't stable. You can't go in there."

"Ray!" She screamed as the house collapsed. The asphalt rose and darkness overtook her.

The world tilted in slow motion.

Ray's bloody face materialized. "Trevor wasn't in there. Breathe, sweetness. Breathe."

Darkness closed in again and her lungs burned. Something pinched her shoulders and her head rattled.

"She's in shock."

"Breathe." The roaring in her ears magnified and Cindy buried her head in Ray's chest.

A sob escaped her, but she didn't have time to cry. "Put me down. We have to find Trevor. Ray, where is he? We have to find him."

Her feet touched the pavement, but strong arms held her tight. "Shhh. I will, sweetness. I will find him."

Detective Simmons jogged over. "How is she?"

"Better." Ray kept his arm around her though she didn't need his support to stand. "What did you find out?"

Ray's cousin glanced at Cindy and frowned. "Maybe you should sit down. The news isn't good."

"Just tell me." Cindy wanted to slap someone when the cousin waited for Ray's nod before he continued.

"Witnesses reported a blond woman in her late twenties forcing Trevor into a brown sedan. Another boy—matching Isaac's description—wrestled with the woman and he too was abducted. We've got an APB out on the vehicle. And an amber alert for Trevor and Jamey."

Another officer ran up to Detective Simmons. "The car's registered to Kyle Maxwell."

Cindy swayed on her feet. Ray's arm steadied her. "We'll find him." Determination lined his face. "If God can protect Isaac through months of street living, he can protect him and Trevor now. I promise you, sweetness. I will find him."

&0C3

Ray helped Cindy to a seat. Enough time had been wasted on searching the rubble. Everything must be focused on finding Trevor.

The Maxwells? Ray didn't know the number to Mr. Maxwell's office. He cornered his cousin. "Can you have someone contact the offices of Maxwell, Bedlight, and something and notify Mr. Alexander Maxwell his grandson has been kidnapped? And also, Senator Maxwell, Georgia's U. S. Senator."

Ray paced the sidewalk praying and pleaded with God to spare Trevor's life. If the boy was dead would Kyle inherit? A wave of grief rolled over him. But Rachel had Trevor, and she wanted him alive.

Ray's nerves threatened to jump out of his skin with helplessness. He must do something, but what? If he went one way in search of Trevor, and Trevor was in the opposite direction, it would take twice as long to reach him.

Chaos churned in his mind. "Hold on, buddy. Daddy will find you. I promise."

"Sir. We've found the car. It's wrecked a few blocks over. An ambulance has been dispatched for the unconscious woman under the wheel. The boys are nowhere to be found. It's our guess they got scared and ran into the woods."

"Where?" Ray grabbed Cindy's hand and they ran for his truck. They raced behind a police cruiser and screeched to a stop four streets over. The front end of a sedan lodged around a light pole. Steam hissed from the radiator.

"Oh, Lord. Why?" Cindy sobbed beside him.

"Sweetness, we trusted God with Trevor's protection this far. Let's not bail on Him now. Give God a chance. I believe He'll come through for us yet."

ଚୖଓ

Cindy eyed the dark faces looking for Trevor and Isaac. The wreck scene was flooded with spectators.

Officers swarmed Ray at the back of the ambulance. They held his arms and forced him away from the closing doors.

Why couldn't they let him go? Ray would beat the whereabouts of Trevor and Jamey out of Rachel. This wasn't a time to be nice. Trevor was probably scared out of his mind. And Isaac. "Trevor, where are you?"

A movement got her eye in the crowd. DZ? Why would he hang around a crime scene? Detective Simmons had atleast four different warrants on him.

He met Cindy's eye with a bold stare. He'd seen something. With one look over her shoulder, she left the crowd and followed the young man behind a row of houses. Except for the two of them, the backyard was empty.

"Ya'll looking for Wingman's boy?"

"Yes." Cindy forgot about Cole's honorary induction into the gang. He'd tried to help Desmond get off the streets, but the teen liked the notoriety of being in a gang. "Trevor is Cole's son. Did you see where he went? Was he alone?"

"Naw." Desmond shook his head. "The preppy kid was with him. Neither of them boys belong on the streets."

"Which way did they go?"

He jerked his head toward the wooded area behind the house. "They shagged out that'll way."

Cindy wanted to run into the woods, but she hurried around the front of the house and screamed. "Ray! Over here! Ray!"

Ray and two other men ran in her direction. "Did you see him?"

Desmond had disappeared. "No. DZ said they ran in there." She pointed to the woods. "I think they're trying to find their way back."

A radio crackled as Detective Simmons set up a perimeter from the wreck sight to Lulu's New Place, which included the wooded area. Ray linked their fingers together and pulled her toward the truck.

"Ray, we have to find him."

He yanked off his tennis shoes and reached behind the seat for rubber boots. "I know, sweetness. Drive the truck back to Lulu's and call me if he's found. I'll check every inch of those woods until he's home again."

"Ray." Fear blurred his image. "All kinds of unsavory creatures inhabit those woods. He's just a little boy."

His arm tightened around her. "He's tougher than you think." A kiss brushed her lips. "I'll find him."

Tires screeched to a halt as James's truck stopped within inches of Ray's back bumper. He jumped out of the truck and ran around the front. "Tell me."

"They're in the woods. Grab a machete or knife and follow me."

Cindy's heart lurched. "Wait, Ray. Please."

Gentle hands framed her face. "It's the man's job to protect the wife and children." His lips brushed hers. "Trust me to do my job." One hand drifted to her abdomen. "Keep the little one safe. Trevor and I will be back soon."

She nodded through her tears. "I love you, Ray."

He winked but his grin waivered. "I love you, too."

The thick branches swallowed Ray, James, and the other men looking for the boys. God, please let him find Trevor before he gets hurt.

"Cindy!" Detective Simmons crossed the street toward her. He waved an envelope in his hand. "Wait."

She paused inside the open door of the truck. "I'm going back. Ray thinks Trevor's trying to get back to Lulu's."

Detective Simmons nodded. "Before you go. Can you verify that this is Cole's handwriting?"

On the outside of the envelope, Cole had written her name in his unique small script. Something fluttered inside her and she pressed a hand to her belly as she looked at Ray's cousin. "Where did you get this?"

"It was found in the car."

Trembling fingers reached in and unfolded the single piece of paper.

*My sweet Lulu,*

*Last night I dreamed I was in heaven with our baby girl. She and I swam from cloud to cloud while surrounded by an amazing warmth of light. The images mirrored my childhood promise from God. I have to admit, it scared me. Especially since the doctor said my time is limited. As much as I want to go to heaven, I'd rather stay here with you.*

A fresh wave of pain washed over her, but relief came in its wake. "This is how Rachel knew. He didn't betray me." The words blurred on the page, and she paused to wipe the moisture from her eyes.

*I haven't found the words to tell you yet, but I have a brain aneurysm. I trust Jesus with my life, and I'll trust him with my death. My only sin is worrying how that may affect you. So, I hope you find this letter when the time is right.*

*I'm so thankful that God allowed me to be your husband. I know your earthly dad wasn't a good example, but you are created in God's image. As long as you are a child of the king, you're a princess. A priceless treasure. So don't let the judgmental negativity of others bring you down.*

*At night, when darkness surrounds you, plead the blood of Jesus and He'll hold you tight.*

*Stay away from DZ and his boys. You have a compassionate heart, but you can't rescue those in love with their captivity. Help those you can at Lulu's place, but stay safe.*

*If I'm gone while you're reading this, please don't cry. Remember that I love you, and your heavenly father loves you. I want you to find a Godly man to keep you out of trouble. One you want to dance with.*

*Be happy.*

*Be loved.*

*Know that I will love you forever, but I'll rejoice in heaven when you rejoice on earth.*

*Little Lulu and I will meet you on the other side.*

*Your loving husband,*
*Cole*

He had freed her to love both men. One lived in her memories and one lived in her future.

"Are you okay?" Ray's cousin stood nearby.

She smiled through her tears. "Can I keep this?"

He slowly shook his head. "We need it for evidence, but I'll make you a copy. And I'm sure the courts will return it after Rachel's trial."

"Thank you." Cindy released the letter and slid in the driver's seat. Trevor could be waiting for her.

Her hands shook as she drove to Lulu's Place. The crew had demolished the fence separating the two lots weeks ago. Vehicles swarmed both buildings. Two local news vans parked on each street. Policemen held bystanders at a respectable distance.

Joni, Maria, and Mrs. Maxwell paced in the dining area. Cindy was engulfed by Joni as she walked through the door.

"What's happening? Did they find them?"

"A local person saw them run into the woods. Ray and James—along with some police—are searching for them now. Other police are knocking on doors between here and there. We thought they may find their way back here. So I came to wait."

The Twin Terrors had their heads bowed on a round table. "Jesus, help Trevor and our brother," one of them said.

Cindy couldn't stay inside. She headed for the backdoor and the women followed her. Mrs. Maxwell included. Cindy turned to her mother-in-law. "What about Rachel? Did they arrest her?"

"Alex said they have to wait until after she gets out of surgery."

"Where is Mr. Maxwell?"

"He's searching from the helicopter with that federal agent."

Figures the man would have friends in high places.

Mrs. Maxwell dabbed the corner of her eyes with an embroidered hankerchief. "I'm so sorry for this. If anything happens to Trevor..."

"If anything happens!" Cindy whirled around. "He was kidnapped. Wrecked. And ran into a forest full of desperate people that would do anything for their next fix. Something has happened."

Joni grabbed her hand. "Where are you going?"

Cindy lifted her chin. "To pray."

ഇരു

"Trevor!" Ray swung his machete, and cut a path through the dense vegetation. "Trevor!" Despite the fall season, the wooded area was thick with undergrowth.

"Isaac? Jamey?" James yelled a hundred yards to his right.

Ray turned. A suspicious looking character stood against a live oak. His cousin had advised posting a reward. Most criminal's ultimate goal was money. If they thought Trevor was valuable, they may not hurt him. Was this guy after a reward?

"Isaac!"

"Trevor!"

"Jamey!"

Ray kept searching all the while calling Trevor's name. After about three hundred yards the flat land dipped. A dry creek bed lined the bottom. On the other side, huge sheets of carpet hung from the branches of a tall magnolia tree.

In the beginning twilight, Ray stumbled over its massive roots, but searched toward the tree. "Trevor! Are you in there? Are you hurt?"

A precious little head appeared from the dirty carpet folds. "Daddy! You found me."

"Oh, thank God. James! Over here!" His heart quickened as Ray ran up the hill and swung Trevor in his arms.

The cold hands squeezing his neck felt like Heaven. Ray's heart exploded as he thanked God for His mercy once again. "Oh, Trev. You scared me. What did I tell you about running off?"

Trevor leaned back and grinned. "But I had to. The looking lady had a gun. She wanted to shoot momma." Fear entered Trevor's gray eyes.

"Trev, momma's fine. She's praying for you."

Trevor's grimy finger pointed at the carpet fort. "That boy is looking for his daddy, too."

With his son safely in his arms, Ray eased to the tree and ducked through the opening. He blinked not trusting his sight. A miracle peered at him with hope-filled eyes.

James burst through the small opening and fell on his knees at Isaac's feet. The boy's hair was a shade or two darker, and he'd lost that baby look, but whiskey colored eyes watered in his father's presence.

"Isaac? Oh, praise God. You're alive. You're here."

Recognition flashed in Isaac's eyes. "You didn't forget me?"

James hugged the boy tight and then held him at arm's length. "I've thought of you every day. Prayed for you every night. Isaac, Daddy loves you. I love you so much."

Hope spilled down dirty cheeks. "I remember, Daddy. I didn't forget."

*Epilogue*

Through the cottage window, water tumbled from trough to trough as the old wind mill turned. Sunlight filtered through the oak limbs overhead as a gentle breeze flirted with the colorful leaves.

An apple tree stood proud at the waters' edge of the mountain spring. Rocks roughed the meadow between the cottage and the church—where Ray waited.

The cottage floor creaked under her slippered feet as she turned from the window. High heels would sink into the ground. Cindy didn't want Ray's first glance of his bride to be of her wobbling down the aisle.

She looked in the full length mirror. Ray would love this dress. Despite the cool mountain temperatures, the short sleeves showed off her tan. Those weeks in the sun paid off.

Violin music penetrated the windows. A knock signaled that Mr. Maxwell waited on the other side of the door.

Trevor stood from a chair in the corner. "Is it time yet?"

"Yes." She inhaled deeply. This wedding had no attendants. Trevor would walk down the aisle first and act as Ray's best man. "Are you ready to make Ray your daddy?"

Trevor grinned. "Can he live with us again?"

Nervous laughter escaped her. She hoped Mr. Maxwell hadn't overheard Trevor. "We're moving into our new house." She held out her arms and twirled. "How do I look?"

"Like a princess."

"Then you must be my prince. Come on. Let's go marry Ray."

❧❧

His tie was choking him. He loosed it and sucked in a breath. Was his tie now crooked? Ray wanted to look his best for Cindy. He straightened and tightened the noose again.

Mawmaw caught his eye and held up both hands. She mouthed the words, "You're good."

He lifted his shoulders and brought them down again stretching his back muscles. The violinist Cindy'd hired played.

Wesley—the preacher marrying them—smiled at the congregation from the wood platform Ray had built.

Where was she? What was taking so long? The women had returned to their seats minutes ago. He released a breath. He should've had his uncle stand up with him. Or Zack? Then he wouldn't feel as if all eyes were on him.

A bit of white flashed at the corner of the mountain cottage. Trevor stepped out first and bounced down the aisle. He was such a great kid—one a father could be proud of. Ray hoped the new baby would be just as good. Trevor stepped up on the platform and stomped on the piece of duct tape marked for him. "Is this my spot?"

Ray nodded as their guests laughed.

The music changed and Cindy stepped beside Mr. Maxwell. Ray sucked in a breath. She was a hundred feet away, but her beauty knocked him for a loop. Bare arms swung slightly as she moved toward him. Her calf played hide-and-seek with the folds of lace. Desire flooded through him.

Creamy flesh disappeared only to tease him seconds later as her long legs moved toward him. His breath quickened and blood surged through his body, quickening a desire to forgo the ceremony and skip straight to the honeymoon.

She moved closer still and the dip of her dress hinted at her curves. The fabric might as well not have been there. He could see every inch of her from memory. He should be thinking of commitment and family. Of babies and grandbabies. But those weren't the images dancing in his mind.

This past month they'd honored God. It hadn't been easy, but with both of them wanting to please Jesus, their common goal had been achieved. They'd waited. But now, she'd be his again.

From five feet away, Cindy's lips curled in a knowing smile. She knew exactly what he was thinking.

The reception would be short.

Ray stepped forward and rested a hand on the curve of her waist, high on her hip. Blue eyes sparkled and he lowered his head. He tasted sweet honey. Chuckles flowed through the congregation.

A little hand yanked on Ray's arm. Trevor whispered, "Not yet."

Ray leaned closer and whispered, "Cindy Maxwell, you are bad."

She winked. "Yes, I am. But you love me anyway."

"Don't forget it."

"Me too?" Trevor reached for Ray. "Love me, too."

Ray swung his son into his arms. "Never forget, Trev. Daddy loves you, too."

_Dear Reader,_

Don't forget! Don't forget that you have a heavenly father that loves you. Don't forget that He gave His Son, so you could have eternal life. Don't forget that Jesus offers the fullness of the Holy Ghost to empower us on our journey. Don't forget that all three are waiting to wrap love and protection around you.

And once you accept Jesus as your savior, don't forget. Don't forget that you are a child of the King. Don't forget that He has a perfect will for you. Don't forget His calling. Don't forget His blessings. Don't forget His glory. Don't forget He has a place prepared for you in Heaven.

Don't forget. Your daddy loves you!

Bridgett Henson

## About the Author

Bridgett Henson was raised in the Deep South by a Baptist mother and a Mormon father. During her teen years, she abandoned the Christian faith altogether. Now, she and her husband minister at a small Methodist church, while holding membership in a local Pentecostal assembly where they raise their three children.

When she's not writing fiction for all denominations, she attends short mission trips, youth conferences, rallies, and summer camps.

Bridgett has a special burden for the youth of today, especially those bound by sex, drugs, and alcohol. She often speaks to those recovering from these addictions.

She hopes that her readers will come to know the God who created and loves them, understand the merciful grace found in the blood of Jesus Christ, and be introduced to the sustaining power of the Holy Ghost.

Visit her website for more information.

www.bridgetthenson.com